A RIVALRY OF HEARTS

FAE FLINGS AND CORSET STRINGS

TESSONJA ODETTE

TESSONJA ODETTE

A Rivalry of Hearts

FAE FLINGS AND CORSET STRINGS

For all the Anne Shirleys whose imaginations run wild and tempers run wilder. Keep that fire ablaze.

A NOTE ON CONTENT

*A **Rivalry of Hearts*** may be a cozy, low-stakes, fantasy romcom, but it does contain some topics that may be upsetting to some readers. Below is not an exhaustive list, but please note the following content:

- Adult situations
- Explicit language
- Overindulgence in liquor
- Fantasy drug use
- Death of parental figure (mentioned)
- Chronic illness of family member with poor prognosis
- Descriptive on-page sex scenes (medium spice)
- Public displays of sexual activity and mentions of voyeurism
- Intended SA/taking advantage of an inebriated person (not explicit; the perpetrator is intercepted and stopped before he can make an attempt)

Welcome to Faerwyvae

The only part of the world inhabited
by fae. An isle united under fae rule
where humans and fae live side by side.
Faerwyvae is protected by a barrier of
fae magic. Fae never leave the isle,
and humans are only permitted
to cross the border under
strict regulations.

Eleven Courts of Faerwyvae

WINTER   SPRING   SUMMER

AUTUMN   EARTHEN

WIND   FIRE   SEA

SOLAR   LUNAR

STAR

Seelie and Unseelie Fae

Most fae have two physical manifestations: an unseelie form and seelie form. Unseelie form is a fae's natural manifestation, whether animal, elemental, or spiritual in nature. Seelie form is a manifestation modeled after human likeness. Some fae shift effortlessly between the two forms. Others claim one form and rarely shift. While there are many exceptions, seelie fae tend to live in human societies, while unseelie fae tend to favor the wilds.

Fae Monarchs

Each court is ruled by two fae monarchs: one seelie and one unseelie, each responsible for separate aspects of leadership. The seelie monarchs oversee day-to-day operations of modern society for humans and seelie fae. The unseelie monarchs advocate for the wild fae and preserve their way of life according to ancient traditions.

LOCATIONS

- ◇ FLOATING HOPE, WIND COURT
- ◇ HYPERION UNIVERSITY, SOLAR COURT
- ◇ VERNON, WINTER COURT
- ◇ LUMENAS, STAR COURT
- ◇ DARLINGTON HILLS, SPRING COURT
- ◇ JASPER, EARTHEN COURT

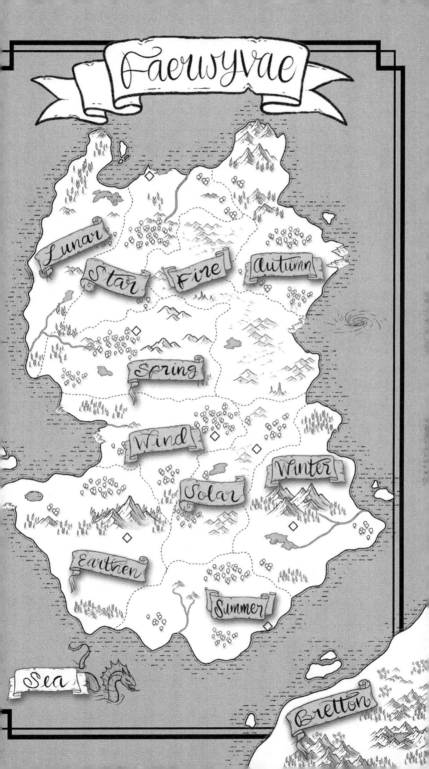

Part One

HOW TO BARGAIN
YOUR VIRTUE

CHAPTER ONE

I've always maintained that a woman in possession of a vast imagination would want for nothing in life. She'd be superior to those with such fleeting virtues as wit, beauty, or accomplishment. The richest woman in the world, if only in her mind.

Today I'd settle for being merely punctual.

Instead, I'm an hour late, rushing through the streets of Floating Hope, my mood not nearly as optimistic as the town's name.

To think I started my morning in high spirits. That, of course, was before I missed my train stop, disembarked at the next one, caught the first train back by the skin of my teeth, got lost in town, and then finally—my most grievous of errors—asked a will-o'-the-wisp for directions.

I was warned about wisps in my visitor's brochure, which included a handy list of dangers a human should avoid while visiting the isle of Faerwyvae. It detailed everything from fae bargains to death-by-kelpie. I found the warnings oddly amusing and promptly restyled them in my notebook under

1

the title *Fourteen Ways to Die in Faerwyvae: An Illustrated Guide*. If only my sketch of the wisp had been even remotely accurate, then maybe I'd have recognized the blue flamelike creature for what it was.

I have three things to say in my defense.

One: I assumed the creature was a sprite or a sylph. This is the Wind Court, after all, and my studies on faekind insist wisps are most frequently found in the courts of Fire or Lunar.

Two: even though following a wisp through swamplands is Way to Die Number Seven due to the risk of death by drowning, the cobblestone streets and charming storefronts that comprise the town of Floating Hope promised safety from said watery demise.

And three: well, the wisp was just so kind to offer a personal escort to my destination.

After which he led me astray, bringing me all the way back to the train station before zipping off with a cackle and taking the slip of paper bearing the address to Flight of Fancy Bookshop with him.

I stand by my opinion that the brochure should have been more specific about the mundane dangers wisps pose, and not just the deadly ones.

Impatience tightens my chest as I double back down streets I've already traversed, the scowl on my face a stark contrast to the wide-eyed wonder I held when I first arrived in Floating Hope. Back then, I still had an hour to spare and took my time to marvel at the storefronts, the pastel-colored buildings with their gabled roofs and intricate millwork, the beautiful people—human and fae alike—in their smart suits or fashionable day dresses. Now I only have eyes for street signs. I may not have the address of my destination memorized, but I do recall it was on Wuthering Avenue. If I can find that, I can find the bookshop. And if I can find the bookshop, then perhaps there's still a chance I haven't completely blundered the most important opportunity of my life.

The weight of my carpet bag soon threatens to dislocate my arm from its socket, so I give up on trying to carry it in a ladylike fashion and heft it against my chest. As I weave through the pedestrians crowding the sidewalks and dart past horse-drawn carriages in heeled shoes not made for walking, my stride shifts into an undignified wobble. Why I chose fashion over comfort on a day like this is beyond me. Had I even an ounce of good sense I'd have chosen my low-heeled boots, an airy blouse and walking skirt, and a hat.

Instead, I'm a panting, sweating mess, the hem of my too-long day dress is filthy, and my already unruly auburn hair has been subjected to the violent whims of the breeze. They don't call this the Wind Court for nothing, and by now half my tresses have fallen loose from their updo. A particularly stubborn lock has even wound itself around one arm of my spectacles. I'd stop to fix my hair, but I really can't afford yet another distraction. I've already had too many for one day.

The first was on the train. I emerged from my sleeper cabin to enter the dining car for breakfast, where I was seated near two fae males dressed in fine suits. I knew they were fae because of their pointed ears. Not to mention one had horns while the other had a long, whiplike tail. Despite my best efforts, I couldn't tear my eyes from them. And not just because they were fae. While I am still getting used to seeing people who are hardly more than myth where I'm from, I was more fascinated by their beauty. They were two of the most beautiful males I'd ever laid eyes on, and the longer I admired them, the faster my imagination began to spin. Before I knew it, I had my pen, inkwell, and notebook in hand, my breakfast forgotten, and I was chronicling a tale of heart-wrenching romance.

I named the characters Johannes and Timothy. Johannes

—the one with the horns—was a surgeon, and he'd saved the life of Timothy with the tail. They fell hopelessly in love, but their budding relationship was struck by a shocking twist of fate; Johannes was the former fiancé of Timothy's best friend! And when I got to the love scene—oh, I just knew Timothy would do something delicious with that tail...

And that was how I missed my stop.

Those closest to me have always said my imagination would be my downfall. They might be right if it wasn't also the very reason I'm here. I was invited to the isle of Faerwyvae *because* of my imagination. Or, more accurately, the books it helps me produce.

Back home in Bretton, I'm a nobody. An unknown author with little to her name. But by some miracle, I'm slightly famous in Faerwyvae, this fantastical isle where humans and fae live side by side. At least, that's what my publisher told me when he proposed a month-long tour for my newest book—the first book I've written about fae characters. This was supposed to be my chance to prove myself worthy of the publishing contract I've secured. A rather generous contract, mind you, especially compared to the meager coins I make in Bretton for my years of hard work. I was hoping my book tour would result in another contract.

Yet my hopes have unraveled every day since I left home. Because today isn't my first mishap. Technically speaking, I am two weeks late to my own book tour.

Two.

Weeks.

I swear, nothing that happened before today was my fault.

I nearly weep with relief once I finally spot Wuthering Avenue and glimpse the sign that reads *Flight of Fancy Bookshop* across the street. The blisters marring my ankles scream in protest as I wait with the other pedestrians for a break in

4

carriage traffic. They scream even louder as I rush across the street. I'm gasping for breath by the time I stop outside the bookshop, and despite the relentless stream of people weaving around me, I abandon all sense of both vanity and pride. I lower my arms, drop my carpet bag onto the sidewalk, and mutter a desperate, "Thank God."

A chuckle emerges from a man I hadn't previously noticed amidst the bustle of the sidewalk. I'm doubled over, catching my breath, as he pushes off the wall he was leaning against and gives me an amused once-over.

He looks to be my age or a few years younger. I'm nine-and-twenty, so that puts him around...five-and-twenty perhaps? He's tall and slender, possessing the kind of roguish beauty that is so haphazard, it must be genuine. His hair is a pale blond that falls in lazy curls over one brow. From the rounded curve of his ears, he's human. Or at least partially so. Only pureblood fae have pointed ears. He wears gray slacks, a matching waistcoat, and a crooked cravat. His sleeves are rolled to his elbows and his hands are tucked in his trouser pockets. Pressed between his lips is a cigarillo, but based on the sweet floral-vanilla scent that fills the air between us, he isn't smoking the cloying tobacco that is popular in Bretton. For all I know, it's some fancy fae herb.

His proximity to the bookstore suggests he's either a shop patron or perhaps a clerk out on his break. Or...maybe he's here to see me? That is my purpose at Flight of Fancy; I'm here to sign books and meet my fans.

The man untucks his hands from his pockets, glancing from me to my carpet bag and back again. He flashes a disarming grin that reveals a dimple in his cheek. "You wouldn't happen to be Edwina Danforth, would you?"

I straighten and attempt to smooth my hair, only to find my tresses are still tangled in my spectacles. "I am," I say with as much poise as one can muster while blowing hair from one's face.

He takes another drag from his cigarillo. "I didn't think you were coming."

"I know I'm late. I'm terribly sorry. Are you...here for the signing?"

His grin deepens as he closes the distance between us and extends his free hand. "Monty Phillips, Junior Publicist at Fletcher-Wilson."

"Oh!" I take his hand with enthusiasm. Fletcher-Wilson is my publisher in Faerwyvae. "You must be in charge of the tour. Please tell me today's signing hasn't been canceled."

"It hasn't." His smile briefly falters. "Did you receive our last telegram?"

Oh no. Not that tone of voice. I can't help but assume bad news is coming. "On the ship, yes. I was informed the tour would continue as planned, and that I'd only miss two dates: the signings for the Summer Court and Sea Court."

"Right, but we sent a follow-up telegram to the Glass-beach Hotel last week."

My stomach sinks. "The Glassbeach Hotel was full by the time I was cleared by customs. I was relocated to the Pink Swan."

"Ah." He rubs his brow. "Well, it's no matter. I can tell you now. Even though Mr. Fletcher decided not to postpone or cancel the tour, he felt it was prudent to make use of the signings you'd miss, as well as secure an alternate author, should you fail to arrive at all."

It takes me several seconds to process what he could mean. "Are...are you saying I've been replaced? But I'm here now. I came all this way." I snap my mouth shut, determined not to say a word more. Discomfort bubbles in my chest, a familiar sensation that always serves as a precursor to me shoving my metaphorical foot in my mouth. I hate being misunderstood and struggle not to defend myself. Yet I've learned time and time again that I'm better off being patient and expressing myself clearly, slowly, and concisely—

"I promise, I would have arrived on time if I could." The words fly from my lips at a rapid pace, and as much as I want to swallow them back, I can't stop now that I've begun. "I wasn't expecting the shipwreck. Though calling it a shipwreck is an exaggeration, I'll admit. But a storm really did hit while my ship was crossing the channel between Bretton and Faerwyvae. Our journey was waylaid for days, and by the time we corrected course and reached the isle, we docked at the wrong port. As you can imagine, it created a nightmare ordeal for customs processing. I was stuck in my cabin for almost an entire week while they sorted out the mess."

"Miss Danforth—"

"And I know I'm late today, which is unforgivable. It's only partially my fault."

He opens his mouth but seems to think better of it, taking a long drag from his cigarillo instead.

Words continue to pour from my lips. "You see, I asked a will-o-the-wisp for directions. Please don't lecture me; I already feel foolish enough. I was here an hour early...before I got lost. And before that, I was going to arrive an entire *three* hours early. But then I missed my stop. That wasn't... well, that was my fault too. I had this brilliant idea for a story, and since it involved fae characters, I thought Mr. Fletcher might be interested in a new proposal—"

"Miss Danforth," Mr. Phillips says, his tone firm this time, "you're not being replaced."

The discomfort leaves my chest and I'm finally able to cease my string of excuses. "I'm not?"

"No, you've merely gained a tour companion." He steps to the side and waves toward an A-frame sign near the book-shop door. At the top reads: *The Heartbeats Tour*. Beneath that is my name, Edwina Danforth, followed by another, William Haywood.

My mouth twitches, begging to frown, but I try to force my lips into a steady grin. As much as it rankles my pride to share what was supposed to be *my* tour, it's better than being replaced entirely. I glance from the sign to Mr. Phillips.

His dimple-framed smile returns, as if that's supposed to placate me. He halfheartedly flourishes his hand. "You write steamy romance, he writes bittersweet poetry. You're a match made in heaven. Like you, he's one of Fletcher-Wilson's newest and brightest authors."

Well, I do like being called new and bright, even if the compliment was placed in conjunction with one for this William Haywood fellow. I study the sign once more, reading the title out loud. "The Heartbeats Tour."

Mr. Phillips takes my bag from the ground and tilts his head toward the door. "Copies of your book are inside and waiting to be signed. Are you ready?"

That refills my well of pride, bringing with it a spark of excitement. I haven't even seen my newest book yet, and I've never so much as signed a copy for anyone who wasn't family.

Right. This is the most important day of my life. I can do this. I can…share my tour. It's not like I'll lose anything. I already have a publishing contract. What's the worst that can happen?

I take a deep breath. "I'm ready."

With a nod, Mr. Phillips turns toward the bookshop—only to whirl back to face me. Frowning, he gestures toward the side of his face, near his eye. "Do you want to…"

I blink at him before I understand what he's miming. Only then do I recall the hair still wound around the arm of my spectacles. "Oh, right." Blushing furiously, I unravel my tangled strands, tearing a few straight from my scalp in the process.

As I replace my lenses, I catch sight of Monty Phillips shaking his head in clear amusement. He takes another drag of his cigarillo, then disposes of the butt in a small metal receptacle by the door. With a wink, he says, "This is going to be a very interesting tour, Miss Danforth."

CHAPTER TWO

I follow Mr. Phillips inside the bookstore and abruptly pull up short. All the awe I abandoned while I was frantically searching for my destination returns. The interior of the shop is unlike anything I've ever seen before. From the outside, Flight of Fancy looked like any other business with its two-story cream exterior and green-and-white striped awning. I was too preoccupied to even look at the window display. Now Flight of Fancy has my full attention.

The interior is a white-dappled blue that resembles a midday sky, the ceilings high to accommodate the tallest bookshelves I've ever seen. A wooden staircase leads to a second-floor loft area, which is so crowded with shop patrons, I can't see what it holds. Chatter fills the air, along with scents of paper and tea, the latter courtesy of the small café located at the back of the first floor. Movement catches my eye from the nearest wall, drawing my gaze to a book that has slid from one of the tall shelves of its own accord. My pulse kicks up as I expect it to fall, but its descent is slow and graceful. The front and back covers splay open, and to my surprise, they begin to flap like wings, its interior pages gently rippling as the book soars from the shelf to the checkout counter.

Behind the counter stands a female fae with blue skin and pastel blue hair that ripples on a wind I don't feel. She's gorgeous, dressed the way I wish I was, in a white blouse, a blue skirt, and a matching waistcoat. She extends her hands, and the flying book alights upon them, going still as it lands.

"That's Arwen."

I jump at the sound of Monty Phillips' voice. I was so entranced I'd almost forgotten the publicist's presence. "Oh?"

"She's the shopkeeper at Flight of Fancy. A sylph. She uses her air magic to make the books seem enchanted when she takes them from the shelves for customers."

I assess the fae woman with new eyes. So that's what a sylph looks like. She might be offended to know I mistook a wisp for her kind earlier today. The blue flamelike creature who sent me off course looks nothing like the humanoid beauty behind the counter. Then again, I read in my visitor's brochure that most fae can shift between two physical forms, what they call *seelie* and *unseelie*. A fae's seelie form is a manifestation modeled after human likeness, while unseelie form often takes on the appearance of an animal, spirit, or element. Most of my encounters have been with seelie fae, as those who prefer their unseelie form often reside in the wild. Ever since disembarking the ship that brought me to Faerwyvae, I've only been in three locations: the port town, the train, and…here. So my experience with faekind in general is quite limited.

"Who is this, Monty?"

Another voice steals my attention from the sylph, this one female. But when I glance before me, I can't locate the source.

"Ah, Daphne, you're here," Mr. Phillips says, his gaze lowered to the floor.

I follow his line of sight and find a small furry creature staring up at me. Before I can think better of it, I utter a yelp and launch a step back.

"Rude, but all right," the female voice says.

I blink at the creature. The voice came from its direction, but I saw no movement from its mouth to suggest the animal had spoken. And…what kind of animal even is this? A weasel of sorts? It's about the size of a house cat, but with a shape I can only describe as an elongated fox with an arched back, small triangular ears, and a long fluffy tail. Its fur is a gray-brown but with a cream throat and underbelly.

Mr. Phillips snorts a laugh that he manages to turn into a cough. "Daph, this is Edwina Danforth."

"Ah, our very late author, gracing us with her presence."

"Miss Danforth, this is Daphne, an intern at Fletcher-Wilson."

"Intern," I echo. Embarrassment heats my cheeks and I face the creature named Daphne. "I'm so sorry. You simply startled me. You're the first unseelie fae I've met."

"Clearly you haven't met a pine marten either," she says, her tone low, flat, and unamused. Again her voice carries from her form despite the lack of motion from her mouth. It must be fae magic that allows her to communicate without the use of lips or vocal cords.

"I haven't," I say, desperate to remedy the awful first impression I've made. I shift from foot to foot, unsure if it would be more respectful to crouch and speak to her eye-to-eye. But since Mr. Phillips remains standing, I do the same.

"Is this all your luggage?" Mr. Phillips asks, gesturing toward my carpet bag he still carries. "Or did you store the rest at the station?"

"The latter," I say.

"Then I'll store your bag behind the counter and fetch the rest while you get settled. You can handle the signing while I'm gone, right, Daphne?"

"Is this your way of sneaking out for another smoke break?" Daphne says with the same unamused monotone she used with me. Perhaps that's just her usual voice after all? I'd rather that be the case than to think I truly offended her.

He chuckles. "Take her upstairs, won't you, Daffy Dear?"

She huffs, but darts toward the staircase. "Right this way, Miss Danforth."

I belatedly follow, my gaze tilted toward the loft and the crowd that gathers beyond the oak railing. It makes sense the signing would be held there. From the look of things, it's already underway.

My tour companion must already be here. He, of course, would have arrived on time, unlike me.

Anxiety tickles my chest at the thought of being put on display before all these strangers, not to mention a fellow author, but I do my best to breathe my worries away.

As Daphne slinks up the stairs, my awe over meeting my first unseelie fae returns. Questions burn my tongue, and it's all I can do to keep them in my head and not utter them out loud. But I'm desperate to know. Does Daphne have a surname, or am I really to address her by first name like Mr. Phillips did? Does she always take unseelie form? Does she have a humanoid form, or is she the type of fae who prefers never to shift? Is a pine marten's fur soft? Would she let me pet her, or is that the most offensive thing I could—

I bite back a squeak, my uncomfortable shoes snagging on the lace hem of my too-long skirt. I trip but manage to catch myself on the rail before I fall completely. Damn this dress and all its lacy layers.

My spectacles slide down my nose as I right myself. I shove the bridge up and regain my composure, but to my

13

humiliation, I've caught the attention of a cluster of shop patrons closest to the upper rail. I give them a forced smile, then resume my ascent. Daphne has already reached the top, where she scurries in between the many patrons' legs and skirt hems until she's out of sight.

I don't bother rushing after her and instead take my time reaching the top step. Once there, I assess the loft. The walls are painted in the same blue and white as they are downstairs, but the bookshelves lining the walls are only chest high. The ceiling is arched and strung with ropes of orb-shaped lights. Their glow is more luminescent than the gaslight we have in Bretton. Faerwyvae is known for its use of electricity, fueled by the ley lines of fae magic that criss-cross the isle. Above the strings of lights flutter dozens of folded paper birds. While the flying book I witnessed downstairs was an illusion of practical air magic, the paper birds *must* be enchanted.

Something snags my hem. I glance down to find Daphne sitting back on her haunches, her clawed paw tugging my skirt. "Come along. Your table is back here."

She darts through the crowd, and this time I try to keep up with her. *Try* being the operative term, for she's small and agile, while I'm short but very much human-sized amongst a sea of figures who all seem to be a head taller than me. They pay me no heed as I weave between them, as all are either locked in conversation with their neighbors or fixated on the back of the room, eager expressions on their faces. Most appear human, an even mix of men and women, though I catch sight of a few pointed ears, vibrant hair or skin, or animalistic features like whiskers or antlers. There isn't a distinct line, but at least half seem to be waiting for their turn to reach the back of the room, while the others casually loiter about. This is the first time I've seen such a vibrant and social atmosphere in a bookstore. I suppose this is also the first time I've been to a book signing. I'm so overwhelmed I almost miss the books many are holding—a clothbound volume in green with gold foil details.

Could that be…

Is that *my* book?

Are they waiting for *me*?

There's a greater chance they're waiting for my tour companion—you know, the author who's here already—but that is far less exciting of a prospect.

Still, the thought of meeting my readers has me pushing toward the back of the room with less trepidation, offering apologies to those I jostle in my rush. The closer I get, the denser the crowd. I can no longer simply slip between the clusters of figures and must firmly tap those in front of me on the shoulder and kindly ask them to step aside. At the disgruntled looks I get, I explain, "I'm the other author. I'm trying to reach my table."

That results in furrowed brows but reluctant acquiescence. My voice is nearly hoarse from this constant refrain until only a few figures stand between me and the two tables I can barely make out just ahead. The tables are set between bookcases that span from wall to wall, and the only way to get behind the two tables is through a gap in between them. A gap which is thoroughly blocked. I glance from the three chatting gentlemen to the left and the tall woman to the right. If one of these four would move a few inches one way or the other, I could skirt around and reach my destination. I choose the woman and reach her shoulder, preparing to tap it, but before my hand can make contact, she bends forward, leaving my fingers in midair.

"Will you sign this too? It's for my sister." The woman retrieves a copy of the green-and-gold book from a bag on the floor. Then another. "And this? It's for my cousin."

I think she adds a third book to the stack but I can't be

sure because my attention has been swallowed by the man who sits behind the table. He's tall, but not in the way that almost everyone seems tall compared to me. Even with him seated, even with his posture tilted slightly to the side in an aura of casual grace, I can tell he'd tower over me. His shoulders are broad, hugged by his emerald-and-sage suit. His cream silk cravat is slightly loose, showing off the cords in his neck and the angles of his decidedly masculine throat. Then there's his hair. Its messy style conjures images of bedroom activities but with a neatness that suggests every wayward strand was placed with precision. His strands are a shade so dark they can't seem to decide whether they're slate, black, or violet. They sweep over the pointed tips of his ears —ears that are decorated in an array of gold piercings, from studs to cuffs to delicate hoops. My gaze drops to his eyes, a hue so aggravatingly blue I could weep.

This is William Haywood? The poet? My tour companion?

I don't know whether to be elated or envious. No wonder the loft is so crowded. They're all here to see *him*, this... goddamn work of art.

The woman before me finally straightens, her stack of books now as high as her chest. I shake my head to clear it and prepare again to tap her on the shoulder. Despite my momentary distraction, I was able to catch a better glimpse of my table. Even now I notice a stack of mauve books growing behind the three still-chatting gentlemen, and the tiny, clawed paw that sets them there. Daphne must be unpacking a crate of my books. The previously empty table certainly speaks to my publisher's lack of optimism over my arrival today.

Clearing my throat, I tap the woman's shoulder at last.

She ignores me.

I tap it again, but it's to no avail. She's prattling on and on to Mr. Haywood. I can no longer see him behind her, but his deep baritone reaches my ears as he utters sounds of interest, the scratch of his pen sliding over paper.

With a huff, I turn toward the trio of men instead. "Excuse me," I say, tapping the nearest on the shoulder.

He shifts to the side, but instead of facing me, he faces my table. His attention snags on the stack of books. Gathering the topmost one in hand, he reads the title out loud. "*The Governess and the Fae.*"

My heart flips in my chest at hearing my book's name read aloud. I'm so desperate to see the cover, to hold it in my hands for the first time. I sidle closer to the man, prepared to force my way between the two tables if I must. Just then, the man with my book whirls toward the poet. I leap to the side so as not to collide with him and bump into another figure instead. The girl with the mountain of books is gone, but the next woman in line has taken her place.

"Excuse me, I was here first," she says, shooting daggers at me with her eyes.

I wave my hands. "No, you don't understand—"

"Is this one of yours?" asks the man holding my book.

I abandon the woman and face him, a glowing grin stretching my lips. "Why, yes—"

"Of course it's not mine," Mr. Haywood says.

My mouth snaps shut. The man had been asking the poet, not me.

Mr. Haywood reclines in his seat, a crooked smirk on his lips. "*The Governess and the Fae,*" he says in a mocking tone. "Do you think I'd write such smut and drivel?"

The man chuckles and tosses my book back on the table without a second glance.

Fury heats my cheeks as the trio of men finally saunter off, my precious book left crooked beside the stack Daphne was so carefully constructing. My fingers curl into fists as I stare after the men. I can't tell whether I'm more hurt, humiliated, or enraged.

"Are you next?" The deep voice shreds my every nerve.

I turn back around and find I'm still standing before Mr. Haywood, the girl beside me nearly growling with impatience.

The fae poet looks up at me, his pen poised above the empty space on the title page inside his book. His head is tilted coyly to the side, a seductive grin on his lips. "And who might you be, love?"

"Edwina Danforth."

He lowers his gaze to his page and begins to scrawl out my name. I skirt between the two tables and settle into my chair with all the grace and trembling restraint of a vengeful goddess.

He frowns, pen frozen, then slowly meets my eyes.

I lift my chin, retrieve the crooked book, and place it neatly on top of the stack. "Author of smut and drivel."

CHAPTER THREE

o William Haywood's credit—or perhaps to his discredit—he quickly recovers from his surprise at discovering my identity. Without looking even remotely abashed, he closes the book with my half-scrawled name, pushes it off to the side, and turns that same seductive grin he'd shone upon me to the next girl.

"I step downstairs for three whole minutes, and everyone forgets how to form a proper line," Daphne says from beside me. Her slinky little pine marten body is inside a wooden crate as she lifts more books with tiny paws and slides them onto the table. I aid her efforts until the box is empty, and then we unpack a second crate. After that, Daphne hands me a pen and two ink pots. "That should be enough for now. I'll see what I can do about organizing the crowd. Again."

Without another word, she bounds off. I wish she'd organized the crowd before I got jostled around and insulted by an arrogant fae.

I can't stop seething over his comment. Smut and drivel. My precious book. I mean, I like smut. Smut is lovely. But drivel?

Drivel?

With a huff, I scoot my chair to the right and arrange all my books to the left of my table, building them as high as I dare to forge a wall between me and Mr. Haywood. Not that I couldn't lean back in my seat and glance directly at him without impediment, but this at least provides me some small sanctuary. Some tangible divide to keep me from marching straight over to him and slamming a book over his head.

To add insult to injury, not a soul has stepped up to my table yet, even with the crowd taking on a more distinct shape and leaving me clearly visible. Many of the loiterers have gone downstairs and a neat line now forms down the staircase. Based on the sharp yelps I hear now and then, I wouldn't be surprised if Daphne was biting ankles to encourage the patrons to obey her directions.

And yet…is no one here for me?

My heart sinks, taking the edge off my annoyance and replacing it with disappointment. With a sigh, I remove the top book from one of my stacks and finally take a good look at the clothbound cover. It's a beautiful shade of mauve with pink-gold foil forming a floral frame around the title: *The Governess and the Fae*. A soft smile curls my lips as I trace the pattern of roses, leaves, and thorns with my fingertips, then brush every letter that forms my name beneath the title. It really is the most beautiful cover I've ever seen on one of my books, the care and quality etched into every line of foil, every stitch in the binding.

My pride swells, consuming all my less pleasant emotions.

This is why I'm here.

This is why I do what I do.

And to think I submitted this book to Fletcher-Wilson on a whim!

I didn't have anything to lose, considering my publisher in Bretton didn't want anything to do with a manuscript with a fae love interest. I hadn't anticipated such disdain, but I often forget the tensions that lie between Bretton and Faerwyvae. It's only been twenty-four years since the last human-fae war. After the fae won their independence from Brettonish rule, they placed strict regulations on Faerwyvae's borders, which impacted immigration and trade.

At least, that's what I learned in my visitor's brochure.

Before coming here, I didn't know much about the fae at all. Growing up, the children of Bretton are taught only what's in the history books. We learn that Faerwyvae is the only place in the world where fae reside, and that humans discovered the isle and the curious people who lived here long ago. We're taught that humans and fae were once friends. That the fae adopted seelie form after tasting human food, donning human clothes, and learning human language. Then we're taught about the human-fae wars, the most recent of which united the humans and fae living in Faerwyvae under fae rule. Even though humans are protected here and seem to be flourishing, visitation is rare—hence the chaos that occurred when my ship docked at the wrong port —and immigration is even rarer.

I am lucky to be here indeed.

Lucky to have this contract.

Lucky to hold this gorgeous book in my hands.

I open the cover to the title page. Then I flip to the next page, which boasts a two-page illustration so stunning it takes my breath away. Leaning forward in my seat, I shove the bridge of my spectacles and study every gorgeous inch of the artwork. I was told the book would include an illustration, but it's one thing to hear about it and another to see it. The piece depicts the most heart-pounding scene from the book, when the governess and the wicked fae succumb to their passions in an enchanted garden. The fae male has long rippling hair, an open shirt, and a musculature that has my mouth watering while the governess stares up at her lover, her form limp and supple in his arms, the sleeves of her chemise slipping from her shoulders—

"They're about to do it, aren't they?"

I slam the book shut, but it's only Daphne who speaks over my shoulder. I didn't notice when she leaped onto the back of my chair.

"Hey, I was looking at that." She still speaks in the same disinterested monotone, so I can't tell if she's being serious.

I angle my head over my shoulder and meet her small dark eyes. "Do you read romance novels?"

"The sexier the better. Ah, there they are." She gestures with her muzzle to the other side of the table.

I face forward in time to see a group of young human women approaching, headed by a plump beauty a few years my junior. All are outfitted in day dresses even more extravagant than mine, their hair styled in popular updos and hats with silk flowers on the brim. They almost look better suited for church than a casual trip to a bookshop.

The leader halts before my table with her hands to her lips. Tears glaze her eyes as she blinks at me. When she speaks, her voice is high and warbling. "You...you're Edwina Danforth."

"I am," I say, sitting up straighter.

The woman finally pulls her hands from her mouth. "It's really you?"

"It is."

"You're my favorite author!"

My heart leaps into my throat. I've never heard those words before. "I am?"

"Yes!"

"Me?"

"Yes!"

I want to ask if she's sure, but her squeal of excitement confirms it. It also draws the attention of those in line at the neighboring table. A fae male with green hair and a top hat sneers in distaste at the spectacle my now sobbing fan is making.

I couldn't be more pleased.

"They were here earlier," Daphne says as she leaps from the back of my chair to the table. "You hadn't arrived yet, so they left. I found them next door at the sweets shop. I'll see if I can find the others who were hoping to see you. They might still be nearby."

She leaps onto the floor and scurries toward the stairs.

There really were people eager to see me.

With a triumphant grin, I rise from my chair. William Haywood comes into view over my wall of books. To my great pleasure, he's watching me with an arched brow. I refuse to meet his gaze.

With exaggerated moves, I uncap my ink pot, flourish my pen, and address my reader. "Can I sign something for you?"

"Please," she says, fanning her tear-stained cheeks. She turns to her friends, who hand over bundle after bundle of books. My eyes widen as she sets them on my table. Not because there are so many, but because these aren't just multiple copies of my newest book like the other young woman brought to Mr. Asshole Poet earlier. These are copies of every book I've ever written and published.

But only my newest book has been published in Faerwyvae. My previous titles were only published in Bretton.

I meet her eyes with astonishment. "How did you get all these?"

She beams at me. "I found a few at select bookstores around the isle that specialize in imports, but most I had to pay an arm and leg to purchase by mail from Bretton. It took me the better part of a year to collect them all."

"But…how did you even learn about me to begin with?" My newest book is a recent release. How has she been collecting my books for a year?

"Queen Gemma's Book Club, of course."

"Queen Gemma's Book Club?" I echo. "What is that?"

Her eyes go wide. "You don't know about it? Queen Gemma is your biggest fan. She's been praising your books since before she married the Unseelie King of Winter."

"King of—you're telling me Queen Gemma is an *actual* queen. It's not just a…cute title? She's a real live queen who… who likes my books?"

"She is! And she hosts a book club in the form of a monthly periodical. She chooses each month's book, we read along and send in letters about our thoughts. She publishes some of our reviews, and a dozen club members are selected at random to join her for an in-person meeting each month. So far, the club has read half of the *Governess in Love* series. I daresay we'd have read them all if she didn't try to play fair and give attention to other authors. But she simply adores you!"

I fall into my chair, my knees too weak to hold me up any longer. A queen. An actual queen is my biggest fan and she's been promoting me for over a year. I…I can hardly process this news.

When my publisher wrote to me with the proposal for the book tour and informed me I'm *slightly famous* on the isle, I thought he meant my new book was making its rounds. I had no clue I'd already established a name for myself here based on my prior works. The meager royalties I earn in Bretton have done nothing to suggest my book sales have increased. My old publisher certainly hasn't treated me like I've become more in-demand. It's always been war with him, each sale a heated negotiation that always ends in me getting less than I think I deserve, followed by his unsolicited advice that I should consider writing *fine literature* or something *targeted for the educated male reader*.

The bastard forgets I did write a literary piece, and he refused to publish it since I wouldn't agree to let him do so under a male pseudonym.

I stare at the spread of books before me, emotion clogging my throat as I experience what it's like to have my work so thoroughly appreciated for the first time.

"Are you all right, Miss Danforth?" the woman whispers, concern etched upon her face. "I hope I haven't upset you in some way."

"No, of course not!" I shake my head to clear it. "It's quite the opposite. I'm just so moved."

I manage to return to my feet. Asshole Poet comes back into view, and I sense him staring at me. This time I meet his gaze and hold it with triumph.

Who writes drivel now, you smug bastard?

I give him too much credit by expecting he'll finally look abashed. A corner of his mouth lifts in a smirk that oddly feels like a challenge.

I grind my teeth and give all my attention to my dear reader and her mountain of books waiting to be signed. With my largest, most genuine smile of the day, I ask, "What is your name, my book-loving friend?"

CHAPTER FOUR

*a*fter two more hours, the crowd thins out and the end of the line is in sight. William Haywood's line, that is. I never manage to gain much of a line myself. In fact, only a few more readers approach my table at all, but each interaction is heartfelt, genuine, and a boon to my pride. It's enough to keep me from being too jealous of Mr. Haywood's incessant stream of fans. Besides, the lack of attention on me provides the perfect opportunity to covertly remove my shoes and rub my aching feet.

I dread the thought of putting my shoes back on. At this point, I'll be happy never to don them again. Perhaps I can get away with going barefoot until I'm reunited with the luggage Mr. Phillips fetched from the station. I haven't seen the publicist or Daphne much at all in the last hour. I reach into my dress pocket and retrieve my brass pocket watch. It's a quarter to three. In a matter of minutes, the signing will come to its official end.

Only one reader remains in the loft, and once he leaves Mr. Haywood's table, it will only be me and Asshole Poet. I decide I'd rather be busy when that happens, so I set about packing my remaining books into the two crates. I only sold a total of five since most of my fans already had a copy of *The Governess and the Fae*.

The last guest says his farewell to Mr. Haywood, then his footsteps sound down the stairs. The silence left in their wake makes my skin crawl. I pour all my attention into rearranging the books in the crate, making far more noise than necessary.

Even with my purposeful distraction, it's impossible to miss the sound of Mr. Haywood's movements as he rises from his chair. Every inch of my body is aware of his footsteps and the shift of his shadow as he leans against the edge of his table.

"I truly didn't expect you to show up."

I bristle. That's how he greets me? No formal introduction? No, *Sorry I made an ass of myself with that poor first impression. I never should have insulted your life's work by calling it smut and drivel. Let's start over*? I know most fae are less formal than humans are. Hell, some don't even have surnames, which is one of the main pillars of formality amongst human society. But I'd have taken even a casual greeting without offense.

I finally bring myself to look up at him, a cold smile on my lips while I bat my lashes. "Were you hoping I'd let you steal my tour entirely?"

"I was." His posture is leisurely, ankles crossed, hands propped at the edge of the table beside his hips. The light from the strings of glowing bulbs that crisscross the ceiling above him catches on his gold earrings. I notice he has more on his right ear than his left, lacking all sense of symmetry.

That, of course, means I'm staring. I shake my head and drag my gaze to my pen and ink pots, which I place in the crate. "You admit it."

He shrugs. "The tour should have been mine in the first place. I was here. I showed up."

That familiar discomfort writhes in my chest, begging me to explain myself again like I did outside the bookshop with Mr. Phillips. This time, I manage to stop myself before the deluge can leave my lips and instead give him a curt, "Well, I'm here now. So don't get too comfortable."

"Oh, I don't think my comfort is at risk. I may have been a tad worried when you first arrived, but you're no competition after all."

His words send fire to my cheeks. I rise to my feet and face him with my hands on my hips. "No, Mr. Haywood, I'm not your competition. We don't write in the same genre. We don't share the same readers. But for some asinine reason, we've been forced to share this tour. What was supposed to be *my* tour. You're lucky to be involved at all, so I suggest you get down from your high horse and thank me for being late and bestowing upon you the honor of being in my company."

His expression goes slack for all of a second before a corner of his mouth lifts. Maybe I'm imagining it, but he almost looks impressed. Or perhaps just amused. But the deeper his smirk grows, the more it makes my skin crawl. It looks a little too much like that seductive grin he first used on me when I arrived. After which he proceeded to shine it upon guest after guest after guest. His cheeks must ache after donning such a contrived expression without end. I can't fathom how I found that look even remotely dazzling when I first laid eyes upon him.

I wish I could say I found him less attractive now that I've gotten the full scope of his personality, yet he remains a work of art. A portrait of a devil, perhaps, but a beautiful one. I can't help but feel the contrast between us, with my dirty hem, bare feet, and undoubtedly wild hair.

He breaks my gaze with a sigh and rubs the back of his

neck in an aggravated gesture that gives the ends of his hair an extra tousle. Then, swiveling to the side, he reaches for something on his table before facing me once more. "A peace offering then," he says, tone brimming with reluctance.

I stare down at the hand he's extended toward me, bearing a green book with gold foil. It's Mr. Haywood's book. The title reads: *A Portrait of June, Etched in Solace*.

I snort a laugh. A pretentious title if I've ever seen one.

He thrusts the book closer to me.

I glance from the cover to Mr. Haywood's face. His gaze hovers somewhere above my shoulder, as if he'd rather look anywhere but at me. I shake my head. "No thank you."

"It's yours."

"It's not."

"It has your name in it," he says, finally deigning to meet my gaze. "I signed it for you and everything."

"I don't want it."

"It's free."

"I. Don't. Want. It."

"Well, I can't use it now." He leans forward and sets it on my table, never breaking eye contact even as he leans uncomfortably close. "Not unless someone named Ed asks for a copy."

I hold my breath, forcing myself not to flinch back. I only exhale once he leans back into his previous position. Belatedly, I process his words. "Ed? What do you mean *Ed*?"

His smirk returns, and this time there's a wicked edge to it. "That's all I had time to write before I realized who you were."

Irritation boils my blood. I lift the book from my table and flourish it before him. "That makes the book even less mine. My name is not Ed. I don't want a book addressed to someone named Ed. And I certainly don't want a copy of *your* book in any form."

With an indignant huff, I slam the book against his chest, which doesn't so much as make him stagger back. I let go and he fumbles to catch it before it can fall to the ground.

I take the opportunity to make my exit and march toward the stairs. I'm almost to the first step when his voice grates upon my ears. "Aren't you forgetting something, Ed?"

I've never felt so much indignation in all my life. I whirl around, ready to spew a thousand insulting nicknames of my own, but the words catch in my throat. He's still slouched against the edge of his table, his book in one hand. In the other, he holds my shoes, which dangle from his fingertips by their laces.

Mortification clogs my throat. It's bad enough that he knows I'm barefoot. Now he's touching my shoes. Shoes I ran around town and sweated profusely in.

He looks at me from under his lashes, taunting me with the ever-growing curve of his lips. "I'm not giving back your shoes until you take the book."

"Then you can keep them both." On bare feet, I whirl on my heel and storm down the stairs, stomping my fury with every step.

I REGRET THE STOMPING AS I REACH THE BOTTOM FLOOR AND find the bookstore silent now that the signing is over. Shop patrons pause their perusal of the shelves to cast me bewildered looks. I shrink down, my expression apologetic. Now that I'm down here, I'm not sure where to go. I'd like to be reunited with my luggage and better shoes, if possible. Or at least my carpet bag, where I can find my notebook. I can certainly think of one new entry I'd like to make.

Fourteen Ways to Die in Faerwyvae: Arrogant Fae Poet Edition.

Oh, wouldn't that be cathartic?

I recall Mr. Phillips mentioning he'd store my bag behind the counter, so I make a beeline to the sylph he'd called Arwen. She's in the process of wrapping a stack of books in parchment and twine, likely reserving them for a customer. I give her an awkward smile as I reach the counter, unsure how to greet her. Is she the type of fae without a surname? Should I formally introduce myself?

She saves me the trouble. "How was the signing, Miss Danforth?"

"Lovely," I say, adjusting my spectacles out of anxious habit more than necessity. "Thank you so much for hosting me. Flight of Fancy is a lovely bookshop."

I pause. Worry my lip. I know we should exchange pleasantries a little longer, but I do so want my bag.

My next question comes out in a rush. "Do you happen to see a carpet bag behind your counter?"

Her blue hair continues to blow on a wind I don't feel, and I make a mental note to jot down her lovely appearance as possible character inspiration. She shakes her head. "Mr. Phillips took your bag to the back room when he returned with your luggage. The room is behind that door, to the right of the café."

I glance at the portion of the bookstore set with tables and chairs, only one of which is occupied; its patron is a fluffy raccoon who is reading a book with one hand and sipping tea with the other. Excitement buzzes in my chest. Another unseelie fae! I saw only one other during the signing, a bear in a top hat who came to see Mr. Haywood.

My mood sours at once as I recall my irritating exchange with the poet.

"Shall I escort you?" Arwen asks.

She's still tying her parcel, so I shake my head. "I can see the door from here. Thank you."

I make my way to the back of the shop, trying not to stare too hard at the adorable raccoon fae but failing miserably. I'm so distracted, I almost bump into one of the tables. Skirting around it more carefully this time, I approach the back door.

"Edwina doesn't really stand a chance against him, does she?" The voice is muted behind the slightly ajar door, but I recognize the flat feminine tone as belonging to Daphne.

"I wouldn't be so sure," says a male voice. That must be Mr. Phillips. "Today is only her first day. I think more will come to see her once word spreads that she's not fully absent from the tour."

I beam at his vote of confidence in me. I reach for the handle but hesitate as Daphne speaks again.

"Yes, but he's already had a head start. Mr. Fletcher is making his decision based on sales during the tour, isn't he? That's what Sandy in marketing said."

"He is," Mr. Phillips says, "and I do believe total sales might be in Mr. Haywood's favor by the end if today's turnout is indicative of future signings. But there's also a choice involved on their end. Mr. Haywood may not want to publish three more poetry books. You've heard the way he talks about his *grand and most illustrious art, that which can neither be forced nor tamed, but danced with like the wind and a blade of grass*, or whatever it is he says."

I'd take pleasure in his mocking tone if I wasn't so confused over their subject matter. What is this about a decision my publisher is making?

"He's expressed great interest in publishing more books with Fletcher-Wilson," Daphne says.

"He has?"

"Do you pay attention to anything?"

"When I must." I can hear the smile in Mr. Phillip's voice. Then he takes on a more serious tone. "Maybe Miss Danforth doesn't want to live in Faerwyvae."

My heart leaps at the mention of my name again, but I'm more confused than ever.

"She'd have to live here?" Daphne says.

"For at least a year. It's the best way to take advantage of the marketing budget that will come with the contract. More tours. More events. Besides, Mr. Fletcher wants any subsequent books we publish of hers to be set in modern-day Faerwyvae, and therefore factually accurate. A year of research would do her good."

"I have to agree with that. Why did everyone in *The Governess and the Fae* have fangs and drink blood? Is that really what they think of us in Bretton?"

I internally wince. Daphne isn't wrong about that inaccuracy. How was I to know better?

"Did you not know?" comes a voice beside my ear.

I jump so high, I'm surprised my soul didn't leave my body. Turning, I find William Haywood behind me. How he snuck up so silently, I haven't a clue.

"What are you doing here?" My voice is a furious whisper as I unceremoniously shove him by the arm until he moves away from the door. I don't want Daphne and Mr. Phillips to know I overheard their conversation.

"Ah, you didn't know." He doesn't bother to whisper like me.

"Did I not know about what? That...that fae don't have fangs? It was a creative choice, and I stand by it—"

"The contract," he says, and my mouth snaps shut. "One of us will be offered a covetable contract based on our sales performance during the tour. *Only* one of us."

I frown. "That can't be true. Mr. Fletcher said he's open to more book proposals from me if they're about fae characters."

"This isn't just any contract. This is a three-book deal with a massive advance and a significant marketing push over the next year. They've never offered a contract like this before and I daresay they won't offer one like it again until they've tested whether it bears fruit. The offer was in your hands until you were late and nearly botched your tour."

I blink at him, nausea writhing in my gut at the thought of what I was nearly given and might have already lost. A three-book contract. A marketing push. Fletcher-Wilson is the primary publisher in Faerwyvae. If they're offering a one-of-a-kind contract, this truly is a rare opportunity. And if what I overheard is true, I'd have the chance to live here if I'm offered it.

I haven't considered whether I'd want to live in Faerwyvae, but with very little tying me down back home, I can't help but be excited at the prospect. Not to mention my publishing advance is worth ten times more in Faerwyvae than it is in Bretton, thanks to the abysmal exchange rate. I could be rich!

And yet...

The contract is not yet mine.

"Now I've been added to Mr. Fletcher's considerations," he says, voicing my exact revelation. He winks. "I hope you won't hold it against me when I win."

Retorts burn my chest, but I'm still too shocked. My words lack the bite I wish they had. "You...you don't know you're going to win."

"Oh, but I do. I need this. I'm getting it."

I scoff. "Is this what your *competition* comment was about? Because you've seen me as a rival from the start?"

He tilts his head to the side and gives me a patronizing

look. "Oh, Ed, you'll have to sell a lot more books to be my rival."

Before I can react, he lifts a finger, taps me lightly on the nose, and saunters off.

My hands curl into fists. I have every intention of marching after him and giving him a piece of my mind when the back door opens.

Mr. Phillips pulls up short. "Ah, you're here. Is the signing over?"

Daphne slinks out of the back room after him. "Do you ever look at your pocket watch or is it just for decoration?"

The publicist chuckles, then gives me a dimpled grin. "Well, then. How about we have drinks and dinner on Fletcher-Wilson's tour budget?"

CHAPTER FIVE

The last thing I want is to have dinner with my new nemesis, but I don't know what the alternative is if I refuse. I'm still new to this situation. I've never been on a book tour before nor have I had a publicist. Mr. Phillips seems to serve as a tour manager as well, and if he's in charge of our room, board, and meal budget, then it's probably best that I stay at his side. Or at least until I'm comfortable enough to go off on my own.

I have my own money, at least, thanks to my generous publishing advance from *The Governess and the Fae*. Eleven pouches full of eleven different currencies—one for each of the fae courts—are packed in my carpet bag.

But...tour budget. I really should take advantage of that, shouldn't I?

Dinner turns out to be delightful, served in the public dining room at the quaint inn we'll be staying at. I've already seen my modest bedroom and confirmed the arrival of all my luggage. Which means I am indeed wearing shoes once more. I never found out what Mr. Haywood did with my uncomfortable pair, but good riddance.

If only I could be rid of him too. I glare at him whenever I unintentionally meet his eyes from across the dining table, but he remains perfectly unflustered. Ignoring me, aside from that infuriating smirk of his. At least I don't have to talk to him. There are plenty of others at our table to engage his attention. Mr. Phillips invited the shopkeeper, Arwen, to join us once Flight of Fancy was closed for the evening, and she brought along two friends who work at nearby shops.

I haven't interacted much with the working class, aside from at my local public house, where I like to write with a pint of ale. Most of my other interactions come from the occasional visits to my parents' estate. My family isn't aristocratic by any means, but they are wealthy. Were they not, I don't think they would have entertained my vocation as a writer. As the middle daughter with six siblings, all of whom either married well or went into business well, I am just expendable enough to be granted some freedoms. I live in my own cramped apartment above a butcher's shop in the city. So long as I keep my own home and don't rely on my family's funds, they won't pressure me to marry. If I ever did move back to the family estate, I'd undoubtedly be forced to marry, for women in Bretton are considered the property of their parents, brothers, or husbands well into adulthood. Unless they have a career like me, which isn't commonplace. But I, the expendable middle daughter, get to devote my entire life to writing.

Yet, as free as I am, this trip is teaching me just how small my world was before. Not just because I come from Bretton or because I've never met fae people or talking creatures before, but because I've missed out on perfectly ordinary experiences, like dining with shopkeepers or staying at an inn. Excitement bubbles inside me. I know that this—all I'm getting to experience—will make my writing richer.

After dinner, the dining room grows crowded, the

atmosphere shifting into lively frivolity as drinks are favored over food. Scents of smoke and alcohol infuse the air, mingling with the laughter and chatter. The others have gone to cavort with strangers while I remain alone at our table, nursing my second pint of ale. It tastes different from the ale back home, but it's delightful, crisp, and refreshing as it fills me with a calm buoyancy.

It's exactly what I need to keep less pleasant thoughts from consuming me. The publishing contract. The promise of fame. The prestige I've been fighting for my entire career. The fact that I might have already lost my chance. Mr. Haywood is clearly superior to me when it comes to sales. Daphne said so herself; he's already had a head start. Even Monty stated Mr. Haywood will most likely garner the most sales by the end of the tour, despite his confidence in me. If I can't find a way to sell more books than him...

I force the stressful considerations from my mind and slump lower in my chair, glad no one is paying attention to me or my undignified posture. My notebook is open to my playful entry entitled *Fourteen Ways to Die in Faerwyvae: An Illustrated Guide*. I'm revising my sketch of the wisp to make Way to Die Number Seven more accurate when a shadow falls over my page. The dining room is already rather dim thanks to the dark oak walls and minimal lighting fixtures that hang from the ceilings. Clenching my jaw, I ready my glare and look over my shoulder. Sure enough, there stands William Haywood, a glass of violet wine in hand.

"Cute," he says flatly, arching a brow at my drawing.

I close my notebook. "Is pestering me really so satisfying that you had to seek me out?"

He scoffs. "I'm not here for you, Ed."

My cheeks heat. "Do not call me Ed."

"Weenie, then?"

I whirl fully around. My voice trembles with the restraint

it takes to keep from shouting. "You will not call me Weenie either. It's Miss Danforth to you."

He leans down and props his forearms—his very bare and admittedly impressive forearms—on the back of the chair beside me. No longer in his suit jacket, his sleeves have been rolled to his elbows. His cravat hangs loose around his neck, his waistcoat is open, and the collar of his shirt has been unbuttoned to his clavicle. There's a flush to his complexion that speaks of his inebriation.

"Oh, come now," he says, voice low and poisonously sweet. He tilts his head in a boyish manner, and I'm struck by the realization that I haven't a clue how old he is. He looks close to Monty's or my age, but fae aging is still a mystery to me. My brochure explained that most fae cease aging when they reach maturity. For all I know, Mr. Haywood could be anywhere from five-and-twenty to two thousand. He takes a sip of his wine, his throat bobbing as he swallows. "We're going to become far too familiar over the course of the month to keep such formalities like surnames."

I blame the ale, but I find myself momentarily disarmed. "Then, if you must, you can call me Edwina."

"Aw, I want to be on a first name basis too," Mr. Phillips says as he approaches the table with an overfull tray. "I'd be honored if you'd call me Monty."

He sets the tray down at the center of our table to reveal an assortment of colorful beverages, some in wine glasses and others in tumblers. William removes his forearms from the back of the chair and plants himself upon the seat. Right next to me. He slumps to the side, legs spread wide, and somehow still manages to look graceful. Yet he's angled too close to me, and I note the way the hem of my skirt brushes the leg of his trousers. I changed before dinner, so at least my skirt doesn't drag on the ground. Though…is the way it touches Mr. Haywood any better?

I abruptly scoot several inches from him.

Daphne hops into the seat at my other side while Arwen and her two companions settle in beside William. Monty remains standing and flourishes a hand at the tray. "Enjoy."

There are twice as many beverages as there are bodies at our table, and I'm the only one who doesn't immediately reach for a drink. Daphne extends her paws toward a tiny cup and brings its contents to her whiskered muzzle.

"What are you drinking?" I ask.

"Blackberry cordial."

Watching a pine marten consume spirits is not something I ever thought I'd see in my lifetime. I assess Monty's beverage next, a clear liquid in a tumbler. "And you?"

"This?" He frowns and takes a drag from the cigarillo he holds between two fingers. "Water. I don't imbibe anymore. I'm a working man now. Responsible." He says it with very little enthusiasm, then throws back a swallow of his benign beverage with the gusto of a man who must have once imbibed a great deal.

There's a story there, I can sense it.

But more interestingly…

Booze.

I study the tray and find another pint of the same ale I've been drinking. But how can I keep drinking ale when there's such a colorful spread before me? Violet wine like William drinks. An entire bottle of blackberry cordial. And several glasses of a rather curious drink that is clear indigo on the bottom half and a creamy pastel blue on the top. I note this is Arwen and her companions' beverage of choice.

"What's that?" I ask, pointing at the one on the tray.

William leans forward and slaps me lightly on the back of my hand. "Not for you."

I burn him with a seething glare. "Excuse me—"

"He's probably right about that," Monty says with a

chuckle. "That's Cloud Dive. It reacts differently with everyone but has a stronger effect on humans."

So it's a fae beverage. I was cautioned about fae fruits in my brochure. Overconsumption of fae spirits is Way to Die Number Nine, but if I remember correctly, the warning was specifically regarding liquor made from *dangerous* fae fruits.

I glance at Arwen and her companions who chat animatedly. The sylph shopkeeper is clearly pureblood fae, but the two women with her have rounded ears. They seem to be enjoying Cloud Dive just fine.

I glance back at the layered beverage with no small amount of longing. I at least want to know what it tastes like—

"Not. For. You." With every word, William inches closer and closer until our shoulders brush, his eyes locked on mine. He blinks at me, his lids slow and heavy. "Trust me."

"Trust you? Why should I trust you?" He's my rival, not to mention he's already more inebriated than I am. I scoot even farther away from him and face Monty. "What exactly are its ill effects?"

Monty shrugs. "Cloud Dive's motto is *It goes to your head*. It's the Wind Court's specialty and represents the element of air. For some, that means a feeling of lightness or ease. For others, it enhances their sense of intellect. Creatives use it to generate new ideas. But that can also devolve into an overinflated ego and delusions of grandeur."

That doesn't sound so bad. Especially the part about enhancing intellect and generating ideas. I need more story ideas! I'll need something to show I deserve a three-book contract. Controlling sales numbers is impossible, but presenting three brilliant book proposals is something I can do. Maybe this liquid muse can help.

William's eyes bore into my profile. If he wanted me to show restraint, he shouldn't have tried to stop me. Now half the reason I want to drink it is to spite him. I reach for the glass. William tries to intercept me, but a slender blue hand falls over the back of his.

Arwen dances her fingertips up his forearm, drawing his eyes to hers. "Let her have fun," she says, batting her lashes in a way that looks far too effortless. She angles herself toward him, and her fingertip glides up his arm until it's under his chin. "Tell me one of your poems."

William forgets me entirely, shifting toward her, and for some reason, that fills me with rage.

Without a second thought, I take the glass from the tray and down its contents.

CHAPTER SIX

I'm walking on air. Cloud Dive is the most delectable drink I've ever had. And I've had three now. The flavor is like blueberries and moonlight while its effects are unlike anything I've felt before. Where wine and ale dull my senses after a time, Cloud Dive sharpens my mind. I've never felt so clear or clever. Every word that leaves my mouth is bloody brilliant.

I'm conversing with one of Arwen's friends, a human girl named Jolene Vaughn who works at the nearby modiste. Turns out, she's a fan of my books.

"Can I ask you something?" Miss Vaughn says, scooting closer to me, a conspiratorial grin on her lips. She occupies the chair Daphne sat in before the pine marten climbed into the rafters, where she now naps. Miss Vaughn's round cheeks are flushed pink, her lids slow and heavy, her golden hair falling loose around her shoulders. If she'd stuck to Cloud Dive like me instead of switching to wine, she wouldn't be so inebriated.

I'm more sober than I've ever been, and my hair looks fantastic. I've already restyled it four times all without the aid of a mirror because I can tell, just by the weight of the pins securing my tresses to the left side of my head above my ear, that I've just started a fashion trend. William keeps glancing at me from across the table where he chats with Arwen, so I know I've increased my allure.

"Can I? Please?" Miss Vaughn bounces eagerly in her seat, hands clasped in a pleading gesture.

Oh, right. She asked me a question.

"Of course you may, Miss Vaughn," I say in my most benevolent tone. "Ask me anything about my books and I will answer."

"First, call me Jolene, please. Second, your sex scenes are phenomenal." She doesn't lower her voice when she says the last part, and it strikes some small and reserved portion of my mind that she's speaking a touch too loudly for the subject at hand. "They're so inventive!"

"Aren't they?" I say, taking a sip of Cloud Dive from glass number four. My gaze lifts to William. He's leaning forward, laughing at something Arwen just said.

"I must know," Jolene says. "Are your sex scenes based on personal experience?"

William's face whips my way and I nearly choke on my drink. Coughing, I set my glass down. "Pardon?"

"Your sex scenes. Do you write them based on things you've done?"

Even though I'm looking fully at Jolene, I can see William watching from my periphery. So I give her the only answer I can. A lie. "Of course they are."

She gasps. "Really?"

"Really. I have a…a very robust sex life."

"And you've done everything you've written about."

"I most certainly have." I face William with a proud look, but he's already back in conversation with Arwen. Perhaps I imagined his interest.

"So even that scene in *The Governess and the Baron*, when he hoists her up the wall by her thighs, kneels before her and...*tastes her*," she whispers the last part. "You've done that?"

"Of course I have."

Of course I have *not*. In fact, I haven't done even a fraction of the interesting positions I've written about. But she doesn't need to know that.

Jolene looks truly impressed. "That's incredible. Here I thought sexuality was repressed in Bretton, and that female freedoms were few and far between."

She's right about that. Before I can get caught in my lie, I change the subject. "Which book of mine is your—"

She waves her hands at me in a hushing gesture, her attention now across the table. "I have to hear this," she says, voice trembling with excitement.

I follow her line of sight to find William standing before a small crowd. When the hell did he gather an audience? He speaks in a sonorous voice.

> "The darkest abyss of ardor's first kiss,
> A transaction of masks and lies,
> Her heart is traded for satin and silks,
> While mine is purchased in sighs."

His audience breaks into delighted applause, but I emit a snort of laughter. William angles his head toward me, and I realize the sound I made was louder than I intended. "Do you have something to say about my poetry, Weenie?"

Not that damn nickname again! He's really earned my ire now. I rise to my feet. "Yes, I have something to say, *Willy*."

"Please, delight us with your clever observations."

I open my mouth to do just that, only to find the effects of Cloud Dive are waning. So I take two deep gulps of my drink, lift my chin, and lock my eyes with his. "Your poetry is pretentious."

He faces the table fully and plants his hands on its surface. Even with him leaning down across from me, he still stands taller. "How so?"

"It's so convoluted. Do you even understand the words that leave your lips?"

"Aw, little Ed," he says, his mouth pulling into a mock pout. "Have my words gone over your head?"

I roll my eyes. "On the contrary, your words are beneath me."

"Think you'd make a better poet? You must be a veritable wordsmith, writing about the duke's massive throbbing member and the governess' mewling whines."

He knows about the duke's throbbing member? Does that mean he's read my books? I'm almost of a mind to ask when my rational side reminds me he's just making assumptions at my expense.

I fold my arms across my chest. "I *can* do better."

He mimics my posture, standing at his full height. "I dare you to try."

"I'll do more than try." My confidence flares, dimmed only by the fact that I have to crane my neck to hold his gaze. Well, I have a solution for that. Tugging the back of my chair, I slide it away from the table and stand upon the seat. Now I'm slightly taller than him.

My attention sweeps over the crowd, full of furrowed brows or half smiles of confused amusement.

Overhead, Daphne stretches in the rafters and peeks down at the commotion. "Oh, I've got to see this," she mutters.

My confidence swells once more. I haven't got a plan for what I'm going to say, but I'm the cleverest woman in the world right now. What do I have to fear?

I use my most pretentious voice as I begin, my pace admittedly slow and clunky while I string words together. But as each sentence falls from my mouth, the next forms.

> "There once was a man named Will,
> He thought he gave women a thrill.
> What he truly gave,
> Was an itch 'tween the legs,
> The kind only ointment can kill."

I erupt with laughter, which is echoed by those around me.

"Ah, you're making fun of my genital hygiene," William says, tone flat. "Such mature humor coming from you."

I'm busy bowing for my rapt audience when Will's voice carries over the clamor. He slowly rounds the table toward me as he speaks.

> "Ed, my dear,
> Little Weenie, I fear,
> My patience for you has passed.
> For who could endure,
> Another encore,
> Of such a persistent pain in the ass."

He stops directly before me as he states the last line, our faces mere inches apart. Another round of chuckles spreads through our audience. My cheeks flush, but I refuse to show an ounce of embarrassment.

"Honestly, that was the best I've heard from you yet," I say. "That one at least made sense."

"Forgive me if you lack the intelligence to understand the finer points of poetry." He lifts his finger to tap me on the nose like he did in the bookshop, but I intercept him, clasping his finger in my palm.

"Forgive *me* if you lack the imagination to appreciate the duke's massive throbbing member. I know it can be difficult when you've never seen visual proof." I glance suggestively at his forefinger still clenched in my hand, then let it go with a sneer. "But, yes, Willy, a cock can be larger than a teaspoon."

He plants his hands on his hips. "A teaspoon. Really?"

"Surprised, are you?"

"I am. I hadn't a clue a cock could be *smaller* than a teaspoon. My experience lies firmly in the realm of the magnus melon." He gives a significant tug to his waistband.

"Magnus melon?" I echo.

"Fae fruit," Daphne says from the rafters. "Very long and girthy."

Jolene leans toward us, her mouth practically watering as her gaze flicks from the front of his trousers to his eyes. "That's my favorite fruit."

William winks.

I jab him in the chest to draw his attention back to me. "Is that how you plan to win the publishing contract? By seducing your readers? Is that how you manage to sell so many books?"

"And how do you plan to win? Your readers are either spinsters or spinsters-in-training. I can't imagine you'd have great success utilizing your skills from your *oh-so-satisfying* sex life."

My cheeks heat. He was listening to my chat with Jolene after all.

I huff. "First of all, how dare you insult my readers by calling them spinsters. There's nothing wrong with a woman being unmarried at *any* age, and I don't appreciate you or society at large trying to make us feel ashamed about that.

Second of all, at least I don't have to fondle my fans to sell books."

He steps closer. As much as I want to flinch back, I dare not move, lest I tumble from my chair. "Even if you did fondle your fans, it wouldn't help you sell more books."

"Yes, you've already slandered my target audience," I say.

"Oh, I'm including everyone. You couldn't seduce the pants off a prostitute."

"That's false. I could pay them." Damn it all to hell, where did my cutting wit go? I turn the subject back to him. "I bet you're all talk. You may be able to seduce with words, but that doesn't mean you're even remotely adequate in bed. I bet you're a lousy lover."

"You think you're better?"

"I know I am. I've written books to prove it."

"Then prove it off the page. Seduce someone. Now. Tonight."

My mind goes blank. Without breaking eye contact, I lean carefully to the side to retrieve my drink and down the rest of the glass. Almost at once my mind grows clearer, lighter. I return the empty glass to the table. "I will. And I dare you to do the same."

"Easy," he says with a lopsided grin. "How about we make it interesting? A bet."

"Oh, did I hear the word bet?" Monty saunters up to the table. I hadn't realized he was missing during our poetry battle. A glance his way shows most of our crowd has dispersed, having lost interest as our conversation turned personal. "I love bets."

"More than your job?" Daphne calls down. She drops to the table, landing with a thud that rattles the empty glasses that litter its surface. "I don't think we should be encouraging this."

Monty waves a hand at her, his eyes locked on us. "Oh, hush. Things are finally getting interesting."

"Fine," I say. "I'll make a bet."

William sweeps his gaze down the length of me. "What are you willing to wager, love?"

I pause to think this through. I've never participated in a bet before, but I can't stop now. Not in this moment when I'm certain I've never been so clever, so bold, or so capable of sheer brilliance. My mind is whirling fast, but one idea stands out as worthy of a bet—something that will provide a solution to my most pressing problem.

"The publishing contract," I say, my voice quavering with exhilarated restraint.

William's face goes slack.

Monty's gaze flicks between us. "What publishing contract? You mean *the* publishing contract?" He looks at Daphne. "How do they know about that?"

"How do you *not* know that they know about it?" she says. "Did you not hear them outside the door when we were talking in the back room?"

"No. Your hearing is better than mine."

William gives me a simpering look. "Weenie, you can't bargain away your virtue for a publishing contract."

"My virtue? I'm sorry, I thought I was in Faerwyvae, where sexual freedoms are respected."

He clears his throat, his confidence faltering. He takes on an oddly serious tone as he lowers his voice. "We may be freer here, but there are many in seelie society who value propriety."

I've never been fond of propriety, especially when it primarily seeks to control and repress women without placing nearly as many restrictions on men. Hearing him push propriety's virtues only serves to inflame me more. "Are you afraid?" I taunt.

"For you? Yes." His tone has returned to normal, his arrogance back in place. "You're going to be humiliated. I'll win as soon as I walk away."

Panic slices through me. I was so wrapped up in the thrill of our exchange that I never once second-guessed the core of our conversation.

A bet.

Of seduction.

For all my talk, that is not my forte.

I've had my share of courtships, some of which included sexual relations, but I've never seduced anyone. Oh God, what was I thinking?

"Hold on. Stop, stop, stop." Monty holds up both hands, and I could thank the saintly man for coming to my rescue. "William is right. This is too easy. We need terms. A good game has clear rules. And you're bargaining something rather important."

"Monty, stop trying to get involved," Daphne says. To us, she mutters, "Ignore him. His personality is twisted."

Monty places a hand over his chest and pretends to stagger back. "You wound me, Daph!"

She rounds on him. "You're the one who said so! It was the first thing you told me when I started my internship. You said, 'I must inform you my personality is twisted. Don't take me too seriously.' Then you gave me that idiotic nickname."

"Daph? Oh, you mean Daffy Dear."

Daphne bares her teeth and then faces us once more with a roll of her small black eyes. "Monty is the kind of person you would absolutely pay to see get struck down by lightning, but...you'd also sort of be sad if they died. Like, I'd laugh if he got hit by a train, but I'd still weep over his remains. You know?"

"Aw, I'd weep over your remains too, Daffy Dear," Monty says in an exaggeratedly sweet tone. Then he rolls up his already rolled-up sleeves, flourishes his hands, and flicks his wavy blond locks from his face. One would think he was about to perform surgery or some other impressive feat. "Now, rules. What exactly does winning entail? Assuming you two know what I think you know, Mr. Fletcher is going to offer the contract-you-aren't-supposed-to-know-about based on sales during The Heartbeats Tour. How will a bet sway his decision?"

"I overheard you saying we'd be given a choice," I say. Wait, why am I entertaining this whole bet idea again? "If one of us refuses, the other will be offered the contract instead, correct?"

Monty wags a finger at me. "Ah, I see what you're getting at. The loser must refuse the contract, if offered. We're taking sales out of the equation and basing this entirely on sex? I like it."

"Let's stop this nonsense," William says with a shake of his head. He's serious again, so unlike his usual self. "We can't stake our careers on one night of sex. It's asinine."

Seeing him flustered urges me on. "What are you afraid of?"

A tic feathers the corner of William's jaw, but he says nothing.

"William is again correct," Monty says. "One night is too easy. So, let's make it…many nights. Whoever can seduce the most lovers by the end of the tour wins."

The word *win* refuels my excitement, as does the prospect of extending the duration of our bet to the end of the tour. That will give me multiple chances to take the lead from William. I could steal back the contract without having to beat him in sales. The clarity sharpening my mind reminds me this was my idea. My most brilliant and clever idea. Of course it's going to work in my favor.

A smile spreads over my lips.

"You're out of your mind," William whispers. "Drink some water. Sober up."

"I've never been more sober," I say, every word as clear and controlled as ever, demonstrating my point. If I were drunk, I'd be slurring my words, which I'm obviously not. "You just don't want to lose."

"I'm not going to lose."

I hold out my hand. "Then let's bet on it."

William reaches to grasp my palm. Before we can shake, Monty leans across the table to separate us with a chop of his hand.

"Now, Miss Danforth," Monty says, "not so fast. A bet with a fae is akin to a bargain. And fae bargains are magically binding. Not wise to agree when we still have terms to define."

Another slice of panic cuts through my floaty sense of confidence. He's right. Way to Die Number Three: making a bargain with a fae that results in accidental death. Such as agreeing to dance at a revel from sundown to sunrise and perishing from exhaustion. I doubt our bet would lead to such a demise, but then there's Way to Die Number Four: breaking a bargain with a fae. That almost always results in death. My brochure didn't specify whether the punishment is delivered by magic or law, but I'd rather not find out firsthand.

I lift both palms in surrender to show I'm not ready to shake on it after all.

Monty gives me an approving nod. "Smart choice. Next, we need to define seduction. We can't force intercourse, for there are ways to enjoy such relations without penetration."

My cheeks heat at his blunt use of words. I may write steamy romance novels, but rarely do I hear such topics discussed out in the open. Faerwyvae truly is a different world.

"How about this?" Monty says. "We'll define seduction as an act of physical intimacy between two parties behind the closed door of one's bedroom. And we need a deadline. These intimacies must take place by midnight on any given night. Or...should we make it less vague than *intimacy*—"

"Keep it vague," William says, tone icy. He really is acting strange. Then his expression softens, turning taunting once more. "For Weenie's sake."

"I don't need your consideration."

"Well, you have it. You're going to need it to beat me. It's not going to take me until midnight to find a willing bedfellow every night of our tour. You've seen the effect I have on others. Do you really want to go up against that?"

Were I not the most brilliant person in the world right now, walking on a cushioned ball of sunshine and rainbows provided by my most trusted friend, Cloud Dive, I might think there was wisdom in his warning.

"Gladly," I say, thrusting out my palm once more. "I agree to these terms."

This time, Monty has no further argument as William secures his hand around mine in a firm shake. His eyes are narrowed, that tic pulsing in his jaw once more. "I agree to them as well."

"This is fun," Monty says.

"This is a bad idea," mutters Daphne.

"This is going to be so easy," I say with a giggle as I drain the rest of my drink.

Part Two

HOW TO SEDUCE
A STRANGER

CHAPTER SEVEN

WILLIAM

*H*ow the hell did flirting with Edwina end in a bet where I'm supposed to sleep with someone who *isn't* her? Did she not understand that when I dared her to seduce someone tonight, I meant me? I made it so obvious. Didn't I?

Not that I want to sleep with her. Of course I don't. I don't even like the woman. She's a nuisance with a temper and my rival in securing the contract I desperately need. That isn't to say I don't enjoy her company. More than anything, I like how much she hates me. Which is why I dared her to try to seduce me. Wouldn't that be a riot?

But no. Instead of reading the subtext of my clear flirtations, she took my bait, added coal and fire to it, and sent it back to me. Of course I had to respond in kind. Add more coal. Add more fire. Again and again.

How the hell did it end in such a ridiculous bet?

I glance at my idiotic little nemesis now. Our party has moved from our table to the bar counter. She's slumped at the far end, her cheek propped in her hand, spectacles askew. Her eyelids droop, and her head begins to tilt. She's about to fully nod off but startles awake at the last minute and mumbles something incoherent.

I'm pleased to see the effects of Cloud Dive have run their full course. It serves her right, ignoring my warning. I almost believed her when she said she was perfectly sober, for she was rather sharp during our verbal exchange. Now her delusions of wit and grandeur have fizzled into drowsy incompetence, as Cloud Dive often does to humans.

I've seen it firsthand when my sister imbibed behind my back. She stayed up all night writing what she thought was the most brilliant stage play, only to spend the next day heaving up the contents of her stomach. And the script was, of course, complete nonsense. I only gave Edwina the benefit of the doubt because she's nine-and-twenty, whereas my sister is only nineteen.

Edwina almost nods off again. Her spectacles slide from her face to the counter, and when she startles awake, she goes to push the bridge of her lenses up her nose, but without them there, she jabs herself right between the eyes. She frowns, jabs again, then searches for her fallen spectacles on the counter. The impish grin she makes when she finds them and replaces them has my lips curling in turn.

Not because she's cute.

There's nothing cute about that foolish smile or her round flushed cheeks.

Or that tangled auburn hair that she managed to pin in what looks like a bird's nest on one side of her head.

Or the way she swings her legs on her too-high stool, humming a stupid little tune—

"William?" Arwen steps into my line of sight, her lovely blue face blocking my view of Edwina.

I shake my head, realizing this isn't the first time she's had to say my name. While I'm well into my cups tonight, I haven't had a drink since Edwina and I made our bet. Word of our bargain quickly spread, which sent a flock of males to my rival. With Monty flitting about the room like a butterfly, someone had to stay sober and keep an eye on Edwina, lest she leave with one of the men.

For the sake of sabotage, of course.

Not for her protection.

Thankfully, it didn't take long for her faculties to unravel, and she lost her male companions. No decent person would try to bed a drunkard who no longer had the means to consent.

I force my attention to settle on Arwen. "Sorry, love, what were you saying?"

"I asked if it's true that you're really a stage actor, as well as a poet."

I don my winning grin, one that is admittedly growing tired on my visage. "It's true. I am a stage actor and have been since my days at university."

"Have you been in anything I would have seen?" Jolene asks.

It takes an effort not to glower at the human girl. She's practically clung to my side since the bet began, and I'd feel much better if she would have stayed with Edwina to give her some female company.

Again, for the sake of sabotage.

"Big productions aren't my style," I say. The words almost burn my tongue, for they aren't entirely true.

Pureblood fae like me can't lie.

Unless you're an actor playing a role.

"I prefer private plays or artistic endeavors," says William

Haywood the Poet, while William Haywood the Stage Actor would give anything to star in a big production.

"I'd love to see a private play," Jolene says, blinking up at me from under her lashes.

Arwen sidles into her friend and steals my attention. "It's getting close to midnight."

I know what she's getting at. According to the terms of the bet, I must enjoy an act of intimacy in my bedroom by midnight. Arwen and Jolene have been engaged in a competition of their own—who can earn their place in my bed tonight.

Little do they know, I have no intention of participating in anyone's game. Not Arwen and Jolene's. Not mine and Edwina's. She and I may have secured our bargain by verbally agreeing to the terms of the bet—that's all it takes to make a bargain with a fae—but this farce will be over by morning, I'm sure of it. The little idiot will wake up, remember all her horrible decisions from tonight, and beg me to release her from our bargain. Easy. Done.

Then I can go back to beating her in sales and win the contract on my personal merits.

I may be eager to win—desperate, more like—but I'd prefer to do so with my dignity intact.

"I am growing tired," Arwen says when I fail to respond. "What I wouldn't give to have a quiet place to sit down."

I lean slightly to the side, stealing a glimpse at Edwina. She's awake, but barely, chatting to someone I can't quite see. Then the figure—a fae male with a mane of golden hair and a feline nose—leans down and whispers something in her ear.

She laughs, then lets out a startled squeal. "Oh, you have a taaaail!" She drags out the last word too long and too loud. Her eyelids grow heavy again, and I catch sight of the tip of a tan, fur-tufted tail tickling her cheek. The male must be a lion fae in his seelie form. She gives a halfhearted chuckle with her eyes closed. "I'm writing a book about a fae with a tail. You wouldn't happen to be in love with a surgeon, would you?"

"Oh, I'd love to sit down too," Jolene says, tugging my sleeve.

"There are plenty of open seats at the end of the bar," I bite out. If the girl would just fucking keep Edwina company—

Jolene's stricken expression snaps me back to my purpose. Shit. I stepped out of my role for a moment and lost my patience. That wasn't something William Haywood the Poet would say to a pretty woman interested in his writing.

I force a sigh and drop my head. "Those were the last words she said to me," I say under my breath.

"Who?" Arwen says. She and Jolene exchange a look. "You mean June? The woman your poetry is about? That's what the title of your book means, doesn't it? *A Portrait of June Etched in Solace*. Such a lovely title."

My gaze is distant as I lift my head. Addressing none of their questions, I say, "Someone I used to know. Blooming hell, it was so long ago now. *I just need to sit down.* That's what she said to me. Then she was gone."

Jolene places a hand on my forearm. "I didn't mean to dredge up such painful memories."

"Memories are like broken glass," I say. "They only hurt if you touch them."

"That's beautiful," Arwen says.

I flash her a mournful smile, then my eyes dart back to Edwina.

Only…she's not there.

I shift from side to side, glancing over the heads of patrons who stand between me and the end of the bar, but I see no sign of her.

Something tightens in my chest. "Where's Edwina?"

The women startle and glance behind them.

Arwen cocks her head. "She was just there—"

I rush to the end of the bar. There's no sign of Monty or Daphne, only strangers. Monty may have left outside to sully the air with his cigarillo smoke, while Daphne is probably dozing in the rafters again.

"Where is the woman who was sitting here?" I ask the patrons who'd been nearest Edwina.

"She left just a moment ago," an older woman says with a shrug, her breath reeking of ale.

"Alone?"

"No, with a gentleman—"

I rush to the back of the dining room where the stairwell to the bedrooms is located. Urgency fuels my steps as I clear the stairs two at a time. I'd tell myself this is about sabotage, but it's more than that. Edwina was nowhere close to being in her right mind. If that fae with the lion's tail seeks to take advantage of an almost unconscious woman...

Rage boils my blood.

I have a sister, for fuck's sake. How could I not get angry at the thought? In this situation, I can't keep up the pretense of being William the Poet. I'm not even William the Stage Actor right now.

In this moment, I'm just Will, and I've had a long fucking day plastering a smile to my face and flirting with strangers. The only real fun I've had is teasing Weenie, but look where that got me. I haven't an ounce of patience left for assholes, so this male better not be one.

At the top of the stairs, the hallway is dimly lit and empty. I sprint around the corner and finally spot who I'm looking for.

Edwina sways on her feet as she struggles to fit her brass room key into the lock of a door. A door that is not hers. Our bedrooms are farther down the next hall. The lion fae stands

61

behind her, his tail flicking back and forth, protruding from the back of his trousers. It's common for fae with animalistic features in their seelie forms to wear clothing that accommodates them. Others can shift certain features at will, and their clothing shifts with them. So the sight of his tail out in the open isn't what sparks my ire.

It's the way his tail tugs the hem of her skirt, brushing her ankles with every flick and swish. Then her calves.

I start down the hall, fingers balled into fists.

Edwina startles, but not at my approach. Neither she nor the lion fae seem to hear my footsteps. She yelps at the brush of the lion's tail and whirls to face him. Her lids are still heavy, but she forces them wider. "Whoareyou?" she says, words slurred together.

"Darling, we've been chatting for minutes," he says, voice smooth. "You need to take someone to bed before midnight. And you said you've always wanted to try the pleasures of a man with a tail."

He flicks it up to brush her neck.

She cringes away, hands raised to block him. "Nope, nope. Not as sexy as I thought."

He swishes his tail back to her hem. She retreats a step but trips over her own feet. She giggles as she tumbles to the ground.

The lion fae chuckles too and flicks his tail toward her once more.

I finally reach them and grip the back of his collar. He's several inches shorter than I am, and when I force him to face me, he pales. I lower my voice to a growl. "And just what the fuck do you think you're doing?"

"I…I was walking her back to her room."

"You're never going to walk again if you don't get out of my sight at once."

I release his collar, and the lion has the good sense to

make himself scarce before I can think better of it. Once he's out of sight, I face Edwina.

She's lying on her back, chortling to herself. "He had a tail. A long, floppy tail. I don't know what Johannes sees in you, Timothy."

I haven't a clue who Johannes or Timothy are, but she's in no shape to find her bedroom. With a grumbling sigh, I kneel before her and heft her against my chest. She complies with my efforts and winds her arms around my neck, letting me secure her in place. She's as light as a petal.

"No, I don't want to fly," she mumbles into my shoulder as I carry her down the hall. We stop outside her room—one I only know is hers because it's directly across from mine. She fights me as I try to pry her room key from her fingers, but her efforts are weak.

"Calm down, Weenie, I'm trying to get you safely to your room."

"Oh. You." She says it with no small amount of disdain but relinquishes her key by shoving it against my cheek. I snatch it before it can slide down my face and into my collar. Then, shifting her weight to one arm, I unlock her door. Once inside the room, I sweep over to her bed, guided by the meager moonlight creeping through the window. I lay her gently upon the mattress and remove her spectacles, not letting my hands linger any longer than necessary. She burrows into the pillows without bothering to undress or get under the blankets.

She's going to regret sleeping in her clothes and corset, but I'm not about to undress her. Instead, I can ensure the room is warm. After I set her lenses on her nightstand, I light the stove, pour her a glass of water, and return to her side.

"You should drink something." I keep my voice soft and low as I crouch beside the bed.

"No more Cloud Dive," she mutters.

"Not Cloud Dive. Water."

With a groan, she stirs and pushes herself up slightly. I aid her efforts to drink until she's taken a few hearty swallows. Then I return the glass to the nightstand.

She falls back onto her pillows. "What's stabbing me in the head?"

"Probably a headache."

She groans again, then begins tugging at her hair.

Oh, right, the nest of tangles and pins she constructed.

"You're making it worse," I say and plant myself at the edge of her mattress. Then, gingerly, I seek out one pin at a time and tug it free from her hair. Another experience I have, thanks to my sister. Once I've removed all the pins—or what I can only assume are all of them with the disastrous mane Edwina has—I smooth out her tangles as best I can. She can do the rest with a brush on the morrow.

"You're not William," she says, eyes closed.

"I'm not?"

"No. You're being nice to me. You must be Monty. You saved me from a wicked villain. You're my hero, Mr. Phillips."

I scoff. "All Monty did was encourage our bet. He's an accomplice in stupidity, not a hero."

She whimpers. "No, I'm too late! It must be past midnight now."

"It doesn't matter," I say, rising to my feet. "We'll dissolve the bargain tomorrow."

She says nothing to that. Perhaps she didn't hear me. There's no point talking about it now anyway. I'll wait until we have a moment to speak in private when she's sober and willing to listen to reason.

"Who did William choose?" she whispers.

I frown. "Hmm?"

"Which girl did William choose? Who did he take to his

64

bed tonight? No, don't tell me. He's a point ahead, either way." Her voice catches on the last words. She sniffles. "He's going to win, isn't he? I've only known him a single day, but it's enough to convince me I can't compete with him, no matter what I do. He's better than me in every way."

The sorrow in her voice lances my heart. I may like taunting her when she's sober, but I take no pride in seeing her upset while she's drunk. "He's not better than you."

"He is. Everyone loves him. Men. Women. I lied when I said he's probably a lousy lover. I bet he's a god in bed. I bet his throbbing member would put the duke's to shame."

I stifle my urge to laugh. Burying my mirth, I step away from her bed. "Get some sleep, Miss Danforth." I make to turn around, but something snatches the leg of my trousers. Glancing down, I find Edwina's fingers pinched around the fabric near my calf.

"Can I tell you a secret, Monty?"

I work my jaw side to side. "Save your secrets for morning."

"I lied," she rushes to say, "to Jolene. I don't have a spectacular sex life. I…I hardly have one at all."

I crouch beside her bed once more. "You weren't fooling anyone with that, trust me."

"I don't do the things I write about." Her voice warbles with emotion. "I only imagine them. My imagination is very impressive when it comes to smut."

"I bet it is."

"But in real life…I'm a fraud. I'm faking it."

Her words resonate deep in my chest. I lean closer, lower my voice, and confess that which very few know. "I'm a fraud too, Edwina."

With her eyes still closed, she reaches up to pat me on the shoulder, her motions sloppy. Then her grip suddenly tightens, and her fingers wind around my collar.

"Oh, no." The dread in her voice has me freezing in place. "What is it?"

She tugs my collar, lifts herself from the bed, and surges toward me. I brace my arms to catch her, unsure of what's happening or what she needs—

She heaves blue liquid all over my shirt.

CHAPTER EIGHT

EDWINA

The first thing I'm aware of when consciousness creeps upon me is pain. Pain in my skull, pain in my gut, pain in my throat. Then the nausea turns my stomach, followed by the distinct sense of the room spinning around me. But…what room? Where am I?

I pry my eyes open, seeing only a hazy blur at first. Then a ceiling forms over my head—dark, save for the shard of pale illumination that cuts across it. I drag my gaze to the window and find the faintest glow of predawn light. I recognize the silhouette of the building that makes up half the view. This must be my bedroom.

Fire sears my throat. I've never been so parched. An inch at a time, I pull myself to sitting, and my vision spins ten times faster. I wince against the jab of pain that erupts in my temple and blindly reach for my nightstand. My fingers brush the curve of a glass. I secure my hand around it and bring the refreshing liquid to my lips. Too soon, my water is gone.

I cast my gaze around the room for the pitcher, unable to remember where it is. I wasn't in my bedroom for long before dinner, so I'm not too acquainted with its layout. My eyes snag on the orange glow burning in the small stove across the room. So that's why I'm so unbearably hot.

I reach for my chemise, determined to remove a layer… but my fingertips meet only skin. Alarmed, I pull my covers away and my bare breasts greet me. I frown. It's not like me to sleep in the nude. I tend to prefer the comfort of at least one layer. When I'm not sweating in a stiflingly hot room, that is. I glance back at the stove, willing my predicament to make a modicum of sense.

That's when I see the wingback chair angled toward the stove.

And the silhouette of the male figure that slumbers in it.

Pulling my blankets over my chest, I erupt with a shriek. One that dies in a raspy croak but startles the sleeping man awake. He leaps from the chair and whirls to face me. Through the scarce illumination and my still-swimming vision, I make out pointed ears, mussed hair, and a bare expanse of muscled chest.

My own nakedness takes on new meaning.

"No!" I shout.

"Weenie," he hisses, "quiet down. You'll wake the whole inn."

Oh God. That voice. I know that voice. And as my eyes adjust more and more to the light, I can make out his face too. Even without my spectacles, I recognize those eyes, those lips.

"No!" I repeat, even louder this time. I pull my blanket up to my chin. "No, no, no. Don't tell me…"

He gives me a withering look. "Is your imagination running wild?"

A surge of memories spills into my awareness. I recall standing on a chair, spouting ridiculous poetry. The insults I exchanged with William. The bold confidence that spurred me on.

Cloud Dive, you traitor! It didn't make me brilliant. It didn't give me any genius ideas, only the opposite. And now...

"The bet," I say under my breath.

"Ah, the mortification sets in." Wicked mirth laces his voice.

"What did you do to me, William? This...this isn't how we were supposed to—"

"I didn't do anything that you're imagining, Ed."

"Then why are you shirtless?"

"You threw up on me."

"Then why am I shirtless?"

"Why the fuck do you think? You threw up on yourself too." Shaking his head, he hastens over to a clothesline strung between the stove and the wardrobe. Two articles of clothing hang from it. He snatches down the larger one and whirls back to face me. "I barely touched you. My worst offense was loosening your corset so you could remove it yourself. Then I spent the next half hour scrubbing vomit from your blouse. I slept in the chair to ensure you didn't hurl again and choke to death on your stomach's contents."

I blink at him. He did all that? For me? Suspicion dampens my surprise. Why was he in my bedroom in the first place?

He heads for the door, his aggravation painted in every long stride. "You're welcome."

"Wait!"

He halts, his fingers frozen on the handle.

69

I swallow the renewed dryness in my throat. "You mean... we really didn't..."

He tips back his head with a long-suffering sigh, then slowly faces me once more. His eyes are narrowed, his lips curled in a cruel smirk. He glares down at me as he approaches the bed like a predator cornering his prey.

My senses are all mixed up because a strange thrill flutters through me.

He stops at the edge of my bed, plants one hand on the mattress, and leans down, giving me a much closer look at the firm musculature of his chest, the hollows of his collarbones, the length of his neck. His eyes lock on mine, and I shrink back, pinning my blankets more firmly to my chest. Still, the thrill remains, my heart thudding as I wait for whatever wicked thing he's about to do.

"Oh, Weenie," he says, voice so soft and deep it makes me shudder, "if we'd been together last night in the way you're imagining, we'd have done more than remove our tops, and I would be in bed beside you, not in a chair. You wouldn't have to ask what we'd done because every inch of your body would remember. You'd still be quaking from the pleasure I gave you. You'd be slick both from our expenditure and your want for more."

A breath leaves my parted lips and I find myself swaying, my grip on my blankets slackening.

He leans ever closer, one knee on my bed now. His free hand inches toward me, then softly lands on the top edge of the blanket I continue to clutch. One I'm growing dangerously close to relinquishing.

"But I don't bed drunk idiots, unlike some people." His expression turns back to annoyance. He gives my blanket a firm tug, and my weakening grip gives way. "That's mine."

Belatedly, I realize my chest is still covered in my sheet, and what I thought was my blanket was his waistcoat.

My cheeks blaze with my humiliation. Why was I snuggling with his waistcoat?

He doesn't look back at me as he sweeps out of my room, his shirt and waistcoat in hand, but my gaze certainly lingers on his wide bare back before my door slams shut.

I'm left blinking in his wake, wondering what the hell almost came over me when he was on my bed. I fall back on my pillows, my mortification growing tenfold as more memories from last night take shape in my mind. Shoving my face into my pillow, I mutter a wail, wishing there was some fae magic that could turn back time and let me erase the last several hours of my life.

LATER THAT AFTERNOON, WE BOARD A TRAIN TO OUR NEXT destination. Thankfully, my nausea has subsided and I was able to sleep until eleven-thirty. Which was thirty minutes past when we were supposed to leave for the station. I've also succeeded at avoiding William most of today. Even now as I settle into my train compartment, I'm awarded further respite, for William and Monty are in the next compartment over. With just me and Daphne, there's ample space to laze about on the plush seats, each bench long enough to fit four passengers and upholstered in an indigo-and-silver brocade so fine I could almost convince myself I'm in some wealthy widow's parlor. The walls are of rich oak and the windows are adorned in silk curtains to match the seats, drawn open to a view of the platform. The bustle of the station has died down, which tells me the train will soon depart.

Just when I'm about to abandon all sense of propriety and slouch over the length of my seat, our compartment door slides open. I stiffen, expecting William has come to bother us from next door...only it's neither of my male traveling companions.

It's Jolene.

"I'm so glad I was able to procure a ticket in time," she says, catching her breath as she drops herself into the seat across from me, beside Daphne. The pine marten, not wanting to share her seat, leaps into the luggage rack overhead. She casts Jolene an irritated glance—one the woman is fully oblivious to—before curling up in a furry ball.

"I didn't know you were coming with us." I resist the urge to more bluntly ask why she's here. My mind conjures images of her hanging off William's arm last night. Did they become...intimately acquainted? Just because he awoke in my bedroom doesn't mean he didn't have time for *certain activities* before he got there. I'm still not sure how my evening concluded or how William ended up in my room. Not all memories have returned to me. Still, I'm not unhappy to see Jolene.

"Oh, I didn't know either until an hour ago," she says. "But I was able to secure leave from my duties at the modiste for a few days, so I figured I might as well join you for your next signing. Mr. Phillips already said it's fine, as long as I room with you and pay for my train ticket, drinks, and meals. I can't wait to have you sign my copy of *The Governess and the Fae*."

Bless her heart, she knows her way into my good graces. I reach into my carpet bag on the seat beside me, extracting my pen and ink. "I could sign it for you now—"

"No," she blurts out. She recovers from her outburst with a smile. "No need. I want to have it signed at the event. Otherwise, what reason do I have to follow you around? Besides, I haven't purchased Mr. Haywood's poetry book either."

She purses her lips but it doesn't hide her coy smile. It's

not so much me she's here for but William. Some smug part of me is gratified that she still refers to him by his surname, at least. But all arrogance drains as I acknowledge what a pretty girl she is. She's dressed in a pale blue skirt and a white blouse with lace gloves adorning her hands. Her golden hair is neatly curled in an updo beneath a dainty hat. She looks so prim and proper without the bright cheeks and loose messy hair from last night.

Heavens, what did *I* look like last night? The countless minutes it took me to brush through my hair this morning wasn't promising. At least I managed to clean up well enough, even in my rush out the door. I opted for a low chignon, so as not to aggravate the pounding headache that has come and gone throughout the day, as well as an ensemble I can get away with wearing without a corset. It's a tartan skirt and matching jacket, the bodice stiff enough to give shape without more structured undergarments, yet roomy enough to allow me to breathe.

The train rolls into motion, slowly at first as it leaves the platform, then gaining speed as it moves along the outskirts of Floating Hope.

Jolene's sigh draws my attention back to her. "I wish I'd have gotten to know Mr. Haywood better last night," she says, a wistful lilt to her words.

"Oh?" I try not to appear too interested as I extract my notebook from my bag. I already have my pen and ink out, so I might as well jot down some story ideas if inspiration strikes me. "Did you not grow as acquainted as you'd hoped?"

Her lips pull into a pout. "Not at all. Well, he did tell me about June."

"June?"

"The great love of his life whom he gave his heart to but lost. She's who all his poems are about. At least, that's every-one's theory. He didn't exactly confirm it, but he shared a story about the heartache that plagues him to this day." She presses a palm to her chest, a dreamy look on her face. "That felt more intimate than a single night of physical passion could."

A twinge of discomfort pinches my chest. I don't know anything about this great love of William's life. But why should I? It's not like we're friends. We're barely acquaintances.

"Still," she says, and the wistfulness leaves her tone, "I would have taken passion, had he offered it. I thought for sure he'd choose me to fulfill the bet with."

I keep my voice nonchalant as I ask, "Did he fulfill the bet with anyone?"

"Not that I know of. By the time he ran after you, it was already a quarter to midnight."

My notebook tumbles from my hands to my lap. I smooth it out over my skirt and pretend I dropped it on purpose. "What do you mean he ran after me?"

"When that lecherous lion tried to walk you back to your room. Don't tell me you were too drunk to remember anything from last night. You seemed so clear of mind."

I frown, vague snatches of memory fighting to become sharper.

"Whatever the case," Jolene says, "Mr. Haywood didn't return after he left to find you, but a fae male slunk into the dining room looking scared out of his wits. By then, Mr. Phillips had come in from outside. Arwen and I apprised him of the situation. He halted the lion before he could leave and told him he needed to have a chat with him in the alley. When he returned, his knuckles were wrapped in his cravat."

My eyes go wide. Is she suggesting Monty scuffled with a male who'd tried to take advantage of me?

"Don't give Monty all the credit," Daphne says from the

74

luggage rack. "I bit the bastard's ankles." She sounds way too pleased about that.

But talk of Monty sharpens something in my mind. I remember! He rescued me. He...he...

No. It wasn't Monty who came to my rescue.

It was William.

More and more memories unfold until I'm mortified all over again. William lifting me in his arms. Me shoving my room key against his cheek. Him helping me drink from a glass of water. That's not all. Conversations I'd be better off forgetting echo in my mind.

I don't have a spectacular sex life.

I'm a fraud.

I'm faking it.

No, no, no. For the love of all things. How could I have said that to him? Now he knows my secret.

A final memory slides into place.

I'm a fraud too, Edwina.

William's use of my full name is more shocking than his words, for I don't understand what he could have meant. Is he only pretending to be a complete and utter rake? Or is there something else he's hiding?

"I admire you, Miss Danforth."

I shake my head to clear it and meet Jolene's eyes. "Me?"

"You're so worldly and experienced. The way you express your sexual freedoms without a care for what society thinks is truly admirable. I would never be bold enough to make such a bet with Mr. Haywood. You must be so confident you'll win."

I force a grin that hopefully hides my guilt. I'm not ready to come clean and share what I unwittingly divulged to William. Yet her words manage to inflate my pride. I like how she sees me. If only I could live up to her expectations.

And yet...

Maybe it's not too late to become the woman she thinks I am. Maybe there's still time for me to live as my heroines do. I may not have the desire for a whirlwind romance, but I could experience the mind-blowing lovemaking part, couldn't I?

My heart sinks before I summon a flicker of true excitement.

Love, courtship, and physical intimacy have always been more interesting on the page than in reality. In life, my suitors always seem to disappoint, either with their unromantic personalities or their views that a woman's career is merely a fancy and must be relinquished after marriage. I've disappointed them too, in how I put my career above all else, regardless of how little it pays, or how adamant I am that I won't marry and become a traditional wife. Even the relationships I've engaged in for the sake of pleasure alone have disappointed me. Sex is nothing like it is in romantic fiction. Kisses are wet and forceful. Intercourse is just a too-heavy body crushing mine, a man grunting and thrusting and asking me if it feels good without any interest in knowing my honest answer.

"It's a shame that lion fae was such a poor prospect," Jolene says. "You could have had fun with him, had he been a decent male. You've never been with a fae male before, have you?"

I stammer to answer, unsure if I'm about to get caught in my lie.

"No, you couldn't have," Jolene says, not unkindly. "There were a lot of inaccuracies in *The Governess and the Fae*, but I can't blame you for that. You hadn't been to Faerwyvae yet. Now that you have, your next books will be that much better. Just think how incredible your sex scenes will be after all the research you're about to do!"

I straighten in my seat. "Research?"

"The bet. You'll have a plethora of romantic experience between now and the end of your book tour. It won't even matter if you lose to William. You'll have gained so much." She begins to fan her face. "I'm getting flushed just thinking about the scenes you'll write next."

I blink at her. Finally, the excitement I couldn't summon before settles over me, lifting my heart and the corners of my lips. Every part of me feels brighter and more buoyant.

"I can use the bet as writing research," I say, my words wrapped in wonder. "You're a genius, Jolene."

I open my notebook and uncap my ink. I may be trapped in a bargain I never would have made were I in my right mind, but there's no going back. Our bet is magically binding. All I can do is try my best to beat William. Which means I need to brainstorm clever ways to win over a lover.

I dip my pen nib into my ink and write a heading on a fresh page in my notebook: *How to Seduce a Stranger: A Research Guide.*

CHAPTER NINE

EDWINA

*I*t only takes a few hours to reach the border between the Wind Court and the Solar Court, where our next destination lies. I keep my gaze locked on the window as rainy windswept plains shift into rolling hillsides. Sunlight casts the landscape beneath a distinctly golden hue, the soft brilliance that comes before sunset, even though sundown is still hours away. It's breathtaking to glimpse such a sudden change in the environment. My brochure mentioned every court has its own climate and terrain, but I never imagined the distinctions would be so perceptible.

Soon the verdant hillsides become dotted with cream stucco buildings with terracotta roofs. The farther we go, the more plentiful the buildings become until the outskirts of a city begin to form. I catch sight of clustered townhouses, storefronts, canals, and stunning cathedrals before our train pulls into the station. I'm brimming with excitement as we prepare to disembark.

Jolene links her arm with mine. "I've never been to the Solar Court."

I'm surprised that someone who's lived in Faerwyvae her whole life hasn't visited the next court over. It makes me feel less alone in this new experience.

We emerge onto the platform and some of my excitement abates. Oppressive heat surrounds me, an unwelcome thing considering my long-sleeved jacket and heavy skirts. I noticed our compartment growing warmer as the train wove through the countryside, but I didn't anticipate it would be this hot outside.

Jolene drops my arm and immediately sets to fanning herself with her hand. "Oh. Oh, this is too much."

"Tell me about it," Daphne says, emerging behind us. She scampers to me and takes refuge in the shade my skirts provide. "At least you can remove your warm layers. I'm stuck in this fur coat."

A thought occurs to me. "Do you not have a seelie form? Are you unable to shift into a humanoid body?"

She doesn't answer right away, and when she does, her voice is almost too quiet to hear. "I prefer not to."

"This is perfect."

I turn at the sound of Monty's voice. He steps onto the platform, face tilted toward the sun, eyes closed. His blond hair practically sparkles under the golden light of the Solar Court, and unlike me and Jolene, he's dressed for the weather. His shirtsleeves are rolled up, his waistcoat open. He wears lightweight linen trousers cuffed at the ankles to reveal his leather loafers, sans socks.

My breath catches as a figure emerges behind him. William is dressed like Monty with a similar style of cuffed cream trousers and bare ankles above pointed Oxfords. But where Monty wears his waistcoat open, William has abandoned his waistcoat entirely and wears a thin blue linen shirt unbuttoned to the center of his chest.

A chest I had in plain sight this morning.

Another flush of heat washes over me, and only some of it is from the sun.

William meets my eyes, a wry smile on his lips. "Feeling a little hot, Weenie?"

I avert my gaze and address Monty. "I didn't expect it to be so warm."

"I apologize," he says. "I should have prepared you. Thankfully, the university isn't far from here."

"University?"

He nods. "Your next signing is at the Hyperion University Library, and we'll be staying in the dormitory while we're there. We'll hail a coach there now. I've already arranged for our luggage to be transported separately."

I frown. Once again I'm separated from my luggage when I need it most. I angle my thumb back toward the train. "Can't I just fetch a blouse—"

"Just remove your jacket," Jolene says, bumping her shoulder into mine. With a wide smile, she unbuttons the pearl closures at her wrists and neck, then proceeds to roll up her sleeves and open her collar. Watching a woman dress down like this would be a scandalous sight in Bretton, but as the other passengers disembark, many do the same, even the women. And those not dressing down are already wearing attire better suited to the heat. A group of young women nearby wear sleeveless white dresses, their shoulders bare for all to see, their ankles and lower calves visible.

I could weep with jealousy, but if I remove my top as Jolene suggested, I'll be left in my chemise. My very corset-less chemise.

The very thought has my cheeks heating until a tall

female fae with long black hair and curves to die of envy for strolls by, her skirt a confection of cotton ruffles, her top a wisp of almost see-through linen. And she is very much not wearing a corset.

If she can wear a flimsy top with such confidence, surely I can too? My breasts, being far less impressive than the fae woman's, wouldn't even stand out that much. I can bear a little social discomfort for the sake of preventing heatstroke, can't I?

"Come along," Monty says, oblivious to my internal conflict. He lights a cigarillo and perches it between his lips. "We'll find our coach on Lonan Street."

He and William start off, Daphne darting just behind. One step after them is all that convinces me I'll perish if I don't find relief.

With a huff, Jolene takes my carpet bag from my hand. "Take off your jacket already."

I give her a grateful smile and unbutton my top as we walk. Once freed from my heavy outer layer, I take back my carpet bag and stuff my jacket inside. I give Jolene a questioning glance.

She studies me, then tugs the sleeves of my chemise down my arms until both sides slouch off my shoulders. In turn, my neckline dips lower, baring a dash of cleavage. "Much better."

"Are you sure?" I mutter, resisting the urge to curl forward.

"I work at a modiste, remember? Trust me on fashion, Edwina."

Something softens in my chest. I wasn't sure how I felt about Jolene last night. While I enjoyed talking to her, especially when she gushed about my books, I felt a little betrayed when she left me to hang all over William. But now I appreciate her companionship. I've never had a close female friend before—or any friends, really, unless you count imaginary ones—so these kinds of interactions are new.

We exit the station on Lonan Street, where a line of coaches stretches from here to the next avenue.

"This way," Monty says, gesturing toward one of the coaches. Neither he nor William has turned around, so I have yet to see if either will react to my state of undress.

When we arrive at our vehicle, the coachman takes Jolene's and my bags. Monty insists on helping him tuck them into the storage compartment at the back of the coach, probably just to steal extra time enjoying his cigarillo. This leaves William to play the role of gentleman and aid us into the coach. Daphne hops inside at once. William waits outside the door, posture slouched, hand extended.

Jolene accepts his aid with a flutter of her lashes. "You're too kind, Mr. Haywood."

The smile he gives her makes my lips curl into a snarl. Does he never stop flirting? I step up to him next with my head held high. He sucks in a breath as his gaze falls on me for the first time since we set off for the coach. His posture goes rigid as his eyes fall on the expanse of skin I've exposed above the neck of my chemise, then trail over my bare shoulders.

Everything inside me begs to curl forward and shrink from his scrutiny. Before I can do anything, his blue irises flick back to mine, his cheeks flushing pink.

I'm so surprised by the color rising in his face that I can only blink back at him for several beats.

Understanding dawns.

I made him flustered.

My urge to shrink in on myself dissolves. No, I will not make myself smaller before my rival. In demonstration of my resolve, I straighten my posture and lift my chest higher, accentuating the subtle peaks I've put on display. His throat bobs. Holding his eyes, I place my palm over his hand and take my time entering the coach.

CHAPTER TEN

WILLIAM

*E*dwina isn't cute. She isn't cute at all. There's no way William Haywood the Poet would find a woman attractive after she threw up on him. So why do I find my eyes flicking back to her again and again in the coach? I went out of my way to sit nowhere near her, which is why I'm across from her beside Daphne and Jolene Vaughn. That, however, was a mistake, for if I look anywhere but out the window, Edwina is all I see.

Her pale shoulders.

The dip of her cleavage.

The swell of her breasts.

The freckles that dance over her collarbones, mirroring the spattering of dots over her nose and cheeks, like a lake reflecting a starry sky.

I realize I'm staring again and firmly look away. What's come over me? I'm no stranger to the amount of skin Edwina is showing. Solar was my home court for four years. I graduated from the very university where our signing will be held. I'm used to seeing women out in public in sleeveless dresses and flimsy fabrics. More so, I've seen my share of naked bodies. Male, female, human, fae. Sex might as well have been my major at university, for I performed in bed as often as I did on stage, just to a different script. One was flesh and fucking, the other was projection and prose.

So why should this strange human woman with her horrible temper and even worse personality fluster me so?

She doesn't, I try to tell myself as she nudges the bridge of her spectacles back in place, but my distraction has pitched me out of my poet's persona. William the Stage Actor can only lie when he's immersed in his role as William the Poet. Why I'm struggling to stay in character in the first place is beyond me. Perhaps it's the lack of sleep. Unlike Edwina, I didn't sleep in until thirty minutes after our agreed time of departure.

I slide my gaze from her—yes, I've caught myself staring again—to Monty. His attention is already on me, his eyes narrowed while mischief plays around his mouth. I didn't like the questions he asked me on the train. What did I do with Edwina last night? Why did I go to her rescue? Why were we avoiding each other on our way to the station?

He claimed his questions were for the good of determining whether either of us made progress toward our bet. He's deemed himself the overseer of our bargain and will keep track of our points on our behalf, though I can't fathom how any of his questions were relevant.

He holds my gaze a beat longer, then scoots closer to Edwina. His legs are crossed toward her and his foot is dangerously close to brushing her tartan hem. "You got creative with your top after all. You fit right in with the Solar Court ladies now."

"It was Jolene's idea," Edwina says, speaking to him

without an ounce of the ire she reserves for me. I'm not sure whether I should feel envy or hubris.

"Brilliant, Miss Vaughn," he says to Jolene, giving her a soundless round of applause before returning his attention to Edwina. "Yes, a lovely chemise. The color reminds me of something. A type of dessert. What is it? Do you know, Mr. Haywood?"

"I can't imagine what you mean," I say with an air of indifference.

"That's because you aren't looking. Just look. You must know what I'm thinking."

I look anywhere but at Edwina. "I do not."

"Ah, I remember," Monty says with a snap of his fingers. "Meringue. That fluffy white dessert."

"I haven't had meringue," Edwina says.

"It's a lovely confection," Monty explains. "You see, my best friend is a baker. He makes the best meringue as a pie topping. I've made it with him before. You take egg whites and sugar and whip them into *stiff peaks*." His eyes meet mine across the coach as he says the last two words.

Bastard. I know what he's playing at now. He's trying to keep Edwina's breasts at the front of my mind.

"I prefer small soft peaks, personally," Monty says, somehow managing to keep his tone somber. "What about you, William? Do you prefer small peaks or large peaks? Of meringue."

"I'm not keen on dessert," I say, fixing my gaze out the window as our coach crosses a bridge over a sunlit canal.

"Mr. Phillips," Edwina says, "may I inquire about the bruises on your hand?"

"Oh, this?" Monty spreads his fingers over his knee. Purple bruises flush his knuckles, and a few are even scabbed over.

"It's nothing, Miss Danforth. I simply petted a cat a little too hard in the alley last night."

The soft look in Edwina's eyes tells me she knows exactly how he got those bruises. Which also means she must remember what happened last night. While I'm grateful Monty taught the lion fae a lesson, I would have done so too if my priority hadn't been seeing Edwina safely to her room. Now he's the one receiving her tender gaze while I was treated like a common criminal for spending the night in her room.

"Don't admire me too much," Monty says. "I was bored last night, that's all. I'd take any excuse to beat a man sense-less. You may not know this, but beneath my smile, I'm a fount of bottomless rage."

He says it all with a dimpled grin, so I haven't a clue if he's jesting. I've only known the publicist for just over a week, and so far he's seemed equally flippant about life and work.

"Still, it is rather heroic," Jolene says from beside me. Her hand falls upon Daphne's back in an idle stroke.

The pine marten stiffens and rounds on the girl, teeth bared. "I am not a pet."

Jolene flinches back. "Sorry! It was just a force of habit. I have six cats—"

Daphne leaps off the bench and bounds to the other side of the coach, planting herself beside Monty.

"Daffy Dear is feral indeed," Monty says to Jolene, then poses another question for Edwina. "How are you feeling about the bet you made last night?"

"Oh, fine. Just fine. Everything is…fine." Her words come out in a rush.

Damn. I still need to find an opportunity to let her beg me to dissolve our bargain. But if I've learned anything in the last twenty-four hours of our acquaintance it's that her pride only swells before an audience. I'll need to get her alone. The less I say about it now, the better.

So I clench my jaw and firmly hold my tongue, even when Monty speaks again.

"Want any tips?" he asks. "I consider myself a bit of a romance expert. An unofficial matchmaker if you will. In truth, it's the job I wanted before I applied at Fletcher-Wilson, but the matchmaking agency didn't take my track record of one seriously."

"You've matched a couple before?" Jolene asks, leaning subtly closer to me. "How much do you charge?"

"You wouldn't believe it by his actions, but Monty already has a job," Daphne says in her dry monotone.

"Clever," Monty says with a smirk at the pine marten before returning his attention to Edwina. "Come, Miss Danforth. Ask me anything."

"Well," she says, reaching for the seat beside her. She frowns when her hands meet only air. Perhaps she was looking for her carpet bag. Or that little notebook I've seen her scribbling in. She smooths her hands over her skirts instead. "What stirs your desire, Mr. Phillips?"

Her cold and methodical tone contrasts her words. They'd sound flirtatious coming from someone else, but she poses the question like an inquiry about the weather. It takes some effort to hide my grin.

"Oh, I'd rather not make you blush," Monty says, rubbing a hand over his jaw. "But I can say, in general, men simply want to please their lovers. We want to do whatever makes you feel good."

"What makes *me* feel good." She echoes his words slowly as if they're foreign to her.

Monty's brows lift. "Don't tell me...do you not know your own preferences? Your favorite positions? The places you like being touched most?"

Edwina's mouth falls open, her cheeks turning pink. She's saved from answering as Jolene sits forward in her seat. "Oh, she absolutely does. She has so much experience. Did you not know? She's done everything she's written about."

Edwina grimaces.

"Is that so?" Monty says, stifling a laugh. "Well, if you're ever curious to explore in a safe and neutral place, Miss Danforth, come to me."

"Swine," Daphne mutters.

It takes all my restraint not to voice my agreement. My fingers curl into fists.

"Oh?" Edwina tilts her head. The moment she comprehends his offer is marked by an even deeper flush of her cheeks. "Oh! That's…rather…"

Monty angles himself closer to her, propping his elbow on the backrest. "I assure you, I would be a fully neutral test subject. I don't do attachments, and I mean it. This isn't one of your little books where love changes a man. I am incapable of love."

I expect her to roll her eyes, but she elicits a gasp instead, then reaches toward the empty spot beside her. "Damn," she mutters when her fingers come away empty once more.

"Did…did you just swoon, Miss Danforth?" Monty's voice is rich with laughter.

Her shoulders slump. "It's just…it's exactly what one of my heroes would say, right before they settle down. I wanted to take a note of your words, but my notebook is in my carpet bag—"

"Trust me, I'm not a hero." There's a somber note in his voice, reflected in the lack of mirth in his eyes.

Edwina shakes her head. "Back to the topic at hand. One I believe you misinterpreted. I wasn't asking about what you like to do with your lover, but more what makes you interested in a lover in the first place? What would make you want to take a woman you just met to bed?"

Monty tilts his head, expression thoughtful. "An eye patch," he says. "A peg leg too."

"Really?" Jolene stares at Monty, then exchanges a confused look with Edwina. "Why?"

"It makes me think she'd be willing to do things that are *arrrrrgh*-rated."

I close my eyes with a groan and rub my brow. A fucking pirate joke.

"I don't understand," Edwina says.

"R-rated," Monty says with a shrug.

"What does R-rated mean?"

"It stands for restricted," I say, gathering my composure enough to speak with feigned disinterest.

Jolene nods emphatically. "It's a new regulation placed on stage plays. Don't you know? *The Governess and the Rake* was the first to earn such a label. It's the reason the regulation system was created."

Edwina bolts upright, eyes wide. "Are you telling me there's a play of *The Governess and the Rake*? And it was so inappropriate for the stage that it required the implementation of a special rating system?"

"Yes," Jolene says.

Edwina gasps. "No."

"It's true."

"No. Are you sure?"

"Yes, Weenie," I say, tone firm. "She's telling the truth."

Edwina's eyes lock on mine. The sweet, elated smile that curls her lips is so open, so genuine, it makes my chest feel tight. I know her smile isn't for me. It's for the stage play she apparently didn't know existed. I open my mouth, about to confess something else, something that might make that smile shine more firmly upon me, but I stop myself. William the Stage Actor may have performed in an adaptation of *The Governess and the Rake*, but William the Poet would never admit as much. William the Poet hates fiction. And romance.

Besides, why would I seek to make her smile?

The coach rolls to a stop. We've arrived at Hyperion University, and as we disembark from the coach to the cobblestone courtyard, the coachman saves me from having to aid Edwina's exit. Thank fuck for that. The last thing I need is a repeat of earlier when I gawked at her, struck dumb as she sauntered into the coach wearing that damn top. My hand still feels warm where she touched it, and I don't think I could maintain a straight face if she touched it again.

I force my full attention to the building before us, my gaze sweeping over the four-story dormitory lined with ivory columns and ending in a domed roof of blue tile. It's the same dormitory I lived in during my four years at the university. Nostalgia settles over me, a mixture of longing, comfort, and the painful dissonance between a past and future forever divided by time.

Edwina and Jolene huddle close together, admiring the architecture as they head for the front doors. Daphne bounds after them, and Monty nearly does the same—before I stop him with a firm hand on his shoulder.

He faces me with an amused look. "Can I help you, Mr. Haywood?"

I step closer and lower my voice. "You will not touch Edwina."

"I won't?"

"It's unprofessional," I say, keeping my voice as level as I can. "You're our tour manager and publicist. It's a conflict of interest for you to start any kind of physical relationship with her."

Monty narrows his eyes, and for a moment I wonder if he was serious about gladly taking any opportunity to brawl. I could take him on with my slight height advantage, but I've never been in a fight that wasn't choreographed. Still, I hold his gaze without falter.

His face breaks into a grin. "That's my boy. Next time, say all that in front of her. Oh, and you still owe me an answer about your preferred size and shape of peaks...of meringue." He waggles his brows, then jogs the rest of the way to join the women.

CHAPTER ELEVEN

EDWINA

*B*eing on time is—unsurprisingly—a rather serene experience. There's no rushing. No running. No pleading with fate to turn back the hands of time. It helps that my lodgings are only a three-minute walk from my destination. The small dorm room Jolene and I shared last night was so quaint, so much like the one I resided in when I was a college student in Bretton, it was hard to remember I was in the faelands at all. I thought perhaps Hyperion University was solely a human college, but as I enter the university library, I'm once again immersed in the splendor of fae charm.

The entrance unfolds into a grand atrium that almost looks more like a greenhouse than a library, with floors of white marble veined with gold and potted plants and flowers surrounding a wide circular fountain. Several floors of endless ivory shelves flank the atrium, lined with walkways edged with marble balustrades and colonnades.

I return my gaze to the atrium and take a better look at the fountain before me. Trickling water creates a soothing symphony as it pours from the marble statues at its center. I step closer and study the three human figures that comprise the statues. I gasp, recognizing the countenance of the closest one. It's Ananda Badami, one of the greatest female writers of all time! With slightly more reserved excitement, I note the two other likenesses beside her. Grant Farthing, poet. Sylvain Rushworth, award-winning novelist. My heart swells to see them centered here, like guardian angels of this most precious place of literature and learning.

It's almost a struggle to tear my eyes away, but fluttering movement catches my attention. I stare up at the glass ceiling, bright with warm golden sunlight, and spot pale blue wings. Birds the size and shape of swallows swoop overhead to perch on the statues near the ceiling or the array of greenery. I'd be alarmed that they'd create a mess of droppings, but the glittering mist that trails in their wake as they fly tells me they aren't regular birds. They must be fae creatures, and the mist…is that what keeps the temperature so cool in the library?

Mr. Phillips informed me there was no need to dress for heat during today's signing, and I feared he'd pulled a prank on me as I made my way from the dorm, but now I can see he was right. My green long-sleeved taffeta dress is perfectly suited for this cool indoor climate.

I'm still not recovered from my awe, but I dare not dally too long. This is one of the rare occasions I'm on time, after all, and I'd like to take advantage of that after I set up my table. I follow Monty's directions to the far end of the atrium. There, I find a modest circular dais, which I imagine must be used for lectures from guests or events like today. Two tables stand upon the platform, and I'm not surprised to see William's already boasts neat piles of books on display. When Monty came to my room to ensure I was ready for the event, William was already here setting up his table. Thank goodness he isn't here now, and for the fact that we aren't seated so close together. This time, our tables face each other from opposite sides of the dais.

I stride over to my table and find several crates full of my books. The boxes have been opened but none of the books have been displayed. I don't have Daphne to help this time, but I can manage well enough on my own. I find a crate that's only partially full—one with leftovers from the Wind Court signing, along with a pen, ink pots...and my uncomfortable shoes. Looks like William was bluffing when he threatened to throw them away if I didn't take his stupid book. Well, he would have done me a favor by discarding them. I'll have to do so myself after the signing. Keeping the shoes-I'll-never-wear-again in the crate, I remove my books and artfully display them on my table. Only to realize one of the books is out of place.

Amidst the sea of my beautiful mauve covers is a volume in green. I scowl, recognizing it at once. Turns out my shoes weren't the only things William returned. I remove the interloper from my stack and aggressively flip to the title page. The first thing I find is a pale pink flower petal, though I haven't a clue how it got there. I remove it, letting it flutter to the ground, and read the page. Sure enough, I find the name *Ed* scrawled upon it, the D ending in a slash of ink. But that's not all that's written on the page. Beneath, it reads: *I like smut and drivel.*

I release an indignant huff. That cheeky bastard. I uncap my ink with far more force than necessary and hastily dip my pen. Beneath William's message, I write: *Well, I don't like you. Or your book. Stop trying to give this to me.*

Then I march over to his table and toss it onto his stack.

After I finish setting up my table, I check my pocket watch. Thirty minutes until the signing. I suppress an excited squeal and practically skip as I go off in search of the romance section. After begging for directions from the front desk, I find what I'm looking for on the second floor. The section isn't quite as large as I'd hoped for such a grand library, but I can't complain. Some of my favorite romances are shelved here, and there's even four of mine! I open *The Governess and the Duke,* grinning wide as I count the names on the borrowing card. To think this many students have become acquainted with the duke's most impressive throbbing member.

I return my book to the shelf and seek out one I haven't read yet. I've spent a good ten minutes here already, which means I'll need to return to the dais soon. In the meantime, maybe I can determine my next read…

There! I spot a title on the clothbound spine of a book I've been meaning to procure. It's on the shelf above my head, and this particular title has been pushed back just enough to put it at the end of my reach. I stand on my toes and extend my arm until my fingertips brush the spine—

I flinch as I touch flesh rather than cloth. My eyes lower to a glower when I find William standing beside me. He already has the book in hand, but instead of handing it to me, he opens it.

"There's a thing called a ladder," William says as he browses the title page.

"I would have reached it if you hadn't intervened. May I have the book now?"

He leans his shoulder against the shelf. "*The Stag King and His Very Large Kingdom.* What kind of title is that?"

96

"It's a parody, but it does the romance genre justice. Quite steamy and enjoyable, but you wouldn't understand." I snatch the book out of his hands and turn my back on him.

"More research into the art of seduction?"

I stiffen, mortified that he's somehow found my notebook. But no, he probably gleaned as much from the questions I asked Monty.

His voice dips low. "Weenie, I know you're in over your head when it comes to this bet."

"I'm not—" I whirl to face him, but I can't say a word when I see the knowing glint in his eyes.

He leans down, bringing his face far too close. "I know your secret, love. You told me the other night."

"I was drunk," I say, turning my nose up at him.

"You were vulnerable and honest." For a moment, the teasing lilt leaves his voice. "You don't have to pretend otherwise."

"Oh, well, what about your secret?"

His posture goes rigid. "Mine? What secret?"

"You said you were a fraud too."

He lowers his head, either in relief or amusement. When his eyes return to mine, there's mirth in them. "It's not what you're thinking. I'm not a fraud when it comes to my romantic experience."

"Then what are you faking?"

He gives me a cold grin. "My secrets are irrelevant to you. What matters is that I'm trying to do you a kindness. I never should have secured a bargain while you were inebriated, and I'm willing to make up for that. Say the word, and I will dissolve our bet."

My eyes go wide. "You can do that?"

"I am the fae party in our bargain. I am the reason our bet is magically binding. But, since this is a bet with mutually binding terms proposed by a third party and not a one-sided

97

bargain I constructed, I need your cooperation to end it. Then all I have to do is verbally release you from our bargain, stating that every term is now null and void. After that, we can act like civilized adults."

Part of me yearns to accept his offer. I already know our bet is madness. I may rail against society's standards for women, but that doesn't change that I was raised in human society. Despite all the actions I've taken to shrug off the burdens of propriety, I still carry layers and layers of all that society tried so hard to instill within me. There's a voice that calls me a spinster. Another that labels my past romantic relationships *unchaste*. I hate those voices, yet I shrink from them nonetheless.

But I don't want to shrink. I want to be bigger than those labels and those voices.

More than anything, I want that contract. If we dissolve our bargain, I'll have to rely solely on sales. With his head start from the first week of the tour, how can I hope to outsell him? We've only had one signing together, but there's no guarantee that the rest will be better. Even after my readers returned to Flight of Fancy when they learned I'd made it, my turnout was laughable compared to William's. And what about my research? This bet serves more than one purpose, and I can't risk losing it now.

I take a bracing breath and meet his eyes. "We're keeping our bargain."

His façade cracks and he releases a strained groan. "Damn it, Weenie. Why are you so determined to...to..."

I bristle, certain I know what he's fighting not to say. "Sully my virtue? Lower my value as a woman?"

"Vex me," he says through his teeth.

I blink at him, at the anger in his cold blue irises, the tightness in his jaw. My pulse quickens.

He braces a hand on the shelf beside us and leans toward

me. "Why do you want the contract so badly, hmm? You've already published...what, five books?"

"Seventeen."

"And at least one was adapted into a stage play. You're successful, aren't you? Opportunities abound. Why must you fight me for this contract?"

Anger sears my veins at how he talks about the contract like he has a right to it. He's the one fighting *me*. The familiar discomfort writhes in my chest, and I don't repress the volley of words that spill from my mouth.

"For your information, Willy, I don't make any money from the titles I publish in Bretton. A few coins here and there. A small print run. I've seen no increase in royalties to suggest I'm earning a damn thing for the stage play adaptation. Every manuscript I bring to my publisher ends in haggling and a reminder that I would earn more if I'd write better books. Do you know what my publisher considers *better books*? Literary works with a moral undertone. Cautionary tales. Novels, according to him, make society stupid, and he only agrees to publish them because there is at least some demand. But do you know what would make my work even better? If I were a man. If I'd cease writing about throbbing cocks and simply adopt one between my legs. At the very least, if I would only remove one letter from the end of my name and publish highbrow moral works as Edwin Danforth, I'd be worth something in Bretton."

He stares at me as if seeing me for the first time, jaw slack, brow furrowed.

I continue. "Do you now see why I might be overjoyed at the chance to be respected as *me*? Why I'd be willing to do anything to take advantage of an opportunity that might take me out of obscurity? I'm not wealthy, William. I've struggled for every coin I've earned and I've never tasted fame until now. Do you know what it's like to have a dream within reach only to have some arrogant bastard saunter in and try to take it away?"

His expression hardens.

"The contract was supposed to be mine from the start," I say. "You're not even supposed to be here."

He scoffs. "You, on the other hand, were supposed to be on time."

"I was shipwrecked. Well, my ship was caught in a storm —I don't have to explain this to you. The truth remains that you're clinging to *my* tour like a barnacle."

"You're wrong," he says with a shake of his head. "This tour was supposed to be *mine*. I was offered one months before you even signed with Fletcher-Wilson. It wasn't in my contract, but a verbal agreement was made. Then my release tanked in sales and the tour was proposed to you. I had to beg Mr. Fletcher in person to reconsider. It just so happened that he'd just received the telegram regarding your delay."

I frown. "How is it possible your release tanked? Everyone has your book."

"Because I made it happen in a matter of weeks. I scheduled interviews in every paper across the isle that I could convince to feature me. I made appearances at local bookstores. I inspired sales with my face, my persona. I sparked my book's rise in the rankings and took that data with me when I pleaded with Mr. Fletcher for a tour. I convinced him I needed more in-person interactions to sell this book to the masses, and I was right."

I give him a withering look. "You really are seducing your readers. With your face and your persona."

"I am."

"No one likes your poetry; they like your attention."

His eyes darken. "The poetry is brilliant and beautiful. You would know if you had any taste."

I shake my head. "I can't believe that's your reason for

wanting this contract. To woo readers with your face rather than your words."

"That's not my reason."

"Oh? Enlighten me then."

"I don't need to enlighten you. My reasons are none of your business."

"What you mean is your reasons are superficial."

He scoffs. "Hardly."

"Then what could possibly be so important—"

"My sister." He says the words so fiercely that it takes me a moment to process them. Then he snaps his mouth shut, eyes widening at his own confession. His jaw tightens as he looks away from me and leans against the bookcase. "I have a sister named Cassie," he says, his tone level despite the frustration etched over his face. "I am her sole guardian. We have a mountain of debt, but it's all in her name. I worked several jobs to pay it down, but it wasn't enough. The sale of *A Portrait of June* saved her from being taken to the workhouse, but some of our debts remain. If we don't pay it off this year, we won't be able to afford her college tuition."

If he was looking for pity, I daresay he's snagged mine. If he's her sole guardian, their parents must have either abandoned them or died. Furthermore, it crushes my soul to think a woman interested in furthering her education might be robbed of the opportunity. "She could always get a job," I say but am unable to hide my grimace. It's not like I have experience with traditional employment.

And there, a well of guilt opens wide in my chest.

I may have struggled in my career and faced my share of injustice, but I can't say I've lived an unprivileged life. My eldest brother funded my years at college. While I pay for my own apartment and day-to-day expenses, I always have the family estate to return to if things get bad. I'd be considered my parents' property and would have to fall in line with their rules, meaning marriage and relinquishing my career. Still, while it may be a fate I abhor, it isn't the worst one I could possibly have.

"I don't want her getting a job," William says. "She…she isn't well. The types of employment available to a young woman without a college education are likely to prove too exhausting for her constitution. More importantly, I want her to live her dream while she has time—"

"There you two are," Daphne says, slinking over to us.

I blink, my mind stuck on what William was about to say. Something about having time. Time for what?

"I expected this one to be late," Daphne says, angling her furry head toward me, "but you too, Mr. Haywood? The signing is about to start."

Alarm ripples through me. I can't be late after I arrived on time! I remember the book in my hands, but before I can stand on my tiptoes to try to return it to the shelf, William does it for me. Without offering him a word of thanks, I dart after Daphne as she heads for the stairs—but something catches my sleeve. I glance at my wrist, where William has lightly taken hold. The sight of his long, slender fingers wrapped around my green cuff sends my heart skittering.

"Ask me to end it," he says, a note of pleading in his voice. "Let's call off the bet."

The worry on his face almost works on me.

Almost.

"You may have swayed my sympathies the slightest bit," I say, "but I'm not calling it quits. I see now we both have reasons to fight, but yours don't invalidate mine."

"Let's at least fight fair."

"Fair? As in the sales numbers you inflated with all the efforts you made before this tour even began?"

"Yes, it's fair. A hell of a lot more fair than our idiotic bargain. It has nothing to do with our art."

"You act like I'm the one who bullied you into the bargain when you're the one who spurred me on! Why are you so against this bet that you have an equal share in responsibility for?"

"It's a matter of pride. I want to win for my efforts in sales, not seduction. Does it not rankle your own pride?"

"It does, but that's only the least of slights against it. You know what rankles it more? That you sell more books than me. That you know my secret and had the indecency to bring it up. That you thought it would be so easy to convince me to end our bet."

He scoffs. "Yes, because I thought you were a rational creature. If not on the outside, then at least at heart."

"Rational. As in, you thought somewhere deep inside I'd realize I could never win a bet against you?" I give him the falsest, coldest smile I can. "Willy boy, never underestimate a writer with research on the brain."

With that, I tug my wrist from his grip and follow Daphne down the stairs.

CHAPTER TWELVE

EDWINA

*T*he signing is similar in many ways to the one at Flight of Fancy. Once again, William is the far more popular author. He constantly has a line or cluster of guests, and it doesn't take me long to glean that he attended Hyperion University for their performing arts program and was a stage actor long before he became a poet. I also learn that he is six-and-twenty years of age, which means the bastard has not only beaten me in sales, beauty, and popularity but in youth too. Though I suppose I can consider myself the wiser and more worldly. He's not some ancient fae with several hundred years of experience under his belt. He's three years my junior.

There are some pointed differences between this signing and the last, and they are all for the better. For one, it's quieter, and our guests seem to have better manners. No one loiters around our tables after getting their books signed, chatting loudly and crowding the walkways. Instead, our guests politely leave to enjoy the rest of their day or peruse the shelves of the library. They keep their voices at library-appropriate volumes, even when squealing over William or catching up on old times. And, best of all, I have the pleasure of meeting three times as many readers as I did at Flight of Fancy. It seems word has spread that I've finally made it to the tour. I'm moved by the genuine interactions I have with those who truly love my books.

What I am not at all moved by is my table placement. I thought it would be better to be seated across from William as opposed to beside him, but with our tables facing each other from opposite ends of the dais, he's constantly in my line of sight. He takes every opportunity to smirk at me, especially when his lines are impressively long. I meet his haughty looks with a sneer, an exaggerated smile, or by pushing the bridge of my spectacles with a subtle display of my middle finger. I'm not sure if middle fingers are a rude custom in Faerwyvae, but it's the effort that counts.

I don't know why he's smirking at me after our conversation in the romance section. His popularity only confirms that I was right in refusing to let him dissolve our bargain. *I* should be the one smirking.

By the end of the signing, I've all but forgotten about William. I'm floating on air, lifted by the love of my readers, my tired wrist a tribute to all the books I signed and all the smiles I inspired. I wish I could bottle this feeling up and keep it forever. It would get me through the hardest days. Though I suppose the next best thing would be…living here. Securing that three-book contract as well as citizenship. A full immersion in the setting I'm writing in. Opportunities for more interactions with my fans. And what I wouldn't give to see a production of *The Governess and the Rake* in person.

"Another great signing, my friends," Monty says, once

William and I have finished packing our leftover books in the crates. Now that the signing has ended and the sun has begun to set, casting the atrium in an even warmer honeyed glow, the library is almost empty.

"It was such a lovely signing," Jolene says, clutching both William's and my books to her chest. She tried to linger at William's table for as long as she could, but when his line extended to the fountain at the center of the atrium, Daphne barked at her to move along. Thank heavens for Daphne's crowd control. Monty spent most of his time on a smoke break. After Jolene left William's table, she settled in at mine, finally letting me sign her copy of *The Governess and the Fae*. Then she insisted on serving as my assistant—not that I needed one with my nonexistent line—after which she proceeded to try to catch William's eye.

The hour she was at my table was the one where I received the least number of smirks from him. I'm honestly surprised he hasn't been entertaining Jolene's infatuation. He can't be oblivious to it. Compared to all the men and women he dazzles with that seductive grin and flirtatious banter, he treats Jolene with mere politeness. I can't imagine he dislikes her. She's young and sweet and gorgeous and everything men normally want in a woman.

For some reason, I feel rather smug about his lack of interest in her.

"We have two choices for how to spend our last evening in the Solar Court," Monty says, pulling me from my thoughts. "The responsible choice is we dine in the cafeteria, retire to our rooms for the remainder of the evening, and then reconvene for our departure in the morning. Or there's the fun choice. We get changed, we eat, we rest, and then go to a party at Somerton House."

"I vote for sleep," Daphne says at once. She's perched on one of the crates, her beady little eyes looking quite heavy. It makes me wonder if pine martens are nocturnal. If so, it might be challenging to keep a diurnal schedule. Maybe that's why she naps so often.

Jolene claps her hands together at her chest. "A party sounds lovely. This will be my last night with you, after all. I take the train back home tomorrow." She casts a hopeful look at William.

He, however, doesn't humor her silent request, instead giving Monty a wry look. "I know what kinds of parties happen at Somerton House."

"Then you'll know it's the perfect landscape to potentially make progress in your bet." He waggles his brows and gives me a questioning shrug. "What do you say, Miss Danforth?"

I've been so elated about today's signing that I haven't thought about the bet in hours. My lungs tighten, either in anxiety or excitement. This could be my first opportunity to begin the research I've resolved to do. My first opportunity to earn a point against William. While I can't be certain he didn't earn one last night, Jolene's frustration when she returned to our dorm just before midnight was a promising sign that he didn't. Apparently, she strolled the hall outside his room for two whole hours and he never once came out. Only Monty left their shared room, and he informed her that William had retired early.

My gaze flashes to my opponent. His eyes widen and he gives a subtle shake of his head. He's obviously trying to warn me to reject Monty's proposal, but it might as well be bait. If he doesn't want me to go to this party, then I definitely want to.

"You're right, Jolene," I say, lifting my chin. "A party does sound lovely."

107

SOMERTON HOUSE IS A LARGE PRIVATE RESIDENCE IN THE CITY, nestled between other grand manors that line the street, just a few blocks away from the university. We pass through the front gate and approach the door. Strains of muffled music—a familiar opera—emanate from inside.

I exchange an excited look with Jolene, whose arm is linked through mine. I've never been to a house party before, only a few public balls and the occasional garden party at my family home. Even in college, I refrained from much socializing and spent my waking hours either studying or writing. I'm not even sure Bretton Ladies College had an active nightlife considering how strictly our activities and curfews were enforced.

Monty takes a drag from his cigarillo and raps the hinged door knocker upon its brass plate. Daphne stayed behind, so we're just a party of four. I shudder, but it's more from anticipation than cold. Night has fallen, but the air remains warm. Not stifling like it was when we first arrived at the station, but warm enough that I've changed out of my long-sleeved dress to a silk evening gown with lace cap sleeves, a loose unstructured waist, and a low square neckline. It's one of the most modern and fashionable gowns I own, its style influenced by the lighter, gauzier fae fashions that have become more prevalent, even in Bretton.

Meanwhile, Jolene wears a scarlet ballgown that makes me wonder if I'm underdressed. On the other hand, William and Monty are outfitted in similar casual slacks and open-collar shirts like they wore when we arrived in the Solar Court, so perhaps it's me and Jolene who are overdressed. After all, the two males seem far keener on what Somerton House is all about.

A butler opens the front door. He and Monty exchange a few whispered words, and the butler bows for us to enter. The opera I heard from outside is even louder now, and as we make our way down the hall and into the main foyer, I discover the source. A female fae with glittering golden skin and bronze iridescent hair stands at the center of the room, her impressive soprano filling the air with a haunting melody of love and loss. My first instinct is to shrink back, fearing we've disrupted her performance with our sudden arrival, but a glance around the room banishes my worries. While many stand and watch the vocalist, there are several others who chat in groups, paying the singer very little heed. Still others lounge on chairs, divans, or against the wall, notebooks and graphite in hand as they sketch the female. Smoke fills the air, as does the scent of liquor. This is nothing like the elegant house party I imagined, with a formal dinner, dancing, and separate rooms for the men and women to congregate. Here everyone mingles freely and the atmosphere is unrestrained.

When William said he knew what kinds of parties happen here, perhaps this is what he meant. He didn't think my delicate human sensibilities could handle such frivolity.

"William Haywood, is that really you?" A human male with a bushy mustache, a pipe, and neatly combed black hair strides to us from across the room. He looks to be about ten years my senior and is dressed in nothing more than a burgundy silk robe. He claps William on the shoulder and speaks through the pipe between his lips. "I heard you were in town but never thought I'd see you at Somerton House any time soon. Are these your friends?"

The man appraises me and Jolene with appreciative looks, then turns his attention to Monty. He removes the pipe from his mouth and sniffs the air. Then, arching a brow at Monty's cigarillo, he reaches into the breast pocket of his robe and extracts a small lavender-scented sachet. With a wink, he hands it to Monty. "Try Moonpetal. Much more relaxing."

Monty's eyes brighten. "Cheers to that." Without waiting for a formal introduction, he wanders off, a skip in his step.

William rolls his eyes, but the man doesn't seem at all offended. "Grayson, that was Monty, Junior Publicist at Fletcher-Wilson, my publisher. This is Miss Edwina Danforth, fellow author, and her friend, Miss Jolene Vaughn. Miss Danforth, Miss Vaughn, this is Grayson Somerton, our host and my former mentor."

"In poetry?" Jolene asks, her expression alight with interest.

Mr. Somerton frowns. "No, in acting. I hosted many performances here and William was one of our brightest stars." To William he says, "I was surprised to hear you made a name for yourself on the page rather than the stage."

William's throat bobs, then a lopsided grin curves his lips. "What is a blank page if not another kind of stage?"

Mr. Somerton takes a puff from his pipe, giving him a meager smile yet making no further comment. He turns to me and Jolene. "Since this is your first time at Somerton House, allow me to acquaint you. Here, in the foyer, is what we call the music hall. The parlor to the left is set with easels. The study hosts my finest liquor. In the library you'll find a makeshift stage for spoken-word performances. Upstairs in the south wing, you'll find rooms dedicated to pottery, painting, pianoforte, harp. In the north wing—"

"They're not going to the north wing," William cuts in.

I glance between William and Mr. Somerton. "Why? What's in the north wing?"

Mr. Somerton busies himself with his pipe and refuses to meet my gaze.

William looks me straight in the eyes. "Do not go to the north wing. I'm warning you."

How has he yet to learn? Telling me not to do something is the surest way to get me to do it. I curtsy for Mr. Somerton. "Thank you for being such a gracious host. I look forward to enjoying your lovely home."

He gives a deep nod and I tug Jolene with me toward a wide curving staircase.

"Where are you going?" William's tone is edged with warning.

I cast a coy look over my shoulder. "To the north wing, of course."

CHAPTER THIRTEEN

WILLIAM

*J*t's not my responsibility to save Edwina from herself. If she seeks the mortification that awaits her in the north wing, that's her prerogative. Who am I to stop her? Yet even as I think it, my legs twitch, begging me to move, my chest burning with annoyance at every step she takes up the stairs. No sooner than she reaches the landing do I charge after her, abandoning Grayson in the middle of his sentence. Not that I was listening to him anyway.

"Miss Danforth," I call out, but the crowd of partygoers is denser here, with guests weaving from room to room or chatting idly in the halls. I call her name again, and this time, she pulls up short. She's probably more startled that I called her by her proper name and not Weenie, but I'm not about to shout the latter in the middle of a house party.

She puts her hands on her hips. "Willy, why are you following me?"

Her question catches me off guard, for it forces me to

truly consider the answer. Why the hell *am* I following her? I can't convince myself this is an act of sabotage, for what she'll find in the north wing won't aid in making progress toward our bet. Not immediately, at least. While I could convince myself this is just another instinct of brotherly protection, something I'd do for my sister, there's nothing brotherly about my feelings where Edwina is concerned. All she ever does is vex me. She's a nuisance.

So what is it? The fact that she's human, and I know humans to be fragile creatures? Their lifespans are short, their bodies prone to ailments I'll never have to suffer.

The latter strikes a hollow pit in my chest. Yes, I know about human frailty all too well.

Maybe that's all this is.

I sink back into my role of William the Poet and lower my voice for only her to hear. "I'm giving you one last chance to heed my wisdom, Weenie Poo."

Her nostrils flare at the newest nickname. "If you wanted me to heed anything, then you wouldn't have called me that."

She's right, but I couldn't resist. William the Poet loves riling her up. It's become the highlight of this role.

"Furthermore," she says, "if you wanted to dampen my curiosity over the north wing, you would have offered to serve as my personal escort. Then I wouldn't have been even remotely interested."

"Fine," I say through my teeth. "I will escort you. Shall we?"

"Such a gentleman," Jolene says, reminding me of her presence. She's been standing beside Edwina all the while, her longing gaze locked on me, but I barely noticed her. When Edwina's around, it's hard to concentrate on anything else. That's how annoying she is.

"Your offer is too late," Edwina says. "I'm still going."

She turns and starts off down the hall. Jolene glances from her friend to me before asking, "Shall we?"

"You stay here." As soon as the words leave my lips, I know my tone was too harsh. Jolene looks like a scolded puppy. I suppose my heart should be moved at the sight, but it's more set on catching up to Edwina. Forcing my most dazzling smile, I face Jolene. "The north wing isn't a proper place for you or Miss Danforth. I'll escort her to sate her curiosity and see to her safe return."

"I would like to come too."

I hang my head in an exaggerated motion before meeting her eyes once more. "I can bear to allow Edwina to enter such an unsavory place but not you. I wouldn't be able to live with myself. Trust me, Miss Vaughn. I will return and we can finally have some time to talk, just the two of us."

She visibly swoons, rocking back on her heels. "You mean it?"

"I do. Now, stay in the south wing and I'll return for you."

"You'll return for me," she echoes, voice breathless. She tips her face toward me, her eyes on my lips, her own parted expectantly.

I step back and give a consoling pat on her shoulder before racing after Edwina.

Getting rid of Miss Vaughn wasted far more time than I hoped, so by the time I catch up to Edwina, she has already turned down the hall leading to the north wing.

She turns at the sound of my footsteps, rolling her eyes when she sees me. "I already told you. Your offer as an escort came too late. I'm going with or without you."

"With me," I say, "whether you like it or not. At least this way, I'll be there to drag out your limp and mortified form when you faint."

"Why would I faint? Oh." She halts in place and whirls

fully to face me. "Are there spiders? Is the north wing an insect habitat?"

The terror on her face has me stifling a laugh. If only I could confirm her fears, then she'd abandon her curiosity at once. Yet, now that we're alone, I find myself slipping out of my role again. I can't lie unless I'm deeply immersed in my William the Poet persona. Besides, if my falsehood failed to sway her and she decided to see the north wing anyway, she'd discover my ability to lie. I'd like to keep that a secret from as many as possible.

"There are no spiders," I finally say.

She sighs with relief and resumes walking. "Spiders are the one creature I cannot suffer to live."

"Oh? So there's one creature you despise more than me?"

"Only one," she says with a solemn nod.

We reach a pair of white doors with gold handles. Two human butlers dressed in all-white suits flank them. Wordlessly, they hand us each a glass vial and open the doors.

"What's this?" Edwina whispers, shaking the vial.

"I'll tell you once we're inside," I say, tucking my vial into my trouser pocket. We cross the threshold and the butlers shut the doors behind us. Dread settles deep into my bones as we enter a dimly lit hallway, the air thick with the heady scent of incense. Muffled sounds emanate from farther ahead and my muscles clench. I'm already desperate to bolt back the way we came. Memories from the one and only time I've been to the north wing surface in my mind, but I try to force them away. This isn't about me. This is about Edwina. She shouldn't be here alone. The sooner she sees what this place is all about, the sooner we can leave.

The sounds grow louder and more distinct with every step, and soon the hallway opens to a wide circular room. The walls are set with several large alcoves containing different pieces of furniture—a divan here, a set of chairs

115

there, a swing in another. Naked bodies writhe in each alcove, a living display of art. More furnishings are set throughout the room where guests can create art of their own. Moans and grunts and sighs mingle to produce a rather unsettling orchestra of public pleasure.

Nausea tightens my stomach. It's not that I find the display repulsive. There's nothing repulsive about sex. It's beautiful. Enjoyable. But I have my reasons for disliking this place, and being here again sends memories rising to the surface. Panic. Humiliation. Shame.

"Oh!" Edwina's shocked voice is a welcome distraction.

I face her, seeking comfort in how she nudges the bridge of her spectacles higher on her nose. I've grown used to the gesture, especially after watching her from across the dais during our signing today, and the familiar sight lulls me into a sense of safety. Then a fierce protectiveness as I remember why I'm here.

Her mouth falls open, eyes wide. "Oh, my heavens. Is this an orgy?"

I rub my jaw, resisting the urge to hide my entire face behind my hand. "It's a voyeurism club."

"It...it's..."

"We can go," I say softly. "We'll walk back the way we came and pretend this never happened. I can hold your hand if your knees are weak, and I promise not to tease you about it—"

"It's incredible!"

I blink at her, caught off guard by her reaction. She strolls over to the nearest alcove, where one human male is seated behind another on a velvet divan. Tapping a finger to her chin, she assesses the couple from different angles.

"That would be Johannes, and that would be Timothy," she says to me as I reach her side.

I don't know who the fuck Johannes and Timothy are or

why she's telling me this, but if I'm not mistaken, she's said those names before, when she was drunk.

She lifts her palm and wiggles her fingers, leaning closer to me as she says, "Do you see the way he cups his testicles like that? It's brilliant. Beautiful. I can use that."

She walks over to the next alcove. I'm...stunned. She's the only person in this entire room commenting on the public sex as if it were nothing but a painting on the wall. Most everyone else either has their hands in their trousers or under their skirts, or have coupled up on the furnishings.

Edwina is the weirdest woman I've ever met.

Belatedly, I follow her to the next display, keeping my eyes on her as much as possible, my hands tucked in my pockets to evoke some semblance of a casual air.

"He has the build of the reclusive baron," she says, pointing at the fae male thrusting into his dark-haired partner whom he has pinned against the wall of the alcove. "And she's nearly a spitting image of my governess from that book. Look at the way he fists her hair."

Like she did with her palming-the-testicles gesture, she mimics the male's hand, curled into his lover's dark tresses.

She shakes her head, her face full of longing. "That would have made the scene in the catacombs so much better. Oh, but the placement of her hands is just as good!"

With her eyes locked on the couple, she turns her body toward mine, her motions stiff and almost mechanical, then steps in close. I suck in a sharp breath as one of her hands lands on the side of my waist. She furrows her brow, still looking at the couple, as she presses her body flush against mine. Then she mirrors the woman's other hand, winding hers behind my neck and threading her fingers into the ends of my hair.

I'm so surprised by this sudden closeness, I freeze. The slam of my heart and the shiver that runs through me as her fingers claw gently against my scalp are the first pleasant sensations I've had since stepping inside this room.

She heaves a sigh. "It's all wrong. I'm shorter than she is and you don't have me hefted against a wall—"

Her words cut off as her gaze finally leaves the couple to meet mine. She utters a stifled yelp, eyes growing round as she takes in our proximity, the placement of her hands. For the strangest moment, I get the urge to remove my hands from my pockets and bracket them around her waist, keeping her there against me. But the moment is too short, and she leaps away from me as if I scalded her.

"Sorry," she squeaks out, hands covering her lips as her cheeks deepen to scarlet.

I clear my throat to tell her it was fine, that I didn't mind being her test subject, when a satyr approaches her. His humanoid upper half is roped with muscle, every inch of his skin glistening as if coated in oil. His bottom half is covered in brown fur, his legs ending in hooves. He gives her a respectful nod and gestures toward an empty sofa. "Would you care to join me?"

My hands are out of my pockets at once, my fingers curled into fists. I'm a breath away from striding between them—but I stop myself. Who am I to intervene? I was wrong when I assumed Edwina was too prim and too human for the north wing. She's enjoying it here, and she has every right to enjoy it more if that's what she wants.

She glances from the satyr to the couch then back to the satyr. Her eyes sweep over him, admiring that impressive display of glistening muscle. I might find it attractive too were I not so fucking uncomfortable here. Her gaze drifts down to where the satyr's fleshy torso gives way to furry hips, and there her attention halts. Snagged on his rather impressive—and rather erect—member. "Oh, you're...you're ready to go. Now."

"I'd love to have your mouth on me," he says.

Her eyes flick back to his, and her rosy cheeks turn ashen. "Me? Mine?"

"Yes, lovely."

She lowers her voice to an anxious mutter. "Should I? It... it would be research, I suppose. But...but, uhhhhhhhh—"

I fear she'll make that sound forever, so I give in to my urge to step between them. Facing Edwina, I say, "If you're thinking this is a good way to earn a point in our bet, think again. Our terms require an exchange of intimacy behind the closed doors of our bedrooms. There are no closed doors in the north wing, Weenie, and our bedrooms are back at the dormitory."

The relief on her face is clear. She leans to the side to address the satyr. "I'll have to decline, but I do appreciate the offer."

He gives her another gentlemanly nod, then saunters off to proposition his next option.

"He should be careful," she says, voice low. "He could poke an eye out with that thing."

Just like that, she has already recovered from the interaction and moves on to admire the erotic display in the next alcove, this one featuring a couple sharing a large wingback chair.

Edwina releases an excited gasp, tugging on my shirtsleeve. "Oh, look at the tender way she pays attention to her lover's nipples! Isn't that just gorgeous? What I wouldn't give to have my pen and notebook."

One of the women in the alcove opens her eyes to frown at how close Edwina has gotten in her visual study.

I pull her back with a light touch to her shoulder. "You know, this club may thrive on voyeurism, but your attention is a little too invasive."

She finally notices the glare the woman is giving her and

clasps her hands in an apologetic gesture. Yet her gaze only grows more intense as the couple returns to their lovemaking. Edwina's voice lowers to a whisper, her words slow and wistful. "She flicked her velvety tongue over the hardened, rosy peak of her pert, teardrop-shaped breasts—"

"Do not narrate," I bite out. "Blooming hell, you're embarrassing—"

"William, is that you?" The female voice has my spine going rigid.

"Fuck." The last person I want to see is Meredith. Spurred by panic, I take Edwina's hand in mine and pull her across the room to the hallway at the other end. The corridor is lined with doorless rooms, all filled with more grunts and groans, louder slaps of flesh, and the whimpers of aroused spectators. I drag Edwina quickly to the other side where we're greeted by a blessedly cool breeze. Here, the lighting is even dimmer and the doorways are lined with sheer curtains.

We rush through one doorway onto a circular balcony, but the balustrade is occupied. A dryad with green leafy hair perches nude upon the rail, her head thrown back, her balance precarious, while her lover—a lizard fae, based on their green scaly skin—feasts between her open legs.

"Oooh!" Edwina says, startling the couple. The dryad almost loses her balance on the rail before she catches herself. "That's so dangerous but so sexy!"

I drag her away as fast as I can. Thankfully, the next balcony is empty. Breathing slow and deep, I gather lungfuls of soothing air. As I reach the balustrade, I plant my forearms on the rail and let my head hang as I recover my composure. I'm so far from being William the Poet right now, it's laughable.

The relative silence on the balcony calms my racing pulse. A light breeze muffles the sounds of pleasure coming from inside while music from downstairs gives me something else to focus on.

After a few moments, Edwina comes up beside me. She leans against the balustrade and assesses me with a furrowed brow. "Are you all right, William?"

Her gentle tone paired with the sound of my name—not Willy, not Mr. Haywood—eases me even further. Still, all I can manage is a nod.

"I was too preoccupied to notice before, but you don't like it here, do you? Is it too stimulating for you? Are your...your masculine urges too strong? I won't shame you if you have an erection. I got an eyeful of satyr cock, Will. I don't think you have to worry about surprising me with what you have."

"Did you just turn an attempt to comfort me into a slight against my manhood?"

"Slight is the word for it—I'm so sorry! I shouldn't tease you when you're in such a sorry state. It's just too easy."

My lips pull into a grin as I shift to face her. She's right. It's easy to tease each other. As easy as breathing and as comforting too. A few barbed words from her, even cleverly veiled ones, and I'm already feeling like my normal self. Not my false persona but just me. It'll do for now.

Her brows knit together and she steps closer. One hand falls on my bicep, and I recall the way she put her hands on me earlier. It makes my pulse kick up, in a far more pleasant way than the frantic racing I experienced after hearing Meredith's voice.

"Really, though," she says. "Are you all right?"

"I am. I just...I have a history here, and it reminds me of things I'd rather forget."

Her hand leaves my arm, making it feel colder without her touch. "That woman who called your name...was she a former lover?"

"No, not exactly." I debate not telling her anything. Why

should I? She doesn't need to know. But I want this bubble of calm to last, if only for a little longer. "I participated in the north wing activities only once."

Her expression brightens. "How was it? Educational? Enlightening? No, damn me." She slaps her hand to her forehead. "Of course you didn't enjoy it. That's what you're trying to tell me, isn't it?"

"Basically, but your first instincts aren't far off. The north wing isn't just a voyeurism club. It also serves to help actors grow out of stage fright. If an actor can participate in, enjoy, and perform something so intimate as sex in public, then surely they can act before an audience. That's always been Grayson's intent, at least. As I told you earlier, Grayson was my mentor. While he isn't affiliated with the university, he's always hosted parties for the students and alumni and does what he can to encourage the various arts. His advice helped me grow into one of the most highly praised actors at the school. I was deemed brilliant. A prodigy in the making. Faerwyvae's next star. There was only one thing I failed at when it came to acting, and that was love scenes."

She frowns. "As in…"

"Whether it was a kiss or a lovemaking scene, I would lock up. Despite my ample sexual experience in my personal life, it was the one thing I couldn't fake on stage. The one thing that turned my acting skills to shit."

"Oh, right," she says. "Because pureblood fae can't lie. Which means you couldn't pretend to be in love. But then… how do fae act at all if they can't lie?"

"The most talented fae actors can say or do anything during a stage performance without being thwarted by the magic that keeps our kind from lying. If they can seamlessly shift into another persona, they can state that which is true for that character, even if it misaligns with their regular self. I was one of those talented actors." I'm dangerously close to revealing what few know—that I can take such talents off the stage too.

"That's fascinating," she says. "So you can lie, but only when you're performing. What was the cause then? I've seen you flirt with strangers. I can't imagine doing so on stage is much different."

"Flirting is easy. Kissing is different, at least to me. I simply can't kiss someone when I don't feel genuine physical attraction, no matter who I'm pretending to be. So I've always settled for roles that didn't involve romance—at least not kissing scenes. Then two years ago, I was granted an audition for a role that could have made me a headline star across the isle. A role that could have changed my life. A role that ended my career."

I clench my jaw. I don't want to say the next part. I shouldn't say the next part.

But the confession leaves my lips before I can stop it.

"The play was *The Governess and the Rake*."

CHAPTER FOURTEEN

EDWINA

*M*y mouth falls open. William has surprised me a lot this evening, first with his discomfort in the north wing, then with how candidly he's been speaking to me ever since we stepped onto the balcony. But I never could have anticipated this. "You starred in *The Governess and the Rake*? The stage play of *my* book?"

He rubs his brow. "My tale doesn't have a happy ending, Weenie."

Oh, right. He's only telling me this to explain the source of his panic after fleeing the voyeurism room. It takes no small effort to bury my vanity and avoid asking him questions about my play. Was it lovely? Did the audience swoon? What were the costumes like? Instead, I give him an encouraging nod.

"As you can probably guess," he says, "the lead role included not just a kiss but a sex scene. Multiple, actually. Not true sex in the stage adaptation, of course, but a rather convincing imitation of it. I knew it would be a challenge for me, but I needed that role. I needed a boost to my career and the income that could make a significant dent in our debt. While I may have been a prodigy at university, out in the real world, I was just a dandelion in a vast garden of curated roses. So I was desperate to get the part. And I did. My audition was exquisite, all because it didn't include a kiss. Yet I knew I couldn't avoid the love scenes for long. I came to Grayson for advice, and he suggested I participate in the north wing. He thought it would help me get comfortable performing intimate acts before an audience.

"I chose Meredith as my partner. We were old friends from university. I didn't have feelings for her, but I was, at the very least, attracted to her."

A prickle of envy jabs me in the chest. Of course he was attracted to her. I saw her myself before he dragged me away. She was tall with pouty pink lips, gorgeous curves, and straight black hair.

William shifts to lean his backside against the railing, arms folded over his chest, eyes distant. "I was so nervous. More than any audition. Any performance. But Meredith did her best to distract me. I managed to initiate a kiss, though I can't say it was a good one. Not even my attraction to her could make up for my terror at having an audience. We progressed to touching, but I hardly felt like I was inside my body. I must have blundered my way through enough to convince Meredith I was ready for more, for she then proceeded to remove my shirt, then her chemise. As soon as her top was around her waist, I had reached my limit. My head was spinning. I hated the way I felt. Hated what I was doing. And that is when I vomited all over her."

My mouth falls open. "You...vomited. On *her*."

"All over those beautiful breasts of hers."

I can't stifle the snort of laughter fast enough. "I'm so sorry."

He gives me a small smile. "Apparently, I am in no way cut out for public lovemaking."

Another burst of laughter leaves my lips, but I cover my mouth until I can recover. With my words half trembling with mirth, I ask, "So, then what? You relinquished your role and quit the show?"

"Oh, Ed, my sordid tale has only just begun."

I find myself leaning closer. "Do tell."

"You're enjoying this aren't you?"

"A little."

I expect him to clam up and realize how much he's divulged, but he still wears that half smile. "Then let me conclude with the worst part yet. No, I did not take the rational route and quit the show. Instead, I powered through every kiss scene as best I could. The director was sorely disappointed in my poor performance, but I promised I would work on it. Then it was time to rehearse the first love scene. And it wasn't just any rehearsal. Our director invited some of his colleagues to watch, a producer, a casting director, and a talent agent. Big names in the industry, ones you absolutely want to make a great impression on. Can you guess what kind of impression I made?"

My eyes go wide. "Please tell me you didn't..."

"I, William Haywood, threw up all over the beloved actress Greta Garter."

"Greta Garter? You were cast opposite *Greta Garter*?" Even I know of the Faerwyvae-born human actress. Her career is new, but her rise to fame has been astounding. So much so that she's even left the isle to perform in other countries. The month before I left Bretton, I attended the theater with my family and was delighted by her performance in the lead role. She's as beautiful as she is talented.

"Not once, Weenie, but twice."

"Twice?" I'm so mortified and amused that I don't know whether to laugh or cry.

He nods. "The first time, I tried to play it off like I was unwell. The second time, the director realized I wasn't cut out for the role. He fired me, but not before lecturing me about my failure to disclose my *shortcoming*, as he called it, when I was cast. He had every right to be angry. I'd wasted his time and created a production delay while my role was recast. And even though what happened was never made public, word spread behind the scenes. I was never cast in anything but a supporting role again."

My shoulders fall. "You never performed in my play after all."

"Oh, I performed," he says. "The director was kind enough to cast me as Gardener Number Three."

"I didn't even write a gardener character in the book."

"I might as well have been part of the set."

I'm starting to understand why he's so determined to make something of his poetry career. His first passion already failed. At least he has a second one. I don't know what I would do if I ruined my chance at being a writer.

He heaves a sigh and I study his profile, the way the moonlight paints the planes of his face. It's enough to make me forget just how at odds we are with each other and see him as the beautiful male I first took him for. My initial impression of him changed so fast, from admiration to annoyance in the blink of an eye. While my opinion of him hasn't completely improved, it has evolved after our conversation. He may be every inch the arrogant asshole he's proven himself to be, but he's also this vulnerable, wounded artist that stands before me now. One who followed me up to the north wing because he feared I'd be as uncomfortable here as he is.

127

Something tender cracks inside my chest.

William's gaze whips toward mine as if the crack had been audible. He angles his body toward me, posture relaxed. He seems to have recovered from his embarrassing memories and he assesses me through slitted lids. Only inches separate us, but I don't feel the urge to step away. "I truly am impressed, Weenie."

I arch a brow. "With what?"

"With your complete lack of fear. It's reckless, and you're as stubborn as a weed, but you charge ahead without restraint. You aren't flustered at all in the north wing. I really was prepared for you to faint at the first sight of a naked body."

"No, it was lovely! It was like seeing my characters come to life. Studying positions I've only ever written about. So badly I wish I'd brought my notebook."

"Do you always approach sex from such a methodical view?"

I bristle, but there's no judgment in his tone. My muscles relax as I take in his open expression. "Well, it is my job. Or part of it."

"Yes, but outside of writing. Do you enjoy physical intimacy? When I first took you out here, you asked if I was feeling too stimulated, but what about you? Does the sight or thought of such acts arouse you? There's nothing wrong if it doesn't. I'm just curious."

I give his question some thought. I realize it must seem strange that everyone else in the north wing was reacting with arousal rather than academic study like me. "I do experience sexual urges if that's what you're asking. It's just easy for me to take myself out of an imagined scenario and look at it from an objective standpoint. When I was studying those couples, I wasn't imagining myself as part of the act, not even as a viewer. Not until—"

I swallow my words, horrified at what I was about to confess. It wasn't until I used William as a prop while trying to replicate that one couple's position that I entered my imagined scenario. When I met his eyes and saw the placement of my hands, felt the heat of his body, I was fully immersed in the act. My hand in his hair, my fingertips clawed against the base of his scalp, my other palm at his waist, pulsing at the flex of his abdomen, the rise and fall of his chest. I thought my heart was going to explode. Even now, as the memory replays in my mind's eye, my pulse kicks up.

"Right," William says, and I fear my every thought is plastered on my face. "You mean the satyr."

I blink at him. "Oh. Oh, yes! The satyr." He's right, of course. The satyr's proposition pulled me into the scenario too, but it wasn't nearly as arousing.

"Did I overstep by intervening?"

"No, I appreciate that you did. I wasn't ready for what he was suggesting. I mean, I want to do those things. For research, of course. I thought maybe I should accept his offer, but..." I shudder.

William leans in and places his forefinger under my chin. I freeze at the touch. He lifts my chin slightly until I lock my eyes with his. "Don't do anything you don't want to do."

"I *wanted* to—"

"I'm not talking about logical wants. Don't do anything that requires convincing."

I narrow my eyes. "Why? Because simply doing something for the sake of doing it is wrong?"

"No, because you'll like it more if you do it for the sake of pleasure, not study. You have experienced pleasure, haven't you?"

I swallow hard, but with him still lifting my chin, the

motion is jerky. His line of questioning sparks my stubborn side. "Of course I have."

"With a partner or just alone?"

"I've had partners."

"But have they given you pleasure?"

My chest heaves. Why does the word *pleasure* sound so erotic coming from him? Why does it make me so light-headed? "I've experienced pleasure, Willy."

"So alone, then. Do you touch yourself?"

"Sometimes."

He releases my chin, then stands before me. I shift to the side, but now my back is against the balustrade. He leans closer, then braces his hands on the rail on either side of me. "Have you never craved a partner in place of your fingers? Someone who will set your heart racing and make you weep with ecstasy?"

"Those kinds of partners belong in my books."

"You don't think the pleasure you write about is attainable off the page? I think you just haven't found the right person. Maybe Monty was right. Maybe you just need to learn what you like."

I can't form a word in reply, not with him standing so close. Not with his head angled to the side as his eyes drop to my lips. Not with the way he lifts his hand from the railing and alights it upon my collarbone. My breaths grow shallow as he sweeps his fingers to the base of my throat, then lowers his palm until his skin is flush with mine. His touch isn't belligerent or groping, remaining several inches above my cleavage, but it's not exactly tame either. Should he raise the position of his hand, he'd be clasping my throat. Should he lower it just enough, he'd be cupping my breast.

And yet...I don't flinch away. Don't cower. Logic has fled me. Like when I touched him earlier, I'm now fully immersed in this moment, in every sensation, every breath. My pulse thuds against his palm.

"Ah," he says, stepping away from me with a wicked smirk on his lips. He tucks his hands in his pockets. "It is possible to get your heart racing."

I nearly stumble in my efforts to gather my composure. With a huff, I smooth out my dress and pin him with a glare. "You're clearly feeling much better."

"I am, thank you." His eyes crinkle with mirth, but his *thank you* sounds genuine.

"Well, I've had about all I can stand of you," I say. "Now, do we walk back the way we came, or can you get us out of here without subjecting you to the horrors of the north wing once more?"

"The wing ends here. There's no other way out but back the way we came."

"Don't you have any special fae magic? What kind of fae are you? Do you have wings? Wind magic? Can you float us down to the garden below?"

He snorts a laugh. "I'm not a useful kind of fae in this situation."

Yet he pointedly avoids telling me what kind of fae he is. If most fae have a seelie and unseelie form, what's his secondary manifestation? Is he an animal? An element? A spirit? Some legendary creature like a banshee or vampire?

"Come, Weenie," he says before I can let my curiosity run amok. "Don't worry about me. We'll go back the way we came."

I give him a teasing pout. "Do you need me to hold your hand so you don't faint, Willy boy?"

"Yes." His answer wipes the pout off my lips. "But only so we can hurry out of here before you're dragged away by some virulent satyr, or you stop to gawk at the next pair of blushing nipples."

I clasp my hands to my chest. "But did you see all those nipples? I didn't know they came in such lovely shapes and colors."

He chuckles and takes my hand in his. "You really love your research, don't you?"

"I do. Oh, speaking of…you never told me what this is." I extract the glass vial I received when we first arrived at the north wing. I'd tucked it into my bodice until now.

"It's a tonic," he explains. "One part contraceptive, one part disease prevention. Anyone who engages in north wing activities with a partner must consume the full contents of the vial."

My mouth falls open as I assess the vial with new eyes. "Are you serious? This is brilliant! How long does it last?"

"One month."

I remove the cap with gusto and down the liquid at once. The flavor is sweet yet herbal, with only a slightly bitter aftertaste.

"Really?" William deadpans. "Have you no restraint? I could have been trying to poison you."

I tuck the empty vial back into my bodice. "Yes, but you can't lie. Besides, if I'm going to win our bet, I might as well prepare myself. You should too."

He rolls his eyes but reluctantly retrieves his own vial and downs its contents with far less enthusiasm. "Oh, yes. Our bet."

Now that I know more about him, I wonder if his reluctance to participate in the bet has anything to do with what he told me. I'm about to ask but stop myself. Our serious mood has ended. He proved that when he teased me about getting my heart racing. So instead, I tease him back. "Now that I know your weakness, Willy, I'm feeling more confident than ever."

He gives me a simpering smile. "Oh, Ed, did you not listen

to a word I said? I can't kiss someone when I'm not stimulated by attraction. That doesn't mean I'm not easily attracted."

But it does, doesn't it? If he was easily attracted, he wouldn't have had a problem kissing Greta Garter. I may have only seen her perform once, but I know for a fact that she's stunning. Hell, I'd kiss her, if only to learn how to write about the feel of such luscious lips. I'd probably do anything she asked, to be honest.

I don't say any of this out loud though.

I arch a haughty brow. "Then let's see which of us is the best seducer. I've learned some things tonight." I lift my palm and wiggle my fingertips in an imitation of the first couple we saw. I'm still so impressed with how he worked his lover's testicles.

"Never make that gesture again," William says as he grabs my hand and pulls me back into the hall. Apparently he was serious about us holding hands.

I could easily pull away…but I don't. And as we leave the main room full of its beautifully writhing naked bodies, I find my eyes trail back to William's face. An amused grin dances over his lips, and I can't help but admit his smile is the best work of art here.

CHAPTER FIFTEEN

EDWINA

$\mathcal{I}$'ve never been so acutely aware of someone I'm not even looking at. Yet William's presence is impossible to ignore, even as we stand on opposite ends of a room with dozens of people between us. I can feel him looking at me. Smirking, more like.

Our unspoken truce has ended. Or whatever the camaraderie we found on the balcony is called. It ended the moment I slid my hand out of William's as we left the north wing. We found Jolene pacing the hall not long after, and when she asked what took us so long, what horrors had befallen us in the mysterious wing, William and I exchanged a look. One that sealed our secrets between us.

After that, I simply said to Jolene, "Spiders."

And that was that.

She's been hanging off William's arm ever since, and there she remains, clinging to him like a lifeline as they chat amongst a small crowd before the enormous fireplace. A fireplace that somehow keeps the room cooler, not hotter, as it burns pearlescent white logs with pale blue flames. Strange fae magic, to be sure, and I'm grateful for it. Even though the nights seem cooler in the Solar Court than the days, with so many guests, so much activity, and so much alcohol, I daresay this cramped room would be stifling without the cooling magic. We're in a recreation room on the first floor, one of the few not dedicated to any art. Unless you count drinking and canoodling as an art. The room seems to be most effective at pairing up couples, which makes it perfect for the purpose of our bet.

I meet William's eyes for what must be the hundredth time since entering the room. A corner of his lips curl as he taps the mantle he's leaning against. My gaze shifts to his fingertips. For a moment I'm struck by the memory of how he'd lifted my chin with that very finger. Before he teased me about pleasure. Then I realize what he's gesturing at. It's the small clock perched upon the mantel. It reads a quarter to eleven.

He gives me a pointed look that says, *Almost midnight.*

My sneer replies, *I know.*

He tilts his head to indicate the girl on his arm. The lofty arch of his brow conveys that his night's win is guaranteed. He's not wrong either. Jolene has both arms wrapped around his, her cheeks flushed from the drink she somehow managed to consume without letting go of William. She's determined to take him to bed tonight and isn't keeping her intentions a secret from anyone. A sharp pinch of annoyance pricks my chest before I snap my attention back to William.

Then pay attention to her, I mouth at him with a dismissive flick of my wrist.

Pay attention to him, he mouths back, jutting his chin at the man whose chair arm I'm perched upon.

I bat my lashes and lean closer to my companion until our shoulders touch. *Like this?*

William isn't the only one who's found a partner for the night. Though mine is still more of a *potential* partner. He's a human named Archie and he's a postgraduate student at the university. He took a liking to me almost as soon as we entered the room. I was initially worried about our age difference, as he's three-and-twenty to my nine-and-twenty, but he wasn't put off in the least. If anything, he was more fascinated.

Archie notices me leaning into him and angles himself toward me. With a disarmingly sweet smile, he lifts his palm and presents a pair of dice. "Will you blow on them, Edwina?"

A blush warms my cheeks. I've hardly known the man for more than an hour, and he's already calling me by my first name. "Blow on them?"

"Infuse them with luck."

I shake my head. "I don't have any magic if that's—"

He chuckles, as do the others surrounding the card table. Archie has been engaged in a game of cards and dice with several male classmates. Most have a female companion with them, perched on the arm of their partner's chair like me, which the players insist is good luck. Archie begged me to be his *lady luck*, but I haven't a clue what this blowing on dice ritual is all about.

"You're so cute, Edwina." Archie blinks up at me, his cheeks ruddy, his chestnut hair mussed. He wears spectacles just like me and might be the cutest man I've ever met. I'd love to cast him as one of my heroines' younger brothers. Or perhaps the hero's much kinder yet secretly villainous rival. "It's not magic, sweet girl. It's just for luck."

I internally wince. No one has ever called me *sweet girl,*

and I daresay no one would if they knew me well. Still, it's refreshing to have a stranger see me in such a way.

I do as he asked and blow on the dice, then I lift my gaze to find William again.

He's hidden at first as a cluster of partygoers saunters past, but as soon as they clear my line of sight, I find William's eyes at once, narrowed to a glare. I give him a haughty shrug and lean even closer to Archie, draping my arm behind his shoulders as he throws the dice, then flips a card. Archie cheers and circles his arms around my waist, pulling me fully into his lap at the same time. My face burns hot, and I'm not certain what to do with my hands. One arm is still thrown over his shoulders, and I place the other hesitantly over the armrest. I've never sat in a man's lap before, and I've certainly never acted so familiar with a stranger in public, but the other women at the card table seem perfectly comfortable in similar positions.

I find William again. His face is slack at first, but his expression quickly sharpens. He scoffs, as if my efforts are laughable, and somehow manages to extract his arm from Jolene's iron-clad grasp to put it around her shoulders. Her expression brightens at once. That might be the first time he's initiated any kind of touch with her. She whirls toward him and drapes both arms behind his neck. His eyes widen as if he hadn't expected her to react. For the briefest moment, his arrogance disappears. Then he lifts his gaze over her head and we lock eyes once more. His haughty façade returns, and he places his hands at her waist. While he doesn't bring her nearly as close as Archie has brought me, it's obvious he's trying to show me up.

So I take things one step further and place a hand on my companion's chest.

William pulls Jolene an inch closer.

I drag my hand higher up Archie's torso until it rests over

his clavicle. Nearly the same place William touched me earlier. Then I slip my hand under the collar of Archie's shirt until only warm flesh lies under my palm.

The way William sucks in a breath, the way his jaw tightens, makes me feel like it's *his* body beneath my palm, his skin I'm teasing. And that, for some strange reason, thrills me. I give him an innocent smile.

William's eyes dip to my mouth and his own parts slightly.

I lift my chin and drag the tip of my tongue over my upper lip. I probably look more like a lizard than a seductress, but the way William's pupils go wide has me uncaring either way. I sit up straighter in Archie's lap, lifting my chest and letting the low-cut bodice of my evening dress do the rest of the work. I may not be the most well-endowed, but I know how to lace my corset just right to make the best of what I have. Showing it off is a matter of posture, which I rarely care to utilize. But now…

William's gaze slides to my chest—

My view of him is cut off, replaced with Archie's face. Before I realize what's happening his lips claim mine in a short but firm kiss. He cheers and the rest of the players at the card table release disgruntled groans. Archie must have won the game, but I hadn't been paying any attention. Without shifting me off his lap, he leans forward and collects the handful of jasper chips and rounds—Solar Court's currency—and pockets them. He grins at me, then kisses me again. "I knew you were good luck!"

I'm so stunned by the two unexpected kisses that I can't form a reply. Thankfully, he's already focused on the next game, as one of his mates begins shuffling the cards.

I slide my hand out from under Archie's collar, feeling more self-conscious now.

William's stare is like a gaping black hole from across the

room, impossible to ignore any longer. Gathering my composure, I meet his eyes with what I hope is a proud look. The kiss doesn't count toward our bet, as our intimacies must be exchanged in our own bedrooms, but it's a step closer to securing Archie as my lover. With how comfortably he touches me and how readily he kissed me, inviting him back to my dormitory feels like a sure deal. My confidence flares, and I taunt William with a coy shrug of my shoulders.

Easy, I mouth.

His eyes narrow to a glare. Then a boldness takes over his expression. He pulls Jolene even closer to him now. Her back is facing me, but I can tell she was in mid-conversation with him. Probably a very one-sided conversation, from how preoccupied he's been with me, but now she stiffens in his arms. He slides his attention to her, and he showers her with that stupid seductive grin. Her form melts against him, and she angles her head, giving me a slight view of her profile. Her lashes are closed, her lips parted in silent invitation.

William goes pale, his demeanor faltering once more. The grimace that tugs his features reminds me of everything he told me tonight. His struggles. His embarrassments. His inability to kiss someone he isn't attracted to. I'm struck by the sudden urge to race across the room and rescue him. I shift in Archie's lap, ready to launch myself out of it, when William's eyes return to mine.

I freeze.

I arch a questioning brow, but that only makes his lips curl wickedly. Archie tugs me until I'm settled fully in his lap again, but I can't take my eyes off William. There's a dare in his cruel grin that makes me breathless. With some strange mixture of terror and elation, I watch as he lowers his mouth to Jolene's, his eyes locked on mine all the while. He doesn't close them, doesn't so much as blink away from me as he gives her a slow and languorous kiss.

My fingertips move to my mouth before I can stop them, tracing where his mouth brushes against hers. His attention on me scalds hotter than any flame. My skin flushes as if burned by his hands, his lips, even though he's nowhere near me. Even though he's wrapped around someone else at the opposite end of the room. Our locked eyes tether us in a way that defies distance, reason—

He breaks the kiss and finally looks down at his partner. Released from his gaze, I gasp.

What...what the hell was that? Why am I so short of breath? Why do I feel like I've been roasted over hot coals? And what is this fiery heat that pulses between my thighs?

William has been hidden from me now that another group has passed between us, and this one has decided to linger at the center of the room.

"Where are you staying tonight?" Archie steals my attention. Only now do I realize he's no longer playing the card and dice game. He must have lost early in the first round.

I blink, clearing my head. "At the university dormitory."

He leans in and whispers in my ear, "Can we stay the night together?"

I don't know why, but I look for William again. All I see is the mantle and the clock that ticks closer to midnight. It's after eleven now.

I rise from Archie's lap and gather all the boldness I can muster. "Let's go back to my room."

CHAPTER SIXTEEN

EDWINA

*T*he last person I expect to see outside my bedroom once we reach the dormitory is William. He leans beside the closed door, arms crossed, one foot propped against the wall behind him. He and Jolene reached the dormitory before us even though Archie and I left Somerton House first. It only took a matter of minutes to run into them. Or, more accurately, for William to come barreling after us, demanding to know why I would leave the party and my roommate without a word. After which I muttered we all knew Jolene wasn't going to be my roommate tonight. Jolene beamed while William looked murderous. He probably hoped he could sabotage my attempt to secure a lover.

Afterward, Archie insisted on walking behind the other couple so we could have some privacy. After a few minutes, they were so far ahead I couldn't see them anymore. I was certain William would be bedding Jolene in his room by the time I even reached mine. The thought made me irrationally angry all the way here, though I'm not sure why. It would have been foolish to hope I'd be the only one earning a point toward our bet tonight, considering Jolene's determination.

But if that's the case, why the hell is he outside my room? There's no way my friend changed her mind.

"Where's Jolene?" I ask.

His gaze shifts from me to Archie and back again but he doesn't push off the wall. "My room."

"Then why aren't you with her?"

He purses his lips, jaw tightening. "I need to ask you something."

"Then ask."

"Alone."

"Anything you can say in front of me—"

"It's about your research," he says, finally straightening and stepping away from the wall. A cruel smile plays on his lips.

I stiffen. The last thing I need is for Archie to know I'm using him for research. He doesn't even know about our bet. I burn William with a glower before turning to Archie. "Go inside my room and wait for me."

Concern etches Archie's brow. "Is everything all right? If you don't want to talk to him, I'll…" He glances at William and visibly deflates. I could have sworn he was about to say something bold and protective, but of course, one look at the towering poet would change his mind. Archie isn't much taller than I am, and he's as slender as a twig. "I'll wait in your room."

I open the door for him. "I'll be in shortly."

He moves to the doorway, then pauses. With one hand bracing my lower back, he plants a kiss on my cheek. I flinch at the unexpected contact, but he quickly pulls away.

As soon as he steps inside my room, I close the door and march up to William. "What the hell do you—"

I'm only a few feet away from him when he steps into my space. I launch back, but he shadows my every move, angling his body and forcing me to do the same. In a matter of clumsy footsteps, I find my back against the wall beside my door, right where William was leaning a moment ago. It's still warm from his body, and as he leans before me, hands planted on either side of my head, I'm struck by a vision of being pressed between two of him. The William before me and the warmth of his shadow against my back.

Oh.

Oh, I'd like to write that down! What if the shadow was sentient? My mouth practically waters as I imagine the fabulous love scene that would make—

"Weenie," he says, snapping me out of my imaginings. His voice is a deep whisper. "Do you really want to do this?"

His face is so close. The dim light of the hall, the way he's half cast in darkness, somehow makes the intensity in his gaze more alluring. But…what is he asking me? His proximity makes it impossible to remember where I even am or what the hell we were talking about. "Do I…what?"

"Do you really want to sleep with him?" he says through his teeth, nodding toward my closed door.

Oh, right. I steel my expression and lift my chin. "Of course I—"

He takes one hand off the wall to cover my mouth, cutting off my words. "Don't just argue. Fucking think, Weenie. Do you want him?"

My lips tingle where his palm presses against them. And now his face is even closer. His eyes dart between mine, his question hanging in the air. He's holding my gaze in a much more serious way than he did earlier when he kissed Jolene. I can't help recalling the heat that surged through me at the sight.

"Do. You. Want. Him?"

My chest heaves, the word *no* blaring inside me. But I can't say that. I have a bet to win, and he is not going to sabotage me. I shove at his arm and he releases my mouth without resistance. "Why is it so hard for you to believe I can make up my own mind?"

He returns the hand to the wall beside my head. "You don't seem attracted to him. Your body stiffens every time he touches you."

I scoff. "Just because you can't kiss someone you're not attracted to, doesn't mean I can't."

"So you admit it. You're not attracted to him."

"Oh, I find him attractive. I think he's very cute."

He gives me a simpering look. "Cute. You mean like a puppy? How arousing."

"I happen to like cute men. They're a lot better than arrogant beasts like you."

"If you prefer cute men so much, then spend your time selecting one you honestly like. You could have your pick of lovers, Ed. Ones you're attracted to. Why just settle for the first person who shows interest in you?"

Is he serious? Does he really think I can have my pick of lovers? What an ignorant fool. Just because he's lived his whole life with no shortage of interested parties doesn't mean the rest of us experience the same. I'm not like him. I don't have a flock of lovers at my beck and call. I'm not as attractive or as likable as he is. Besides, even if I'd wanted to choose a lover who isn't Archie, I was too distracted by William tonight to do anything but settle for the first man who liked me.

"That's hypocritical coming from you," I say. "You expect me to be particular about who I take to bed when your bedfellow of choice required no effort at all."

One of his hands balls into a fist against the wall, and a

frustrated growl rumbles in his chest. "You know nothing about my *bedfellow of choice*."

He punctuates the last words, but I don't know what he's getting at. Does he think I'm insulting Jolene?

"Blooming hell," he says, shaking his head. "You know nothing at all."

"Which is why I'm doing research. Now, if you'll excuse me." I turn to dip under his arm, but he moves it, planting it beside my waist now. I press my back into the wall again. His other hand is just above my shoulder, his body caging in mine. My heart slams against my ribs.

"He's human," he says with a frown. "I thought you wanted to research fae lovers."

My mouth falls open. How does he know? But of course he does. He heard the same conversation I did. He had to have overheard Daphne and Monty talking about my fae characters' inaccuracies in my book.

"There's research, then there's our bet," I say, keeping my voice as steady as I can. I can't give him the satisfaction of making me flustered if this is a repeat of what he did on the balcony. "If I can't get both from the same partner, I'll be happy with one."

He lowers his head and blows out a slow sigh. "There are other ways to research. Safer ways. If you're going to have meaningless sex with someone you don't even like, then…" He finally lifts his head and meets my eyes again. There's heat in his gaze, mixed with something that reminds me of the vulnerability he showed me on the balcony. His next words send my pulse skittering. "Use me."

I blink at him, piecing his words together.

He steps closer, our bodies mere inches apart. "Use me," he says, his tone firm. Resolute. "Use me like you did in the north wing. You want a fling with a fae lover and a point in our bet? I'll give you both. A free pass. Just say those two words, Weenie. *Free pass*."

He's so close, his breath mingles with mine. I can taste it, the faint liquor that infuses it, and I find myself leaning closer, wanting more. Would his lips taste the same? If I say those two words, *free pass*, would my curiosity be sated?

Intellectual curiosity, of course.

That's all.

I tell myself this, but the fluttering in my stomach says this might be more. This might be...desire.

He speaks again, and I go limp against the wall, more pliant with every word. "Say it. Say it and I'll give you a point without taking one myself. I give you my word. A fae promise. Position me however you want and I'll make sure it's for more than academic study. I'll let you find out exactly what touch you like best, what position, and then I'll withhold it from you. I'll tease you, torment you, until you're begging me, whimpering and whining like one of your blushing heroines. Just when you can't take it anymore, I'll give you what you want. I'll touch you in every way you like. Then I'll make you come."

I bite my lip to stifle the gasp that rises to my throat. My breaths are sharp and short, my knees going limp.

"Use me," he whispers over my lips, and heavens above, I can't remember a single reason not to do exactly what he says. Not even the thought that his lips were on someone else's so recently can cool the sudden fire burning in my core. I can't stop the irrational certainty that he'd kiss me better. That I'd kiss *him* better than Jolene or anyone else ever could.

The hand beside my waist creeps closer on the wall until it rests against my side. Just the slightest angle of his wrist would allow him to grasp me. I wonder how firm his hand would feel at my waist. Wonder whether it would rove over my hip and bottom first or curve over my breast—

"William."

I stiffen at the distant voice. It's Jolene, and she's coming from the men's dormitory farther down the next hall. While the memory of William kissing Jolene only made me crave him more, the thought of her actual presence banishes the illogical ardor I'd been filled with. I straighten and expect William to push off the wall, but he doesn't. He remains in place as if he has no shame in getting caught by the woman he's supposed to be wooing. His brow is arched in question, the memory of his last words still dangling between us.

Use me.

How close I was to falling for that. But...but there's no way he truly meant it. The fact remains that he kissed Jolene. Which means he's attracted to her. She's the one he wants to spend the night with.

I put a hand on his chest and force him back. He lets me, despite being strong enough to resist my greatest efforts.

"You're a really good actor after all," I say, a tremor in my voice. "But you're just trying to sabotage me."

"Is that what I'm doing?"

I launch myself toward my door, desperate to put space between us. I cling to the handle as if it's a life raft. "Go focus on your own sex life and stay out of mine."

Jolene calls William's name again, and this time she comes into view. He glances toward her, and I take the opportunity to rush inside my room.

As soon as I slam the door behind me, I slump against it, throwing my head back with a heavy sigh. Even with the door and several feet between us, I can still feel William's presence. I can still feel the memory of hands that never quite touched me. Can still taste the liquor on his breath. I'm hot all over and desperate to remove some layers.

I reach for the clasps at the back of my dress when movement stills my hand. My attention whips to one of the two beds in the room. Archie reclines on one, arms propped behind his head, fully nude and fully aroused.

He winks. "Hey, sweet girl."

My stomach sinks. I'd forgotten about him.

I give him a tired smile, my gaze sliding to his unimpressive erection. "Oddly enough, this is the second time this has happened today."

CHAPTER SEVENTEEN

WILLIAM

I slam my bedroom door behind me and immediately start pacing. The room is small with two beds, two desks, and a wardrobe, and doesn't allow for more than a few strides before I'm forced to turn and pace the other way. My fingers curl into fists, my heart raging against my ribs. I feel like I'm about to claw my way out of my skin.

"What do you think they're doing?" I mutter as I run a hand through my hair, not caring how it falls. "Is she really going to go through with this? The nerve! I told her she could have a free pass, but she chose him. I could snap him like a twig."

"William, I don't know what you're talking about."

I freeze and face the girl in my room. The girl I haven't paid the slightest attention to since we left Somerton House. She shifts anxiously from foot to foot, wringing her hands at her waist. Her question pierces my flustered mind. She's right, what *am* I talking about? Why am I pacing about the room like a storm cloud?

She steps closer. "Are you worried about Edwina? Is he yet another unsavory character like the lion fae?"

"No," I say, and it's true. I'm not worried about her in that way. She didn't consume any alcohol tonight, so her means to consent is sound. Yet my chest remains coiled with fury. But fury over what? She's in no danger. Am I simply annoyed that she didn't fall for my seductions?

My chest screams, *Yes*.

Is that really it? I'm...jealous.

Of that tiny fucking weed named Archie.

"Then...then why are you so upset?" Jolene asks, interrupting my thoughts once more. "Did I do something wrong?"

The worry on her face cools some of my ire, and I'm left with a well of shame. How careless I've been with this woman. Now my evening's actions have come to collect my guilt. This was all my doing, bringing her into this. I was never attracted to her, yet I wooed her tonight. I even kissed her. That wasn't for Jolene, but she doesn't know that. She has no clue I only kissed her to rile up Edwina. It was only because I'd been looking at Edwina that I was able to kiss Jolene at all.

That's the first time I've ever done that. The first time I've delivered a convincing kiss to someone I'm not attracted to.

Blooming hell, I *should* be attracted to Jolene. She's pretty, I can admit that, but true attraction is different. Ever since the incidents with Meredith and Greta Garter, my tastes have grown more distinct. In my university days, when I slept my way through half my acquaintances, attraction was purely physical. Now there's an emotional aspect too. Being pretty or handsome or sexy isn't what constitutes attraction anymore. Not for me. It remains a factor, of course, but what matters more is an unmistakable pull. A longing. A desire for more.

But wait.

Doesn't that mean…

I'm attracted to Edwina?

I run a hand over my face and resume pacing. Her visage fills my mind. Her fiery hair, always a mess. Those spectacles, constantly being shoved higher up the bridge of her nose whether they've begun to slip or not. The dirty hem of her dress the day we met. Her bare feet when she refused to take back her shoes. Her temper. Her pride. The way she lies.

My heart echoes with every vision. Every memory.

Thud.

Thud.

Thud.

Even as my annoyance burns, so too does something else. It's the pull. Longing. Desire. Want.

No, no, no. This isn't possible. I can't be attracted to her.

I'm *not* attracted to…

I'm not…

"Fuck," I mutter, rubbing my jaw with more force than necessary.

How the hell did this happen? Before I met Edwina, I was determined to dislike her. She was the wicked author behind the stage play that destroyed my career, and her appearance at Flight of Fancy was an unwelcome one. It meant I no longer had sole possession of The Heartbeats Tour. Our first interactions sparked my competitive drive. Not only that, but she drew my attention to her again and again simply because her dislike of me was so blatant and amusing. She was a source of entertainment, nothing more.

Nothing.

More.

Right?

I may have been protective a time or two, but the first instance was brotherly instinct over a maiden in distress. The second instance—shielding her from the horrors in the north wing—was out of consideration for her fragile human nature.

But in the hall outside her room...

The way I spoke to her. The offer I made. The things I said I'd do to her. The things I wanted to do to her. The things I *still* want to do to her.

That was neither teasing nor protection.

That was jealousy and desire.

For fuck's sake, I no longer have the luxury of denial. I'm attracted to the weirdest woman I've ever met, and just acknowledging as much opens a chasm in my chest, one painful and pleasant at once. The former outweighs the latter as I recall how she misread my every flirtation, just like she did the night we made our bet. She even taunted me about my *bedfellow of choice*, when she's the one I was trying to tempt into my bed. She's the one I was fucking with my eyes across the room at Somerton House. How did she misread that? How does she not know?

I suppose I didn't know until now either—

A touch on my arm has me leaping in place. I whirl to find Jolene beside me, the turmoil in her expression more pronounced. What the hell am I supposed to do with her? Not once did I consider sleeping with her. There's no way I could kiss her again. The thought alone has my stomach turning, sending me back to my experience with Meredith in the north wing, with Greta Garter at rehearsal. I take a deep breath, debating how to let her down easy without soiling my reputation as the poet she admires.

"Is this about June?" she asks, tone gentle.

"June," I echo, and as soon as the word leaves my lips, my mind clears. That's right. I can use this. Forcing away thoughts of Edwina, I settle into my role as William the Poet. I don't bother shifting my outward mood, for the frantically pacing man she witnessed will serve me just fine.

"I can't stop the memories," I say, letting my voice warble. She reaches for me, but I lift my hands. "Please don't touch me. I…I can't let you touch me, not when I'm trapped in the past like this. It wouldn't be fair to you. Oh, how I wish I could be present with you right now, but the pain…"

She presses her hands to her heart. "You can tell me about it. I'll listen."

I unfocus my eyes and lower my voice. "There are things I haven't told anyone. If I tell you, you must keep it to yourself."

Eagerly she nods, pleased to be granted such exclusive access into William the Poet's innermost thoughts and traumas. I proceed with my performance with ease, insisting we keep our distance and sit on separate beds while I talk. She eats up my every word, and it serves me well too. The more I talk and the more I immerse myself in my role, the more I can distract myself from the thought that Edwina is likely—at this very moment—making love to another man down the hall.

CHAPTER EIGHTEEN

EDWINA

I wake with a start and find not a pillow beneath my cheek but parchment. Wincing, I lift my head, blinking into the morning light. The muscles in my neck and back revolt as I straighten in the chair I fell asleep in. I squint at the sight before me, gathering my bearings. I'm dressed in only my chemise and corset while my notebook lays open before me on the desk, my ink pot uncapped.

"Good morning," says a cheery voice, reminding me of why I awoke in the first place.

I swivel in my chair, despite the protestations of my still-aching muscles, to find Jolene flouncing into our room. She glances at my bed where Daphne dozes on the pillow that should be mine. "Oh good, I'm glad it's just Daphne. I didn't want to walk in if someone else was still here. I knocked, but you didn't—"

Her words cut off as she meets my eyes. She blinks a few times before her lips quirk at the corners.

I stiffen. I've seen that look before. It means I've done something embarrassing. My hands fly to my face. Sure enough, there's a smear of moisture that has the suspiciously familiar viscosity of drool.

"No, Edwina, it's all over your cheek."

Frowning, I shift back to the desk and the small circular mirror propped off to the side. My reflection reveals what so amused Jolene. Across my cheek is a splotch of ink. As I rub at it, I find my fingertips stained with ink too. The latter isn't unusual, considering I was writing all night, but I don't usually make a habit of falling asleep mid-sentence.

With a chuckle, Jolene sets a steaming pitcher on the desk beside me and hands me a cloth. "I picked these up on my way to our room. I don't have time to visit the student baths before I catch my train back home."

Thinking about whose room she just came from—and why she'd be so eager to wash—spears my chest with something hateful. But Jolene is my friend and I should be happy for her, so I breathe the emotion away. That doesn't mean I'll ask her how her night went. It would be akin to prodding a bruise.

I accept the cloth and pour some of the water into the washbasin on my nightstand. Wringing out the lilac-scented water, I ask, "You're leaving?"

"Yes, I'll be taking the morning train back to Floating Hope. But enough about me." She sits at the edge of my bed. The movement jostles Daphne awake, who in turn grumbles and repositions herself on my pillow. Jolene beams at me. "How did your night with Archie go?"

I keep my gaze on my reflection as I wipe the ink stains from my cheek. My stomach drops at her question. "Uh, well...we kissed."

"And?" She scoots forward, eyes alight with expectation.

When I say nothing more, her face goes slack. "Wait, that's all?"

I grimace, glad I have an activity to distract myself with. I rub my cheek more vigorously as I give her a nonchalant, "That's all."

I purse my lips, hoping she'll get the hint that I don't want to talk about it. How can I explain it to her? How can I admit that my mind was so full of William after I returned to my room that every time I closed my eyes, I saw his face, felt his hands, heard his words? It was like I was pressed against that wall all over again, and William was whispering all the things he'd do to me. It filled my imagination, obliterating my view of the naked man in my bed and replacing him with William. And to my horror, I was titillated. Not by Archie, but by William.

Because that bastard was right. I wasn't attracted to Archie. Not in the least. Sure, he was cute. Charming. The most adorable man I've met. Yet there was nothing between us that sparked desire.

Nothing but thoughts of William.

William! Of all people.

It was useless to fight the fantasy, and I even tried to let it fuel my enjoyment with Archie. But every time I felt Archie's cold thin lips, his probing tongue that he unceremoniously shoved into my mouth with the gusto of a man digging up treasure in my tonsils, his hands that plunged under my skirt before playing with other parts of me first, I'd be pulled back to my less pleasant reality. I tried again and again, tried to sink deeper and deeper into my fantasy while he kissed me, touched me. Yet the deeper I went, the further my mind wandered. When it wandered back to the recreation room at Somerton House and the moment William locked eyes with me while kissing Jolene, excitement flooded me. The sexual kind, yes, but another kind too. The kind that sparked inspiration. Words on a page. A scene between Johannes and Timothy played out in my mind's eye, and I had to write it down at once.

I pulled away from Archie, who'd already stopped kissing me and was asking what was wrong. Apparently I'd begun staring into space. I barely recall what happened next because my muse took over. I rushed to the desk, asking Archie to excuse me for just a moment. The next thing I remember is the sound of the door closing behind him. I was vaguely aware when he said goodbye and gave me a gentle kiss on the cheek. Even now the memory is hazy with how deeply distracted I was, but I know he was disappointed by my abandonment.

I dip the cloth in the basin, watching the liquid turn cloudy with ink, and wring out the excess water with violent precision. I'm such an asshole. I wish I could say this was the first time I've done something like that, but it's not. I've always chosen my writing over romance, but this experience—this research—was meant to support my writing.

William is to blame for this. He succeeded in sabotaging me, just like he wanted.

"That's a shame," Jolene says. "I'm sure you were looking forward to a much more thrilling night. Still, if you kissed, you've earned a point in your bet with William. I suppose that means you're in the lead."

The cloth falls from my hands with a splash.

I whirl to face her. "What do you mean I'm in the lead?"

She stares down at her hands. Though a soft smile graces her lips, there's no excitement in her posture. "We didn't sleep together last night. Well, I slept in his room, but in Mr. Phillips' bed."

"Did that idiot never come back from the party?" Daphne mumbles from her curled-up position. "I only get promoted from intern to editorial assistant if he vouches for me. I'd prefer he wasn't dead today."

Come to think of it, I didn't see Monty even once after Mr. Somerton gave him the sachet of Moonpetal. Whatever that is. But I don't care about Monty. Not after what Jolene said. I sit on the bed beside her. I'm not great at faking sympathy—or any soft emotion, really—but I do my best now.

"You must be disappointed," I say. "You put a lot of effort into spending the night with him."

"Yes, but—no, I can't be disappointed." She heaves a sigh, a wistful look taking over her face. "What we shared was deeper than sex. He told me things he hasn't told anyone. Confided in me like he's never been able to do with another soul before." She lowers her voice to a conspiratorial whisper. "He told me more about *her*."

"Her?" My mind goes to Meredith and Greta Garter. I don't know why, but the thought of him sharing that same vulnerability with Jolene makes my heart sink.

"June, of course!"

I furrow my brow. "June?"

"Well, he still hasn't confirmed if that's her name. Nor did he give me concrete details…" She frowns as her voice trails off. Then she shakes her head. "Whatever the case, he was so distraught after seeing you safely to your room with Archie. I was certain I'd done something to offend him. But it wasn't me at all. It was June! Painful memories must have arisen inside him. For a time, it was like he didn't even know I was there! I was finally able to reach him, and we shared the most beautiful night. He recited poetry that made my heart ache, all about the longing he feels, his desire to be close to someone yet feeling dragged back by his past. With us divided by separate beds, I felt like we were star-crossed lovers from a tragic epic. It was an experience I'll never forget."

I'm not sure what to say about that. It's strange that William was so upset over his lost love in Jolene's presence but didn't once mention her to me last night. He had ample chances to when he shared about his embarrassing past.

Jolene rises from my bed. "I better get ready to catch my train. I think I've stayed away long enough to make my fiancé lose his mind. He'll be wondering where I've gone."

My mouth falls open. "You have a fiancé?"

She strolls over to her bed and begins packing her few items into her carpet bag. "Yes. He's an investor in my father's business. A stranger, practically. I have a choice to remain a working woman or marry, and I'm choosing the latter. I've enjoyed my job at the modiste, but I'd much rather run my own household. Especially if said household is a grand estate."

"I see." There's no judgment in my tone. While I wouldn't choose marriage over independence, the choice she's making is a valid one.

"He's handsome, and I already know he wants me, so I'm not worried about a lack of desire between us. But until our wedding day, or until he's won my heart, I'm a free woman. I'm going to enjoy my freedoms in every way I want. You know all about that, though. We're two of a kind." She winks.

I smile back. I still don't have the heart to tell her she's wrong about me. After learning more about her, I see she's the far more experienced of us.

"Now that I no longer have a personal stake in your bet with Mr. Haywood," Jolene says, "I can fully root for your win. You're in the lead now. Only by one point, but it's something."

Her words send my pulse quickening. Unless William has gathered secret points I don't know about—which would be impossible with how closely Jolene has been stalking him since she joined us—I have one more point than him. If I can stay ahead of him, I'll win the publishing contract.

She lowers her voice. "Maybe this is underhanded of me to say, but I'll say it anyway. If you were the cause of William's distress last night...well, maybe do exactly what you did again. You were the last person he talked to before he lost his mind over June. It's safe to conclude that when he's upset about June, he gets too lost in his emotions to be intimate with anyone else. So..."

Our lips curl at the same time, two wicked conspirators coming to the same conclusion. I'm still not convinced I triggered his emotions in the way she thinks I did, but I know what she's getting at. She's encouraging me to sabotage him.

"Maybe it's selfish of me," she says as she closes her bag, "but ruining his chances at romance serves me well too."

"How so?"

Her grin widens. "I'd like to be the last person he kissed for as long as possible."

My mirth is pierced by another spear of...something. Whether it's rage or envy, I know not. All I know is that I'm suddenly back in the hall with William, his hand over my mouth, then his breath caressing my lips as he whispers two words that send a shiver up my spine.

Use me.

Then before that.

Free pass.

Say it and I'll give you a point without taking one myself. I give you my word. A fae promise.

This time, I'm grinning wickedly alone. Poor Jolene won't be the last person to kiss William Haywood for long, for I know exactly how to get even further ahead in this bet.

Two little words.

One fae promise.
I am going to ruin my rival.

CHAPTER NINETEEN

WILLIAM

*E*dwina practically radiates smugness as we settle in our train compartment, heading for our next destination. I can only assume Miss Vaughn detailed her evening with me. An evening that was entirely without kissing or touching. An evening that resulted in a win for Edwina and a loss for me.

If I'd been thinking straight when I returned to my room with Jolene last night, I could have forced myself to simply kiss the girl. Just a quick brush of my lips to ensure I remained tied with Edwina in our bet. Even a hug could have constituted physical intimacy.

But the fact remains that I was not thinking straight. I was thinking about Edwina. Obsessing, more like. While my state of mind has leveled to neutral, allowing me to slip back into my poet persona, there's one thing that hasn't changed.

My attraction to the woman sitting beside me on the train.

Monty and Daphne sit across from us. I didn't argue when I entered the compartment and found the only open seat was beside Edwina. I figured sitting beside her would be better than sitting where I could easily look at her time and again. But such assumptions were folly, for I'm all too aware of her proximity, her scent, her every motion from the corner of my eye. I can't stop myself from gauging any change in her aroma, can't stop myself from trying to smell the other male on her. As a fae, my sense of smell is stronger than a human's. Furthermore, the type of fae I am—one I don't care to bring up if I don't have to—makes me particularly attuned to certain bouquets.

To my relief, Edwina's scent is mostly unchanged. Either she bathed well, or Archie didn't leave much of a mark—

Why the fuck am I assessing her smell? Her bathing habits? It's none of my blooming business, attraction or no. And...since when am I so attuned to her scent in the first place? I've never made a habit of smelling people, not even ones I'm attracted to. Everyone has a scent, and it's meaningless. Merely data, the same as the shade of someone's hair or eyes. Yet hers strikes me like a blow to the skull, a tantalizing blend of ink, parchment, and air after a lightning storm. A bouquet that has me breathing deeper, yearning to lean a little closer...

"Last night was great, wasn't it?" Monty's voice has my spine going rigid. Only now do I realize I *was* leaning closer to Edwina.

I shift my posture until I'm angled toward the window instead. The outskirts of the city speed by as the train moves east.

"Where were you all evening, Mr. Phillips?" Edwina asks. The joviality in her voice has me equal parts bristling and melting. Bristling because her jolly mood reminds me why she's so damn happy. Then melting because...because something is fucking wrong with me, and now I find myself liking her voice.

I don't even like her as a person, yet now I like her scent, her voice, and am inexplicably attracted to her face and body. And want to spread her naked form beneath mine and taste every inch of her flesh—

With a shake of my head, I shift a few more inches away from her. William the Poet doesn't melt for anyone. He's sharp and brooding and seductive. He only has eyes for his painful past.

"I spent the night on the dormitory roof," Monty says. "Mr. Somerton was right about Moonpetal. I haven't been that relaxed in months."

"Wish I'd slept on the roof," Daphne mutters with a pointed look at Edwina.

Edwina grimaces.

Monty glances between them. "Oh, what's this? Did I miss something?"

Edwina shakes her head profusely, but Daphne rises to all fours and bares her teeth. "Miss Danforth, it seems, forgot my existence last night. As a result, I was rudely awoken by activities I shouldn't have been privy to."

I clench my jaw. What I wouldn't give to leap off this train right now. The last thing I want to hear are details of what Edwina did with Archie.

Monty releases an exaggerated gasp. "You forgot about Daffy Dear?"

Edwina's face twists with apology while she wrings her hands in her lap. "I'm so sorry. I gave you my pillow as payment, though. Remember?"

The pine marten huffs but settles back on her haunches. "You did give me your pillow."

"To be fair," Monty says to Daphne, "you should have seen that coming. Miss Danforth has a bet to win."

"I didn't want to see anything coming," Daphne says. "Thanks to this workaholic, I didn't have to."

My gaze whips to Daphne, my pulse quickening. My mouth falls open, a question burning my tongue. I need her to clarify at once, but...but...

I release a steadying breath. William the Poet doesn't care. William the Poet doesn't need to know.

Monty chuckles, and I find his narrowed gaze is locked on me. Then, with a smirk, he shifts his attention to Daphne. "Care to elaborate?"

"Oh, I think Edwina should explain," Daphne says.

"We kissed and that was enough for me," Edwina says. "He left, and I decided to get some writing in."

Daphne's mouth falls open in the pine marten equivalent of a teasing grin. "She fell asleep on her notebook and woke up with ink all over the side of her face."

Edwina absently rubs her fingers over her cheek.

Yet I'm still lingering over what she said. She's finally given me something I can latch onto without coming across like a besotted fool.

I turn toward her with an arched brow. "So, you only kissed? After all that research you were so adamant to do with him?"

"I told you last night," she says through her teeth, a ready glower on her face, "it didn't matter if Archie provided material to study, so long as I could earn a point in our bet. Something not even you were able to accomplish." She says the last part under her breath, a victorious smirk on her lips.

Monty leans forward, propping his elbows on his knees. "This is getting interesting. Back up just a touch. What did the two of you talk about last night?"

Edwina and I both go still. We meet each other's eyes at the same time. My face is slack, but she recovers first. That triumphant grin is back on her face and she shifts her gaze to

Monty. "Mr. Phillips, correct me if I'm wrong, but is it true that when a pureblood fae states the words *I promise*, what follows is as binding as a bargain?"

"Why are you asking me?" Monty says. "You have a pure-blood fae beside you."

"Daphne then." Edwina glances at me sidelong for only a moment. "I want the answer from someone who isn't a talented actor."

Fuck. Has she gleaned the truth? That I can lie, not only when I'm on the stage, but when I'm playing a more subtle role in everyday life?

"It's true," Daphne says. That teasing baring of her teeth returns. "Why? What did Mr. Haywood promise?"

Edwina gives me another sideways look, her smugness growing like a rose in bloom. It draws out my competitive side. Makes me want to wipe that look off her face. She purses her lips, then mutters, "I wonder if he even recalls."

I scoff. If she wants to play this game, I can play too. Angling my body toward her, I cross one knee over the other until my foot brushes against her silk skirt, then I prop my elbow on the backrest. "Oh, I recall, Weenie. You don't have to be shy about sharing. Tell them. Tell them what I promised you."

To my great delight, her smile falters and her posture stiffens. I keep my eyes on her profile, daring her not to shrink away. Finally, she angles her head to lock her gaze with mine. Her breath hitches, the motion visible even through the pleats and folds of her high-collared white blouse.

"On second thought," Monty says, rising from the bench, "I think I'll visit the smoking car. Join me, Daph."

Daphne leaps off the bench. "Is it because you smell what I smell?"

"Yes, my little mustelid friend," Monty says as he reaches

the door to our compartment. "That is the smell of sexual tension. We'll leave you to it."

Edwina's cheeks blaze crimson as they close the door behind them. "That is not what this is," she says as she shoves the bridge of her spectacles.

I lean closer. "Is it not?"

Her chest heaves again, her composure shattered. "You... you don't even like me. Why—"

"I offered to fuck you, Ed, not marry you."

"Yes, but after everything you told me, surely you can't... do things with me unless—"

"Weenie."

Her expression deepens to a scowl. "What?"

"If you want me to keep my promise, stop overthinking it. Don't worry about whether I can adequately perform based on what I shared with you on the balcony. Simply trust that I can."

Surprise flutters over her face. Is she beginning to understand? That attraction—or rather, lack thereof—won't be an issue between us? The way her breaths continue in sharp bursts emboldens me. After how flustered she's made me up until now, I'm pleased with how easily I can do the same to her.

I angle my head slightly, and my eyes fall on her lips. "Do you still not believe me? I can show you right now."

"There's no point," she says, though there's an unsteadiness to her voice that belies her words. "The doors to the compartment may be closed, but this is neither of our bedrooms. If I redeem my *free pass*, as you called it, it wouldn't count toward our bet."

My lips curl at one corner as my gaze sweeps back to hers. A spear of sunlight flashes over her lenses, obscuring her brown irises for longer than I like. When the glare passes, I say, "We could practice."

She huffs. "This is a public space. I know how you feel about making love in public spaces."

"It doesn't seem so public to me."

Her lips part, and for the briefest moment, she looks like she's truly considering my offer. Then she shakes her head and averts her gaze. "You're trying to distract me. All I wanted to know is if you were serious about your promise. If you are, that's all we need to discuss. I'll use my free pass against you when you least expect it. For research." She tacks on the last part with a stern look before averting her face again.

"You may be finished talking about my promise, but I'm not."

She rolls her eyes, still not looking at me. "You can't take it back now."

"Oh, I'm not taking it back. I only want to rework the terms. If you get a free pass, I want one too."

She whips her gaze back to me, eyes wide. "Pardon?"

"I want a free pass to use against you too. One without an expiration. I propose we create a single free pass that we exchange between us. Meaning, you are currently in possession of it, but once you redeem it, I will get to use it next. Then so on and so forth."

"Why would I agree to that? As it stands now, I can redeem my free pass the next time you've found a lover, and I'll have two points to your zero."

"Yes, but think how many more opportunities you'll be given to sabotage me."

She blinks at me a few times. "I'll only have those opportunities if you redeem the ticket and place it back in my possession."

"Exactly."

Her eyes narrow to slits as she assesses the possibilities.

"If we're constantly trying to sabotage each other, we might never accumulate points with any other lover."

I don't know if I'm imagining the relief on her face, but I certainly feel it in my chest. Still, I do all I can to mask it behind an arrogant front. "I may have made it sound like you have a choice, Weenie, but you don't. While I'm bound to keep my promise, I didn't agree to any binding terms that constitute a formal bargain. That means I can alter my conditions for keeping said promise, which I now have. I will let you redeem your free pass, but only if I get one as well. Do you agree to these terms?"

She narrows her eyes again, her fingers anxiously tapping her lap. Then her hands go still, face slack, as understanding seems to dawn on her.

Yes, I realize it too. If we continue to sabotage each other, and neither accumulates any points with anyone else, she'll always remain one point ahead of me, thanks to her kiss with Archie. And if I never return the pass to her after she uses it with me, she'll have a two-point lead, at least for a while.

It's a gamble for both of us, but I still intend to play with her to my advantage. The truth remains that I am the more capable and experienced seducer between us. I may have failed to keep our bet in mind last night, but I'll be prepared next time. Edwina isn't the only person on the isle I'm capable of being attracted to. I *can* accrue points. And if she refuses to rise to my bait with the free pass, I'll do everything I can to torment her. Aggravate her. Arouse her. Until she's begging me to let her redeem it.

"Fine. I agree to the terms for the free pass." Her tone is grudging, but the tightening of her lips tells me she's hiding a smile. She thinks she's already won, but our game has only just begun. Lifting her chin, she faces forward again.

A dark smear stands out against the pale skin of her neck,

just above her lacy collar. I furrow my brow, tilting my head to the side for a better look.

She frowns as she catches me staring. "What?"

I tap the side of my neck that mirrors where the stain is. "You have something here. Ink, maybe."

Her cheeks flush and she rubs at the spot on the wrong side. I shake my head, and she scrubs at the other side. The stain doesn't so much as budge.

"Let me." Before I can think better of it, I remove my arm from the backrest, push her hand out of the way, and rub my thumb lightly over the smear. Just like her efforts, mine are fruitless.

Or...not quite. In a different way.

I glance at her profile just in time to see her lashes flutter shut at my touch. Her pulse leaps beneath my thumb, the column of her throat trembling from the force of it.

Something about that racing pulse sends my own skittering. My stomach tightens, half with desire, half with the pride of knowing a simple brush of my thumb has that much sway over her. How much more can I ruffle her?

"Hold still," I say, voice low. Inch by inch, I lean in, half expecting her to pull away as I bring my face closer to her neck. She freezes, even as I lower my mouth to her collar. Even as my lips press against her flesh. Her pulse beats faster now, and her scent fills me. I part my lips and slowly drag my tongue over the stain, tasting bitter ink, the salt of her skin, and something floral like soap or fragrance oil. She releases the smallest squeak, a sound that borders on a whine. My breath hitches as I imagine what other sounds I could coax from her. I'm almost of a mind to try...

But no. That won't come for free. If she wants more of me, she can beg me with those two words.

Free pass.

I pull away from her, the ink stain no longer visible, and return my arm to the backrest.

She swivels her face to mine, her expression some mix of terror and elation. "You just licked me."

I run my thumb over my bottom lip. "You're welcome," I say with a wink.

I've never seen a shade of crimson like the one that blooms in her cheeks. She slaps a hand over her mouth as if recalling the sound she made, then looks pointedly away from me, her gaze locked on the compartment door.

I finally angle myself away from her, sobering from our heated taunting, and slip out of my role...

Or back into it?

It dawns on me what I just did. Everything I said. I hadn't planned any of that. How does she draw out this side of me? The side that dares her to be bold, only to raise the stakes and act bolder myself. The side that competes with her again and again, not to crush her, but to watch her clash against me.

Who the fuck am I when I'm with her? Am I the confident seducer I was a minute ago? Or the foolish fae male who's hyperaware of her proximity and scent, like I'm returning to now?

Maybe both.

The compartment door slides open, and Edwina leans forward in her seat as if desperate for the interruption. Monty saunters in with Daphne at his heels. "Oh, good. No one came to blows." With that, he tosses two dark green velvet blankets at me and Edwina.

She assesses hers. "What is this for?"

"Did you not read the itinerary?" Monty says as he settles in across from us. Daphne nestles into her blanket while Mr. Phillips spreads his over his lap. "It's about to get cold once we cross the border."

171

"Oh, right," Edwina says, spreading the blanket over her skirt and taking the opportunity to put more space between us. "We're going to the Winter Court next."

Her neutral tone tells me she doesn't realize the significance of our destination.

I shift uncomfortably in my seat, the blanket folded beside me. William the Poet dreads our next stop. He has from the start. He hoped Edwina might never find out what awaits her there. Because the Winter Court is home to Edwina's biggest and most influential fan. A queen. The woman who propelled *The Governess and the Rake* to fame in Faerwyvae. William the Stage Actor dreads our destination as much as the poet does, for how could he not resent both Edwina and her famous fan for the stage play that stole his career?

Meanwhile, Will…

I release a slow sigh, aware of Edwina's movements as she nestles beneath her blanket. The taste of her skin sizzles over my tongue.

Will thinks Edwina is brilliant.

Beautiful.

A thorn in his fucking side, yet it's somehow a delight.

As I watch the scenery shift from blue sky to puffy white clouds, I let myself admit that Edwina is so much better than she realizes.

I suppose it's time she knew it too.

Part Three

HOW TO ROMANCE YOUR RIVAL

CHAPTER TWENTY

EDWINA

*A*fter my eventful time in the Solar Court, I need a few days to relax and recover. With our next signing not scheduled until mid-week, I'm given exactly that. What better way to enjoy leisure time than at a luxury hotel in the middle of winter? Nothing screams *stay cozy indoors* more than the Verity Hotel at the center of downtown Vernon, Winter Court.

Our rooms are plush, richly furnished, and heated to perfection. Every meal is hosted in the elegant public dining room or brought straight to our doors. The view outside our windows—falling flakes, streets and shops blanketed in white, towering snow-capped mountains far in the distance —provides a perfect way to enjoy the lovely weather without needing to step outside.

More relaxing than anything, however, is my respite from William. The room I share with Daphne is next door to the one William shares with Monty, but we see little of each other over the next couple of days. I'm at very little risk of William gaining points in our bet. Monty informed us that Vernon is a resort town that caters primarily to human tourists. Here human propriety is valued. There are no rowdy gatherings in the hotel, no opportunities to mingle with unknown parties without formal introductions first. This is not the place to solicit strangers for a casual fling.

Still…

It wouldn't hurt to check.

A glance at the clock on the mantle tells me it's just after ten in the evening. I dined with Monty and William a few hours ago, and I watched William enter his room afterward with a tired yawn. A yawn I mirrored just for show. It's been this way between us for the last couple of days. Faking yawns. Silently emphasizing that another uneventful night shall pass.

Though is it *really* uneventful?

I know mine is.

But what if William is faking it?

He knows I won't use my free pass unless it's for the sake of sabotage. If he wants to steal a point when I least expect it, it would be now.

I pad across my room's soft cream carpeted floors to the oak wardrobe. From inside, I extract one of the burgundy velvet robes stocked within. I wrap it around my chemise and proceed to my door. Pressing my ear against it, I listen for footsteps in the hall. Thankfully, Daphne isn't here to poke fun at my strange behavior. She's spent much of her time outdoors since we arrived in Vernon. Turns out, the pine marten is fond of snow.

Hearing nothing out of the ordinary in the hall, I crack open my door and peer out. The lamps are dim, casting the ivory-and-sage brocade walls in a soft golden glow. An hour ago, I heard the telltale sound of William's door closing,

175

which means either he or Monty—or both—left their room. I tried peeking then, but all I caught was a flash of movement as a figure rounded the hall. It's possible it was only Monty leaving to join the men smoking and drinking in the dining room after hours, and it's equally possible he returned without me hearing him.

But what if it was William?

What if he managed to subvert the hotel's strict rules of propriety and secured himself a lover? If both he and Monty left at the same time, William could have returned before his roommate for a quick tryst. I've been writing at my desk all evening, my attention half attuned to the adjoining wall. No sound has stood out, but what if the walls are well insulated? What if they're enchanted to muffle sounds? Just because I heard William's door close once doesn't mean I've caught everything else.

I open my door wider and glance down one end of the hall, then the other. Empty. On silent feet, I tiptoe to the next door over and press my ear to it. I listen.

Listen.

Listen.

But all I hear is the pounding of my heart. I slow my breathing, angle my head, press in closer—

"What are we listening for?"

A strangled yelp erupts from my throat as I whirl around. How the hell did William sneak up on me? Even going so far as to press his ear to the door right beside me without me hearing a damn thing? He chuckles and takes a sip from a tumbler he holds in one hand, then reclines against the door frame.

He arches a brow. "Spying on me, love?"

I take in his dark mussed hair, his open collar and waist-coat. Terror surges through me as I consider whether he dallied with someone in their room instead of his. Don't the terms of our bet require that our acts of physical intimacy are exchanged behind our own bedroom doors? Yet that doesn't mean William can't seek pleasure for the sake of it alone. A tide of fury washes over me at the thought, so sharp I have to cross my arms over my chest to keep it contained.

"Goodnight, Mr. Haywood." I march past him toward my room, but his arm comes around my elbow. Halting in place, I glare up at him. "What?"

He smiles down at me, swirling the emerald-green liquid in his tumbler with his free hand. "Aren't you here to tell me something?"

"What could I possibly have to say to you?"

He pretends to ponder, then takes a sip of his drink. "Oh, I don't know. Two words, perhaps. That's the reason you're listening at my door, isn't it? You want to redeem your free pass. You're ready to use me."

"That's not it at all," I say, but my words come out thick.

"Then why are you here?"

"I...I was just wondering where you and Monty might be."

He downs the rest of his libation. "We were drinking. Well, I was drinking. Monty was smoking."

I glance at his loose state of dress again, then the fall of his hair, sticking out at odd angles behind his pointed ears, in a way that looks more alluring than slovenly. The infuriating fae is sex incarnate, whether he's dressed in a full suit or with liquor on his lips and his buttons undone. "That's all you were doing?"

A corner of his mouth curls. He blinks at me, slow and heavy. "I was drinking *a lot*."

My chest loosens, and my breaths come easier. Now that I think about it, I haven't seen him in such a state since our first night in Floating Hope before I got acquainted with Cloud Dive. He was adorably drunk that night...until I got more drunk. At Somerton House, he only had a few drinks and didn't seem at a loss of faculties. But now...yes, I suppose inebriation explains his mussed state. I hate how charmed I am by it. How relieved I am that he wasn't with a lover.

Then again, I have every right to be relieved. I'd like to keep my one-point lead for as long as I can. After I redeem my free pass, I'll have a two-point lead.

That's all the comfort I need for now.

I uncross my arms and square my shoulders. "I'll let you get back to it, then."

"Weenie."

I ignore him and continue to brush past. He reaches for my elbow yet again, but his moves are clumsy. His fingers come around the belt of my robe instead. My momentum has my sash untying with the next step I take. I pull up short, but the burgundy velvet is already falling from my shoulders. My first instinct is to cover myself, but I'm distracted when William fumbles his empty glass. I abandon my concerns for my robe and reach to catch the tumbler. He lunges for it at the same time. Our fingers collide, knocking the glass to the side. It falls safely and unharmed to the soft rug beneath our feet.

While my fingers are tangled in William's.

I don't know how to react. My eyes lift to his, only to find him slack-jawed and drinking me in from head to toe. Shit. My open robe. Again, I think to cover myself, but his expression has me reconsidering. The sight of *me* put that look there. Did it also make him clumsy? Did he drop his glass because he was so shocked at the sight of my robe unraveling?

Instead of pulling the velvet closed over the front of me, I shift slightly, encouraging it to slide further down my shoulders, revealing even more of my chemise. Let him see all of it. Every inch of the white muslin that covers all that he cannot have tonight. His fingers tighten around mine.

I step back slightly, giving him an even greater view, but his eyes are on mine now. "I'll have my hand back, William."

Wicked delight plays over his face, and he tugs my palm, forcing me to take a step closer. "Let me give you a proper goodnight first."

I swallow hard. "What do you mean?"

He holds my eyes and lifts my hand. Then he lowers his mouth to my knuckles. I suck in a breath, recalling how he licked my neck in the train compartment. Hardly an hour goes by without me thinking about it, and now the memory caresses me like a lover. The thought of memory-lovers reminds me of the shadow-lover I fantasized about when William had me against the wall outside my dormitory room. Now there are three of him in my mind. A shadow of heat at my back, a tongue flicking up the column of my neck, and the version of him who stands before me, radiating his undeniable allure. He brushes his lower lip over the curve of one knuckle, then the next. A gesture that should be chaste yet is somehow one of the most erotic things anyone has done to me. Heat pools between my thighs, and his earlier words blare through my mind.

Use me.

Use me.

Use me.

He presses his mouth fully over the back of my hand. I nearly protest when he straightens, but I let my fingers slip from his.

"Goodnight, Weenie." With a wink, he turns away, retrieves his glass from the floor, and strides to his door.

Belatedly, I force my feet to move, fleeing to my own door. I pause, gripping the handle but not turning it. A glance to the side shows William is doing the same. He lifts a brow in question, a silent dare to redeem my pass. To call him over to my room so he can show me all the other places he might caress with his lips. I've already lost my senses at the feel of them on my neck and hand. How much better might they feel on—

I clench my jaw and force the thoughts to recede. Force the heat pulsing at the apex of my thighs to stop giving me unnecessary ideas and save them for when I can truly sabotage William with my free pass.

My desire doesn't relent, it only builds and burns, but I at least gather the resolve to open my door.

"Goodnight," I mutter and rush inside my room, slamming the door behind me harder than I intended. My legs are weak and trembling as I scurry to my bed. I fall upon the plush blankets and cast a glance around the room to ensure Daphne is still out. With no sign of my furry roommate, I plunge one hand under the hem of my chemise, seeking the slick aching center of me. The other hand I bring to my lips, pressing them to the place William kissed, stifling my panting breaths while I work my much-needed release.

CHAPTER TWENTY-ONE

EDWINA

The next morning, I leave the comfort of the Verity Hotel for the first time since arriving in the city of Vernon. Three things surprise me next. The first is that our destination is right across the street, at a bookshop. The second is that even though I've seen no break in the snowfall outside my hotel room window, only the lightest, most perfect dusting of fluff coats the streets, and the sidewalks aren't at all slick, filthy, or icy. It's nothing like the snow in Bretton, wreaking havoc on the roads, sending coaches and automobiles careening into each other.

The third thing that surprises me is the massive line that starts at the bookshop door and winds all the way around the next corner. Maybe that shouldn't come as a shock. This may be the first time I've seen a line out the door in advance of our signing, but William has been popular everywhere we've gone, whether it's a signing, a party, or a pub.

"Let's go around back and enter through the alley," Monty

says as we cross the street from the hotel. Today, I am not on time, having woken up a half hour later than I was supposed to. William and Daphne are already inside, so it's just me and the publicist. Thankfully, I still have twenty minutes to spare before the signing begins.

Monty leads me down the opposite end of the street from where the line is going, then guides me behind the row of buildings to a snow-dusted alley. I rub my gloved hands over my arms to generate heat. Even in my warmest wool coat and the long-sleeved tartan day dress I wear beneath it, the chill is pervasive. We stop at a door and Monty raps his knuckles on it. My breath comes out in misty puffs of air as I bounce on the balls of my feet—anything to distract myself from the cold.

The door opens and an elderly man with gray hair and watery blue eyes greets us. "Come in, come in!"

I could weep from the delectable warmth that surrounds me as we step into the back room of the bookshop. Crates upon crates fill nearly all the available space, some haphazardly stacked, but there's a charm to the clutter. Not to mention the scent of paper that always sets me at ease. How could it not? The smell of books is universally loved and I'll fight anyone who says otherwise.

Monty introduces me to the man. His name is Mr. Cordell and he's the owner of the bookshop.

"It's such a pleasure, Miss Danforth," he says, his tone gentle yet refined. His expression turns bashful. "I'm a big fan of yours. The *Governess in Love* series is one of my all-time favorites."

My mouth falls open. "Really? Which book of mine do you like best?"

"Oh, don't make me choose. But please allow me to take your coat and gloves. Then I'll warm you up with a nice cup of cider." He grins and his eyes crinkle at the corners.

What an adorable man. A kindred spirit if I've ever met one.

I hand over my outerwear, which he hangs on one of three coat racks that stand in the back room amongst the crates. He places my dark-green coat beside a much larger black one. I can't help wondering if that's William's. Monty didn't bother to wear a coat to cross the street, so there's nothing of his to take. Mr. Cordell leads us out of the back room and into the main portion of the bookshop.

The first sight of bookshelves has me relaxing even further. My eyes dart this way and that to take it all in. The shop is nearly as cluttered as the back room was, with overstuffed shelves, clusters of bookcases used to section off different genres, and tables stacked with featured titles. Handwritten notes are interspersed throughout the shelves with personalized recommendations from Mr. Cordell or the other employees.

The bookshop may not have the whimsy of Flight of Fancy or the elegance of the university library, but there's a charm to it that makes this my favorite stop yet.

"We're over here," Monty says, peeking out from behind a bookcase. I must have gotten distracted in my admiration of the shop, for I have no recollection of losing him or Mr. Cordell. I hurry over to Monty and the maze of shelves opens to the most beautiful sight I could ever hope to see. The romance section. It consists of an entire wall of shelves flanked by two smaller bookcases to create a comfortable little nook. Two tables are set inside it, where William and I will be signing. Spines in every color march along the shelves, and I nearly have a heart attack at the sight of my *Governess in Love* series featured with their covers facing out and taking up four whole shelves directly behind our tables.

Movement draws my eye to where Daphne's tiny paw sets

a copy of *The Governess and the Fae* on the table from behind. I'm about to help her but Monty does first.

"I told you not to unpack the crates alone," he mutters as he crouches behind the table and stacks my books, several at a time, upon it.

I still can't see much of Daphne behind the table, but I catch her monotone. "I wouldn't have had to if you were on time."

"Weenie."

I stiffen at the sound of William's voice. My pulse skitters. With all the composure I can manage, I face him. His appearance greatly contrasts with how he looked last night. Though his hair maintains the same reckless abandon it normally does, it's less mussed. His blue eyes are clear instead of heavy-lidded. He wears a full suit, charcoal gray this time, and his cravat is neatly tied. The jewelry in his ears is now silver, the same shade as his brocade waistcoat.

There's no sign of discomfort or embarrassment in his posture or the crooked curl of his lips. Why would there be? He may have taunted me to use my free pass while he was inebriated, but it's not like he wouldn't do that while sober. And even though I flustered him when he caught sight of me in my chemise, he recovered faster than I did.

I'm the one who stayed flustered. I'm the one who busied my hands between my legs while thinking of him, something I've never done before. By that, I mean I normally fantasize about imaginary lovers, letting scenes from my books play out in my mind. Last night, though…

I absently rub my fingers over the back of my hand. The place he kissed. The place *I* kissed while I came last night. My breaths grow shallow at the memory.

Thank heavens he can't read my mind.

"Mr. Cordell asked me to give you this." He hands me a porcelain mug, one of two he's holding.

I accept it, looking anywhere but at him. The steaming mug fills the air with the delectable scent of apples and cinnamon. The taste is even better, tart and sweet with the perfect balance of spice. I take another sip, letting it distract me from the heat of William's proximity.

"Did you see the line?" he asks, tone casual.

"It's a little early to boast, isn't it?" When he doesn't answer, I hazard a glance at him.

He's staring down at me, a bemused look on his face. "You still don't know, do you?"

"Know what?"

William opens his mouth, but Mr. Cordell's voice cuts off whatever he was going to say. "Ah, good, you got your cider. There are only a few minutes before I open the doors for the ravenous readers. First, though, you have a very special guest, Mr. Haywood. One I took the liberty of inviting inside early."

Mr. Cordell steps to the side and waves someone over. From behind one of the bookcases emerges a stunning creature—a tall, slender fae with wide brown eyes and the longest, feathery lashes I've ever seen. Their skin is tawny with light-tan freckles over their nose and cheeks. Two dainty antlers protrude from either side of their head, while their russet chin-length tresses are arranged in a loose wave. They're dressed in flowing white trousers and a blue silk robe-style top with long, trailing sleeves.

William's face breaks into a jovial grin. He sets his cup of cider on his table and greets the newcomer with a warm embrace. "Zane, what are you doing here?"

"I performed at the Verity Hotel last week. I saw your name on the sign outside the bookshop and decided to stay for your signing."

"We've been in the same city and the same hotel this entire time? You should have found me sooner."

"I couldn't abuse my influence and force the hotel staff to divulge your room number."

As I stare between the couple, something tightens in my chest.

Mr. Cordell beams. "My bookshop is full of famous people today. A true honor."

That's when I realize who Zane is. This is the famous opera singer, one whose reputation has crossed the channel to Bretton, despite them never performing outside of Faerwyvae. Only humans leave the isle, and only under strict guidelines. Fae remain safe within the magic-infused border of standing stones that mark the perimeter of the isle. One that prevents humans from entering without a designated fae escort, all to prevent Faerwyvae's bloody history of war from repeating.

Yet somehow this famous fae whom I've heard so much about, from their incredible vocal range to their beauty…is friends with William? I was already jealous that he was cast opposite Greta Garter.

"Ah," William says, his mood sobering as if he only now recalls he has an audience. He introduces Zane to me, Monty, and Daphne, then adds, "Zane and I went to university together."

"Another school chum," Monty says. "You really got around at university, didn't you?"

Zane scoffs and elbows William in the arm. "Get around, he did."

William's gaze slides to mine, but I avert my face before I can read too much into it. My chest continues to tighten. Am I truly so envious that William has such famous acquaintances? Or am I envious of…

I shake my head before I can finish that thought and occupy myself with setting up my table. I stack my books in several different ways until Daphne slaps my hand and tells me to stop ruining what she's already made perfect. Then I settle into my chair, watching William do the same from my periphery. He and Zane are still chatting amicably, and the latter perches at the edge of his table.

After a few more minutes, Zane says, "I should go. I don't want to occupy your time once your fans arrive."

"Are you not among my fans?" William quips.

"No comment. You on the other hand…" Zane swivels on William's table until they're facing me. "I'm really excited to read your newest book."

I straighten. "Oh! Oh, thank you." For the love of all things, Zane—the famous Zane—is looking at me. Smiling at me. Wanting to read my book. I flutter my fingers, eager to smooth my hair, or…do something.

Then I catch William's glower. "Don't let it get to your head, Weenie. Zane is merely a hopeless romantic. They'll read anything with a kiss or a tryst."

I give him an exaggerated smile. "They have wonderful taste then, unlike you."

Zane chuckles and rises from the table. "I'm off—"

"No, Z," William says. "Please stay. Save me from boredom."

I frown. Since when has any signing been boring for him?

"Fine," Zane grumbles and settles back on the table. "Just for a while."

"It's time!" Mr. Cordell says, glancing down at his pocket watch. He returns the timepiece to his waistcoat pocket and scurries away.

Daphne darts after him. "I'm on crowd control."

Monty crouches beside my table. His blond curls fall over his brow as he gives me a pleading look. He speaks in a whisper. "Can I stay in your room tonight?"

My heart leaps at the question. "What? Why?"

187

He gives a significant look to the chatting pair beside me. "I think we both know how tonight will end."

I swallow hard. "You think William and Zane…"

"Look at their body language," he whispers. "They're more than old friends. That is the aura of two people who've fucked. Forgive me. Two people who've *courted*."

He doesn't need to watch his language on my account. I glance at the couple with fresh eyes, taking in William's easy smile, devoid of the seductive mask he wears for his fans, the way Zane swats his arm as they tease each other. They do seem closer than university friends. Could Monty be right? Are they old lovers ready to rekindle their flame?

Am I at risk of losing a point to William tonight?

"I'm sleeping with you and Daph tonight," Monty says, drawing my attention back to him. "Not in a sexual way, of course. Unless you ask nicely." With a coy grin, he saunters off. Just then, a flood of chattering bodies fills the bookshop, jostling each other in their excitement to reach our tables. Daphne growls and threatens ankle bites to corral them into a line. I expect the line to extend from William's table.

But it doesn't.

Instead, dozens upon dozens of figures line up with mauve books in their hands, tears in their eyes, and squeals of anticipation on their lips.

For me.

The line outside the door, the buzz of excitement…

It's all for *me*.

The crowd goes quiet as the leader of the line approaches my table. She's a tall human female outfitted in a deep crimson day dress lined with black lace, her hands tucked into a fur muff. Her black hair is pinned in a low chignon, and her expression is somehow exuberant and dignified at once.

"Hello, Miss Danforth," she says, her voice trembling slightly. "I cannot express how pleased I am to meet you."

Something clicks in my mind, a reminder of what one of my readers said at Flight of Fancy Bookshop. I study this woman's appearance all over again, from her elegant state of dress to the way she carries herself. How the guests who stand behind her cast awed looks her way. How they don't seem afraid of her yet maintain a respectful distance.

"You wouldn't happen to be…"

"Gemma Rochester." She extends a hand for me to shake, her beautiful smile growing even wider. "I'd like to think I'm your biggest fan."

My mouth falls open as I rise to my feet and grasp her hand with maybe even more excitement than she has for me. Gemma Rochester isn't just any reader. She's Queen Gemma of Queen Gemma's Book Club. She's the wife of the Unseelie King of Winter.

And she's my biggest fan.

Pride flares inside me, and my eyes find William's at once. He shrugs as if to say, *Now do you get it?* I lift my chin with a smirk and expect him to do the same, but there's no arrogance in his eyes. No taunting. Just a soft smile, a tip of his chin in a subtle nod, and a strange flutter in my heart.

CHAPTER TWENTY-TWO

WILLIAM

*E*dwina glows when she's smug. Figuratively, of course, yet she's as blinding as the sun. Her diminutive stature takes on the commanding presence of a sunflower in a field of daisies, her petals unfurling for more praise. I'm half convinced she could subsist on adulation alone.

"Your books changed my life," Queen Gemma says, her eyes glazing. "They consoled me during one of the hardest experiences I've endured and helped me weather a scandal with my head held high. I hardly have words to express the comfort your books have given me. Please know how much I —and all your readers—cherish you."

Edwina's jaw slackens at the queen's praise, and the crowd visibly swoons, their expressions captivated.

Zane leans toward me and whispers in a wry tone, "Has anyone ever told you that? That your book changed their life?"

"Yes, Z," I whisper back. "My sister."

They smirk. Zane knows certain facts about me and my situation that few others do. "Right. You're funding Cassie's dreams."

"College," I specify. "And I'm keeping her out of the workhouses."

Zane's expression softens and they make no further comment. As much as we like to tease each other, my family is a sensitive topic, and Zane knows it.

"I don't want to take up too much more of your time," the queen says, "but I hope you'll stay for my book club meeting. We'd love for you to do a reading for us if you're open to it."

"Of course I'm open to it." Edwina's voice is rich with wonder. "I'm more than open to it. I insist!"

"Lovely. Oh, and…" Queen Gemma pivots toward me as if she only now recalls this signing hosts two authors. "You as well, Mr. Haywood."

I bow my head in acquiescence, for what else can I do before a queen? She may not be the reigning monarch of any of the courts—only one with fae blood can hold such a position—but she is the wife of Elliot Rochester, Unseelie King of Winter. To be honest, I'm a little starstruck.

As the queen turns away from the table, the guests in line step aside, offering curtsies as she passes.

Edwina sucks in a gasp. "Oh God. I didn't curtsy. William, I didn't curtsy!" She looks at me with wild eyes. "Should I run after her? Apologize? Throw myself at her feet and beg for forgiveness?"

She's so frantic, I'm almost of a mind to tease her, but I don't have it in me today. "It's fine, Weenie. She wasn't upset, and she's not even your queen."

She deflates a little. "Ah, I guess you're right. I suppose none of the fae royals are my monarchs."

Am I imagining the disappointment on her face? Edwina

is from Bretton, which means she only needs to respect the fae and follow our rules while visiting. After our tour is over, she'll return home.

Unless she wins the publishing contract, that is.

Which I can't let her do.

I need the contract. Cassie needs it. I will not fail my sister.

Something tightens in my chest, a sharp thing that claws at my bones. I shift in my seat to distract myself from it. Luckily, Edwina doesn't notice my discomfort as the line has surged forward in Queen Gemma's wake, and her next guest is chattering her ear off over her love of Edwina's books.

I force my eyes off her and face ahead. At my nonexistent line. At the very empty space in front of my table. Only then do I feel Zane's gaze burning into me.

"What?" I snap.

Zane looks from me to Edwina. "Nothing," they mutter, their lips curled with a mischievous grin.

THE SIGNING IS UNBEARABLY SLOW. FOR ME. NOT FOR Edwina. Our roles have reversed, with her enjoying an endless line of excited guests while I have the occasional visitor. It's nothing less than I expected. I knew all along that Winter Court would be Edwina's domain, and she continues to glow with every book she signs, every word of conversation.

My only entertainment comes from a game I've created. It involves seeing how many times I can covertly slip my book onto her stack and get her to unwittingly take it and almost sign it. It's the same copy I've already tried to give her. Over the last several hours, as day has crept toward evening, the title page has grown more and more clustered with writing. When she first discovered the book in her hands, her pen poised to sign, she found my reply that I wrote to her: *Well, I don't like you. Or your book. Stop trying to give this to me.* Beneath that I'd scrawled: *You don't have to like me to use me, Weenie.*

She slammed the book shut so fast she startled her reader, cutting off the young man's effusive praise. Edwina set the book on her lap until she had a lull in her line. She glared at me while writing her next message, which ended up being a crude rendering of a penis with my name under it. It was so juvenile, I could only meet it with an equal measure of immaturity. The next time I passed it back to her, I wrote a page number on the title page, and when she flipped to it, she found not only a handful of flower petals that fell upon her lap, but a poem I'd edited, crossing out lines and replacing them with insults. My favorite of which compared the shade of her hair to a boiled carrot.

She hastily went to work making edits of her own, changing the part about carrots to reflect the size of my cock. And it was a baby carrot this time. Predictably.

I'm enjoying this game more than I should. As the signing is nearing its end, I probably only have one more chance to trick her into taking my book again. I edit another poem for her, turning a brooding love sonnet into an explicit ode to a girl with carrot-colored hair, from the perspective of an amorous shriveled carrot.

I do this while half listening to the man standing in my line. Zane has been chatting with Monty and Mr. Cordell at the front counter, leaving me alone with my insufferable reader, a Mr. Gavin Aston. I've given up on playing my part as the seductive poet, as Mr. Aston seems more interested in hearing himself talk, rather than speaking with me. He's been droning on about his favorite piece of Brettonish literature, a pretentious work called *Infinite Suffering in the Garden of Happenstance*. I nod as he speaks—because of course William the Poet likes the same trite shit as Mr. Aston—and continue scribbling new lines over the sonnet. Once it's complete, I covertly lean toward Edwina's table and slide the book onto her stack. She's so immersed in speaking with her current guest, the same way she is with every reader, that she doesn't even glance at her stack of books as she gathers one to sign. Her eyes crinkle at the corners, her grin as sweet as nectar—

Until she finds my book's title page beneath her hands yet again.

Baring her teeth, she cuts me a murderous glare.

Blooming hell, I could live for that look.

I purse my lips to keep from laughing and force my attention back to Mr. Aston. He's been listing all the ways he's similar to the main character in *Infinite Suffering*, and it's a miracle he hasn't floated away from the sheer mass of his inflated ego.

Disappointment sinks my chest as I don't catch Edwina writing anything else in the book. Has she finally tired of our game? Her last guest leaves and—thank the All of All—so does Mr. Aston. Only a handful of guests remain, and Queen Gemma has returned. With the shop closing for the evening, it must be time for the book club meeting.

Edwina and I leave our tables so Mr. Cordell can rearrange the nook for the meeting. She has my book in her arms, hugging it to her chest. My breath hitches at the sight, and I'm suddenly jealous of an inanimate object.

"I'm keeping this," she says, hugging the book tighter. "Otherwise, you're going to continue to annoy me."

"Then I've finally won. You've accepted my gift at last."

"I'm only going to throw it away the first chance I get," she says, yet the way she cradles it in her arms makes me think otherwise. Or perhaps that's only what I hope. "In fact, I'll dispose of it right now."

She flounces off in the direction of the back room, and I join Zane just outside the nook. My friend hands me a steaming mug, scents of chocolate and peppermint wafting from it. I accept the cup and take a sip. It's warm, the flavor a delectable blend of sweet and bitter mingling with the unmistakable—and not unpleasant—burn of liquor.

"Mr. Cordell informed me that book club hour is synonymous with drinking hour," Zane says, taking a hearty sip of their own mug. "I approve."

They must be right, for everyone who gathers in the nook holds an identical mug, and the mood is growing livelier by the second.

Edwina returns from the back room, her coat draped over her arm. I squint at it, smirking when I catch a sliver of green poking out from one of the pockets. She didn't throw my book away after all. Little liar.

"You aren't leaving, are you?" Queen Gemma strides up to Edwina, two mugs in hand.

"Of course not," Edwina says. "I just wanted to gather my belongings."

"Good. Are you still open to doing a reading for us?"

"Absolutely."

"You truly are a treasure, Miss Danforth. This just might be the best day of my life. Just don't tell my husband. Or my children." Gemma winks and hands Edwina one of the mugs.

Just like she did with Cloud Dive, she downs a hearty sip without hesitation. Part of me wants to chastise her for accepting a drink before even knowing what it is, but at least the liquor is of the human variety this time. She won't suffer any effects that are out of the ordinary.

"Oh!" Edwina licks her lips, slowly running her tongue

over the chocolate that stains them. Now I'm jealous of this damn drink too. "I like that indeed."

Gemma links her arm through Edwina's and leads her into the nook. Monty, Daphne, and Mr. Cordell settle onto the chairs at the back of the meeting area while Zane and I remain standing just behind them. I lean my shoulder against the nearby bookcase, watching Edwina's eyes light up as Gemma formally introduces her to the ladies that comprise the book club. Not that they didn't already meet her during the signing. After introductions, the book club members settle into their chairs, facing Edwina.

She wrings her hands, the first sign of nervousness she's shown all evening. "What would you like me to read for you?"

"What's your favorite scene?" asks one of the women.

"That's a hard choice." Edwina furrows her brow and taps a finger to her chin. "I suppose if I had to choose, it would be the scene in *The Governess and the Earl*, when Sarah realizes she deserves to be loved by a man of high standing."

"That's one of my favorites too," Queen Gemma says. She hands Edwina a copy of the book in question from her personal signed stack. "I'd be honored if you would read it for us."

Edwina's cheeks flush, but she accepts the book and seeks the chapter. She nibbles her thumbnail, another sign of her nerves, but when she speaks, she seems to forget her anxiousness. The bookshop is silent as she reads the chapter, her voice soft yet carrying the depth of emotion the character portrays. Her tone falls when the character speaks of her longing and fears, then rises when she voices her worth. Chills run down my spine. I've been surrounded by performers for most of my life. My mother, Lydia, was an actress. Though not related to me by blood, she was Cassie's mother and was the woman who raised me. We practically lived in the theater for most of my life. Then there were my years at university. Edwina may not have the honed skill of someone who spent her life studying the performing arts, but she has a raw talent in the way she reads from her character's point of view. The way she sinks into the role and captures emotion with the slightest inflection.

I'm mesmerized.

So much so that my heart plummets when she speaks the final word of the chapter and closes the book. Reality sharpens around me, pulling me from the pages she'd drawn me into.

For fuck's sake, she's...

She's incredible.

Applause erupts all around, and I set my mug on the nearby shelf to join them. Edwina's gaze flicks to me, her eyes widening as if she'd forgotten I was still here. I give her a smile devoid of taunting, and the one she returns—so wide and genuine—nearly takes my breath away. Then her attention falls back upon the book club members.

"I'm sure of it now," Zane says, keeping their voice low.

"Sure of what?"

"You like her."

The blood leaves my face. "I don't..."

Zane chuckles. "You can't finish that sentence, can you? Because it's a lie. You *do* like her."

I tug at my cravat, loosening it and unbuttoning the top of my collar. Why is it suddenly so hot in here? I lower my voice to a whisper. "I...may be attracted to her."

"She's not your usual type. I would know."

"No, she's not," I say. Zane *would* know. Zane witnesses my sexual exploits during my university days and even joined them a time or two. Zane and I never exclusively courted, as we were both of a mind to enjoy only casual flings while at school. Yet once our physical relationship ran its course, a deeper friendship remained. They've been my closest friend ever since, even though we haven't seen much of each other since their opera career took off. We still keep in touch by letter.

"She's different," Zane says. "Quirky. Cute. Chaotic. I like it."

"She's annoying," I mutter.

"And you like it."

What's the point of denying it? Zane has seen through me. "Yes. For whatever reason, I want to bed my rival."

Zane arches a brow. "Is that all it is? Just physical?"

I refuse to even contemplate that question.

"Will you read something else?" Mr. Cordell asks.

"Chapter Eighteen," Daphne calls out.

"Chapter Fifty-five," says one of the ladies.

"I'd love for you to read Chapter Thirty-two of *The Governess and the Rake*," Gemma says.

My shoulders tense. I know exactly which chapter that is. The heated kiss that precedes the love scene. The very one that ended my acting career.

The book club members voice their agreement. One adds, "Remember when King Elliot read Alexander's lines at one of our meetings?"

Gemma laughs. "He was terrible at it."

"Yes, but his grumpy demeanor certainly added nuance to the character that wasn't on the page." A wave of laughter rumbles from the ladies.

Edwina sighs. "What I wouldn't give to hear Alexander's lines read by a handsome male."

"Might I make a suggestion?" Zane says, and my heart stops at once. I know what they're about to say before they even say it. "William will read the lines."

"Z," I bark under my breath, but the sound is drowned out by exclamations of approval.

"He's an actor, isn't he?" one of the ladies says to another.

"He's as handsome as Alexander."

"No." Edwina's voice silences all the rest. My eyes meet hers, and I expect to see annoyance or embarrassment in them. Instead, it's concern that etches the firm line of her mouth. Concern...for me.

A crack wends through my heart as I understand the source of her distress. She knows what this play means to me. What this scene means. And it's that care that emboldens me. That care that burns away my trepidation and replaces it with my competitive spark. I adore her for her concern, but I don't need it. Not truly. Not when she's here. Not if I've been presented with an opportunity to shatter her expectations and rock her off her feet.

I release a long and steadying breath, then tuck my hands into my pockets. With my signature seductive grin, I say, "I'll read the role."

Edwina blanches. She gives me a significant look. "Are you sure?"

"Positive."

The book club members squeal with delight as I make my way to Edwina. I cast a look at Zane, who gives me a taunting grin. Monty turns in his seat and mutters to my friend, "Nice work. I think we're on the same team."

"Shut up," Daphne says, standing on her chair to get a better look at me and Edwina. "Things are about to get smutty."

Gemma retrieves her copy of *The Governess and the Earl* from Edwina and gives her *The Governess and the Rake* instead, while a young woman offers a copy of the latter book to me. Her voice is soft and shy. "So you can read the lines."

I grace her with a smile but wave away the book. "I won't be needing it."

Edwina worries her lip as I face her. She arches a brow in a silent question. *You really think you can do this?*

I step in close and hold her gaze, my unspoken answer written in the wicked curve of my lips. *My beautiful bespectacled hellion. I'll make you pay for doubting me.*

Out loud, I say, "Tell me, dearest, how would you like me to make love to you tonight?"

CHAPTER TWENTY-THREE

EDWINA

*M*y mind goes blank at the question. Why would he ask me such a thing? And in front of so many people—

Oh right.

My book.

He's reciting a line from my book.

Apparently, we're not merely reading the excerpt like I did before. We're...

Acting it out?

The thud of my racing heart reaches all the way down to my hands, making the book shake as I open it to the right chapter. I may have written *The Governess and the Rake*, but I don't have the whole thing memorized. William stares at me, frozen in character, as he waits for my reply. I take a few moments to gather my composure. Once I think I can face William without losing my senses, I pivot toward him.

I scoff. "Make love to you? Why would we go straight to lovemaking when we haven't even kissed?"

William steps toward me, a wry grin curving his lips. "Allow me to amend that."

As William reaches for my cheek, I pause, glancing at the book again. He freezes once more, holding patiently in place with his hand hovering in midair while I scan the scene. There are several lines of the heroine's internal thoughts as well as descriptions of body language, but William is already embodying the rakish hero's every move. The stage play must have kept its script quite close to its source material. If I do what William's doing and act out the body language, I don't need to read anything but the dialogue. Well, I have that memorized at least.

I place the book on one of the nearby shelves and fall back into the scene. William resumes motion, and his fingers brush my cheek. I knock his hand away and step back. "Don't you dare touch me like that. Without affection. With that cold and loveless look. I know what you're doing. You're trying to scare me away. Trying to convince me your feelings are merely physical. That I'm nothing more than the dozens of women you've dallied with before."

The book club ladies utter sounds of approval, which calms my nerves.

I'm no actress, and I know my performance is stilted, but I doubt anyone's paying attention to me when they can simply watch William. I'm even stunned by him. By the way he reacts to my words with every part of him—expression, posture, motions. He truly is a brilliant actor.

He snatches his hand back and turns to the side. "You are nothing more than another dalliance, Dolly. If that isn't enough for you, then you can leave."

"Leave? Leave your room or...or the manor?"

He shakes his head, jaw set. "How can you perform your

duties as my nephew's governess when you're constantly lusting after me?"

My mouth drops to show Dolly's indignation. "Lusting after you? Is that all this has been? Lust?" I approach William and he turns his back to me. "I healed you, Alexander. I stitched your wounds after your duel with Lord Herringbone when everyone else would rather see you punished for your recklessness. And I...I healed your heart."

"You know nothing of my heart." William's voice trembles in a perfect imitation of Alexander's poorly hidden emotional state.

"If that's really what you think, I'll leave. I'll leave the manor, my position as governess, and we can go our separate ways." I force a quaver into my voice. "I've had enough of your moods. Of feeling your love only to have it torn away again and again. If you won't accept my love now, you'll never get a chance again. Goodbye, Alexander."

I whirl on my heel and take a step away. I ensure my right hand is within reach, for William is supposed to grab me by the wrist—

The front of his body collides with the back of mine and his arms wind around me. I'm so startled, I let out a squeak. Well, I suppose that's a valid response from Dolly, but why is William holding me around the middle? Did the script change this part of my scene?

He clutches me against him, squeezing me tight as he buries his face in my neck. Another action I didn't write. "Forgive me, Dolly. Don't leave. You know me too well. You know the very core of my being."

A shudder runs through me at the feel of William's hot breath on my neck, the way his muffled voice reverberates through me. It takes me a few moments to recall what I'm supposed to say next.

"I won't fall for your hot and cold demeanor anymore," I

say, voice breathless without any effort on my part. "Tell me how you feel once and for all."

He releases my middle and takes me by the wrist instead, spinning me to face him. He steps toward me, forcing me back until I come up against the bookshelf. With my wrist still in his hand, he pins it over my head, against one of the shelves.

This is exactly like it is in my book, aside from the bookcase behind us. It's supposed to be a wall. And I'm finding it increasingly hard to keep my pulse from racing.

William stares down at me with a tortured expression. His throat bobs, right on cue. "You know how I feel."

I'm supposed to lift my chin, but I'm so flustered I can't meet his eyes. At least I can deliver the right line. "I don't."

William brings his forefinger under my chin and lifts it. An action that isn't written in my scene because I'm supposed to be looking at him. My breath hitches as he forces me to meet his eyes. He brings his face mere inches from mine. "Then may I show you?"

My lips part, my answer ready. I know what I'm supposed to say and what happens next. But...but shouldn't we cut the scene here? We're in public, after all, and...bloody hell, there's William's issue to consider! He can't kiss someone he isn't attracted to, nor is he comfortable performing intimacies in public. Maybe I should—

His fingers lace through mine, still pinned over my head, and he gives my hand a squeeze. It isn't an action expressed in my scene, and there's something reassuring about it.

I release a slow breath, calming my panicked thoughts.

William leans ever closer until our noses touch, just the lightest brush of skin against skin. Another action not in this scene. Then, with his voice so low there's no way it could carry beyond me, he whispers, "May I, Weenie?"

Finally, I deliver Dolly's response. "Yes."

William leans the rest of the way in, and his lips press against mine. They're soft yet firm, perfectly warm. Nothing cold or probing like Archie's mouth was. Our lips linger together for a long moment. My mind empties. Spreads out into a beautiful blank page. I don't remember where I am. Who's watching. I'm only aware of William's lips. The scent of his skin. The taste of chocolate and peppermint between us. The squeeze of his palm. The way our lips part at the exact same moment and he kisses me again, harder this time. The way I angle my head, craving just a little more—

Applause erupts, splattering ink across that blank page in my mind. I stiffen. William lingers just a second longer, exhaling against my mouth, then pulls away. I blink into the space he occupied, my spectacles fogged from our breaths. Our audience has risen to their feet, their applause even louder now. William faces them and bows. Belatedly, I do the same, my motions stiff and clumsy.

William has finally earned the attention and approval of the book club members, who now surround him, begging him to autograph that scene in their copies of the book. The meeting dissolves into casual chatter, and I participate in it, answer questions, laugh at the right times. Yet half my mind remains wrapped in that kiss, my gaze constantly seeking William in the small crowd. He doesn't meet my eyes like he did at the party at Somerton House. Instead, he seems truly engaged in the conversations around him.

"You don't have to worry about my request earlier." Monty's voice shatters my train of thought.

I don't know how long he's been standing beside me or how long he's been watching me staring at William, but I force myself to shift all my attention to him. "Pardon?"

He lowers his voice. "About spending the night in your room."

"Oh." Right, he did make that request earlier. Because he

assumed William and Zane would spend the night in William's room. Does he no longer believe that's the case? My heart flips with relief.

"Zane and I had a chat just now," he says.

I find my gaze has strayed to William again, and Zane has joined him. They whisper something in his ear, which elicits a furrowed brow from William. Then his eyes lock on mine. I avert my gaze back to Monty. "Is that so?"

Monty takes a cigarillo from a slim silver case and tucks it over his ear. Thankfully he knows better than to light that thing in a bookstore. Then why does mischief play in his eyes? "We came to some similar conclusions."

I frown. "Like what?"

"Like the fact that I won't need to spend the night in your room after all. I can spend the night in Zane's."

More relief floods my heart. Was he wrong about William's relationship with Zane? Did Monty find himself a lover instead? A genuine grin warms my lips. "Did you and the opera singer hit it off that well?"

"We did indeed, but I think you have the wrong idea. I'll be spending the night in Zane's room alone."

I puzzle over his words...until their meaning becomes clear. He'll stay in Zane's room tonight because Zane will be staying with William.

The smile falls from my face. "Oh."

Monty lets out a heavy sigh. "It's a shame that kiss wasn't behind bedroom doors. It didn't count toward your bet. Now William's going to take away your one-point lead for a tie."

My gaze shoots to William. His eyes are already on me, and I wonder if he's been watching me talk to Monty this entire time. Zane angles their head toward the front of the store. William's mouth lifts in a taunting curl, his eyes glinting with menace.

He gives me a pointed nod and leaves the crowd with Zane.

Hurt and rage boil inside me as I watch them walk away. Disappear from view. I imagine them crossing the street to the hotel, hand in hand.

I'm frozen in place, my imagination alternating between thoughts of them together with thoughts of he and I together.

After that kiss, I…

I…

Well, I don't know what I was thinking. What I was feeling.

William didn't kiss *me*. That was Alexander kissing Dolly. He was playing a part. Just because he kissed me before an audience doesn't make me special. He's already confessed that kissing me wouldn't be a problem. He's merely proved it.

Now he's going to spend the night kissing someone else.

And…more.

I've never felt such a blazing envy. Everything inside me wants to march after him and sabotage him with my free pass, just like I said I would.

Monty releases another exaggerated sigh. "If only there was something you could do to stop them. Then you could keep your lead."

It's like he read my mind. What he doesn't know is that there *is* something I can do to stop them.

Do I dare?

I want to, but there's one thing that holds me back.

A small, shriveled piece of my heart that shrank even more when I saw the way they looked at each other. William and Zane have history. Whether as friends or lovers, it's clear they know each other. Like each other. Want to spend the night together. I can't ruin that. I can't come between them or what they have together. What if it's love?

My chest constricts further, but I don't fully understand the source. Am I conflicted because I want to maintain my lead in the bet? Or is it more personal than that? Is my envy for academic reasons? Or romantic ones?

I recall the feel of William's lips against mine. The way he squeezed my palm. The way he asked permission, soft enough for only me to hear.

Desire floods me, followed by another spike of rage, and I can no longer convince myself it's for the sake of our bet alone. Perhaps I'm petty. Perhaps I'm half out of my mind. Whatever the case, I want to be the last person William kissed. I want what Jolene wanted. I want what I already stole from Jolene, and I want to keep it for as long as I can.

Clenching my jaw, I march away from Monty.

"Oh, did you think of something?" The lack of inflection in his tone makes me wonder if he knows about our free pass after all.

I stride to where I draped my coat and wrap it around me.

"Are you leaving now?" Queen Gemma's voice fills me with guilt.

I face her with an apologetic smile, only to find most of the book club members looking at me too. I shouldn't leave them. These are my fans. My readers. People who admire and respect me.

I know what I should do.

And yet…

"I'm so sorry," I say. "I hate to leave in a rush, but…but I need to ruin someone's night."

With that, I turn on my heel and race from the bookshop.

Outside, I pull my coat tight around me, bracing myself against the cold. It must be past ten in the evening now, and the streets are quiet save for the music and chatter streaming from the late-night establishments serving dinner, drinks, and entertainment. It's a far more subdued atmosphere than either of the cities we've been in before, which makes sense for a winter resort town that caters to polite society. As I cross the street toward the Verity Hotel, my boots crunch on fluffy snow, only an inch deep despite the enormous snowflakes that trickle down. My heart races with anticipation, my lips curling. A giddy mood takes over me, fueled by the thrill of my purpose.

It's that giddy mood that almost gives me pause. I've felt this way before—determined, light on my feet, a flutter in my heart—and it didn't end well. Yet that was different. That was a matter of love. This is a matter of sex. Sex and sabotage.

Oh, what a fun book title that would be!

The doorman allows me entry with a respectful nod, and it takes all my restraint to slow my pace as I move through the elegant lobby, past reception, and toward the staircase. Only then do I pick up my pace again, climbing the stairs to the second floor as fast as I dare. I'm out of breath by the time I reach our hall, but it only adds to my excitement.

I'm going to sabotage William.

Redeem my free pass.

Earn a point in our bet.

Secure my two-point lead.

Keep my two-point lead.

Win the three-book contract.

Move to Faerwyvae.

Live in a place where I'm famous and respected and surrounded by admirers.

Kiss William.

Kiss…William.

Kiss…touch…make love to…

William.

My cheeks burn hot, and it isn't only from the strain of activity. I stop outside his bedroom door and raise my fist, poised to knock. That giddy flutter in my chest intensifies, my mind still swirling with thoughts of what I'm about to do with my rival. My mind lingers on the way he kissed me in the bookstore, and for the love of all things, I want that again. I want more of that.

With a deep breath, I let my fist fall in a rapid knock.

My heart hammers so loud, I can't hear if there's motion coming from inside the room. William and Zane must already be inside. They left a few minutes before me. What if I'm already too late? What if they're entangled in each other's arms, each other's lips? What if I have no right being here? What if I'm taking our game too far by interrupting what might be love—

The door swings open just a crack. Inside, the bedroom is dim. The sliver of William I see reveals an open collar and waistcoat, no jacket, his cravat hanging loose and crooked around his neck, his lips quirked sideways.

My lips.

Those are my fucking lips.

I ball my hands into fists and finally say those two words he's been taunting me to say. "Free pass."

William opens the door wider, snakes his hand around my waist, and pulls me into his room. "I thought you'd never ask."

CHAPTER TWENTY-FOUR

EDWINA

*W*ith one arm, William pulls me against him. With the other, he shuts the door behind us. My hands come to his chest as he shifts to the side and leans against the closed door, pulling me with him. His posture is loose and relaxed. Maybe even relieved. He now has both arms around me, and he throws his head back, an easy chuckle escaping his lips.

I frown up at him. What's come over him? He's grinning like he's won when I'm the one who redeemed my pass. Sabotaged his plans.

Or...

I glance around the room. It's identical to mine, with two beds and an assortment of fine furnishings. Only one lamp is lit on one of the bedside tables, casting the room in a dim warm glow. There's no sign of anyone else.

I return my gaze to William and narrow my eyes. "Where's Zane?"

He lowers his chin until those blue irises fall on me. His triumphant smile remains. As do his arms around me. The way he holds me, his grip firm yet relaxed, the way he stares down at me with that smile, almost feels like a weathered embrace. Familiar. Comforting. Like it's effortless for him to touch me like this.

It's *my* posture that's tense. *My* hands that burn against the firm musculature of his chest, even with the linen shirt that separates our flesh. *My* breaths that are short and jagged. I'm the only one of us who's discomposed.

He shrugs. "Zane is probably in their room by now."

"Their room? Weren't they planning on staying in yours tonight?"

"Nope."

"But Monty said..." Suspicion darkens my thoughts. I recall wondering if he knew about the free pass after all. "Monty tricked me."

"Did he now?"

My posture slackens, my eyes going unfocused. "Whose side is he on?"

"Yours, obviously. He wanted you to sabotage me and maintain your lead. Zane, on the other hand, is on my side. They proposed I stir your jealousy. Though...that might have been Monty's idea. They were whispering together for some time. Come to think of it, Monty might be on my side too..."

His grin turns smug. He's clearly enjoying this.

I level a glare at him. "You tricked me. You *all* tricked me. I redeemed my free pass for nothing."

His gaze grows heavy, flitting from my eyes to my lips and back again. "Oh, I wouldn't say this is nothing, Weenie."

I push off his chest and he releases me. "Now that you've all had fun at my expense, I'll be on my way." I step back and plant my hands on my hips, waiting for him to move away from the threshold.

He doesn't.

Still leaning against the closed door, he folds his arms and crosses one ankle over the other. "You said the words. You redeemed your pass, and it is now in my possession. Yet you haven't claimed your act of physical intimacy, which means you've yet to accumulate a point."

My mouth falls open, and I gesture at his body. "You hugged me."

"That wasn't much of a hug." Finally, he steps away from the door. "If you really want to waste your free pass, by all means, leave without claiming your point."

I glance from him to the door. I could stride past him and leave my humiliation behind. But my pride is greater, and he knows it. I can't leave without taking advantage of the lead I so badly want.

And there's still another flicker of want inside me, the same excitement that drove me to his room tonight. He may have succeeded in tricking me, but I still desire more of him, for reasons I've yet to fully acknowledge.

"Fine," I say, doing my best to keep my voice steady. "Let's…perform an act of physical intimacy."

The triumph returns to his expression. "What act shall it be? You redeemed the pass. You get to choose."

"Did we establish that rule?"

"I just did."

He's really going to make me say it. I bite the inside of my cheek as I gather the courage to speak. "A kiss, then."

He steps closer, his voice dipping low. "Take the lead. Show me what you like. Show me where you want me to kiss you."

I nearly sway on my feet at the last part, conjuring thoughts of the less obvious places I could get him to kiss. He's already pressed his mouth to my knuckles, my neck, and now my lips. Only now do I picture that mouth trailing over my stomach, my breasts, then between my legs.

Heat burns at my core, screaming, *Yes, that.* But I can't request that. I'm not brave enough. Not yet. More than anything, I want to start with a true kiss. I want to experience an encore of what we began in the bookstore.

I hold his gaze, trembling as I step closer to him. He's so much taller than me that even if I stood on my tiptoes, I couldn't reach his mouth without his aid. He seems to realize this at the same time, closing the remaining space between us and bracketing my waist in his hands. Then he leans down, angling his head until our faces are only inches apart. He freezes then, like he did during our performance when he was waiting for me to catch up with the scene. Damn him. He's really going to make me make the first move.

My heart pounds faster. Harder. My head swims. I lift onto my toes and press my lips against his. My courage leaves no sooner than our lips meet, along with the strength in my legs. I pull away and take a step out of his grasp, my head light, my breaths short. What the hell is this? Am I fucking swooning? Is swooning a real thing?

"All right, well..." I wring my hands, wincing at the quaver in my voice. "There it is. That was the kiss. I have my point, so—"

"No." William's stern tone has my mouth snapping shut. "That wasn't a real kiss."

"Uh, I think it was," I mutter, looking anywhere but at him.

"I thought this was what you wanted," he says. "Don't you want to know what it feels like to be kissed by a fae? *Really* kissed by a fae?"

A fae...right. My research. In this moment, I couldn't care less about that. I want to know what it feels like to be kissed by *him.* And maybe that's the problem. Initiating the kiss myself made my head spin, while being kissed by him only filled me with desire.

I take a few deep breaths, gathering my resolve. "Show me a real kiss then."

"You want me to take the lead?"

I wring my hands again. "Please."

A gentle smile warms his lips as he places his hand over mine, stilling my anxious motions. "So, we've learned something you like already."

I swallow hard. "I suppose we have."

Tenderly, he takes one of my hands, brings it to his lips, and brushes a soft kiss over my knuckles. Then he brings his fingers to my neck, dipping them beneath the collar of my coat before he slides it down my shoulders, my arms, letting it fall to the floor at my feet. His hands find mine again, and he guides one behind his neck while pulling the other to his chest. His heart slams against my palm, a rhythm that matches my own. It's a comforting tempo, lulling me back into my body and out of my head. With my arms remaining where he positioned them, he winds his own behind me, one hand bracing my lower back, the other cradling my neck. He pauses here, holding my eyes as I catch my breath. Then, ever so slowly, he lowers his mouth to mine.

I close my eyes at the warmth of his lips, sinking into the feel of him against me, the strength of his hands pressing me close. He angles his head, and I do the same, deepening our kiss. Without meaning to, I slide my fingers up his neck, into the ends of his hair, much like I did in the north wing. He releases a throaty sound against my mouth, one that has my lips parting. His tongue sweeps in and brushes against mine in a languorous caress. There's nothing forceful or probing about the way he kisses, unlike my former lovers, Archie included. With William, it feels more like a dance, a conversation. A reaction between our needs, our wants. A song and echo. His mouth somehow does exactly what I want it to, our kisses deepening only when I'm ready. Wanting. Silently begging to taste more of him.

His fingers weave into my hair, sending pins falling to the ground. His other hand roves my bottom, and I'm cursing myself for the warm layers of petticoats I wear beneath my dress. I let my hands wander too, one rounding the curve of his shoulder while the other explores the planes of his chest, his torso. His muscles flex against my palm, which sends a thrill through me. I let my hand move lower, down to his waistband. He sucks in a breath, emboldening me. I kiss him harder, move my hand lower, until my palm cups the firm length straining against his trousers.

Bloody hell, it's a mammoth handful.

And...and it's straining like that for *me*. My touch. My kiss. We're still fully clothed, yet he's hard for me.

I run my hand further down his bulge and back again, assessing the full scope of what he's hiding.

He groans, sucking my lower lip between his teeth. So he likes that.

I tighten my grip and stroke his length again.

He releases my lip and pants against my mouth. His hand leaves my neck to linger over the clasps at the back of my dress. His words come out stifled. "How far do you want this to go tonight?"

I pull back slightly, taking in his heavy-lidded eyes, the need written over every inch of his face. "What do you mean?"

His fingers dig into the back seam of my dress. With the flick of his forefinger, my top clasp comes loose. "I can have you out of this dress and spread naked beneath me in ten seconds flat. If you don't want that, tell me now."

I suck in a sharp breath at his words, at the images they conjure, at the restraint in his tone.

Pride swells inside me. "You want that?"

"You know damn well I want that," he says, rocking against my hand to remind me of the proof in my palm. "But if you're not ready...fuck, just tell me. I'll hold myself back."

I've never felt so powerful. So desired. So in control. I needed him to take the lead, but now that I've found my footing, I don't want to cede to him. Cede this power.

And as much as I want what he wants, I should leave him yearning for something more to redeem his free pass for.

"Let's keep our clothes on," I say, voice breathless. "Just kissing and touching."

"Can I touch you?"

"Over my clothes," I say, delighting in his groan of frustration, the way his fingers curl into a fist against my back, fighting not to flick open another clasp. I move my hand up the length of him again, then to his waistband. He bites his lip as I tuck two fingers beneath it. I give him a teasing smile. "Can I touch you?"

His eyes dance with cruel amusement. I can almost see his thoughts on his face; he's considering denying me the same way I denied him. He blows out a shaky breath before answering me. "This is your free pass. You get to make the rules for what we do."

"Good." I press my lips to his again, just as I plunge my hand into his trousers. I suck his lower lip between my teeth, something I've never tried before but want to experience now that he's done it to me. He aids my efforts to untuck his shirt from his trousers, flicking open the top buttons of his fly.

A moan escapes my lips at the feel of his hard flesh fully in my palm. His cock is somehow larger than it felt from the outside. I slide my hand up and down that smooth length. I'm half tempted to cup his testicles like I saw in the north wing, but I'm too afraid he might laugh, shattering the moment. The last thing I want to do is something he doesn't like. Not when I have him at my beck and call. Not when he's panting, moaning—

"Edwina," he says through his teeth at the next slide of my hand. "Wait. Fuck."

He surges against me, his cock pulsing in my palm. He tugs down the hem of his shirt to bury his release, his other hand closing tightly around the length of my hair that's escaped my updo. It takes me a moment to understand what happened. The reason he's frozen against me, catching his breath, head thrown back, eyes closed, his muscles quivering.

Then he lowers his head, heavy eyelids fluttering open. I slide my hand from around him, and my gaze drops to the hem of his shirt. My mouth falls open. "You...you came. Because of me. I did that."

A slow smile melts over his lips, and when he speaks, his voice is rich with mirth and the dregs of desire. "You seem quite pleased with yourself."

"I didn't know that was possible. Drawing out a man's release with one's hand, I mean. I've written about it, sure, but I've never done that before. I didn't know I could make it feel good."

"It doesn't normally happen that way," he says. "As in I normally last longer. Much longer."

My eyes go wide as I analyze the new information. Already, a potential scene for my next book plays out in my mind. "To confirm what you're saying, I made you come quickly? That was fast for you?"

"Yes, would you like a medal?"

I smirk. "If there was one, I'd take it on a plaque." I shift to the side and angle my hands like I'm framing something over a mantle. *"Edwina Danforth made William Haywood come with her hand in three seconds flat.* I'd hang it in my parlor for all my guests to see."

He snorts a laugh. "I've lost you now, haven't I?"

I lower my hands from my imaginary award and arch a brow in question.

He sobers from his mirth and shakes his head. "I thought we were only getting started, but that damn pride of yours has overridden your desire."

I blush, realizing this probably isn't the reaction he expected from me. Or perhaps he did. I've always handled sex differently than I assume other people do, and William saw a hint of that in the north wing. Yet it doesn't mean I'm devoid of desire. I felt it, hot and heavy with him, and it's still there. Alongside it, though, is a well of exhilaration. Wonder. Power. I now have firsthand experience—in the most literal sense—that I can use in my writing. My fingers itch to draft out some ideas.

William brushes a strand of hair off my brow, and I recall how that same hand struggled not to rip open my clasps. "There were things I wanted to do to you tonight," he whispers.

My pulse quickens. Maybe my need to write hasn't overridden my desire after all.

Then again, I like the way he's looking at me. The yearning in his eyes as he studies my lips. The quavering restraint in his touch as he brushes his hand over the length of my tangled hair.

I still hold power over him, and I'd like to keep it a while longer.

I tilt my chin and part my lips. He starts to lean in when I press my forefinger to his mouth. "If you want to do such wicked things to me so badly, you'll have to redeem your free pass."

He groans against my finger and heaven above, I almost give in. Almost beg him to let me coax more moans from him. Beg him to take me to his bed and show me everything he wants to do to me.

With a heavy sigh, he steps back. "Let me change my shirt. I'll walk you to your door."

"You don't have to be such a gentleman," I say as I sink down to gather my coat from the floor. I drape it over my arm and rise to my feet. "I only touched you—"

My words lodge in my throat as my eyes find him, back turned to me as he tugs his half-unbuttoned shirt over his head. The dim lamplight illuminates the peaks and valleys of his muscled back, the flex of his shoulder blades as he tosses his shirt to the side and gathers a fresh one. He turns to face me as he throws his arms through the sleeves, and I get a full view of the front of him. My gaze slides down his pectorals to the deep V above his still-open trousers.

I've seen him shirtless before, the morning after I got drunk on Cloud Dive and allegedly threw up on him.

But I didn't desire him then. Not as deeply as I do now.

He catches my open-mouthed stare, and his lips curl in a teasing smile. Making no move to button the front of his shirt or his trousers, he says, "Changed your mind?"

I blink and tear my eyes from his physique. "Nope."

He chuckles to himself and finishes getting dressed. I'm still amused by his insistence on walking me to my room, but I make no argument as we leave his bedroom and cross the short distance to my door.

I seek my key from my coat pocket, my hand brushing his poetry book in the process. I grin, recalling all the ridiculous writings we exchanged today. After I unlock my door, I shift to face him. "Well…that was—"

He bends down and silences me with his mouth. His hand cradles my jaw, and I part my lips, inviting his tongue at once. The kiss is deep and demanding. Heat sparks inside me, from my chest to the pulsing want that reignites between my legs. Even after everything we already did, after I thought I'd cooled my ardor, I still want him so badly.

Too soon, he breaks the kiss, panting as he rests his forehead against mine.

"You didn't redeem your pass," I whisper, my hands clenched around his collar, ready to tear off his buttons should he say those two words. "This doesn't count."

He brushes his thumb along my jawline, then over the bottom curve of my lip. "It's just practice," he says, pressing his lips to mine once more before pulling away completely and returning to his room.

CHAPTER TWENTY-FIVE

EDWINA

*T*he world outside my hotel window feels different the next morning. Bigger. Brighter. And it isn't just from the fresh layer of snow glistening beneath the surprisingly clear and sunny day. Nor is it my ego in the wake of the great feat I performed on William's cock last night. While that continues to give me no small amount of satisfaction, I've sunk into a steady calm I haven't experienced since I set off on my journey to Faerwyvae. After so much went wrong in my efforts to make it to my book tour, and then the tension between me and William, it feels like things are going right.

Not only have I officially secured my two-point lead in our bet, but—for the first time—it doesn't seem impossible to beat William for the publishing contract without the bet. Yesterday's signing showed me I truly am as popular in Faerwyvae as my publisher said I was. Maybe I was being hasty in deeming William the clear winner in book sales. Maybe his overwhelming popularity at our first two locations was a matter of circumstance alone.

At our signing at Flight of Fancy, my readers didn't even know if I'd show up. Rumors of my absence had already circulated. At the university, William was a favorite for personal reasons, due to his alumni status.

Maybe I undervalued myself from the start of this tour.

By afternoon, it's time to leave for our next destination. I'm buzzing with excitement as we gather on the train platform, waiting to board. To solidify my new sense of confidence, Queen Gemma has come to see us off. And by *us* I mean *me*.

We chat about books and I give her some personal anecdotes about my writing process. She eats them up, hanging on my every word.

I still can't believe a queen is this enamored with me.

Time and again, I catch William's eye. He's not too far from me, conversing animatedly with Zane, Monty, and Daphne. Heat simmers in his gaze whenever our eyes lock, which makes my breath quicken. I wasn't sure if things would feel awkward between us today, or if his behavior toward me would change. We haven't spoken much, but things do feel different. Better. Softer.

Or maybe this is yet another shift in my perception. He proved he meant it when he said he could kiss me. Which means he's attracted to me. More than that, he...

He wanted me.

He wanted me so badly, I hardly had to touch him to get him off.

I can't help the grin that curls my lips. I meet William's eyes and his narrow, as if he can read my mind. Yet the smile that remains on his lips is warm. Perhaps even a little bashful.

Gemma folds me into a spine-crushing hug as boarding begins.

"Thank you for coming to Vernon," she says, releasing me. "I hope you know how deeply I appreciate you and your work. Your books really did change my life. They were an anchor to happiness when I needed it most."

My throat tightens at the praise. As much as I could bask in it for hours, I realize I've yet to lavish praise of my own. Praise she very much deserves. "I hope you know you've changed my life too. I've heard from so many of my readers in Faerwyvae that you championed my books. I don't think I'd be here if not for you. So thank you."

Her eyes glaze as she presses a hand to her heart. "I'm going to repeat that for bragging rights to anyone who will listen."

"Please, brag away," I say with a chuckle.

With a final wave, Gemma departs and I join my companions on the train.

OUR NEXT DESTINATION IS ONE OF THE NORTHERNMOST CITIES in Faerwyvae. It's a city I read about in my brochure: Lumenas. Nestled at the very tip of the Star Court, it's famous for its entertainment and nightlife, with a focus on the performing arts. And it's a two-day train ride from Vernon.

Thankfully, we procure a luxury compartment. It's three times as large as the ones we've ridden in thus far, with wide cushioned seats, footrests, and accommodations to transition to a sleeping compartment, courtesy of the fold-out cots, the bunks that pull down from the walls, and the privacy screens that slide into place. I suspect we have Zane to thank for the upgrade. They've decided to join us on our journey. Turns out Lumenas is the city Zane calls home.

All the envy I felt for the beautiful antlered fae yesterday has died, and now I'm back to being starstruck. After how they conspired to get me alone with William last night, I no longer suspect there is anything romantic between them and the poet.

The mood is light between our party as our train rolls along for the next two days. We chat. We drink. We eat. When we're bored, we play cards or charades. When we're tired of each other's company we read or nap. At night, I claim one of the bunks and Daphne curls up beside me. During the day, I can't keep my eyes off William, and I suspect it's the same for him. He always has a smirk ready for me, sometimes a wink too.

I smile back most of the time, though once—when he meets my eyes over the porcelain cup of coffee he's sipping from—I display a crude gesture for only him to see, involving my right hand fisting an invisible girth. After which he chokes on his coffee, his cheeks blazing.

Bad girl, he mouths across the train compartment, our exchange lost on our distracted companions.

I give him an innocent shrug, then let my eyes dip suggestively to his lap.

When my gaze sweeps back to his face, I catch him biting his lip as he shifts in his seat. Then, keeping each word slow and exaggerated, he mouths, *When I get you alone, I'm going to—*

I never find out what William's going to do to me, for Zane catches sight of him. "Hmm? Did you say something?"

"Hmm?" William blinks a few times. "Nothing."

I purse my lips to hide my laugh and watch as he falls into conversation with Zane. He seems so different than he normally does, and I think a lot of it has to do with his

TESSONJA ODETTE

friend's presence. He's discarded his aloof demeanor, his arrogant quips. He smiles more. Jokes more easily. Teases in a less cutting way.

I'm a bit stir-crazy by the last leg of our journey, so I nearly weep with relief when our train finally pulls into the Lumenas City Station. The morning is bright, the weather mild and refreshing. Warm compared to the Winter Court, but not nearly as sweltering as the Solar Court.

Outside the station, our group splits up between two hansom cabs, as each compact carriage only has room for two human-sized passengers. I ride with Monty, Daphne in my lap. My nose is practically pressed to the window as we enter the heart of the city. Even before noon, the streets are crowded with other horse-drawn cabs and coaches, while the sidewalks teem with people. The buildings tower high overhead, taller than any I've seen before.

I release a gasp. "This city is beautiful."

"If you're impressed now," Monty says, "wait until you see it at night. Lumenas was made for its nightlife."

I can't imagine how much more stunning it could possibly be. Morning sun glints off the windows of the tallest buildings, illuminating jugglers and other performers who grace the street corners. We pass glittering storefronts, opera houses, restaurants, and luxury apartments. Meanwhile, the people appear to be an even mix of human and fae, pointed ears, animal features, and extravagant costumes standing out in equal measure to modestly dressed, round-eared patrons. It's the most diverse blend of people I've seen in any of the cities we've been in.

I bring this up to Monty.

"Lumenas attracts tourists," Monty says, fiddling with an unlit cigarillo, "many of which are human. Yet a great number of the performers, residents, and staff are fae, and certain areas in the city discard human propriety entirely. There truly is something for everyone here."

"I know why you like it, Monty," Daphne says from my lap. "One of Lumenas' nicknames is Den of Debauchery."

He casts an affronted look at the pine marten. "I, a debaucher? I'm insulted."

She scoffs. "You've been flipping that same cigarillo between your fingers since we got here. You're just wondering where you might find more of that Moonpetal Mr. Somerton gave you, aren't you?"

"Right you are, Daffy. A little Moonpetal, an amateur boxing match. I'm already planning the perfect night."

"You better not try to claim a boxing match as a business expense."

"I have money of my own, you know."

I grin as their banter continues, and I take in every street, every sight, every building. Finally, our cab stops outside a hotel so tall that I couldn't count the number of floors if I tried. William and Zane exit their cab behind us, and our party reconvenes.

William sidles into me as we enter the hotel lobby. "How do you like Lumenas?"

"I love it." I turn in a circle as we walk, staring at the marble floors, the white-and-gold papered walls, the crystal chandeliers. "Monty went all out when he picked this hotel. This must be the finest hotel in the city."

"You love it, hmm? Is that all it takes for you to fall in love? A single glance?" William's question has me tripping over my own feet. His hand comes to my elbow to help me regain my footing. We pause our steps. He leans in, his body closer to me than it's been since our time alone in his hotel room. "I didn't think you were one to fall in love at first sight."

I recover my wits and give him a haughty look. "That's

because you've only been on the receiving end of my hate at first sight."

His hand still holds my elbow. He brushes his thumb over my sleeve before letting his fingers fall back to his side. A devious glint sparks in his eyes. "That didn't feel like hate when you were pumping my cock."

My heart flips in my chest. Thank heavens our companions are now several feet ahead. I clear my throat before I deliver my answer. "I barely pumped it more than three times if you'll recall. Besides, I was pretending it was your neck."

"Mmm. I might like that."

My cheeks burn hot as we finally rejoin our party. Almost at once, I can tell something is amiss.

"What do you mean there's something wrong with our booking?" Monty says, his tone serious for once. "I made these reservations months ago. I sent a telegram last week to confirm we would need a second room."

I study the stern receptionist. Her skin is covered in glittering green scales and her eyes are aqua blue, devoid of any discernible whites or pupils. She flips through the ledger on her desk. "I don't see any record of your telegram, Mr. Phillips. We sent one as well to confirm but never received a reply."

"What does that mean?" Monty asks. "Do we have at least one room?"

"Oh no." Realization dawns at once, and I give the receptionist a solemn look. "I know what this is. I've written about it. There's only one bed, isn't there?"

"I liked that one," Daphne says, staring up at me from near my feet. "Your attention to detail in that scene was impeccable. I particularly appreciated the emphasis you put on the headboard slamming against the wall and creating hairline fractures in the brick. It really demonstrated—"

"There are *no* beds," the receptionist says. "We've been overbooked due to clerical errors and can only accommodate those who confirmed their booking last week. You'll receive a refund and a voucher for free Lumies from any vendor in the city."

"What are Lumies?" I ask.

Zane answers, their expression brightening. "You must try Lumies. They're delicious."

Monty runs a hand through his pale hair, sending his curls in charming disarray. "Can you transfer our booking to another hotel?"

The receptionist shakes her head. "We can't guarantee vacancy at a comparable hotel. There are several large events this weekend that have attracted even more tourists than we're used to this time of year."

Pride flares in my chest. "You mean like our book signing? Is it such a large event?"

"I'm not aware of a book signing."

"It's called The Heartbeats Tour."

William leans in with an amused grin, blocking my view of the receptionist. "I doubt our little book tour is big enough to be highlighted amongst the massive events occurring this weekend. Have you any idea what caliber of famous musicians and actors perform here?"

I glare, but he's probably right.

"Your ego knows no bounds," he whispers, but there's a softness to his teasing, and his eyes linger on mine for an extra-long beat.

Monty opens his mouth to speak again, but Zane taps him on the shoulder. He turns to face the antlered fae with a questioning glance.

"I've got it covered," Zane says. "I live in this city, remember? You'll stay with me."

CHAPTER TWENTY-SIX

EDWINA

*J*ust when I think we missed out on staying in the finest accommodation in all of Lumenas, Zane's offer makes me eat my words. Their apartment building is several floors higher than the hotel and boasts twice as many chandeliers in the lobby. The walls are painted black with multi-hued sparkles that evoke a likeness to starlight and nebulae. The floors are onyx, and with the chandeliers casting dancing light all around, I feel like I'm walking straight through the night sky as we proceed through the lobby.

"Love at first sight again?" William whispers in my ear. He's stayed near me ever since we left the hotel and navigated the streets to reach Zane's building. Several times he's had to drag me away from sidewalk performers—spectacles I'm expected to openly gawk at, unlike the north wing—lest I get so distracted I lose my party.

I'm too enamored with the building's interior to spare him a glance. "Yes."

We reach the far end of the lobby and I find yet another reason to be impressed. Three open alcoves await, each smaller than a private washroom. A muscular fae stands beside each—a centaur, a fae with gray skin and barrel-shaped legs, and a more humanoid fae with a chest twice as broad as William's, straining the buttons of his fine black-and-white suit. A trio of guests enter one of the alcoves before us, and a silver grate slides shut, followed by a black sliding door. The centaur reaches for a large lever and begins to turn it.

I glance at Zane. "Are those elevators?"

Zane nods and guides us toward the next open alcove over, beside the gray male—an elephant fae perhaps? A rhino? I've only ever seen paintings of such creatures, so what do I know?

We pack ourselves into the elevator, and the grate closes, then the door. The first lurch of motion has me clutching the rail that lines the wall. It creates a sensation in my gut that is nauseating yet thrilling. We don't have elevators in Bretton, and I doubt we have a single building even half this tall, but I've heard of the technology. The fae truly have some impressive advancements. I suppose it makes sense considering they have magic and fae creatures with unique abilities on their side. It's inspiring. Amazing. Incredible. My fingers flinch, craving the notebook I left in my carpet bag with all my other luggage, stored at the station.

Fourteen Ways to Fall in Love with Faerwyvae.

My next just-for-fun illustrated list.

Yearning fills my chest at the thought, cracked open by my awe. It takes me a moment to understand where it's coming from.

Then I realize...

I don't want this feeling to end. I want to see more. Experience more. I want to stay here. To live here in Faerwyvae, and I want it for more reasons than just the publishing contract. This magical, eclectic, and fantastic isle...I think I might belong here. I could thrive off this kind of inspiration.

"Maynard is the fastest elevator operator," Zane says, interrupting my thoughts. "He can get us to the top floor in three minutes."

My mouth falls open. "You live on the top floor?"

"I do, and I suggest you steer clear of Mr. Tibbets if you value your time. He's the operator at the far right. He takes at least five minutes to lift the elevator to my floor."

"I imagine the stairs aren't an option?" Daphne asks, a slight quaver in her voice.

"If you have the stamina," Zane says, "then certainly—oh, dear."

I follow Zane's line of sight to where Daphne is. She's lifted herself on her haunches, her back pressed into one of the corners. Her paws are splayed out on either side of her, and her little chest heaves with short sharp breaths.

Monty crouches beside the pine marten and extends a hand. "Come here, Daph."

Reluctantly, she leaves her corner and lets Monty lift her in his arms. As he stands and cradles her against his chest, she tucks her face into his jacket. After a few moments, she pulls her head back and looks up at him. "You sort of...smell good."

He snorts a laugh. "Why must you sound surprised? I do bathe, you know."

"Could've fooled me," she mutters and shoves her face back in his jacket.

The elevator ride is long indeed, and I must admit its charm wears off by the end. But once the door opens, my awe returns. A wide, luxurious space greets us, with the same glittering black walls and onyx floors that the lobby had. Chandeliers stretch from the ceiling, but none are lit. Instead, the noon sunlight fills the room, shining through the row of enormous windows that comprise the far wall. My gaze shifts to the decor. Several different living areas have been arranged, though no walls divide them, only silk screens or just the layout of the furnishings. There's a gilded fireplace with a tea table and pair of indigo wingback chairs, a dinner table before a wall of painted vases on display, several divans, an enormous gold harp, and a glossy black pianoforte.

"Welcome to my home," Zane says, strolling to the center of the space with their arms out wide.

I think my eyes might fall out of my head. "This whole place is your apartment?"

"Yes, and I should confess something now since you brought it up earlier. There is only one bed."

"I knew it," I say under my breath, and my eyes briefly dart to William at my periphery.

Zane chuckles. "But I have plenty of couches, cots, and blankets. Make yourselves at home. Eat. Relax. Rest. Then tonight, I'll show you my city."

AFTER EVENING FALLS, I CAN HARDLY TEAR MY GAZE AWAY from the view outside Zane's windows. Our surroundings are aglow with electric bulbs, bright marquees, and the light from neighboring buildings. The streets far below are even busier than they were during the day, swarming with pedestrians, performers, and coaches.

Zane sidles up next to me. "That's Halley Street, the

busiest and most chaotic street in Lumenas. The most famous theaters on the isle are just a few blocks away."

No wonder it's so vibrant here. "That's incredible."

"Ready to see it for yourself?" they ask. "Once everyone wakes up, that is."

I cast a glance at where our companions doze on the furniture around us. Monty is slouched in one of the chairs by the fire while William naps on a divan, hands laced on his chest, a book covering his face. Daphne is…somewhere. My grin spreads wide as I return my attention to Zane. "I can't wait."

"I already know where we should go, but…" Zane assesses my attire through slitted lids. I shrink a little under their scrutiny, as I don't look nearly as impressive as them. Zane is outfitted in wide-legged slacks and another flowing robe-style top—red silk this time, decorated with white cherry blossoms that are so delicate they must be hand-painted. Matching blossoms twine around their antlers and weave through their russet waves. A spattering of glitter adorns their cheeks, dancing with their pale freckles.

Meanwhile, I'm dressed in a simple blouse and walking skirt. I changed from my travel attire after washing up in the largest, most luxurious bathtub I've ever had the pleasure of using, but I haven't done anything else to enhance my appearance. No cosmetics. No fancy updo.

Zane winks. "Come with me."

I follow them from the wall of windows. I take only a few steps before Daphne drops from the ceiling, nearly startling me out of my wits. Was she napping in one of the chandeliers?

"What are you up to?" she asks, stretching her front legs with a yawn, her curved back arching toward the sky.

"You can come too," Zane says, waving us forward.

We enter the bedroom area, partitioned by tall screens.

Past the bed, vanity, and dressing table, are another set of screens. Beyond them stand several racks filled with an array of clothing in every color I could imagine. Everything from ballgowns to frock coats to articles I have no name for hang from the racks. My eyes snag on glittering gold sequins, iridescent silks, impossibly fine lace, and gorgeous brocade.

Daphne darts from rack to rack. "Are these for your performances?"

"Some of them," Zane says, approaching a rack with the most varied collection of articles. "Others are gifts from designers. They send them to me, hoping I'll wear them to an event or performance."

I join Zane at the rack as they lift a slim black dress covered entirely in fringe.

They hold it up toward me as if imagining it on my figure. With a shake of their head, they return the article to the rack. "Some of the ensembles don't fit me. Antlers, you know."

I assess Zane's clothing with fresh eyes. No wonder they favor the robe style with sashes or other frontal closures. I never considered how difficult it might be to get dressed with antlers.

Zane lifts the hem of their trousers, revealing toned calves that end in hooves. "I don't wear shoes either, and yet…"

They stroll to a wall beside one of the racks and pull a crystalline knob. A drawer slides from the wall, filled with leather oxfords. Then they pull another drawer out from beneath it, this one filled with silk dancing slippers. Another contains low-heeled, lace-up ankle boots like I favor.

Daphne hops into the drawer of dancing slippers and assesses a pair in yellow silk adorned with pink roses. "Designers just give you these without considering whether you can wear them?"

With a wry grin, Zane shrugs. "I think they just want an excuse to gift me things. If I like their style, I commission custom clothing from them later, so it's a win-win. It also provides me with ample gifts to send my friends home with whenever I have guests."

I'm still marveling over Zane's hooves. "May I ask…is this your seelie form or unseelie form?"

"Seelie," Zane says as they return to the rack of varied clothing and rifle through the articles again. "I'm a deer in my unseelie form. I only take that form when I visit extended family who live in the forest, though."

Zane pauses over a cream lace gown, then removes its hanger from the rack. The style favors fae conventions, with loose lines, a dropped waist, and what appears to be an open back. They hold it out for me and angle their head toward one of the free-standing dressing screens around us. "Try this on."

I blink at them, then at the gown. "You…want me to wear that?"

"And if you like it, keep it."

I wave my hands. "I couldn't."

"You can. It's going to waste here. Think of it as payment for staying at my place."

My lips quirk. "You want me to take a dress from you…as payment for staying at your place."

Their grin widens. "Correct. Trust me, in that dress, you'll fit right in once we're out on the town. You'll regret it if you wear what you're wearing now." There's no taunting or judgment in their tone, which makes me believe they might be right.

My gaze drops back to the gown. Even at a glance, I know the lace is finer than any I've worn, and my earlier yearning returns. I want to know what it feels like to wear something so elegant. So different from the style I normally favor. Slowly, I reach for it. "If you insist."

"I do," Zane says, shoving the hanger into my hand and practically forcing me behind the screen. As I begin to undress, Zane adds to Daphne, "You can try something on too. Do you like that yellow silk?"

Daphne's monotone replies with a wary, "Kind of."

"Here, take that behind the other screen."

I'm curious what Zane sent Daphne away with. Do they have anything small enough to fit the pine marten? How adorable would that be?

I manage to change into the lace gown all on my own. With its open back, it's obviously meant to be worn sans corset. That gives me some pause, though it won't be the first time I've gone without a corset in public since arriving in Faerwyvae. I wore nothing but my chemise as a top when we arrived in the Solar Court, after all. This, at least, was meant to be worn this way.

Once dressed, I emerge from behind the screen. Zane brings their hands together, beaming at me. They take me by the shoulders and angle me toward a mirror. "I knew it would be perfect."

I worry my lip as I assess my reflection. The dress is every inch the gorgeous confection I thought it to be on the hanger, and seeing it grace my figure makes me equal parts anxious and elated. It does suit me well, the cream lace complementing my blushing complexion and auburn hair. Even my spectacles manage not to look out of place, as the dress' unique features and flared hem draw the eye most. The front of the gown boasts a high neck, like the everyday blouses I wear, but my shoulders are bare. I shift to the side, where the gown takes another departure from the norm, the sides dropping away to reveal bare flesh. The front is wide enough to drape elegantly over my small breasts, but the sides show off the barest curve. It's a play on cleavage I've never seen before—side cleavage.

I turn further around to assess my back and nearly blanch. The high neck of the gown ties at my nape, but there's nothing beneath that aside from the trailing ends of the bow until my waist.

I dart a glance at Zane. "Am I showing too much skin? Is it perhaps missing a portion?"

"No," they say, unable to hide their laughter. "That's how it's supposed to be worn. Don't fret. You look incredible."

I smooth the front of the dress, then give my shoulders a shake. Thankfully, everything stays in place.

Footsteps sound behind me, and I turn—

A yelp leaves my lips as an unfamiliar female strides out from behind the other dressing screen. She freezes at my reaction, her shoulders rising to her ears. She's not much taller than me with shoulder-length black hair, dark eyes, and a tan complexion. Then I see the gown she's wearing, one of yellow silk with pink-and-white flowers. The top half is modest and bordering on plain, with cap sleeves, an empire waist, and a straight neckline. It reminds me of fashions from the last decade, a style still popular in Bretton. Then the bottom half ends above her knees, spreading out wide with layers upon layers of cream lace beneath the yellow skirt. This would be a shocking sight, for one rarely shows their legs in public—certainly not back home in Bretton—if I wasn't starting to understand who I'm looking at.

I take in her hunched posture, the curl of her fingers that she holds near her waist as if she doesn't know what to do with them.

"Daphne?" Her name comes out with a gasp. "Is...is that your seelie form?"

She grimaces. "Yeah." It's the first time I've heard her

words while seeing her mouth move. In her pine marten form, her voice simply emanates from her.

I assess her all over again, admiring the points of her ears, her dark eyes, and her long black lashes. Unlike Zane, Daphne's humanoid form reveals no hint of her animal manifestation. She looks slightly younger than me, but with fae aging the way it is, she could be older. I resist the urge to ask—because even I can hold my tongue for the sake of not being rude—and instead say, "You're stunning."

Another grimace, then a sigh. "Yeah."

"You don't seem to think that's a compliment," Zane says, tone curious.

Daphne shifts from foot to foot. "I haven't taken this form often, and when I do…well, people expect things of me. Poise. Accomplishments. They usually end up disappointed."

My heart sinks. I know how that feels. I too have disappointed people who had high expectations of me. The most painful time was with a man who thought he loved me. In my case, it was my looks that disappointed him, after my words on a page painted a much prettier picture.

Daphne wrings her hands, then shakes her head. "I'm not going out tonight." A shudder rips through her, and the next thing I know, her humanoid form is gone, replaced with the pine marten. Then, just as fast, she returns to her seelie form. She clasps her hands in an apologetic gesture as she faces Zane. "Oh, sorry! I'll change first."

"Keep it," Zane says. "You don't have to wear it tonight or go out with us if you don't want to, but please take the dress. It suits you."

Daphne wrings her hands again. "All right." She shrinks back down to her unseelie form and darts away.

I watch her every move, marveling that I've witnessed a fae shifting between her two forms before my very eyes. And her clothing remained in place on her seelie form without

239

affecting her unseelie form. What a delight to witness firsthand!

Daphne slips from view, but she's replaced with a new figure. William halts and whirls in place, staring after a scurrying Daphne, before proceeding forward. "Z, are you in—"

He pulls up short as his eyes fall on us. They settle on me, sweeping from my head to my feet and back again. His throat bobs, and it seems to take great effort for him to speak. "Are…we…uh, leaving soon?"

Zane purses their lips but doesn't successfully hide their grin. "We are. Is Monty awake?"

"He's already gone." William's attention is on his cufflinks, the buttons of his dark gray suit not fully fastened, but his eyes keep flashing to me.

I try to maintain an innocent expression, though triumph sizzles in my chest. So, he likes my new dress.

"Gone?" Zane echoes.

"He said something about a boxing match."

"He did mention that earlier," I say.

"It will be us four," William says.

"Three," I correct. "Daphne doesn't want to go out tonight."

William shrugs. "That's fine—"

"Two, actually," Zane says. "I'm not going either."

William and I shift our eyes to them.

Again, Zane tries to hide their grin, but it's no use. "Turns out…there's this thing."

William levels a knowing look at his friend. "A thing?"

"A thing. But you know where to take her, right? You two have fun."

"We were supposed to all go together."

Zane strolls past us with an exaggerated shrug. "Yes, but…there's this thing. And…look at the time. I simply must be off."

William scowls at their back. "I know you're up to no good when the only true thing you can say is *there's this thing.*"

"There's this thing," Zane says again, their voice farther away now. I can't see them beyond the partitions around the dressing area, but I imagine they must be near the elevator doors. "Have fun!"

William heaves an aggrieved sigh, then turns to face me. His expression softens as his eyes meet mine. "Looks like it's just you and me," he says, voice low.

"Looks like."

He angles his head away from the dressing area and his lips curl in a sideways smile. "Shall we?"

CHAPTER TWENTY-SEVEN

WILLIAM

I try not to show just how elated I am to be left alone with Edwina tonight. And in that fucking dress. Bless my luck. Bless Zane. Maybe bless Monty too. I'm starting to suspect they conspired against us yet again. Or are they conspiring *for* us? Whatever the case, it takes all my restraint not to outright stare as we ride the elevator down to the lobby, but I still manage to drink my fill whenever she isn't looking.

Blooming hell, this is the first time I've seen her in anything like this. Even the dress she wore to Somerton House was in the human style, modest compared to the expanse of flesh on display behind her, the way the cream lace hugs the curve of her ass before flaring slightly at the knee. Don't get me started on the front. The sides. I'm equally as turned on by what the lace hides as by what it reveals. Peaks, valleys, the barest curve of her outer breasts.

She cuts a glower my way, and I realize I've been staring. "What?"

I resist the urge to avert my gaze and instead assess her while she's looking this time. Her hair is styled in its usual updo, loose wild tendrils already escaping to brush her shoulders. I reach for one of the strands and tuck it behind her ear. "You look nice."

Her eyes widen behind her lenses, and a flush creeps from her neck to her cheeks. She nudges her spectacles and quickly fixes her attention on the closed door of the elevator. "Thank you."

I tuck my hands in my pockets to keep from touching her again. What I wouldn't give to reach for that tie at the back of her neck and tug it loose. My trousers tighten at the thought, and it's all I can do to remind myself we have plans. Important ones.

Outside the apartment, the noise of Halley Street crashes around us. Horse hooves, carriage wheels, chatter, music. We immediately get swept up in the flow of the crowd. I clasp Edwina's gloved hand as a figure tries to step between us, tugging her close to my side and forcing the pedestrian to go around. "Let's stay together," I say over the noise.

I keep her hand in mine as we navigate Halley to the next corner. As we turn down the cross street, the chaos is cut in half. It's still loud and crowded and packed with pedestrians and performers, but it's easier to walk without getting separated.

Yet I don't give Edwina back her hand.

She doesn't seem to mind, as her attention is more on our surroundings. Her eyes constantly bounce from the buildings to the storefronts, jugglers, musicians, sword-swallowers—there's so much to see and she marvels at every sight. I'm almost certain my hand around hers is all that keeps her from getting swept away and stolen by her own awe.

After a few more blocks, the bustle dies down further, and I catch sight of the sign I've been looking for: Orion Street.

"We're almost there," I say, giving her palm a squeeze as we turn down Orion.

She finally pulls her gaze from our surroundings to look up at me. "You still haven't told me where we're going."

"That's because it's a surprise. But trust me. You'll like it."

She's back to staring at lights and people, which is good because I don't want her to see the small A-frame sign outside the building just ahead. I shift so I'm in front of her, blocking the sign as we stop outside the midnight blue façade of a theater called Vulture's Prose.

"We're here." I release her hand and open the door for her. As she enters ahead of me, I'm graced with another delicious view of her bare back. Blooming hell.

We enter the narrow foyer and are greeted by a ticket taker. I retrieve two tickets from my waistcoat pocket and hand them over. The young man bows and gestures for us to proceed. The theater is small and quaint, so there's no grand lobby, no extravagant auditorium. Instead, we enter a wide space with several rows of chairs and a modest stage at the far end.

An usher guides us to our seats—front row, thanks to Zane. Most of the seats have already been claimed, as we're only minutes away from curtain. We're cutting it close, but I didn't want to arrive too early lest Edwina overhear what play we're about to see. I really do want this to be a surprise.

The stragglers fill the remaining seats in the audience, and whispers of excitement spread as we wait for the curtain to rise. Nostalgia falls over me. Vulture's Prose reminds me of the kinds of theaters I spent my youth in. The kinds of theaters my mother, Lydia, preferred to perform in, often in this very city. I preferred them too, as a child, for everyone seemed like family. The actors would let Cassie and me try on costumes and wigs. It's where I fell in love with acting myself.

If only I'd stayed in settings like these. With Lydia. With Cassie. If only I hadn't strayed so far to attend university.

Then maybe Lydia would still be alive.

The curtain finally shifts, and a fae male with aqua hair and a top hat emerges. With a flourish of his hand, he says, "Vulture's Prose proudly presents *The Governess and the Rake*."

Edwina sucks in a breath, sitting forward in her seat. As the curtain parts, she swivels to face me. Her eyes glisten beneath the glittering stage lights. "Will."

My heart cracks at the sound of my name. The name only those closest to me use. Does she even know? Is she so overwhelmed that she hasn't realized she's shortened my name? Does she have any idea how much it makes me want to fucking kiss her and taste that name on her lips? My truest identity. The stripped-down version of me that isn't playing a part.

I give her a taste of what she gave me—her truest name without games, without teasing. "Edwina," I say back.

"Is this really what I think it is?" she whispers.

I shift in my seat, angling myself closer to her. "It is. And more."

She turns her gaze back to the stage as a young woman with short black hair is lowered on an aerial hoop. She's dressed in a white leotard with a short silk skirt. The first strains of music begin, and a blonde woman in a bland gray gown steps onto the stage beneath the aerialist. Her trilling voice sings the opening lines of *The Governess and the Rake*, while the aerialist moves and sways on her lyra, her languid motions evoking the somber tone of the first chapter.

Edwina glances at me again. "It's a musical."

"A burlesque musical."

She furrows her brow and I wonder if she's heard of burlesque in Bretton. It might be too racy for society there. Yet I've learned enough about Edwina to know it won't be too racy for her. She's going to swoon once the performers start shedding layers of clothing, though it won't happen until later in the play.

Excitement dances in her eyes as she faces the stage again. After the opening musical number, the aerialist descends from the lyra and flounces off stage left.

The next scene is a more traditional performance and sets up the first meeting between Dolly and Alexander. The following is another musical number paired with an artistic, seductive dance between two figures representing the couple.

Edwina relishes every moment, her eyes glued to the stage, her lips tilted in a permanent smile. I'm glad she's enjoying herself. This version of *The Governess and the Rake* may not be the kind of grand production normally hosted at one of the larger theaters, but it doesn't make it any less worthy or impressive. You can hear the passion in every song, see it in every move the dancers make. The acting is exaggerated and dramatic, and the burlesque elements enhance the source material without making a parody of it.

I find myself leaning closer and closer to Edwina. Finally, our shoulders touch. She offers me a soft smile before returning her gaze to the chorus line that shimmies and sways behind Dolly as she reaches her pivotal moment where she deems herself worthy of Alexander's love. She sheds layers of silk, lace, and feathered boas until a form-hugging dress remains, sheer scarlet silk bedecked with crystals.

Edwina's mouth falls open and a single tear slides down her cheek, catching the light from the stage. I lean ever closer and brush my gloved hand over the tear, gathering it on my fingertip. Her lashes flutter as she leans slightly into my touch, though her gaze remains fixed on Dolly's dance. I lower my palm and place it between us.

Edwina's hand leaves her lap at the same moment and lands on mine. She flinches, and I expect her to pull away.

She doesn't.

My pulse quickens. With bated breath, I turn my wrist. There's a chance the movement will make her retreat, but I take that gamble, turning my palm over until it's fully beneath hers. She spreads out her fingers, and I freeze, wondering if this is the moment she pulls away. Instead, her fingers lace through mine. I release a slow sigh, my mouth curving as I more securely take her hand.

With her warmth against my palm, her fingers tangled in mine, I can hardly focus on the play, even when Dolly slides off her dress to reveal her flimsy glittering underthings as her empowering number comes to an end. All I can think of is Edwina. Even with gloves between us, our touching palms steal every inch of my awareness. This is different from when I held her hand on the way here, pulling her from distractions. It's different from when I did the same to take her out of the north wing.

I don't know how it feels for Edwina, or if she's even aware of what we're doing. For all I know, she's simply using me to anchor her emotions.

Isn't that what I'm here for though?

I'm the one who told her to use me.

AFTER THE PLAY CONCLUDES, I TAKE EDWINA BACKSTAGE TO meet the cast. They greet her with delighted squeals, and several ask for her autograph. It's incredible how Edwina can so easily come out of her shell in certain situations. Sometimes she seems so unsure of herself, so reserved. Other times, she chatters nonstop without a care in the world. Though I've learned if there's anything that can summon Edwina's charisma, it's talking about her books.

When we finally leave Vulture's Prose, the streets are far quieter than they were before. Edwina, on the other hand, won't stop talking. I don't mind it. She prattles on about her favorite scenes, her favorite musical numbers. We take our time heading back toward Zane's apartment, keeping to the calmer backroads, and I listen to her every word with an idiotic grin on my face.

We're a few blocks away from our destination when I take a short detour to a food vendor. Scents of fried dough, sugar, and cardamom fill the air as I exchange a handful of citrine chips for two bags of Star Court's most famous confection. I hand one to Edwina.

"What are these?" she asks.

"Lumies."

She reaches into the bag and extracts one of the round pastries. "Are these what Zane was talking about?"

"The very thing."

She beams and pops the pastry between her lips. A muffled moan follows. "Oh, these are good," she says with a full mouth.

I watch those lips, dusted with loose sugar, as I devour my own pastry. I'm almost of a mind to buy ten more bags just for an excuse to linger. Once we return to Zane's place, we won't be alone anymore.

Yet the end of our night is inevitable, and once we finish our confections, we resume our walk. I keep my pace purposefully slow.

"Ah, I can't stop thinking about the sex scene," she says

with a wistful sigh for probably the hundredth time. "It was phenomenal, wasn't it? They barely even touched, yet the striptease and the dance spoke volumes. And did you see her breasts? They were as perky as two pyramids. What a lovely shape."

"You seem to have a fondness for breasts."

She shrugs. "Why wouldn't I? They're stunning, in all shapes and sizes. Maybe it's because mine are so small that I have such an appreciation for their variety. Though sometimes I wish mine were larger." She mutters the last part under her breath as she glances down at her chest.

Maybe I'm scum, but my eyes fall there too, landing on the sliver of skin between her lower ribs and the front of her dress. That delectable curve. She has no reason to wish her breasts were anything but what they are. They're fucking perfect.

Her gaze whips to mine and I freeze. Shit. She caught me ogling her.

She narrows her eyes, a taunting smile lifting her lips. "Were you—"

"I like small peaks," I rush to say. At the last moment, I add, "Of meringue."

Her mouth snaps shut. "Pardon?"

I blink at her. Why the hell did I even say that? I clear my throat. "I...I'm ready to give Monty my answer. About his... dessert query."

"I see." A furrow knits her brow, but she doesn't ask me to elaborate. We resume walking. "I just remembered! Did you know Daphne has a seelie form?"

I heave a breath of relief but turn it into a laugh. Thank the All of All her mind has already darted to another topic. "Most fae do, Weenie."

"Yes, but hers is stunning." She lowers her voice when she says this, as if it's a secret.

"You actually saw her in her seelie form?"

She nods. "Today, while we were getting ready. She's quite cute, but she doesn't seem comfortable about that. That reminds me of something else. What kind of fae are you, William? Do you have an unseelie form?"

I hesitate before I answer, and when I do, I draw out the word like a question. "Yes?"

She halts, hands on her hips. "That's not a full answer. I asked you two questions. What kind of fae are you?"

I mutter a groan and lean against the nearby building to free up space for any fellow pedestrians who might stroll by. There aren't many others around us, as most of the after-hours nightlife is reserved for Halley Street, which glows from just ahead. "Must I?"

My reluctance only intrigues her. "I'm too curious not to know. All you said about it before is that you're not a useful kind of fae. So what kind are you? If you tell me your secret, I'll tell you one of mine."

Begrudgingly, I remove my gloves and tuck them into my jacket pocket. Then I hold out one hand, palm up.

She frowns, eyes flicking from me to my open palm. "What are you..."

"Just watch." I focus my attention on my palm, on the tingling that starts at the center. The tingling grows, spreading into a comfortable warmth that fills every inch of my palm. I narrow my focus further, willing my fae magic to respond. Obey. Create.

Finally, a single pink petal sprouts from the center of my hand.

Edwina gasps.

Another petal forms. Then another. Soon my palm is filled with a pink peony, its petals unfurling in the delicate night breeze.

I hand it to Edwina and she cradles it in both hands.

"I'm a flower fae," I say without enthusiasm.

She studies the flower with wide eyes before lifting her gaze to me. Her mouth parts, but whatever she was about to say turns into a startled squeak. She blinks several times as she takes in my visage. Or, more specifically, the pink petals that line my eyelids.

"This is my unseelie form," I say, tone flat.

Her gaze finally leaves my face to scan down to my toes then up the length of me. When her eyes return to mine, she arches a questioning brow.

"That's all," I say with a shrug. "My birth mother was a flower sprite, but I didn't inherit much from her or my father. Not every fae can shift fully into another form, especially those like me, born in later generations, closer to the isle's unification when the magic began to change. All I've ever been able to do is make flowers and conjure pretty lashes." I blink, and the weight of petals shifts to the fine hairs I'm used to.

"Why do you seem ashamed?" she asks. "Why don't you like talking about your unseelie form?"

"Like I said, it's not very useful. Other fae actors have unseelie forms or fae magic that contribute to their roles. My biggest contribution was as Gardener Number Three."

"That's why you were cast as Gardener Number Three?"

I release a mirthless chuckle. "It's probably the only reason I retained a part in the play at all."

"It's nothing to be ashamed of. Human actors don't have anything but their own talents to recommend them to a role. And I wouldn't call *this* useless." She drops her gaze back to the flower.

My heart thuds heavily in my chest as I watch her admiring my work. My secret. What I don't want to tell her is that I haven't made many flowers since Lydia died. Lydia may not have been my birth mother—in truth, I have no memories of the flower sprite I was born to—but she was my truest mother. And she was Cassie's mother. We were a family despite our lack of blood relation. We should have stayed a family. But Lydia grew ill while I was at university. By the time I returned home, she was at death's door. There was nothing I could do. Nothing but make her flowers. Useless, beautiful flowers that put a smile on her face but did nothing to prevent her passing.

Edwina's head whips back up, eyes narrowed. Her voice takes on an accusing tone. "Is this where the flower petals have been coming from?"

I blink my darker thoughts away and relish the distraction. My lips curl. "Whatever could you mean?"

"You keep putting flower petals in that damn book of yours. One time I opened it and had an entire lapful of pink petals fall all over my skirt."

I can't help but laugh at her chagrin.

"Does that also explain why you're so quiet when you move? How you've been able to sneak up on me a few times?"

I shrug. "Flowers are quiet."

She gives me a curious once over before she returns to studying the flower. "What is this even made of?"

"Fae magic," I say.

"Yes, but how? Is it made from your skin? Does it grow out of your body? Do you shed petals like waste material?" With a gasp, she looks up at me again. "Is this poop?"

I nearly choke on my own laughter. "I just made you a beautiful flower, and you have the nerve to ask if it's poop?"

Her smile is so coy I want to kiss it off her face. "Well, is it?"

"No, Ed." I push off the wall and resume walking toward Halley Street, my cheeks pained from the smile I can't seem to banish. I shake my head. "*Is it poop*, she asks. You know, the fae don't seek to explain everything with science. We just call it magic."

She strolls at my side, then tucks the flower in the loose bun at the top of her head. "I suppose I wouldn't want to know if it's poop anyway. Now that it's in my hair."

I snort another laugh. "What am I going to do with you? Blooming weirdo."

CHAPTER TWENTY-EIGHT

EDWINA

I know I've acknowledged this before, but William's smile is a work of art. I've seen it quite a bit the last few days as I've watched his genuine interactions with Zane, but this time, it's just for me. It's never looked brighter. I'm so dazzled by it that I don't notice he's taken us down a detour until I realize I no longer see the blaring lights of Halley Street just ahead. The street we're on now is livelier than the ones we strolled down on our way from the theater, but not so lively as Halley. Only half the establishments are open this late, most of which appear to be vapor houses or pubs. The stragglers on the sidewalk are either stumbling to their next haunt or smoking and chatting outside their place of enjoyment. Of course, there are a few pairs like William and me, who seem to be on their way back home.

"Weren't we almost there?" I ask. "Why did we turn down this street?"

"We're not done talking yet," he says, his smile still

twisting his lips. The green glow illuminating the sign of a nearby vapor house catches on the silver jewelry in his pointed ears. "You owe me a secret."

I wince. I may have offered him that trade but I didn't have a secret in mind. "I think you know my darkest secret."

He smirks. "Oh, you mean how you haven't done literally every sexual position and activity you've written about? That's not a secret, love. Anyone who expects that of you should reassess their relationship with reality."

My heart stutters when he calls me *love*. It's not the first time he's called me that, and I've never thought twice about it. He calls other women *love* too. But with that smile on his face, his casual tone of voice, and the evening we've enjoyed thus far, it strikes me in a different way. I force my focus back to what he said. "Jolene expected that of me."

"Yes, well, Jolene is gullible." There's no warmth on his face when he mentions the woman he kissed and spent a night with. It may have been a platonic night, but Jolene was moved by it nonetheless. He told her about June, someone he still hasn't brought up even once with me.

I clench my jaw to keep from asking about this great love of his. It's my turn to share a secret, not his. Maybe after I've shared something personal, I can get him to agree to another trade. Eager to get my part done with, I say, "Ask me anything."

He lifts his chin and assesses me from under his lashes. "Anything?"

"Anything reasonable," I amend.

He tucks his hands in his pockets and tilts his head in thought. Then he meets my eyes in an almost bashful way. "Have you ever been in love?"

My cheeks burn at the question. I'm almost of a mind to tell him that's too personal but I suppose it isn't. I bite the inside of my cheek before answering. "I thought I was in love once."

William's gaze burns into me, and I can tell he wants me to elucidate. Still, he doesn't pry. Maybe that's what makes me want to tell him more.

"It was during my college days," I say. "I won an award for a short story, which resulted in its publication in one of the biggest papers in Bretton. This was before I found my passion for writing romance, so the story wasn't sensational. It was more of an imitation of the great writers we were encouraged to evoke in my college writing program. Somehow it was impressive enough to win an award, publication, and the admiration of a young man named Dennis Feverforth."

"I already don't like him," William says, teasing in his tone.

That helps ease the tightening in my chest. "Dennis was so enamored with my writing that he sought me out by way of letter, going so far as to procure my address at college. I was honored to attract such a dedicated admirer, so I wrote him back. After that, we began a friendly correspondence. One that soon turned romantic. He professed to have fallen in love with me through my words. The things he said to me, the way he truly seemed to read into my very soul, convinced me that was true. I started to fall for him in turn, and for the first time, I got to experience the whirlwind romance many of my peers had already had."

"Were you never courted before that?"

I shake my head. "I've been late to everything, it seems. I debuted in society years later than most girls. People were already calling me a spinster by then. My first social season was so horrendous, I refused to participate ever again. That's when I set my mind to furthering my education. I had no proclivity for matrimony and still don't. Dennis was the only exception. After I fell in love with him, marriage and romance were all I could think of. I couldn't write. I could hardly sleep. I just wanted more. More sweet letters. More professions of love. Most of all, I wanted to meet him in person."

"Did you?"

A heavy sigh escapes my lips. "Eventually, yes. He lived on the other side of the country, but he was just as desperate to meet me as I was him. We set a date and exchanged letters daily. He wrote about all the things we'd do together, the way he'd sweep me in his arms and pepper me with kisses. I'd never been so excited in my life. The world looked brighter. My heart was constantly flipping. My grades suffered, as did my writing, but I thought it would be worth it. Maybe I'd soon be married and would no longer be interested in a career. Maybe I'd want to run a household like my married sisters did. Like my parents wanted me to."

William furrows his brow. Even he can tell where my story is going. "What happened?"

"We met," I say, my voice cracking slightly. "Turns out, my words are more beautiful than I am."

Silence falls in the wake of my confession, and it takes me a few moments to realize William is no longer at my side. I halt and find him stopped several feet back, an agonized look on his face. Then his expression hardens. "Explain."

I'm startled by his reaction, by the curl of his fists, the hard set of his shoulders. I can't bring myself to meet his eyes. "He took one look at me, and...and there was nothing but disappointment on his face. We'd exchanged portraits, but..."

My words get lost in the tightness in my throat. I still remember the way Dennis looked at me. The way he pulled his chin back. The way his smile turned into a grimace. I shared some of his disappointment, for it was one thing to stare at a man's unmoving portrait and another to see him animated, expressive. To hear his voice, so stilted compared to the lovely flow of his pen. So nasally when I'd imagined a rich baritone.

I clear my throat. "We proceeded with an incredibly awkward date, and we even spent the night together. That was the end of it. He never contacted me again. Never renewed his confessions of ardor. It was over, and I wasn't even heartbroken. Not really. It felt more like waking up from a dream. The love I thought I felt wasn't real, and I was almost relieved. I shifted my focus back to my studies, my writing, and I never looked back. Ever since, I've vowed to put my words first, for he was right. My words are more beautiful than me, and I'm all right with that. My words deserve all my time and—"

"No." William runs a hand over his face, rubbing his jaw before he locks eyes with me, expression brimming with agony once more. "Edwina, no. Please tell me you don't truly believe that."

I wave my hands in a reassuring gesture. "I'm really all right with it. It's just the truth and one I can handle. I love my career—"

"Edwina." The sound of my name, so harsh on his lips, silences me. He strides up to me, anger flashing in his eyes. "Don't say another idiotic word and listen. I'm only going to say this once."

He's so close I have to angle my head to meet his eyes. I swallow hard and give him a nod.

"You are beautiful," he says, voice deep and melodic. "Your words are beautiful. There is no *this is more beautiful than that* when it comes to you. Your beauty and the beauty of your work are separate entities. Dennis fucking Feverforth was an idiot. He put you on a pedestal. He didn't deserve the eyes he assessed you with or the heart he professed to love you with if he couldn't separate himself from the fantasy he built around you and take you for the prize you are."

His chest heaves as if he couldn't release the words fast enough. Meanwhile, I'm frozen in place, reeling.

I blink at him. Once. Twice.

A blaze of heat melts over my cheeks. I shake my head. "You...you called my words smut and drivel."

He throws his head back with a heavy sigh before returning his gaze to me. "I didn't mean it," he whispers. "It was a wicked thing to say, but it was more of an act. You must know by now that I present a specific persona to my readers."

I have noticed, and I've liked seeing more and more of the real him recently. Still...

"You said the words, William. If you can't lie, then it must have been true at the time."

"Technically, I stated no direct lie."

I open my mouth to argue, but as I think back to our first meeting, I realize he's right. He didn't outright say he disliked *The Governess and the Fae*, even though he did insult it with his flippant attitude and harsh words. Fae are famous for their deception, and an indirect insult he didn't mean doesn't count as a lie. While I'm annoyed he finds it pertinent to put on an act around his fans, I can't say I'm any better. I'm the one who pretended to be an expert seductress, and that wasn't a matter of deception. My lie was outright.

He steps closer, pulling me from my thoughts. "I like your books, Edwina Danforth."

Nothing could have shocked me more. The way he stated those words...

He nods as if reading my mind. "I couldn't say that if it wasn't true. I like your books and your words and your passion for your writing. While I may have resented you for a while, as I associated you with my horrible experience in the play, I don't feel that way now. I don't resent you at all. Weenie, I—"

My heart thuds against my ribs as I wait for him to finish that sentence. His gaze is so intense I don't know if I want to shrink away from it or bask in it forever. The silence that stretches on in the wake of his unfinished statement grows heavier with every breath. His shoulders are tense, his fingers curling and uncurling at his sides as his blue irises dart from my eyes to my lips, then down the length of me. His fingers flinch again.

Does he...want to reach for me? Touch me? Or am I reading too much into this?

Finally, he moves, slipping his hand effortlessly into mine. I'm almost disappointed when all he says is, "Let's go home."

We reach the lobby of Zane's apartment building, and William releases my hand. He approaches the elevator operator at the far right and passes him something. Currency, perhaps. I frown as I follow William into the elevator. Isn't this the operator Zane warned us about? Mr. Tibbets, the slowest?

My legs are tired after so much walking, so I lean against the rail on one of the side walls. William leans against the opposite wall, and the elevator door closes. He holds my gaze, running a thumb over his bottom lip as the lift begins to move. We haven't exchanged a word since he took my hand, yet the air between us remains taut and heavy, as if whatever he left unsaid back then continues to plague him now.

Meanwhile, I'm stuck on the things he *did* say.

William called me beautiful.

He called *me* beautiful. My work too.

My lips curl at the corners.

He arches a brow. "What are you grinning about?"

I shrug. "You're not the worst after all, William. In fact, it sort of feels like we're becoming friends, don't you think?"

"That's where you're wrong." He pushes off the wall and saunters toward me. He doesn't stop until only inches separate us. "A friend wouldn't want to do the kinds of things I want to do with you."

My breath hitches. That intensity has returned to his eyes along with no small amount of hunger. He leans forward, eyes never leaving mine, and slides his hands down my hips until they reach my thighs. Then, in a sudden movement, he hefts me up, props my bottom on the rail behind me, and steps between my legs.

He brings his lips close to mine. "Free pass."

CHAPTER TWENTY-NINE

EDWINA

*M*y breaths come out sharp and jagged as my hands land on his chest. Inch by inch my skirt rises higher all on its own, hiking up my thighs as William steps in even closer. I press my back firmer against the elevator wall. My legs have nowhere else to go but around his hips.

His words hang between us.

Free pass.

"You can't use it here," I say, voice breathless. I'm not even sure why I'm arguing. Either my rational mind is overriding the desire tingling in my lips and core, or my wicked side is trying to delay William's gratification. "This is neither of our bedrooms."

"I'm adding a new rule." Now that my legs are locked around his hips, he's dropped his hands to the railing on either side of me, as if to keep himself from touching me more until I agree to let him. "The free pass can be redeemed in *any* private space, so long as it is after ten in the evening."

His heart slams against my palm, even through the thick brocade of his waistcoat. I lick my lips, a movement he follows with his eyes. "What if the elevator operator stops to let someone else on? This is quite the compromising position."

He leans in and drags his nose up the side of my face, then along my jaw. His hot breath has my lashes fluttering. "He won't," he says into the crook of my neck. "I gave him five citrine rounds to stop for no one."

Five rounds? A single citrine round is worth ten chips. I tilt my head back, allowing him to burrow deeper against my neck. He still hasn't kissed me, only grazed his nose and lips over my flesh. One of my hands moves up his chest to rest at his nape. My words become infused with a breathy whine. "You paid Mr. Tibbets to get me alone?"

He pulls back to hold my gaze, his mouth quirking at one corner. "We have at least five minutes if he takes us at his usual pace, but I told him to take his time. I intend to use every minute wisely. Now, do you agree to my new rule?"

My natural instinct is to argue more, but for once I don't want to. I have no desire to delay his gratification. The heat searing between my legs tells me I'd only be delaying mine.

Which leaves me with only one answer I can give. "Yes."

His lips crash into mine, and I part my mouth for him. My legs tighten around his hips as his tongue sweeps into my mouth in a welcome caress. He brings one hand to my cheek while the other skates up my bare side. I arch against him as his hand moves higher, grazing my ribs. He tucks his thumb beneath the front of my bodice, then traces the outer curve of my breast. Heat burns at the apex of my thighs, and I squeeze him tighter with my legs, desperate for some friction. Too many folds of my lace skirt remain between us, giving me only the slightest relief when I rock my hips.

The motion reminds me of the railing I'm propped on and I suddenly picture us from a distance, hyperaware of how sexy this is. I can imagine one of my heroines doing this, though I never could have envisioned an elevator before seeing one first-hand. Yet as I continue to picture how we look together, a scene unfolds in my mind's eye. Maybe between Johannes and—

"I've lost you, haven't I?"

I blink, finding William's face before me. His lips are pink and swollen, his eyelids heavy. Only now do I realize I've stopped kissing him and have been staring into space, lost in my imagination.

"I'm sorry," I rush to say, my words still tangled in breathlessness. I may have stopped kissing him, but my arousal hasn't abated. I merely drifted elsewhere in my mind. I worry my bottom lip, finding it slick with moisture. I release a few panting breaths. "I do this sometimes when I'm aroused. I start getting scene ideas."

He tilts my chin gently with his fingertip, expression warm and still rich with desire. "You don't have to apologize. It's my duty to bring you back to me and keep you present in your body."

I'm taken aback. I expected him to step away, set me down, and give me the cold shoulder. It's happened before. I've lost many a lover that way.

He keeps his fingertip under my chin while his other hand slides from my ribs to my back. He reaches one of the long ends of the bow that secures the neck of my gown. His hand leaves my skin. Then there's a tug at my bow. With a second tug, the ribbon unravels, and the front of my gown drops to my waist. Cool air skates over my bare breasts. "Do I have your attention now, Edwina?"

I suck in a breath. This isn't the first time he's used my real unabridged name but hearing it while he stares at my naked chest, drinking in the sight of me like a starving man, sends my head spinning. Oh, I'm here all right. And as he leans down and takes my hardened nipple into his mouth, a shock of pleasure brings me close to the edge. This has never happened before. I've never experienced such heavy want that I'm at risk of release before a lover has even touched my sex.

A whine escapes my throat, and I throw my head back against the wall, eyes closed. One of his hands finds my calf, then my knee. It trails up the inside of my thigh, pulling my skirt out of the way in the process. His hand doesn't stop until it reaches the outer hem of my silk panties. I've never been so grateful to be wearing the flimsy fae-style undergarments and not the ruffled pantaloons most women wear in Bretton.

He releases my nipple from the agonizingly delightful ministrations of his mouth to press a kiss to my neck. "I want to give you what you gave me the other night."

My lips part to say yes. Oh, how I want him to do exactly that, but reason weaves its way through my desire. "We don't have time," I gasp, even as I roll my hips. Even as I silently beg him to touch me already.

"We have time, love. I'm not going to need much."

"You're awfully sure of yourself."

"I am." He brings his lips to mine, just as he slips his hand beneath my panties. The pad of his thumb finds my seam, stroking it, painting me with the slickness of my own arousal.

A moan escapes my lips. I encircle my arms around his neck, my fingers clawing into his hair.

"Fuck, Edwina," he says against my mouth. "You're

already so wet. Is that for me? Or is that from watching your play?"

"Wouldn't you like to know—" My words end on another moan as he draws circles over my sensitive apex. Bloody hell, he wasn't wrong. We're not going to need even five minutes, for I can't possibly last much longer. He shifts closer, angles his hand, sliding another finger over me. He palms my sex, then dips one finger into my center, curling it deep inside me as he gently thrusts. I hug him closer, waves of pleasure coursing through me, gathering around that expert finger. I'm panting harder now, and he devours every breath with a kiss. I throw my head back again as the pressure builds. A cry erupts from my lips. "Will!"

He thrusts in a second finger, his thumb circling my clitoris, and I unravel around him, my climax radiating through my core, my very being. He dances with my orgasm, letting me ride his hand in waves until my shudders subside. Once I'm nothing but a limp, spent heap of flesh, he continues to hold me, planting gentle kisses on my cheek. After a few quiet moments, he helps me down from the rail and sets me on my unsteady feet.

"Turn around," he whispers, gently guiding me until my back is facing him. He presses a kiss to my neck, then reaches for the fabric at my waist. Right, my top. He drapes my bodice over my torso, the lace skating over my sensitive nipples, then pulls both ends of the ribbon behind my neck. With slow, careful movements, he secures the bow. There's something sweet about the gesture, about his gentle touch, in the wake of what he just gave me.

I'm about to face him again, to thank him—whether for the orgasm or for tying my bow, I know not—when he clasps me around my waist and pulls my backside against him. He hugs one arm over my middle, while the other slides under the front of my bodice to cup my breast. He brings his mouth to my neck, lightly grazing it with his teeth.

A thrill moves through me at the heated one-sided embrace, and it only grows when I feel the hard length of him pressed into me, straining against his trousers.

"Please use me soon," he says into my neck. "I need more of you."

I angle my head and meet his lips with a kiss. What I wouldn't give to use him right now. To hike up my skirt and let him take his pleasure however he wants it. But I think we both want more than what the remainder of our elevator ride can provide. Our time must be close to its end.

Sure enough, the motion of the elevator stutters, slows.

We break our kiss and William releases me, sliding his hand out from under my dress and leaving my skin cold in his absence. A second later, the door opens and Zane's apartment comes into view. I don't see anyone as we step into the room, which sets some wicked ideas into motion—

"You're back." Daphne's voice greets us from one of the chandeliers. Its light has been turned down to the faintest glow.

Just like that, my devious plans to finish what William and I started evaporate. We're not alone, and the others will be back soon if they aren't lurking around this enormous open space already.

William's hand grazes my back in a comforting gesture, along with a smile. One that holds sweetness and secrets and the promise of more to come. Another night. I return the grin, and he gives me one last lingering look before he saunters away, loosening his cravat.

"What did you two do tonight?" Daphne asks as she drops to the floor. There's no innuendo in her voice, but my cheeks heat just the same.

"Oh, uh, we saw a play. A burlesque adaptation of *The Governess and the Rake*."

"Hmm, maybe I should have gone." She springs across the floor and settles onto one of the windowsills at the far end of the room. She lowers her voice to a curious whisper. "I wonder when Monty will be back. He better not be up to something idiotic."

I stroll to the nearest divan and lay back upon it, unable to pay attention to anything but my racing heart and my need to sprawl out in the wake of my pleasure. I throw a hand over my eyes as I slow my breaths, but William fills my mind.

That was...incredible. I've never experienced such full-body immersion with a lover before. Such euphoria. Such need. I want more, and not just the pleasure. I want to exchange more secrets too. I want to learn more about him and tell him more about me. I want to hear him tell me I'm beautiful and rage at those who've slighted me.

He's right about what he said earlier; whatever is going on between us feels like more than friendship. It's warmer than a rivalry, and what we did in the elevator wasn't even close to hate-sex. If I take any ideas of hate or rivalry away, doesn't that leave just sex? The way my heart continues to flutter feels more than *just* anything.

What is it then? What can it even be? It's not like there's a future between us. Only one of us will win the publishing contract. If I lose, I won't have Mr. Fletcher to advocate for my citizenship, for he has no reason to unless I'm going to write more books for him. Which means I go back to Bretton. Sure, there's a chance I could eventually secure a lesser contract with Fletcher-Wilson or apply for citizenship on my own. But how long could that take? I've fallen in love with Faerwyvae. With the different courts, the freedoms, the variety. And, yes, even my own fame. I need to live here.

I must win the contract.

But if I do…

Will William's resentment return?

Or would he be happy for me?

Could we find a way to make this work between us?

I bite my lip as a giddy lightness sweeps over me. The fluttery feeling lasts for all of a minute before it drains beneath my dawning terror. I've felt that bubbly excitement before. I told William about it tonight. It's a feeling I hate. A feeling I fear. I can't let myself go down that road ever again. I can't fantasize about a future William hasn't offered. I've already had one offer of love revoked, so even if William did claim to want more than sex from me, can I even trust those desires will last? Sooner or later he'll see the side of me that Dennis Feverforth saw. Some way I'll fail to measure up to his expectations.

With a sigh, I calm my racing thoughts, my overactive imagination, and remind myself what this really is.

Research and a pleasurable escape.

That's all it needs to be.

CHAPTER THIRTY

EDWINA

I wake to a startled yelp from nearby. Early morning light pours through the wall of windows as I shift on the divan I slept upon and roll onto my side. After locating my spectacles beside my pillow, I visually seek the source of commotion. I locate it near the gilded hearth. Monty sprawls crookedly in one of the wingback chairs while Daphne stands frozen on all fours upon his chest, her curved back arched even higher than it usually is.

With another yelp, she leaps off his chest onto the floor. "This isn't what it looks like."

Monty frowns, eyelids heavy. He rubs his temples, and I catch signs of cuts and bruises on his knuckles. Just what did he get up to last night? With a yawn, he says, "What were you thinking it looks like, Daph?"

She skitters back a few steps. Her normally even voice is pitched high. "We slept together!"

Monty snorts a laugh, straightening in his chair with a

stretch. He's still fully clothed, though his waistcoat is open, as is his collar. "You fell asleep on my chest. That's not the same thing as sleeping together."

"We spent the night on the same piece of furniture with our bodies touching," she says. "This is humiliating."

"You do know how sleeping together in the carnal sense works, right?"

"Of course I know how it works. I'm centuries older than you. I've been through more mating seasons than you've been alive."

I'm surprised to hear about her age. She's centuries old after all. Pushing back my borrowed blankets, I swing my legs over the side of the divan and rise to my feet. As embarrassing as this moment must be for Daphne, maybe she'd feel better if I acted as a mediator. Though her reaction is rather amusing, I can at least relate to her embarrassment. I've been there, after all, when I woke up with William in my room. I could at least stand beside her and voice my support. Or remind them that they aren't alone and might wake up Zane and William, the former of whom dozes in their bed while the latter is nestled on a couch in a quiet corner of the apartment.

I cross the floor toward the bickering pair. The onyx floors are chilly beneath my bare feet, and I tug my robe tighter around my chemise.

"I'm not talking about unseelie mating," Monty says. "I'm talking about sex."

"I know about seelie sex," Daphne hisses back. "I read books."

He levels a wry look at her. "Well, you must also know I have a type. Four legs and furry isn't it."

Daphne gasps, visibly shrinking back as if his words struck her like a blow. When she speaks next, her voice is small, quavering. "I'm not some pet, Monty. I'm a person."

I halt in place. The hurt in her tone is so palpable it makes my chest ache. While Daphne's humiliation seemed silly—albeit relatable—at first, a deeper layer of comprehension dawns. This isn't about Daphne misunderstanding sex. It's that she sees Monty as more than her colleague. More than just another human. She sees him as a man. She's aware of him in the way I'm aware of William. Meanwhile, Monty only sees her as a pine marten. He dismissed her as *not his type* without considering he only knows one side of her. Her unseelie side.

Monty's expression falls, as if he realizes it too. His tone takes on a gentler quality. "No, of course you're a person. I know that."

"I have another body."

"I'm sure you do." Tenderness washes over his face, and for the briefest moment I think Monty might recover from his blunder all on his own. He opens his mouth but seems to think better about whatever he was going to say. The softness leaves his face, replaced with a cold, taunting smirk. He shifts in his chair, taking on a lazy posture. "You're making too big a deal out of this, Daffy. We didn't sleep together in any way that counts. It meant nothing."

A long stretch of silence follows. Finally, Daphne bites out, "You're an ass." She scampers away and out of sight faster than I can react.

"And I was sleeping so well, too," Monty mutters under his breath as he rises from his chair, cigarillo case in hand. He offers me a nod as he notices my presence.

I give him a withering look. "You were insensitive on purpose just now. Why?"

He removes a cigarillo from his case and tucks it behind his ear. Everything from his motions to his expression and his voice seems worn. Tired. "I told you once before, Miss

Danforth," he says on a slow exhale as he heads for the elevator. "I'm no hero."

THANKFULLY, THE ARGUMENT DOESN'T INFLICT ANY LASTING damage on our party. Soon Daphne returns from wherever she went to hide, and while she doesn't go out of her way to talk to Monty more than usual, she doesn't outright ignore him either. Neither William nor Zane mentions anything to suggest they overheard the argument, which is a relief for Daphne's sake.

If anyone is acting strange, it's me and William. I can't stop the fluttering in my chest every time he meets my eyes. Which is constantly. Across the room when he first woke up this morning. At the dining table when we gathered for lunch. And now, as he and I occupy the two chairs near the unlit hearth. I'm jotting story ideas in my notebook while he reads today's broadsheets. Time and again, as he turns a page, he glances at me over the top of his paper, his lips curling at one corner. The mere sight of those lips reminds me of how they felt on my skin, and how his fingers felt inside me. The way he pulled me against him and whispered those words in my ear.

Please use me soon. I need more of you.

I find myself smiling back without any reservations, and the same giddy feeling from last night sweeps through me. Over and over I remind myself that I can't assign any meaning to this fluttery, melty feeling.

Try telling that to my heart.

By afternoon, a messenger arrives with mail. "These are all for you," Zane says, handing them over to Monty.

"Ah." He accepts them, thumbing through an assortment

of envelopes. "I sent a telegram to Fletcher-Wilson about our change of accommodations, so these must have been forwarded from the hotel."

Monty approaches me and William, handing us each an envelope. William stiffens, abandoning his chair and broadsheets to stand by the wall of windows.

I turn my attention to my own envelope. It's addressed from Bullard and Sons, my publisher in Bretton, and is postmarked from the week I left for Faerwyvae. It must have taken quite the journey to reach me, considering I have no permanent address in Faerwyvae.

My heart sinks to my stomach as soon as I read the first sentence of the letter inside.

> Miss Danforth,
>
> We regret to inform you that Bullard and Sons has decided to terminate your contract on all previously published works and will not accept any new manuscript submissions henceforth. Your works are now out of print and surplus stock will be destroyed.
>
> We wish you the best in your endeavors elsewhere,
>
> John Bullard

I read the letter several times over, my heart plummeting deeper and deeper with every refrain. My contract terms were never favorable to begin with. Bullard and Sons wouldn't agree to publish me without allowing them to terminate my contract at will. And while Mr. Bullard has never made a secret of how much he frowns upon my genre, he's never given me a reason to believe he'd want to terminate my contract any time soon. He's always accepted new submissions from me. After haggling over royalties, yes, but—

My breath catches.

Mr. Bullard accepted new submissions...until *The Governess and the Fae*. He'd made his disdain for the fae clear then, and it opened my eyes to the prevalent hostilities in Bretton regarding Faerwyvae. Could it be…

Daphne hops onto the arm of my chair, and I allow her to read my letter. "Oh dear."

"Do you think it's because I came here?" I ask. "Because of the tensions between Bretton and Faerwyvae?"

"I wouldn't be surprised," she says.

With a heavy sigh, I lean back in my chair, eyes unfocused. I never considered coming here could compromise my career back home. Mr. Bullard gave me no warning that something like this could happen. Once I saw how many of my readers had purchased my imported titles from Bretton, I figured my popularity here could only benefit my publisher there.

But I gave him too much credit. Of course a man who refused to offer me higher royalties unless I published under a male pseudonym would be so petty as to punish me for my dealings with the fae.

Daphne lays a consoling paw on my shoulder. "It can't be all bad. You have your rights back now. You could find another publisher for your previous works."

She's right, I suppose, though I'm not so sure I'll find that opportunity back home. It was already hard enough finding a publisher who'd take me in the first place, and I wouldn't be surprised if others hold the same prejudice against the fae. Which means Faerwyvae is my best hope. I don't have many options, considering Fletcher-Wilson is the primary publisher of fiction here, but Mr. Fletcher might be open to acquiring my now-out-of-print titles. Yet the publishing industry takes time. Time I didn't realize was slipping away. My income is effectively gone, leaving me with no way to pay for my apartment in Bretton. Sure, I have my advance from *The Governess and the Fae*, plus whatever royalties I'll eventually make once I earn out said advance, but the exchange rate between Bretton and Faerwyvae is laughable. The money I make here is better *spent* here.

I must make this my home.

I need that contract.

"Fuck." William's outburst has me turning in my seat. He stands at the wall of windows, leaning against the wide black frame between two of the enormous panes, head thrown back.

Looks like I'm not the only one who received bad news.

Daphne leaps from my chair to settle on the sill beside him. "What happened?"

On tentative feet, I follow, curious to hear his answer.

He lowers his face and pinches the bridge of his nose. "My sister's scholarship application was rejected. I'll have to fund her college tuition in full, and the payment is due next month."

"What about other schools?" Daphne asks.

"The Borealis School of the Arts is the only college she was accepted into."

The pine marten perks up. "That's here in town. You could talk to someone—"

"I've talked to them already. The scholarship was our last chance."

I stop a few feet away as William's eyes flick to mine. The gleam in his irises is gone. He has no taunting smirk for me. No wink. No reminder of what we did in the elevator last night. There's something more like an apology in his face.

And I know what he's apologizing for.

I feel it down to my bones. The reminder that—despite everything we've done together and how we've grown closer —we're still rivals. Both of us are equally desperate for the publishing contract, and if one of us wins, the other loses. Even if the runner-up is offered a lesser contract, only one of us will be given what we truly need.

Either William can afford to put his sister through college.

Or I have a career and a place to live.

Neither of us can wait. Neither of us have time.

William's tuition payment is due in a matter of weeks.

Meanwhile, I have nothing to go home to if this tour ends without a new contract, without Mr. Fletcher advocating for my citizenship. I no longer have a publisher in Bretton. I can no longer afford my apartment. My only option will be to tuck tail and return to my family estate. I won't be the expendable middle daughter anymore if I'm relying on my parents for financial support and a roof over my head. I'll have to submit to their wishes at last. Marry. Give up my career to be a traditional wife.

These thoughts don't spark my competitive nature like they would have before.

Instead, they carve a splinter in my heart.

CHAPTER THIRTY-ONE

WILLIAM

*H*ow can so much change from one night to the next? How can one night be filled with shared secrets, longing glances, and an unraveling of desire when the next is filled with doubt? Fear. Regret. Not that I regret last night with Edwina. Only that I let myself want her so deeply that I lost sight of why I'm here. But I recall my purpose now. I recalled it when I received the letter from my sister this afternoon, and I haven't gotten it out of my head since. It hammers at the back of my consciousness, even as our next signing begins. Even as I smile and flirt and sign book after book. On the outside, I'm William the Poet. On the inside, I'm a mess.

Tonight's signing takes place under the open evening sky, on a rooftop above a bookshop on the outskirts of Lumenas. The heart of the city remains a beacon of light, but it's calmer here, the buildings not so tall. The rooftop terrace hosts a casual atmosphere, with plenty of room to chat and mingle.

There's even a bar for libations. Overhead, strings of glowing orbs crisscross the space, creating a glittering canopy that evokes starlight brought closer.

Edwina and I are on opposite ends of the rooftop, our tables tucked in corners that allow only meager glimpses of her when the crowd parts. Which is for the best. I need to not stare at Edwina tonight. What I need is to get my head on straight.

I finish signing a stack of books for my current guest, and when she leaves, hugging the stack close to her chest as I give her a seductive wink, Zane takes her place. I let my persona slip, which brings a breath of relief.

Zane perches on the corner of my table. There's no one in line behind them, as the easy mood has resulted in a less formal process. That doesn't mean it's been slow. The flow of guests has been steady, and I still get long lines before my table now and then.

"I finally got Edwina to sign a copy of *The Governess and the Fae* for me," they say, flourishing the mauve book in their hand.

My pulse quickens at the mere mention of Edwina's name. I clear my throat to ensure my voice is even as I speak. "I'm sure she would have signed a copy at any time."

"Perhaps, but I couldn't support your rival until I was certain you had enough support as well. You know, after your pitiful turnout at the Winter Court signing."

I snort a laugh. "You were worried about my lack of popularity and thought one book would make a difference?"

"Well, I am your best friend. And I'm happy to see you do, in fact, have fans."

"I appreciate your vote of confidence," I say dryly. But they're right. This signing is far better for me than the last. In fact, for the first time since our tour began, Edwina and I are evenly matched in popularity. Not that I'm surprised. I knew our first two shared signings would be in my favor and that the Winter Court would be in hers. From here on, we may be well-balanced.

"Sooo…" Zane taps their nails anxiously on my table, which tells me I won't like the subject they're about to bring up. "What are you going to do?"

"About what?"

"About Edwina. The bet."

My stomach turns. Another thing I've been thinking about all day. Before today, I was enjoying our bet, our free pass. Our game of seduction and sabotage. But Cassie's letter reminded me of what will happen if I lose our bet. And I'm dangerously close to doing so. I'm already a point behind. We can continue to trade our free pass back and forth, but I'll never get a point ahead of Edwina. The only way I can is if I gain points with someone who isn't her.

The thought makes my skin crawl.

"I don't know," I say under my breath as I rub my brow.

Just days ago I was confident I could be attracted to someone else, and perhaps that's true. But something has shifted between us. It may be small, but it's enough to make the thought of being with anyone else feel like a betrayal. Not just to her but to my heart.

"I don't want to play this game with her anymore," I admit.

"Then don't. Ask her to agree to dissolve the bet. Then tell her how you feel about her."

"How I feel." I huff. "I'm not even sure how I feel or if it matters. I need to win this contract, Zane."

"And you think winning the bet is the best way?"

I shrug. "It's the surest way. You see how popular she is. I can no longer convince myself I can win at sales."

"Yes, but can you win this bet? Can you bring yourself to do what you'd have to do?"

My stomach churns again, and Zane knows it. They know all about my downfall as an actor. My inability to perform intimate acts with people I'm not attracted to. Yet the terms of our bet don't require anything more than a single exchange of physical intimacies. It could be something small. Just a kiss. I'd be forcing myself to do something I don't truly want to do—the very thing I cautioned Edwina against.

But in turn, I would win the contract.

I could continue to pay off our debts. The mountain of bills we accumulated after Lydia's death, from the cost of the medical treatment that couldn't extend her life. The bills that landed firmly in Cassie's name—not mine—as her only living blood relative.

I could free Cassie from that financial burden for good. Then she could turn all her attention to enjoying life. She could attend college and pursue her dreams. While she still has time.

It's almost enough to counter the sinking in my heart. Almost.

"You like Edwina," Zane says. "More than you care to admit."

"Perhaps," I confess, "but Cassie's letter has reminded me how dangerous loving a human can be."

Zane's expression falls, their pity so palpable it could stab me straight through the chest. They shift on my table until they're facing me more fully. "Love, Edwina is not Lydia. Nor is she Cassie."

"Yet she's fragile nonetheless," I say with a sigh. "She deserves someone who won't break her."

The story she told me last night, about her past and Dennis fucking Feverforth, should have reminded me of that. Of how badly humans can shatter when others are careless.

It's more than the fact that humans have naturally short

281

lives. Or that they're susceptible to illnesses the fae will never experience. Our kind have discovered a miracle—that a human in a close and loving relationship with a fae will experience an increase in lifespan. It's impossible to know how long, as human-fae couples were nonexistent before the isle's unification twenty-four years ago. But it's been proven true thus far.

As has the opposite—that neglect can also impact a human's lifespan. Negatively.

Zane's expression hardens. "You are not your father."

I swallow the lump in my throat. "Which is why I'm doing everything I can for Cassie."

"Cassie wouldn't want—"

"I made a promise."

"Did she ask you for that promise?"

I shake my head. "It doesn't matter. She's my sister. I'm giving her the life she deserves. The one she'd have had if my father hadn't failed her mother."

"You can't carry that burden forever."

"No, because Cassie doesn't have forever."

Zane opens their mouth but they don't say a word more. They know I'm right. We've had this argument before. No matter how many times Zane has tried to convince me otherwise, the truth remains that Lydia got sick as soon as my father left. She already had a weakened immune system, but his presence in her life made her well. He loved her into perfect health.

Then I went to university, convinced everything would be fine. That my father had outgrown his wandering ways, his playboy nature. That he loved Lydia enough to remain by her side. That he considered Cassie his daughter, even if not by blood, the same way I considered her my sister. That he'd stay.

By the time I returned home after graduation, my father

was gone and Lydia was dying. And all I could do was make her flowers. My presence wasn't enough. Not like my father's was.

It's not even enough for Cassie.

Cassie, who is fully human and has the same degenerative disease as Lydia. The same weakened immune system. The same stubbornness.

I can't extend her life the way a loving romantic fae partner can.

But I can give her the life she deserves. No matter how long or short that ends up being.

Zane heaves a slow breath as they rise from my table. "You were different," they say, not looking at me.

"When?"

"This week. There was a light in your eyes I haven't seen in some time. There was love."

My heart aches at the word *love*. "Because I forgot what matters most."

Zane shakes their head, a sad smile on their lips as they turn away from me. "No, I think it's because you *remembered* what matters most. I hope you remember again."

AFTER OUR SIGNING COMES TO AN END AND THE ROOFTOP clears of guests, I hazard a glance at Edwina. I've managed to keep my eyes off her the last couple of hours, but now I let my gaze linger, taking in the glow of the orb lights that catch on her fiery hair and the lenses of her spectacles. She finishes packing her leftover books into the spare crates, halting when our eyes meet.

She gives me an uneasy smile. We both received bad news today, and neither of us seems to know how to act with each other. To think how much easier it was last night. Or even this morning, when I grinned at her over my broadsheets and caught the flush of color that swept over her cheeks each time.

I banish the thoughts from my mind and steel myself to do what must be done.

Tucking my hands in my pockets, I stroll to her side of the rooftop, facing the low wall behind her table. She joins me. For several long moments we simply stare at the view—the dark streets below and the bright illumination from the heart of the city beyond.

She breaks the silence first. "It's peaceful on this side of town, yet still lovely."

"Yes," I say, shifting my face to her profile. "Lovely."

With a soft smile curving her lips, she meets my eyes. I untuck my hands from my pockets, and she glances down at them before sidling slightly closer. As she brings her gaze back to mine, she inches her hand nearer until our pinkies touch. It would only take the slightest movement to grasp her hand in mine like I did last night. Then just another move to kiss her. To voice the words I didn't have the courage to say out loud last night...

I take a subtle step back. "Edwina."

She flinches, smoothing her hands over her skirt as if she hadn't been reaching for me. "Yes?"

"Let's call off our bet," I rush to say before I lose my nerve. "Let's call off the free pass. You and I can't afford to play this game anymore."

Her face goes slack as she studies me. Then she narrows her eyes, a cold edge to the smile that was so warm just a moment before. "What happened to *please use me soon?*"

Just like that, I feel like I'm back in the elevator, her body flush with mine, my cock straining against her backside while I whispered those words. My heart pounds at the memory. I want to tell her she can still use me, to do more than use me. To maybe fall for me the way I'm falling for her. But if she falls, I'll fall deeper. And if I fall any deeper than I already have, there will be no coming back. I *need* to come back.

I need to stay here with my feet on the ground, where it's safe. For both of us.

My voice comes out tight as I relay my next truth. "We can't keep doing this. Playing a game of seduction and sabotage. It's been a beautiful and pleasurable distraction, but if we keep at it, I'll never gain traction. You know I need this win."

Her expression softens, and for a moment, I think she understands. Then her face shifts into a mask I've come to know like the back of my hand. Her belligerent and stubborn pride. She steps back, folding her arms over her chest, as if hiding her heart. "I need this win too. My reasons aren't any less valid than yours."

I clench my jaw. It was too much to hope she'd let this be easy. "Either of us can win by sales, Edwina. Don't you see that now? You're just as capable of winning Mr. Fletcher's contract as I am. Let's dissolve our ridiculous bet already and play fair."

For several long moments she just stares at me. I hold my breath, silently begging her to see reason.

My hope shatters as she shakes her head. "I can't risk playing fair. You're right about us being closer in sales and popularity than I first thought, but it isn't enough. You still have the advantage of having had this tour all to yourself the first week. I might never be able to make up for what you sold then. I need a sure bet. A win I can control with my own actions."

Rage and hurt funnel through me. I step closer to her, fingers curled at my sides to keep from touching her. I'm not sure whether I want to hold her or shake her. "Do you understand what that means? What you're making me do? If you refuse to let me dissolve our bet, I have only one choice. I have to play the game in earnest. Do you want that?"

Her eyes widen, and I can practically see her imagination running wild as understanding dawns.

Good. If it shocks some sense into her, I'll make it even clearer.

I allow myself to touch her at last, lifting her chin with my thumb and forefinger. My touch remains gentle but my tone holds an edge. "Let me spell it out for you, Weenie. I may be willing to play fair and leave our win up to Mr. Fletcher's choice, but that doesn't mean I'm going to roll over and let you win this bet. Push me into a corner and I'll fight. Refuse to play fair and I'll play dirty. You want that? You want me to fuck someone else? You want me to do all the things I did to you last night with a stranger?"

Her eyes widen further, her chest heaving.

I brush my thumb over her bottom lip. "You want my touch on someone else's skin? My lips on someone else's throat? My fingers coaxing their pleasure? My cock filling them to the brim?"

She shakes her head, a subtle yet jerky motion.

I bring my face close to hers. "Then let me call off our bet."

She leans slightly closer, her breath mingling with mine.

Fuck, this is dangerous. I didn't mean to taunt her this way. I was supposed to draw a line between us. Get my head out of the clouds. Remember why loving a human is dangerous. Why I can never be enough. Why my goals for Cassie matter more than my heart. But already I feel myself crumbling at her proximity. Balanced on the precipice over the depths of my heart.

Maybe I can fall.

Maybe we can dissolve this bet and simply see where this goes without the pretense of our free pass. Maybe there's a chance for something brighter, even if only one of us wins. Maybe—

"No." Edwina steps back so abruptly that I freeze in place. She refuses to meet my eyes as she speaks. "No, we can't call off our bet. I…I need this. I can't leave it up to chance."

My heart splinters. Cracks.

Then I force myself to acknowledge this is for the best. She made her choice. The choice I should have made, because she's right about the bet. It's the only way either of us can fight for the win with our own efforts.

She steps back again, eyes downcast so I can no longer see them behind the glare over her lenses. Though she can't hide the quaver in her voice. "Do what you need to do. I will too."

She turns on her heel to flee. I reach for her, desperate to stop her retreat.

But my sensible side roots my feet in place.

My fingers close over air.

Part Four

HOW TO FALL IN
LOVE WITH A FAE

CHAPTER THIRTY-TWO

EDWINA

I miss William. He sits beside me on the train yet it's not really him. Not the version I've come to know, at least. The one I've come to like. Maybe it's because Zane is no longer here to coax him into a casual mood. Or maybe it's the aftermath of our rooftop conversation. Whatever the case, William has been every inch the arrogant poet since we left Lumenas and began our journey to our next destination. He speaks seldom and when he does, his tone is snide or disinterested.

Or flirtatious, but only in the case of interacting with his admirers. We've accumulated two during the final leg of our train ride, a newlywed couple who recognized William as the poet who's been gaining fame around the isle. They haven't left us alone since they planted themselves in the seats across from us beside Monty. Since this train offers only public cars for daytime travel, there's no polite way to escape them. I wouldn't care to escape them at all if they'd give me an ounce of attention, but they only have eyes for William.

At least I'm not alone in my annoyance. Daphne curls on my lap, her back pointedly facing our guests. Though I suppose she could be annoyed at Monty more than our guests, for he hasn't stopped chattering either. To be fair, I'm less annoyed with our guests and more with William. Now that he's admitted to putting on an act with his fans, I can't help noticing the contrast. His haughty tone. His stilted laugh. His controlled smile. He sounds nothing like how he does with me.

Or…how he *did* sound.

Before what happened on the roof.

It isn't that he's been cruel, just distant, even when he's next to me. What else can I expect after I rejected his plea to end our bet? Bloody hell, how I wanted to do exactly what he asked. The way he stepped close, taunting me with the wicked things he said he'd have to do with someone else, nearly had me giving in to him. *Begging* to give in to him.

Which is exactly why I refused. William and I are dangerous for each other, and we both know it. The more I'm with him, the more I want to be with only him. The less I want to earn points in our bet with anyone else. Which works well enough for me. If I take not a single new lover, and William does the same, I win.

And William loses.

All he wants is to play fair, and part of me wants that too.

So why can't I be a fair and reasonable person?

I glance at his profile, at the grin that doesn't meet his eyes, at his stiff posture, curated to look casual while being anything but. So badly I want to see his carefree smile again, to feel his sizzling touch, to taste his lips, and explore all the parts of him we've kept hidden thus far. I want to drown in that giddy fluttery feeling he inspires within me.

That, of course, reminds me of all the reasons I can't give William what he wants. What my heart wants.

Because winning the contract is more important than romance. I can never—will never—put romantic notions ahead of my career. That was my vow after Dennis Feverforth. I may not be magically bound to honor promises like the fae are, but I know it's for the best that I do.

I need to get over William and win this damn bet.

My lashes flutter open, but my view is blurry. The rolling motion of the train continues but the sound of chattering no longer assaults my ears. I blink a few times, my mind clearing before my eyes do. I must have fallen asleep.

I shift, finding something soft yet firm cushioning the side of my head. I lift my face from my makeshift pillow…only to discover it's William's shoulder. My body flushes from head to toe. Without looking at me, he hands me something. My spectacles. I set them in place, and my vision sharpens. We're alone; Monty and Daphne are gone, as are our two guests, though plenty of passengers remain in the car around us. Perhaps our companions went to the dining car. I straighten, putting inches of space between me and William as I tuck a few loose strands of hair behind my ear. To my horror, my fingers brush a smear of moisture on my cheek. Mortification floods me as I realize I was drooling in my sleep. On William.

He hands me something else. A silk handkerchief.

Everything inside me wants to disappear into a dark void, but I accept the cloth and dab it over the side of my face. Then, wincing, I wipe at the dampness on William's jacket.

"Sorry," I mutter.

His eyes meet mine, a grin on his face that's somehow wry and sweet at the same time. He places a gentle hand over mine to halt my scrubbing. "It's all right," he says, laughter in his voice.

I freeze, my heart melting, thudding, flipping beneath the glow of that grin. The first genuine expression I've seen him make since we left Lumenas. The first real laugh. If that isn't enough to make me hate myself and my stubborn pride, I don't know what is.

As he holds my gaze, his amusement fades, a sadder smile taking its place. My chest tightens and I'm pierced by a sudden need to bring that sweet grin back. Even if I have to kiss it there. Even if I have to give up everything—

"The next stop is ours," Monty says, shattering the moment.

I startle away from William as Monty and Daphne settle across from us, pastries in hand and paw. William removes his fingers from over mine and promptly averts his gaze. Damn it. How close was I to kissing him just now? And in a public space, no less.

"We'll be in Darlington Hills in less than an hour," Monty says.

I can't bring myself to meet his eyes, lest there's a knowing look in them, and instead turn my attention to the window. My breath catches as a field of sunny daffodils speeds by beneath a perfectly blue sky painted with the fluffiest clouds I've ever seen. I knew our next signing was in the Spring Court, but I must have been asleep when we crossed the border. Now I take it all in. The fields of flowers. The bright groves of fruit trees. Snowcapped mountains in the distance.

It's just the distraction I need from the heat of William's closeness. From the memory of that smile.

WILLIAM IS BACK TO HIS BROODING POET PERSONA AS WE reach our destination in Darlington Hills. Meanwhile, I'm enchanted, my eyes glued to the windows of our coach as I admire the town. It's different from the others, the buildings comprised of dark rich woods with sloping tiled roofs. Along the sidewalks and between every building are blossoming trees in the most stunning array of pink, red, and white. The fresh scent of cut grass and cherry blossoms fills the coach.

Just when I think I couldn't be more impressed with the Spring Court, we arrive at our hotel.

My mouth falls open as we exit the coach in a circular courtyard before the largest tree I could ever imagine. It's as wide as a mansion and as high as the tallest building in Lumenas. Its trunk consists of twisting, twining wood that curves to shape ornate windows, doors, and balconies. Its branches curve overhead in an enormous canopy, bedecked with pink blossoms. There's a natural flow to the structure— a living, breathing architectural feat.

"This is our hotel?" I say with a gasp.

Monty takes a drag from a freshly lit cigarillo. "The Darlington Hills Hotel. Host of this year's Faerwyvae Literary Society Spring Court Gala."

When I heard our next tour stop wouldn't be a signing but a charity ball, I never imagined it would take place in a location such as this. I pictured something more like the Verity Hotel in the Winter Court. Not that I'm complaining. Finding more and more reasons to be amazed with Faer-wyvae is exactly what I need. A reminder of how badly I want to win the contract at all costs.

"So many nice places to sleep," Daphne says, her tone as awed as mine as she stares up at the enormous branches.

"We have real rooms, Daph," Monty says with a chuckle. She huffs but follows him as he leads the way from the courtyard down the tiled walkway toward the hotel. I proceed behind them, casting a glance at William over my shoulder. My heart stutters as I find him smiling at the cherry blossoms overhead, his posture easy. When his gaze meets mine, he masks his expression.

I narrow my eyes to a glower. "You don't have to pretend you're not impressed. None of your fans are here to put on an act for."

He smirks but says nothing.

"Tell me what you're really thinking. It's amazing, isn't it? Even to a fae like you?"

His gaze slides back to mine. My breath hitches as he steps closer and brings his lips beside my ear without touching me. "You want to know what I'm really thinking? I'm thinking I want to prop you upon one of those balconies and bury my face between your thighs like that couple we found in the north wing."

I halt in place, too afraid I'll trip over my own feet. His words send a shudder through me as my imagination runs wild. My eyes flick to one of the twisting, twining balconies high overhead. I can picture myself propped upon one, William's strong hands safely bracketing my waist while he strokes my sex with his tongue, my head thrown back in pleasure—

"Too bad I'll have to pick someone else."

I shake my head, forcing my vivid imaginings to recede. Monty and Daphne have reached the hotel's entrance, and William gives me a cruel smile before following them through the door.

I clench my jaw as I rush to catch up. Damn that William. I know what he's doing. He's trying to tempt me into dissolving our bet. While he hasn't outright refused any further intimate acts between us, his intentions are clear. If I won't dissolve our bet, he'll play the game the way we originally intended. *Not* with me.

Which means all the things I've been craving to do with him I'll never get to do. I may be in current possession of our free pass, but I won't use it against his will. Especially when I understand him so well. I know he wants to win as much as I do.

But my reasons are more pressing than his.

We enter the lobby of the hotel, which is just as awe-inspiring as the exterior. The walls are composed of the same rich wood as the outer trunk, curved and decorated in elegant whorls. Chandeliers of twining, flowering branches extend from the tall ceilings. Everything from the spiral staircases to the chairs in the lobby and the reception desk at the far end appear to have grown from the floor and walls.

Monty makes a beeline for the desk, outpacing the rest of us—likely fueled by panic that we might encounter a repeat of the mishap at the hotel in Lumenas. The rest of us head toward the seating area.

"William!" An excited female voice has us pulling up short. A young woman leans forward in one of the flowering chairs, her gray eyes glittering when they land on William.

He stiffens. "Cassie?"

Cassie. Isn't that…his sister's name?

The woman looks nothing like William with her waif-like frame, her pale complexion, her straight silvery hair tucked in a low chignon. Her ears are round, which tells me she's at least half human. Come to think of it, William never explained their parentage, only that he's her guardian. Cassie rises from her chair with the assistance of a black lacquered cane, a wide smile on her lips. She's dressed in loose trousers that remind me of Zane's while her top is a white blouse and gray waistcoat.

William strides toward her at once. "What are you doing here?"

She holds up a hand to keep him at bay. "Don't even start fussing with me. I feel perfectly healthy."

"You took the train? Alone?"

She levels a glare at him. "I'm nineteen. I know how to ride the bloody train."

"You were supposed to stay with Mrs. Hansen until the end of the tour."

Cassie gives an innocent shrug. "Mrs. Hansen tired of my services. I figured what better time than now to visit my dear brother on his Heartbeats Tour?"

"Cassie," he says between his teeth, "what did you do to Mrs. Hansen?"

"I did as I was told. It's not my fault she made me read *The Pauper and the Golden Lute* out loud to her. Every day."

He pinches the bridge of his nose. "As her paid companion, you were supposed to read whatever she insists. To sit and listen to her drivel, or read her drivel, or do whatever the hell she wants."

"*The Pauper and the Golden Lute* is a cautionary tale. I hate cautionary tales."

A smile spreads over my lips. Sounds like Cassie is a girl after my own heart.

William narrows his eyes. "What did you do to *The Pauper and the Golden Lute*?"

Another innocent shrug. "All I did was add a love scene, a battle to the death, and a happy ending."

"Of course you did."

Cassie puts her free arm on her hip, her other leaning on her cane. "She also called me a spinster."

"Well, fuck her then," William says flatly. "Might as well quit your job over it."

"That's exactly what I said!" Cassie grins, enjoying William's suffering.

I can't stop the laugh that escapes my lips, which in turn catches Cassie's attention.

Her eyes widen, as does her smile. She extends her free hand. "Oh, I'm so rude. You must be Edwina and Daphne."

I shake her hand, surprised by her firm grip despite her slender build. "It's a pleasure to meet you."

"The pleasure is mine," she says, then leans down to shake Daphne's paw. "Though I'm sure you can't say the same about having to spend so much time with my annoying brother. Does he fuss over you all the time?"

I glance from Cassie to William. His façade has fully cracked, showing yet another side of him I haven't seen before. He watches his sister with a mix of tenderness and apprehension, his hand braced behind her back without touching her, as if he's ready to intervene should she lose her balance. There must be a reason she walks with a cane. And now I think I understand a few more things about him that I never considered before.

"While I can't say he's fussed over me, as you put it," I say, returning my attention to Cassie, "he has tried to protect me a time or two. The first was to protect my honor from a lecherous male."

"You didn't exactly need my protection the second time," he says, and I'm graced with a return of that sweet smile I glimpsed earlier. "Though the performers in the north wing probably appreciated my intervention to save them from you."

"Don't keep secrets," Cassie says, swatting her brother's arm with her free hand. "Explain."

"It was an orgy," Daphne says.

Cassie's eyes brighten. "How delightfully scandalous!"

"Daph," William says in a scolding tone, "don't tell her that. How do you even know about it?"

Daphne shrugs her furry shoulders. "Monty told me."

"How does Monty know?"

"I make it my business to know everything." The man in question strolls up to us, a dimpled grin on his face as he extends a hand. "You must be the infamous Cassie Haywood."

"Infamous. Now that has a ring to it." She squeezes his palm in greeting.

"Are our rooms situated correctly this time?" William asks.

"Perfectly. Though I didn't realize we'd have an extra guest with us."

Cassie waves a dismissive hand. "I'm not staying here. I'll attend the gala, but I'm staying with friends."

William whips his face to his sister. "You have friends?"

She scoffs. Twice for good measure. "Yes, my dear cynical asshole brother, I have friends."

He rolls his eyes. "I meant friends in town."

"Lola and Rosie are visiting their aunt before college—don't bring up the scholarship." She cuts a glare at William, whose expression falls. "I'm not going to cry about it, so don't you dare brood about it either."

William's eyes flick to mine, and guilt sinks my heart. He shifts closer to Cassie and lowers his voice. "Is that the real reason you came?"

"I had to make sure you weren't moping about," she mutters. Then louder she says, "Well, I better be off."

"Do you have your—"

"Tinctures, tonics, remedies. Yes, Will, I have all of that. And I meant what I said. I feel great."

"You know how quickly that can change."

"I'm fine," she growls, then faces the rest of us with a

smile. "It's been lovely meeting you, and I hope to get to know you better. Especially you, Miss Danforth. I've heard a lot about you from Zane."

"Oh," I say, taken aback. "Good things, I hope."

Cassie gives me a conspiratorial wink, though I don't know what we're conspiring about. "Very good things. Very good and interesting things." The way she enunciates each word makes me even more uncertain.

William pulls his head back. "When did you talk to Zane?"

"We exchanged a telegram the other day. By the way..." Cassie leans in close to William, though her eyes remain on me. She whispers just loud enough for me to hear. "Does she know about June?"

My breath catches.

William gently turns her away from me. "No," he whispers back. "She doesn't need to know."

Cassie nods, her shoulders slightly slumped. When she faces us again, she gives us an exuberant wave.

William won't look at me, not even after Cassie is through the front doors and out of sight. Not even as we follow Monty up the stairs to our rooms.

My heart sinks with every step. In part because of what he said about June. That I don't need to know about this great former love of his. I can't pretend I'm not jealous that he's shared about her with others. With Jolene. Why not me?

But another part sinks not with envy but guilt.

Because now that I've met Cassie—now that I've been charmed by her, even after such a brief meeting—I understand a piece of William better than before.

The piece that makes him so desperate for that contract.

The piece I'll have to crush to win.

CHAPTER THIRTY-THREE

EDWINA

The last thing I need is to be close to William right now. What I need is a distraction. Peace in his absence. Which is exactly why I arrived at the ballroom early this evening to help the staff prepare for tomorrow's gala. William and I already agreed to reconvene at nine to meet with the event coordinator. I figured if I was early for once, I wouldn't have to risk meeting William on the way. Or getting stuck in an elevator with him and remembering all the delicious things that happened the last time we were alone in one.

So how the hell did I end up setting tables with him? And not just tables in general, but the very same table. Again and again.

At first, it's enough to simply ignore him. The ballroom holds plenty to admire and keep my awareness of his presence at bay. It boasts more of the hotel's organic charm, with its curved twining walls that sprout flowering branches at intervals where ornate lanterns hang. The floor is a gleaming cherrywood inlaid with a spiraling floral pattern. The layout for the event is only partially set up, with tables on one side, an empty stage on the other, and a dance floor in between.

But there's only so much of my surroundings I can admire before they pale against William's beauty. My eyes are trained on his every move, transfixed as his capable fingers lay out plates and utensils. The air seems to sizzle between us, like a current that fights to drag me closer to him.

"Must you follow me, William?" I say when he tails me to the fourth table in a row.

He arches a brow as if he can't fathom my annoyance. "It's faster if we work together." He retrieves a white silk cloth from a nearby cart and spreads it haphazardly over the bare table. With a nod, he gestures for me to take the other end.

Gritting my teeth, I clasp the edge of the cloth and tug it over my side of the circular table. "Why are you even here?"

"Aubrey mentioned a shortage of staff to help set up tonight, so I offered my services."

I frown. "Who's Aubrey?"

"The event coordinator."

"You met her already? I thought we weren't meeting her until nine."

"She visited my room to propose an idea for my auction, but there's still more to discuss."

Something hot flares inside me at the thought of an unknown woman coming to his room. I tug the tablecloth so hard, William loses his grip on his side.

A wicked grin spreads over his face. "Are you jealous, Weenie?"

"Of course I'm not jealous. Why would I be jealous?"

His chuckle tells me he's not at all convinced. He tugs the

cloth back toward his side until it's even. "You have all the power here. You hold the free pass. You hold the ability to let me end our bet and keep me from straying to anyone else."

I scoff, smoothing out the wrinkles over the tabletop with more force than necessary. "You're the one who said you don't want to play with me anymore."

Silence falls between us until I dare to meet his eyes. His expression has my lungs tightening. It's the same way he looked at me from across the elevator that night. "I want to play with you," he says, voice low. "I want to play with every inch of you from now until sunrise, but I don't want it to be a game."

I grip the nearby chair to steady myself. "What do you mean by that?"

His throat bobs. "This isn't a game for me."

My heart rackets against my ribs. Does he mean...his feelings for me?

He shakes his head and smooths out the cloth on his end. "The contract," he says as if reading my mind. "It's not a game. I need it."

My shoulders slump. Whether with relief or disappointment, I know not.

"Yet I have to play to win, right?" His tone is bitter, and his smoothing motions turn rough. With a heavy sigh, he plants his hands on the table, head hung low. "I *really* need this."

I bite the inside of my cheek and retrieve a stack of plates from the cart. I approach his side of the table and hand him half the stack. "For Cassie?"

He doesn't meet my eyes as he accepts the plates. "Yes, for Cassie."

Guilt plagues me as I spread out the fine porcelain items. I'm fully aware that my desires stand in the way of those belonging to someone so special to him. He must know it isn't personal. I have nothing against her. Or him. "She's a charming girl. I like her."

"Charming is a word," he says with a huff of laughter. "She's a troublemaker."

"You care about her."

"She calls it fussing."

We finish setting out the plates and move on to utensils. I nibble my bottom lip before asking a question I know might be too invasive. "You mentioned before that Cassie is unwell. That you didn't want her to get a job because of her constitution. Is it a chronic condition?"

He doesn't answer at once, but when he speaks, his tone holds a serious quality. "She has a degenerative disease, one the medical community doesn't quite understand. Her immunity is weak. She's just like Lydia."

"Is that your mother?"

"Cassie's mother by blood. Mine by love. Our parents met when Cassie was still a baby. Lydia conceived her with a costar from one of the plays she acted in, but he wasn't interested in compromising his career to raise a child."

"She was an actress?"

He nods. "That's how she met my father. He was obsessed with the arts. And women. I thought he'd stay with Lydia. Well, I suppose their relationship held a record for him by the time he left."

I note the way his tone darkens when he talks about his father. The way he clasps the spoons in his hand a little tighter.

"I wouldn't wish my father on anyone," he says under his breath, "but if Cassie shared his blood, she'd have some fae healing."

The pain in his voice has my heart softening. Cracking. Flooding with warmth and hurt and sympathy. Before I can think better of it, I round the table until I'm at his side. He won't meet my gaze as he continues to set out flatware, so I lay a hand on his arm, stilling him.

My brows knit as I look up at him. "You're *really* worried about her. It's more than just fussing, as she calls it, isn't it?"

He meets my eyes and his expression is so broken, so open and vulnerable, my throat constricts.

I swallow the tightness as more and more understanding falls into place. "Did Lydia...did she die from the conditions she shares with Cassie?"

He gives me a slow nod.

My bottom lip trembles. "Will..."

"It scares me that humans can be so fragile," he whispers, his eyes locked on mine. "I never thought I'd love one—"

He snaps his mouth shut as footsteps echo over the floors behind us. His vulnerable expression disappears behind a calculated mask, one so convincing it makes me question whether I imagined the soft moment we just shared.

He turns to face the interloper while I'm stuck on what he left unsaid. What was that about love? He was on the verge of confessing something important, I just know it.

Could it have been about June?

Or...could I be so vain as to think it might have had to do with me?

"There they are," says a feminine voice.

It takes no small effort to draw myself out of my head—until I lay my eyes on the female fae who must be Aubrey. She's as stunning as the ballroom around us with a curvaceous figure, enormous violet eyes, and blonde hair that melts into a pale blue at the ends. She's outfitted in a blouse and skirt in a similar style to mine, but the folds and pleats suit her hourglass frame so well they must be custom made. Then there are the iridescent wings folded down her back. They remind me of a dragonfly's but much larger to match the proportions of her humanoid form.

She stops before us and introduces herself to me. I give her a cordial greeting and hazard a glance at William, seeking any sign of lingering distress after our conversation. He looks fully at ease.

Maybe I imagined it after all. Maybe he was tugging my heartstrings on purpose. Maybe the game we're playing has changed.

I do my best to cast the interaction out of my mind and remain rooted in the present.

Aubrey details tomorrow's gala. "There will be dinner, dancing, and over a hundred auctions, all of which you are welcome to participate in. And I do mean all of you, even Daphne and Mr. Phillips, especially when it comes to dancing."

She hands me two floral-patterned cards, each strung with a silk ribbon. I open one, finding a list of dances and an open space beside each. I haven't held a dance card in years. Not since my debut social season.

"Please give one of these to Daphne," Aubrey says, "so she can participate as well, should she so desire. Everyone who turns in their dance card at the end of the night will raise ten sapphire rounds for every dance that is filled. All proceeds go to the Faerwyvae Literary Society to support literacy outreach in rural towns, for seelie and unseelie children alike."

"That's a cause I can get behind," I say as I tuck the cards in my skirt pocket.

"Lovely. Now, as our honored guests, you need to confirm your featured auction. William, have you considered the date I proposed?"

My heart leaps into my throat. A date? What does she mean by that?

"I've thought about it." He glances at me sidelong. "Do you mind explaining it again?"

"Of course. My proposed auction for you is a date with a fan. Bidding starts at ten sapphire rounds. The highest bidder gets to spend an afternoon with you. In public, of course, and you can set the agenda. How does that sound?"

It takes several rapid beats of my heart before my mind catches up with what she's proposing. My first thought was that she was asking William on a date. I'm only a tiny bit relieved that she was presenting an idea for an auction. There's still a piece of me that burns to think of him alone with anyone else. Anyone who participates in his auction will surely have romance in mind.

"Sure," William says after a stretch of silence, sending my stomach plummeting to my feet.

Why did I hope he'd refuse? What reason does he have when I wouldn't let him dissolve our bet? If this date takes place before the end of our tour, he can turn it into an opportunity to earn a point. That's why he asked her to repeat his proposal out loud. He's trying to get under my skin.

"Great," Aubrey says, then turns to me. "For you, I was thinking of an annotated copy of one of your books."

A sliver of disappointment strikes me. After her idea for William's auction, I thought mine might be something a little more sensational or exciting. Something that might make William as jealous as I'm feeling.

I shake my head to clear it. "Yes, that's…great."

"You already have an annotated copy." William bumps his shoulder into mine, and it takes all my restraint not to shudder at the touch.

I blink at him, blinded by the crooked smile he gives me.

"It's a copy of *my* book," he says, "but it is annotated by both of us."

Heat floods my cheeks as I realize what he's referring to. The book we've exchanged back and forth, now filled with insults and crude altered poems. I tucked it in my carpet bag after the Winter Court signing and haven't looked at it since.

Aubrey's gaze volleys between us, amusement dancing in her eyes. "What's this about? You annotated a book together?"

William turns his attention to the coordinator, his false persona firmly in place. His tone comes out haughty. "It's sort of a silly game we've played, writing notes back and forth during our signings."

That contrived tone paired with how he called it a *silly game* ignites a wave of ire in me. Not to mention the fact that he told a stranger about it. I don't know when our book became a precious secret to me but hearing him dismiss it like that sends a spear of betrayal straight through my chest.

"I love that idea," Aubrey says with a decisive clap. "Is that your choice of contribution, Miss Danforth?"

"Yes, Miss Danforth, what do you say?" William faces me with a smile that doesn't meet his eyes. It's a look I can't read. Is he challenging me? Taunting me? "Might as well get rid of it for a good cause."

"Fine," I say curling my fingers into fists while I force a shrug. "One person's trash is another's treasure."

"If it was trash," William whispers, leaning slightly closer, "you should have thrown it away back when you said you would."

My pulse quickens. As far as he knows, I threw it away after our Winter Court signing. So how the hell does he know I still have it? Was it just a lucky guess? Or was he baiting me to find out? Damn him. First he stirs my sympathy. Now he sparks my annoyance. What is he playing at?

"Fantastic," Aubrey says. "Well, that's everything. Except… William, would you like to have a drink with me? Either my room or yours?" She beams a smile at him so bright it's impossible not to read the subtext in it. Or in the sway of her hips as she tilts her head coyly to the side.

She…wants him.

This isn't another case of me misreading the signs or being manipulated into overthinking like what happened with Zane at the Winter Court signing. No, this is obvious. This is unmasked seduction.

"A drink?" William echoes, his façade slipping.

Her violet eyes turn hopeful. Pleading. "We can discuss ideas for your date."

"Right," he says. "Give me a moment?"

"I'll head to the lobby." She offers me a parting smile, devoid of all malice. It tells me she hasn't once considered me a rival or that there could be anything between me and William. She's the epitome of cool, collected, and confident.

William faces me as soon as her back is turned. His haughty mask is gone, and the heat I saw in his face earlier—before our conversation turned somber—returns. He plants one hand on the table and leans toward me until our eyes are level. "Give me a reason not to go."

My breath hitches.

"Give me one reason, Edwina. Just one."

There's pleading in his blue irises. A challenge too.

I open my mouth before I can find the words to say. Then anger heats my chest. I lean closer too, a scowl on my face. "No, William, *you* give me a reason."

His eyes widen in surprise.

But he can't pin this all on me. He can't taunt me to risk my heart when he hasn't given me anything concrete to hold on to. As far as I know, this is all about attraction. Seduction. Nothing real or lasting. At least not for him.

For me…

I'm too scared to know what this is for me.

Too scared of that giddy feeling and everything it might mean.

"Fine." He straightens with a slow sigh. My heart drops with every inch of space he places between us. "Go get rid of that book."

Without another word, he leaves the ballroom and heads for the lobby.

CHAPTER THIRTY-FOUR

EDWINA

*W*hy couldn't he have given me a reason? Just one damn reason? Why does he fan my hopes and desires, again and again, just to leave me dangling on the precipice like this?

Better yet…why didn't *I* give *him* a reason?

Nausea and shame churn my stomach as I make my way from the ballroom to my hotel room. I don't know if I should be relieved or repulsed that I don't see William and Aubrey in the lobby. If they aren't in the lobby, I don't have to witness them flirting or touching. But their absence means they're probably in one of their rooms by now.

Why am I so upset? I knew this was coming. This is the price I paid for refusing to let William dissolve our bet. The price was him, and it was supposed to be worth the reward— a contract I can win with certain, summable efforts. Maybe part of me thought William wouldn't earn any further points, despite his taunting. That he'd be unable to perform intimate acts with anyone but me. That I'd keep my one-point lead and win our bet without either of us taking new lovers.

How vain can I be?

And how can I still question my decision when I know I was right to make it? When I know I can never let romance take precedence over my career?

Because you're wrong, some small part of me taunts as I climb the final flight of stairs to our floor. I can't bring myself to even look at an elevator right now.

I can't be wrong, I say back to that quiet voice. *Even if I am, what's the point if it's one-sided? If William can't give me a reason?*

That bolsters my nerve, just in time as I reach our floor. My companions and I have a full suite, even larger than Zane's apartment, and just as beautiful as the rest of the hotel. Each of us has our own bedroom as well as a shared common room, recreation room, and enormous bath. I stop just outside the door to the common area, taking a bracing breath in case William and Aubrey are on the other side. But as I open the door, I find the suite empty. Quiet. All the surrounding doors are closed, and I don't dare look too long to check if there is light emanating beneath any of them. It's not my business. It can't be my business.

On swift feet I stride to my bedroom, slamming the door behind me without meaning to. I seek out my carpet bag at once, settling in on the edge of my four-poster bed and shoving the curtain of cherry blossoms out of the way. This room was charming when I first arrived, but now everything annoys me. Even pretty things. Especially pretty things. Like Aubrey. Like William. Very much not like me and my vile, thorny heart.

You are beautiful.

Your words are beautiful.

I grit my teeth at the echoes of William's voice and rifle through my bag. Why did he have to say that to me? Why did he have to show me a side of him that makes my heart race, skip, and flutter?

I find what I'm looking for at the bottom of my bag. A green book with a gold-foiled title. Tenderness wars with hurt and anger as I study it. I favor the latter emotion and shove the others away. William told me to get rid of this book, so I will. I'll take it to the ballroom right now so they can set it up for tomorrow's auction.

With the book clenched tight in one hand, I stomp back to my door.

But as I reach it, my feet stall. My hands refuse to reach for the knob.

With a frustrated groan, I lean against my closed door and stare down at the book. That tender feeling returns, along with a sharp ache in my chest.

As annoyed as I was when William first started pestering me with this damn book, that changed at the Winter Court signing. A lot of things changed then. He kissed me during our reading of *The Governess and the Rake* at the book club meeting. I used my free pass for the first time. And this book…

It turned into a treasure. A collection of insults, immaturity, and crude drawings. A sad smile tilts my lips as I open the title page. It's a mess of both our handwritings.

Ed—

I like smut and drivel.

Well, I don't like you. Or your book. Stop trying to give this to me.

You don't have to like me to use me, Weenie.

TESSONJA ODETTE

There is also, of course, the penis I drew and labeled with William's name, along with an assortment of page numbers we wrote to direct each other to poems we'd altered. I grin as I study each one, but as I'm about to flip to one of the indicated pages, I notice an annotation I don't recognize. It's in William's handwriting, but the page number he wrote is neatly penned at the very top, standing out against the haphazard scrawls from before. Did he sneak one last edit in? And why does the ink look fresher?

I flip to the page number in question.

At the very top above one of his poems are two words.

Don't forget

At the corner of the page is another handwritten number. 87.

I flip to it.

That you are

Another page number. 56 this time.

Beautiful.

Next, I'm directed to page 128.

And

Then page 37.

I think I should confess...

Page 212.

I'm

Page 114.

Falling

Page 235.

For

Page 6.

You.

I can hardly breathe. Can hardly comprehend the words I put together. There's nothing after this. No more page numbers. Nothing to suggest this is just the start of a joke.

But it must be.

Right?

This can't be real…can it?

No, William, you *give me a reason.*

Go get rid of that book.

I slam the cover shut, my mouth falling open. Did he want me to see this? Was *this* his answer? His reason? Because he's…falling for me?

My head spins, and my feet move before my mind tells them to. Before I know it, I'm standing before William's bedroom door, my knuckles rapping on its surface. My whole body shakes from the force of my racing heart, but its cadence turns to terror as only silence echoes back.

He isn't in his room. Which means he must be in Aubrey's. Can he even earn a point toward our bet in her room? Our terms state the intimate act must take place in our own bedroom.

But...

If he plans to stay the night with her...

Doesn't that make her bedroom his for the evening?

My stomach drops. I didn't consider that possibility when we were at Somerton House, but now it's all I can think about.

I slam my hand against his door one last time.

"Is everything all right?"

I startle at Daphne's voice and whirl to face her. She pads across the floor toward me, her tiny black eyes filled with worry.

"Have you seen William?" I rush to say.

She pauses and sits back on her haunches. "He's in the recreation room," she says, pointing a paw toward the farthest room.

My gaze narrows on the pair of double doors and the light glowing beneath them. Hope sparks in my chest. "Is he alone?"

"No, he's—"

I rush to the doors and throw them open, not caring about what I might walk in on.

Two sets of eyes lock on me at once, and two bodies go still.

But it isn't William and Aubrey.

It's William and Monty. Playing billiards with easy grins.

Their expressions slip in their surprise at my sudden intrusion, but Monty recovers first. He takes a long drag of his cigarillo, eying me with a knowing smirk, then places his cue on a rack. "I can guess whom you're here to see, and it isn't me."

Daphne reaches us just then. "What's going on?" she whispers to Monty as he picks her up and carries her back the way she came. "I was just about to get a bottle of cherry blossom cordial."

"I'll pour you a drink in the kitchen." Monty closes the doors behind us, leaving me alone with William.

My frantic mood begins to calm, and I take in the room with fresh eyes. It boasts the same rich woods as the other rooms in the hotel, the same sprouting chandeliers and elegant furniture. Aside from the billiards table, there are several card tables, a tea table, and a floral-printed couch. The room is vast enough to host a large party, but there isn't anyone else here. Just William.

The more my anxiety cools, the stronger my suspicion grows. I hug the book to my chest as if it can shield me against any possible pain he might inflict. "Was this another trick? Like with Zane?"

With a weary sigh, he sets his cue on the billiards table and braces his hands on the table's ledge. His eyes are downcast. "Not a trick."

"Then where is she?"

Silence. Then, "I couldn't do it."

"Why not?"

Finally, he lifts his gaze to mine. "Why do you think?"

I hug the book tighter, then cross the room toward him. When I reach the billiards table, I drop the book on its surface. There's nothing to shield my heart now. "Why can't you just say it?"

His jaw tightens before he answers, voice tight. "Because it's terrifying."

"Why? Because I'm human?"

He nods. "And I don't know what to do with this. With whatever we are. I don't know where it goes from here or if I'm enough. If I'm brave enough."

The tightness in my chest softens. Unravels. I tap my finger on the book. "When did you write this?"

He doesn't ask me to clarify. He knows I found his hidden message. "After the elevator. I knew you didn't get rid of the book. I saw it in your pocket after our Winter Court signing."

I fold my arms. "You rifled through my things just to get a secret message to me?"

His lips curl with a mischievous grin. He holds my eyes without shame. "Yes."

My first instinct is to wipe that smug look off his face and chastise him for digging through my bag. But I don't feel my usual ire. I didn't come here to argue. "Is it true? What you wrote?"

"Yes."

"You haven't changed your mind?"

His expression softens. "Why would I change my mind?"

I hug my arms tight to my chest, another protective shield, before I forcibly drop them to my side. "Because I'm stubborn," I say, voice trembling. "And we're supposed to be rivals. And I didn't give you a reason not to go with Aubrey."

He pushes off the edge of the table and tucks his hands in his pockets. He slowly rounds the corner of the table toward me. "I didn't need a reason. I wanted one from you, but I already had one of my own."

My fingers flinch, ready to reach for him. But instead of stopping before me like I expect him to, he heads for the set of double doors. My heart falls, even as his words lift it up.

"I want *you*, Edwina," he says over his shoulder, fingertips on one of the handles. "I'm falling for you. That's my reason."

"Don't go," I say to his back, my voice rich with pleading. "I'll give you a reason this time. It's this: I don't want you to be with anyone else. I don't want you to kiss or touch or do anything with anyone. Just me."

His back remains facing me, his fingers still on the handle.

I take a step toward him. "Please stay."

He shifts to the side and meets my eyes with a soft smile. "I wasn't leaving, love."

That's when I notice the green flowering vines emerging from his palms, twined around the handles and locking them together. That's when I notice the heat in his gaze. The desire on his face.

He releases the vines and strides my way. When he stops before me, he frames my face with his hands. "But please, beg me to stay again." His voice is deep and rough, and his touch on my cheeks trembles with restraint.

I tilt my chin and part my lips. "Stay."

He devours that word with a kiss.

CHAPTER THIRTY-FIVE

EDWINA

*W*illiam's kiss is hard and demanding, and I meet his lips with equal fervor. His tongue slides into my mouth, and I tilt my head back, savoring his taste, some bittersweet spirit on his breath. His hand winds to my nape, then claws into the base of my hair, loosening my tendrils from their updo. I encircle my arms around his neck, pressing myself against him as if we could melt into one. Now that he's in my arms—mine and no one else's—I don't want to let him go, even for a breath.

He steps in even closer, urging me to step back. Without breaking our kiss, I let him guide me step after step until my backside comes up against the edge of the billiards table. Only then does he release my lips, hoisting me up and propping me on the edge. With unexpectedly gentle motions, he removes my spectacles.

"Is this all right?" he whispers.

My vision blurs, but I don't mind it if it means removing one more layer between us. "Yes."

He sets my lenses aside and brings his lips to my neck. My lashes flutter shut as he trails kisses over the high collar of my lace blouse, then along the edge of my jaw to the corner where it meets my ear. Then his lips are on mine again, and I'm already open for the sweep of his tongue, the sharing of breaths. He lifts the hem of my blouse, untucking it from my skirt before roving his palms over the front of my corset, rounding the curve that covers my breast.

I've never had anything other than neutral feelings when it comes to corsets, but I hate them now. Hate the thick material for hampering my ability to feel more of his touch. His fingertips wander to the top of my corset, running over the lace trim and making my skin pebble when I'm finally graced with his skin against mine. I arch against his hand, signaling what I want from him.

His smiles against my lips. "Feeling greedy, Weenie?"

"Yes. I want you to touch me. All of me."

"Oh, I'll do more than touch." His hand slides to the back of my corset and begins tugging at the laces. I move my fingers to my collar and undo my buttons with clumsy haste, uncaring if I pop them off my blouse entirely. By the time my blouse is open, William has untied my corset. I shrug off my top and let it slide down my arms to the billiards table beneath me. William's fingers come to the front of my corset, unhooking the top clasps until the garment gapes open. He slips his hand beneath the structured ivory brocade and cups my breast, his thumb circling my nipple, hardening it to a stiff peak. I brace my hands on the table and arch back. My other breast crests the top of my corset, and he takes that nipple into his mouth. His tongue flicks over the sensitive bud, and I throw my head back with a moan. I want him to lift my skirts and step closer so I can hook my legs around him, gain some relief from the heat coiling at my center.

His teeth graze my nipple as his mouth leaves my breast to trail over my collarbone, then up the column of my throat until our lips meet again. My hands leave the table to find the clasp at the back of my skirt.

William steps back, his heavy-lidded eyes drinking me in. I expect him to unclasp the rest of my corset to see me fully bare, but instead, he takes another step away.

"Lay back, love."

I do as I'm told, falling back until I'm propped on my forearms. Just when I think he might help me out of my skirt by tugging the waist down, he lifts it from the hem instead, baring my calves. His expert fingers find the laces of my boots, and he holds my gaze while he removes them. Then my stockings. Finally, he trails his touch up my bare leg to my knee, then my inner thigh. His eyes are still locked on mine as he reaches the outer hem of my panties. He strokes the silk covering my already slick center. His grin turns wicked as he watches my lips part. My forearms turn to jelly at his next stroke, and I let myself collapse fully onto the table. But there's still a layer between us. I want his skin on mine.

"More," I beg, voice breathless.

He gives in to my demand, sliding the flimsy silk down my hips, my legs, and drops the undergarment to the floor. Then he hikes my skirt higher and glides a finger straight over my sex, parting my seam. My lashes flutter shut and I release a soft moan.

"You're aching for my touch, aren't you?" William whispers. With his free hand, he braces my knee, gently guiding my legs wider. "How long have you been aching for me?"

"A while."

His thumb slides up my folds, then glides over my clit in

achingly slow circles. Pleasure shoots through me, and I roll my hips, yearning for a deeper touch. He stills his hand. His voice deepens, turns taunting. "How long is a while?"

He's torturing me on purpose when all I want is more of him. All of him. I want him on top of me. Inside me. Yet he's still standing at the edge of the table between my legs, fully clothed while I'm half undressed, only the most vulnerable parts of me—my breasts and my sex—bared. Yet his hand remains unmoving over my center, even as I rock my hips against his fingers. I open my eyes to scowl at him and find a ready smile on his face.

"William, please," I bite out.

"Well, you asked so nicely." He steps in closer, leans over me, and drops his mouth between my legs.

I gasp as he slides his tongue over my folds in a languorous sweep. Every nerve at my core is on fire, and he stokes it with every brush of his mouth, his tongue. His fingers work in tandem, parting me, filling me, coaxing moans and whimpers I didn't even know I could make. Release builds hotter inside me, and I run my hands through his hair, rolling my hips against his mouth. My thighs tremble in anticipation of my orgasm—

He pulls back, slowly, tauntingly, drawing his fingers out from inside me as he lifts himself away.

My voice snags on a whine. "What are you doing?" I say through panted breaths. My entire being thrums on the precipice of the release I almost had.

He steps back, and I lift myself on my forearms to keep my eyes on him. A corner of his slick mouth quirks as he undoes his already loosened cravat, then the top buttons of his waistcoat and shirt. "I recall promising you torment."

I blink a few times through the haze of my arousal until his voice echoes through my head, words whispered in the hall outside my dormitory bedroom.

I'll tease you, torment you, until you're begging me, whimpering and whining like one of your blushing heroines.

I arch a brow. "Haven't you made me whimper and whine enough?"

He shrugs off his waistcoat, then his shirt. My gaze locks on his toned torso, the flex of his muscles as he tosses the article to the ground. "Oh, love, we're just getting started."

He returns to me, stepping to the outside of my legs and lifting my back the rest of the way off the table. I wind my arms around his neck as he pulls me against his chest, drawing me fully into his arms. He smiles down at me, then lowers his lips to mine in a slow kiss. The taste of me on his tongue sends a strange thrill through me.

Our momentum shifts as he strides across the room with me in his arms. Then my back presses into something soft. As he pulls away slightly, I see we've moved to the couch. His fingertips come to the front of my corset, finally unclasping the bottom closures and freeing me from the garment. I'm already sliding my skirt down my hips when he tugs it the rest of the way down.

He pulls back even more, his body propped beside me on the couch, and lets his gaze sweep over me. His eyes follow the trail of his palm as he glides it down my neck, my breasts, my stomach, then skates past my center and down my thighs. When his eyes return to mine, I lace my hands behind his neck and pull his mouth to mine. His kisses are soft and light now, and I take my turn to explore his body with my touch. My hands rove his chest, then his back, rounding the curve of his still-clothed backside until I palm the front of his trousers. His length strains against his fly.

"You're aching for my touch, aren't you?" I say, using his own words against him.

He rocks against my hand in answer, a groan building in his throat.

"How long, William? How long have you been aching for me?"

"It feels like a fucking lifetime," he says against my lips, and he finally undoes his trousers and lets me shove them down his hips.

Our kiss deepens, but as I try to wind my legs around him and pull more of his waist against me, he hardly budges.

"More," I beg, fisting his firm length and delighting in the hiss of pleasure he releases. "I want you. I want you so bad I can't take this anymore."

He brings his lips to my ear. "Then say it again, Edwina. Tell me you don't want anyone else to touch me but you."

I pull my head back and meet his eyes. "I want you all to myself."

"How much of me?"

My breaths grow sharp and heavy. Then, gently, I push my palm against his chest. He obeys my silent command, lifting away from me. I shadow his every move, not letting more than an inch of space between us as I guide him into a seated position on the couch and straddle his hips. His erection is firm against my inner thigh, so close to where I want it but not close enough. I raise myself slightly, then bring my mouth to his. He lets me take the lead as I kiss him. "These lips are mine. This…" I stroke my palm down his length, then guide him toward my entrance. He bites his lip as the tip of his cock enters my slick warmth. Then, in a slow move, I lower myself onto him and take him fully inside me. As I rise back up the length of him, my next word comes out with a gasp. "Mine."

He pulls me against him, burying his face in my neck as I guide our rhythm, riding his cock and rocking my hips to hit all the places I'm learning I like. The way he fills me, stretches me, feels like he was made for me. Pleasure writhes through my very being, cresting as he cups my breast and circles my nipple with his tongue. My release builds all over again, but this time I'm the one keeping it at bay, slowing my pace just when I think I might fall. Our bodies grow slick with sweat, and William's grip on my hips tightens. The way his hips rock harder, I can tell he's close too.

I draw back and meet his eyes, drinking in the tormented need written over his face. "What about me, William? Do you want me all to yourself? Do you want to keep me from touching another man? From kissing him? From riding him like this? From taking all this pleasure you're teaching me and using it with someone else?"

His expression darkens, and his grip on my waist holds me in place. "Don't even say those fucking words. I want you and only you. I want my scent coating every inch of your skin. In your hair. I want you so fully wrapped in me that every fae male will smell me on you for miles."

His possessive words send a jolt of excitement through me. I rock my hips, the only move I can make with him holding me in place. It's enough to make his lashes flutter. I take on a taunting tone. "Your scent may keep fae males at bay, but what about human ones? How will you keep me to yourself when humans have such weak senses?"

He draws one hand away from my hip to cradle the back of my neck. Then he brings his lips to mine without kissing me. "I'll ruin you for every man who comes after me," he says against my mouth. "I'll fuck you so deep, satisfy you so thoroughly, you'll never be able to touch another without thinking of me. I'll reach a place no one ever will again."

His other hand leaves my hip to splay over my upper breast. My heart. "Do you want that? Do you want me to ruin you?"

I draw my tongue over his bottom lip. "Yes."

He kisses me firmly, then guides me off his cock. I'm granted a glimpse at his length, slick from our shared arousal, before he turns me around to face the back of the couch. I brace my hands on the ornate wood above the floral cushion. He embraces me from behind and brings his lips to my ear. The tip of his erection finds my center. "Say it."

I swallow hard, angling my head over my shoulder to meet his hungry eyes. Then I arch my back, lifting my hips and widening my legs. "Ruin me."

In one stroke, he enters me to the hilt. I gasp, clutching the back of the couch as he fills me deeper than before. Deeper than I knew was possible.

Then another long stroke out. There he pauses, and I know what he's waiting for.

"Ruin me, Will."

He thrusts into me again.

"Ruin me."

He picks up his pace and I meet him stroke for stroke, slamming back into him with every thrust of his hips.

"Ruin me. Ruin me." His fingers slide down my front to circle my sensitive clit, and my refrain slips into a whine, then a moan, leaving only my mind to carry my chant.

Ruin me.

Ruin me.

His other hand grips my breast, but the way my heart slams into his palm, it feels more like he's clasping the treasure that lies behind my ribs.

Love me.

Love me.

Release builds inside me again, and this time, neither of us do anything to prevent its crash. I grip the couch harder, my moans growing louder, more frantic, while his throaty groans reverberate through me, increasing my pleasure. Finally, the tight coil of need unravels from my core, melting over his fingers, his cock. And as I cry out my climax, his rhythm drives harder, faster, his orgasm chasing mine until it spills inside me.

Together we ride the falling wave until we're both spent. Until he slips out of me from behind and pulls me to face him, cradling my head against his chest as we collapse over the length of the couch.

CHAPTER THIRTY-SIX

WILLIAM

*T*here's something so perfect about the feel of Edwina in my arms. Our bodies are slick and entwined as we catch our breath on the couch. Edwina's eyes are closed, her cheek pressed to my chest. She must be graced with a riotous symphony from how frantically my heart beats against her ear. I don't think it's ever raced so fast. Nor do I believe I've ever felt so spent and satisfied.

I've had more lovers than I can count, but with Edwina...

Fuck, this is different. The mere thought of her saying *mine* while gliding down the length of my cock is almost enough to ready me for a second round, but I keep those urges at bay. She's so peaceful right now, the way her lips curl in a sweet smile. The way her messy hair falls around her shoulders.

I angle my face and plant a kiss on her forehead. She makes an unintelligible sound, and I smile down at her. I've never wanted someone so bad. Never had so much of my heart involved with attraction. My only regret is that we didn't talk as much as I wanted before my desires took over. We didn't solve anything. Didn't state what exactly this is that we have together, or how to navigate our competition for the contract going forward. But do we need a plan? Isn't it enough that we feel the same? Doesn't that mean we can work through whatever comes next together?

The fact that Edwina didn't use her free pass to do what we did tonight gives me hope. It means it was as real for her as it was for me. Not a game.

Once our breathing calms, Edwina lifts her cheek from my chest and props her chin there. I keep an arm wrapped around her, drawing circles over her back with my fingertips. She studies my face, tracing the edge of my jaw, then my pointed ear. She circles her thumb over the gold stud in my lobe, which summons visions of when I did the same to her clit.

My cock stirs at the memory, but when she releases a slow sigh that carries too serious of an edge, I sober from such notions.

She gives me a sad smile and laces her fingers over my pectoral, then props her chin on her hands. "What should we do, William?"

I'm not the only one who realized we still have problems to solve. I brush my hand down the length of her spine, resisting the urge to palm her ass. "About the contract?"

"Our feelings for each other don't change the fact that we both need it."

She's right. And whatever is blooming between us is still too new to attach any promises to it. Even though part of me wants to blurt out that if I win, I'll take care of her. We'll get married, if we must, for that's one way to secure citizenship on the isle. But I wouldn't want that for us—a union built on necessity—and Edwina wouldn't either. She's already not fond of traditional matrimony, and her pride is too bold, bright, and beautiful to be dimmed. Yet dimmed she would be if she had to become dependent on a lover. She won't thrive unless she earns what she wants for herself.

However, I can't simply hand her the win either. I need it as much as Edwina does. Cassie needs it too.

Which leaves the solution I proposed before.

I shift to the side, cradling her head in the crook of my arm, until I'm facing her. "Let's dissolve the bet."

Her eyes turn down at the corners and she nibbles her bottom lip. I can't summon even a flicker of annoyance over her hesitation, for I understand why she wants to cling to this advantage. She still has a one-point lead, and she knows now that I can't play the game. I proved that tonight, to us both.

After our conversation on the rooftop, I thought I'd resigned myself to do what needed to be done, but I was wrong. I couldn't stand the thought of sharing a drink with Aubrey, much less a kiss. The last thing I want is to lead anyone on when my heart is wrapped around Edwina.

She drops her gaze from mine. "It's the right thing to do, isn't it?"

"It is," I whisper, brushing my fingertips over her cheek. She still won't look at me. "If you need more time, we don't have to do it now."

She burrows her face into my chest. "Do you think I'm a terrible person? For not being ready to let go of my lead?"

"Of course not."

"It's just...I want this so bad. This one point I have over you guarantees my win if we forgo further progress in our bet. I'll get the contract, and I'll get to live here. Which... which is also the only way I get to be with you."

My chest tightens. I hate that she's right. What will happen to us if I win? She'll have to move back to Bretton, and then what? We carry on a long-distance romance while she applies for citizenship and hopes it's approved? Or I finally win her heart enough that she opens up to the idea of marriage and she claims her citizenship that way? And what of her financial situation in the meantime? What of her career?

Blooming hell, these are the kinds of questions those in longstanding relationships would struggle to answer. This affection we've confessed to is too fragile, just a seed without roots. We're not ready to make these heavy choices.

Her voice quavers and she speaks again. "Then what if I win? What if you hate me—"

"Edwina." I pull back and gently lift her chin with my forefinger until she meets my eyes. "I promise with all my heart that I won't hold it against you if you win. My feelings will not be changed by that."

There. A promise I can give that she'll readily accept.

She holds my eyes for several long beats of my heart before she finally nods. I release her chin and she nestles against my chest again. We're quiet for a while, but the silence grows weighted. Her breaths are suddenly too soft. Her arms too stiff around my waist.

"Will you tell me about June?"

Her question carves a fissure through my heart, draining it of every pleasant feeling I've been basking in. It's the last thing I was ready for. A truth I've withheld. I've hinted at it, but I haven't outright stated the facts.

Up until now, it seemed too soon. This secret wasn't meant to be given to someone who was merely my rival, no matter how much I wanted her to be more. If she wasn't going to be more, then she didn't need to know.

But now...

Fuck. Now it seems too late.

My heart thuds an anxious rhythm.

Edwina pulls back again, looking up at me with a furrowed brow. "You've told others. You told Jolene. Won't you tell me too?"

I swallow the sudden dryness in my throat. "That story isn't for you."

"Why?" She shifts in my arms to a seated position. "Why did they deserve to know but I don't?"

"It's not about deserving or not deserving. I'm just... afraid. That everything will change. That you'll look at me differently once you know."

She shakes her head. "I won't be jealous if that's what you're worried about. I just want to know this final piece you've kept from me. I want to understand why you're keeping it."

I lift myself up to sit beside her, rubbing my jaw. Now it's my turn to avoid her gaze.

"Who is June, William?"

My pulse rackets, and I wish my clothes weren't so far away. I'd give anything to cover myself. To hide the vulnerability I feel now.

She tilts her head, inserting her face into my line of sight. "Who is this great love of your life that you write all your poems about?"

I release a weighted sigh, then let my eyes lock on hers. "I don't write poetry about some great love."

She frowns. "Then who..."

"I don't...write poetry."

Her frown deepens.

"I don't write."

I catch the moment realization dawns, draining her face of color.

"I act."

Edwina is frozen, not even stirred by her breaths. Meanwhile, my pounding heart has me trembling from head to toe. I'm so fixated on Edwina's every move, so afraid of her reaction, that I don't miss the narrowing of her eyes, the tightening of her jaw.

"You didn't write the poetry book."

I give a slow shake of my head. "Cassie did."

"Your sister wrote it. And you…took credit for it?"

"It's not like that," I rush to say. "Cassie submitted her poetry book under my name without telling me. When she was offered a contract, one with a favorable enough advance to pay off most of our debts, she begged me to accept it and publish it as William Haywood."

She narrows her eyes. "You say that like it's not your real name." A long pause. "Is it?"

"Not all fae have surnames, and I'm one of those fae. Haywood is Cassie's surname. Lydia's too. I'm just…Will."

"Then who the hell is June? What is this story you told Jolene?"

"That's all it is. Just a story. It's part of my act to support the poetry book. William the Poet is a role I play, and he comes with a backstory. I admit I've used that to my advantage, mostly to keep interested lovers at bay. That's why I never told you this fabricated tale. Because I didn't want to keep *you* at bay."

Edwina stares at me for a long moment. The longer she holds my gaze, the more obvious her anger becomes. She rises from the couch and gathers her discarded clothing on her way to the billiards table. There she replaces her spectacles, then dons her skirt and blouse, not bothering with her undergarments. I follow her, pulling my trousers over my legs as I close the distance between us.

"You lied to me," she says as she secures the buttons of her blouse with trembling fingers.

I stop before her and frame her shoulders in my hands. "It's not like that."

She leaves her blouse only half buttoned as she glares at me, fingers curled into fists. "You lied to me, and you lie to your fans. What else have you lied to me about? Was everything you've said to me an act? Was this…was what we just did together part of some game?"

I clench my jaw. "That's a stretch to assume I've lied about *anything* else. I've rarely acted when it's just the two of us."

"Rarely?"

"I can only lie when I'm fully immersed in a role, Edwina, and I'm not acting now. Which is why I can only say *rarely*. Because, yes, I have acted around you in the past, particularly when we first met. But as I've gotten to know you, to care for you, I've been nothing but the real me."

"How am I supposed to trust that? You could have told me the truth at any time but you didn't."

"Would you have judged me for it? Like you're judging me now when you still don't fully understand the situation?"

She shrugs her shoulders from my grip. "Don't you dare blame me for judging you. Of course I am! We're competing for a contract you don't deserve. The poetry book isn't yours. You made me feel bad for you, claiming you were acting in your sister's best interests. That you were putting her through college. Fulfilling her dreams."

"I am."

"No, if you were doing anything for her sake, you would have supported her work."

I throw my hands in the air. "Is that not what I'm doing? We needed the money, and she asked me to do this for her. No one wanted to publish a nineteen-year-old girl's sexy poetry. Not until she attached it to my name and credentials as an actor. She was overjoyed when she received the publication offer."

"That's not what it means to show your support. That's

TESSONJA ODETTE

reinforcing the idea that a young woman can't succeed on her own."

Her words slap me across my face. Cassie has never expressed anything but enthusiasm over our arrangement, but is Edwina right? Was I wrong to agree to this opportunity?

I shake the doubts from my mind. "She doesn't want the spotlight. She just wants her work appreciated during her lifetime, even if it isn't attached to her name."

"Everyone wants their work appreciated, William, and we all fight for it. No one gets a ticket for an easy life."

Rage boils my blood. An easy life. That's what she thinks we have?

"Not everyone can afford the pride of being a starving artist," I say through my teeth. "Not everyone shares your ideals. Ideals don't feed your family. Ideals won't keep my sister alive long enough to enjoy the fruits of her labor after she's spent her final years striving and fighting for renown. Not everyone wants that fucking life!"

Her cheeks flare crimson. "Is that how you see me? Just a ball of stubborn pride living off ideals?"

I close my eyes and run a hand over my face, doing all I can to cool my temper. I don't want to yell at her. I want to pull her against my chest and bring us back to that beautiful place we were in when she first stormed into the room. But when I open my eyes, she's no longer before me. Instead, she's tugging at the door, both handles still wrapped in my vines.

I stride after her. "Where are you going? Are you done with me, just like that? Without giving us a chance to work through this?"

She keeps her eyes pinned to the door. "I don't know. I just...I knew this was going to happen." She mutters the last part under her breath.

336

"You knew what was going to happen? That we'd fight? That you'd find a reason to push me away? Is that why you asked about June before you agreed to dissolve our bet? Were you just looking for any excuse to keep this advantage over me?"

She whirls to face me. "This isn't just about the bet. But maybe you're right. Maybe I was waiting for this to happen because my past has taught me it will. Men lie. They present themselves one way and then turn out nothing like their pretty promises—"

"Do not compare me to Dennis Feverforth," I say, dropping my voice. "This has nothing to do with him or your past. This is happening now, and you are running away."

She releases a groan as she tugs the handles again. "I'm not running away. Just let me out. Get rid of these vines so I can get away from you and breathe for a minute."

The panic in her voice slices through my chest. I hate the thought of her leaving while things are like this, even if she's only going to her room. Every instinct in me yearns to cling to her, to hold her while we yell and talk and fight until we come to a solution, even if only a temporary truce. Even just a promise to try to understand each other. But she isn't me. Maybe she processes hurt differently than I do. Maybe she processes it alone.

I can't force her to be anyone other than who she is.

Because I love who she is.

I love her.

Even if she hates me now.

Slowly, I lower my fingers to the handle. My chest tightens at how she flinches away, yet I extend my magic and dissolve the vines.

"I won't keep you here," I whisper, "but please come back to me if you find it in your heart to want to work this out. I know you're hurt, and I understand why. I know this fight

337

feels fucking horrible, but please, Edwina. Please don't let this end what we've begun."

Her throat bobs and she gives a single jerky nod.

The last of the vines fall to the floor, and she turns the handle at last. She storms out of the room, leaving me colder than I've ever been before.

338

CHAPTER THIRTY-SEVEN

EDWINA

By morning, I've alternated between seething in rage and feeling like a complete asshole a thousand times over. I'm so mad William kept his secret from me. So angry on behalf of his fans, whom he's lied to. And his sister, who's been relegated to the shadows because no one valued her work until a man presented it. I've been there, and I can't shake my anger over it.

But then again...he was right about me. Not everyone is privileged enough to cling to ideals as tightly as I do. Having well-to-do parents and siblings has always given me a safety net. I can strive for my career and take risks, knowing I can always go home. At the cost of my independence, yes, but I won't starve.

Meanwhile, William and Cassie faced crippling debt—a situation I've never been in—before they were offered the publishing contract. Agreeing to the deal kept Cassie out of the workhouses. Now that I've met her, I can't help but agree that William was right to go to any lengths to protect her from such a fate.

Yet it still hurts. And there's a jagged piece of my heart that says *I told you so*. Taunting me that everything I've cherished between me and William was never real to begin with. It was always a lie. Always an act.

No, the rest of my heart argues. *No, that's not true. You know which side of him is real. You've seen both.*

Then why did he keep this secret so long? Why did he have to wait until I gave him my body? Until I begged for the truth?

I don't emerge from my room until close to noon, and even then I'm not sure of my feelings, or how I'm supposed to face William. Luckily, by the time I enter the common area, he's nowhere to be seen. There's only Daphne, who lounges on one of the kitchen cabinets. She opens her eyes when she sees me, then stretches with an adorable yawn.

"You slept a long time," she says as she hops down to the floor. "Probably from all the moaning last night. Followed by yelling."

I blush at her words. When I stormed out of the recreation room, I found Monty and Daphne in the kitchen. Monty was sprawled on his back over the kitchen island, smoking a cigarillo, while Daphne sipped cordial from a tiny wooden cup. Neither said a word as I stomped to my room, but the silence was enough to tell me they probably heard everything.

I grimace. "Is…anyone here?"

"Monty and William are helping set up the gala."

Relief heaves through me. The gala doesn't begin until this evening. Maybe I can make myself scarce until then and avoid having to face William at all. My heart plummets when I recall the last thing he said to me.

...please come back to me if you find it in your heart to want to work this out.

I do. I really do. At least...I think I do.

But I'm still so torn over how I should feel. I'm not ready to talk to him about it yet.

"Did you choose an item for the auction?" Daphne asks, stealing me from my thoughts.

Panic lances through me. I obviously can't get rid of my annotated copy of William's book. Or...Cassie's book. "Oh, uh, I suppose I'll offer a personalized copy of *The Governess and the Fae*."

"That's not nearly as exciting as William's date."

My mouth goes dry. Shit. His date. I forgot all about that. Now it sends my stomach roiling. I don't want him to go on a date with anyone else. Even if it's not a *real* date.

Of course it won't be a real date.

Unless William has changed his mind about me.

Unless his heart has shifted now that he's seen my ugly side. My rage and pride.

I bite the inside of my cheek to divert myself from feeling the tightness in my lungs. A welcome distraction comes to mind. "I just remembered something I'm supposed to give you."

I return to my room and rifle through the skirt I wore last night. It takes no small effort to force away all the memories of what happened when I last wore it. The male who lifted my hem and tortured me just shy of climax. The way he finally dragged my skirt down and let me ride him—

I squeeze my thighs together, and my fingers finally close over what I was searching for—the two dance cards. I tuck one into the pocket of my day dress and return to Daphne.

"The event coordinator asked me to give this to you," I say as I hand the second card over. "The charity receives funding for every space filled by a dance."

Daphne turns the card over a few times, her furry brow knitting in curiosity. "I've never danced before."

I shrug. "You don't have to. I know you aren't comfortable in your seelie form, and I assume the gala caters mostly to humans and seelie fae. But I wanted to give you the card just in case."

"Hmm." She turns the card over in her paws again.

A knock sounds at the main door. I have half a mind to hide in my room for fear of encountering William, but the caller can't be him. He wouldn't need to knock.

Still, I gather a deep breath before I open the door.

"Miss Danforth!" Cassie's bright expression greets me on the other side of the threshold.

Damn. That's almost as bad as seeing William.

She pulls her chin back with a wary look. "Did you mean to frown at me just now?"

My cheeks flush and I wave an apologetic hand. "I'm so sorry, I just wasn't expecting you. If you're here for William, he isn't in."

"Actually, I'm here to see you."

I shift awkwardly from foot to foot. "Did William send you here to talk to me?"

She scoffs. "On the contrary, I doubt he'd have let me take so much as a step out of his sight. He doesn't know I'm here. Will you go to lunch with me in town?"

I'm tempted to refuse, but maybe talking to Cassie is exactly what I need. Maybe getting to know her better will help me understand their arrangement. And my feelings about it.

"Let me get my coat."

OUR DESTINATION IS A FEW BLOCKS FROM THE HOTEL. I OFFER to hail us a cab, but she insists on walking.

"I feel really great today, I assure you," she insists on our way. "The cane is mostly for days when my legs feel weak or painful. But I keep it on me in case of dizzy spells."

"William told me a little about your condition," I say, mindful not to appear like I'm fussing over her. "He said your mother had the same degenerative disease, and that it's a mystery to the medical community."

"A mystery, yes, but I have plenty of tonics and fae remedies that lessen my symptoms."

We arrive at a café located on the bottom floor of a small building nestled between two taller ones, its circular windows framed with green vines and tiny pink rosebuds. The vines remind me of the ones William locked the door with last night.

I breathe away the memory, a mixture of pleasure and pain.

We sit at a table near a sunny window. Cassie orders food for us, as she's been here before. Lunch consists of tea, an assortment of tiny sandwiches, and little round confections that are soft and gummy on the outside but filled with a sweet, cherry-flavored bean paste on the inside.

"It's delicious, isn't it?" she asks when I taste one.

"It is," I say with a full mouth. Her expression suddenly falls, making my anxiety rise in tandem. "What's wrong?"

She purses her lips before speaking. "I lied to you. Sort of. William doesn't know I came to see you, but I did see him at the hotel already. We had a conversation."

I halt my chewing. "About?"

"About the secret he told you last night. And your reaction."

"Oh?" I take a nonchalant sip of tea, but my hands tremble.

She leans toward me and braces her elbows on the table. Then, lacing her hands, she props her chin upon them and watches me through slitted lids. "Miss Danforth—actually, can I call you Edwina?"

"Please."

"Edwina, then. Do you have feelings for William?"

I nearly choke on my tea. Once I recover, I give her a nod. I do have feelings for her brother. Whether those feelings are good or bad—or both—I'm not sure.

"I thought so," she says. "Just one look at the two of you yesterday, I suspected Zane was right. That you and William like each other."

I can't tell whether her tone is accusatory or merely curious, but my guilt flares just the same. Despite being ten years her senior, I can't help feeling like I'm in trouble and wanting to do anything to get back on her good side. So I say nothing and wait for her to speak again.

"What William told you last night wasn't his secret to tell," she says. "It's *ours*. Mine and his. I made him promise to share the truth about our arrangement only with those who either need to know for business purposes or will listen and accept us with an open mind."

My guilt grows deeper at those last words. They suggest William only told me because he thought there was a chance I would react in an understanding manner.

"Does Mr. Fletcher know?" I ask.

"He does. After I received his offer on the book and got William to agree to my proposal, I confessed that we are a writing duo and explained our arrangement. He was still willing to publish the book and let William be the public face. Though, after the book's release, he was hesitant to promote it with a tour. Mr. Fletcher wasn't sure my brother could pull it off, even with William's acting skills. That's why his promised tour never came to fruition. Not until he proved himself capable and earned a place beside you on The Heartbeats Tour."

I don't know whether to feel vindicated now that I know Mr. Fletcher is aware of the truth. If he approves of their arrangement, why should I be so offended by it? Yet there's more to my annoyance than that.

"I hate that he lies to his fans, obscuring the truth from them. Doesn't it bother you that he's turned your title into a farce? Making up a story about some great lost love named June?"

She snorts a laugh. "For one, we aren't completely obscuring the truth. The copyright page discloses me as the author and William as the performer. For another, William didn't make up the idea of June as a former lover. *June* in my title refers to nothing more than a month. It's our fans who've made the leap. Yes, he's used it as fuel for his role's backstory, and he makes vague statements or provides broody anecdotes that allow our readers to continue believing as they already do. They're going to speculate whether we want them to or not."

"Wouldn't you rather they knew the truth? The real meaning behind your words? The real stories that live behind your poetry, and not the act William puts on?" I don't mention that if I'd known the truth I might not have ridiculed *A Portrait of June* so relentlessly. I never thought the poems were bad, in my heart of hearts. Only that William was pretentious and—as an automatic result—anything he said or did was too. Including what I assumed was his poetry. For the love of all things, how did he hide his anger when I made fun of his sister's poetry to his face?

"Do you want your readers to know the truth?" Cassie says with an arched brow. "Which parts of your books come from the deepest aspects of your soul and which are mere whimsy?"

She has a point. I remember how embarrassed I was when Jolene assumed I've experienced every sexual scenario I've written about. "No, but I write fiction."

"So? Who says poetry must be autobiographical? If I want anonymity, I should be allowed to have it. It's no one's business who my poems are about or if they are based on real experiences. Those words and emotions are mine. You see William as a fraud but he's more like my shield. He bears the brunt of everyone's expectations and speculations, while I get to create. That's all I want to do. Please don't hold that against him."

The hollow ache in my chest abates the slightest bit. Maybe I have judged William too harshly. Yet so much pain remains.

I blow out a heavy sigh. "I hate that he lied to me. William Haywood isn't even his real name."

Her expression turns hard. "He's my brother, Edwina. He may not have been born a Haywood but he deserves my family name. It just so happens that it's his stage name and our pen name. That doesn't mean he's been dishonest with you about his identity."

The edge in her tone slashes through my indignation, making my argument seem as frail as a worn piece of parchment.

"You're judging him too harshly," she says, and everything inside me echoes that she's right. "This isn't some grand scheme; it's our shared art. He's the public face, and I'm the creator. We're a team. I don't want the spotlight. He does. He wants this for me, but I want this for him too. The popularity of our book will breathe life into his career."

My shoulders slump. I know all about his failing career, but not once did I consider how much this might save it. "I just...I suppose if he told me from the start, I wouldn't have been so hurt."

She gives me a withering look. "If he told you from the start, you might never have given him a chance. You're clearly prejudiced against our arrangement."

Normally I'd bristle at such an accusation...but she's right. I never gave William the chance to explain before I shoved a wall of my ideals between us. While I still feel like it's dishonest to their fans, I do understand both William's and Cassie's side better now.

I give her a tight smile. "I'll try to have an open mind. Can I ask you something out of a genuine desire to better understand?" At her nod, I say, "Is this really your dream? The poetry book? This arrangement you have with William?"

"It's a step toward it," she says. "I want to attend college and I want to write a play that my brother stars in before I die. The doctor gave me a prognosis of six more years."

Shock surges through me, even more so by the nonchalance in her tone. "Six years? What do you mean?"

"My symptoms have progressed much faster than my mother's, plus I have my own additional ailments I've had to deal with."

I stare at her open-mouthed. Is this why William has spoken about her not having time? Why he's so desperate to make her happy? It's not just that she's human and fragile compared to him. It's not just that she suffers from ailments. It's that she has a tangible prognosis. A timeline.

She gives me another withering look. "Don't look at me with such sad eyes. I have every intention of living to a ripe old age."

I sit back in my chair, dumbstruck.

"There's something you should understand about William," Cassie says. "Did he tell you about Lydia? My mother?"

"He told me she died. That his father left her."

347

"Do you also know how fae and human aging work in Faerwyvae?"

"I know fae used to age slowly," I say, "but have begun aging as quickly as humans do. Yet most still cease aging once they reach maturity. Meanwhile, some humans have experienced slower aging."

"Those who are in romantic partnerships with fae," Cassie clarifies. "There has been proof that platonic fae partnerships —like friends or family—can slow human aging, but romantic relations are the most effective. When Lydia met William's father, she experienced a drastic improvement in her health conditions, but he left us when William went to university. My mother didn't want William to know because she knew he'd worry. So he didn't find out that his father left or that Mother was ill until after graduation." Cassie's gray eyes glaze, and her voice takes on a quaver. "William blamed himself for not being able to do more. For not being enough to make Mother well."

My own eyes fall under a sheen as I imagine what that must have felt like for him. He probably hated himself for having enjoyed his time at university while his mother was suffering.

"He never should have felt responsible for her health," Cassie says. "No one should be put in that position. To be honest, I can't even blame his father. I never want someone to love me and stay with me just to keep me alive. But William can't let that go. He carries guilt that he wasn't enough for Lydia and that he isn't enough for me either. He hates that all the debt we accumulated during Mother's final years of medical treatment fell under my name after she died. Since our parents never married, neither William nor his father held any legal burden for me or the debt. That made William feel guiltier than anything. Nothing I can say will lessen his sense of shame, which is why he dotes on me like he does. Why he wants to be responsible. He wants to give me everything while I'm alive."

A tear trickles down my cheek. How can I blame him? Even I want Cassie to have everything, and I hardly know her. It crushes my heart that William considers himself inadequate just because he isn't all-powerful. At the same time, I realize what a marvel it is that he was brave enough to open his heart to me. Me, a human he's worried he could fail.

Me, who fled from him at my first chance.

"He's afraid he'll be like his father," Cassie says, speaking straight to my heart. "He's afraid that if he has a human lover, his love won't be enough. Which is why I worry for him almost as much as he frets over me. I fear he'll be too preoccupied with making someone else happy that he'll sacrifice his career and all the things that make him who he is. Two people shouldn't need to be so entwined."

I study her face, her wary expression. "Are you telling me this to warn me away from him?"

She shakes her head. "I'm asking how much you care about him. It's one thing if you love him. It's another if he's just a fleeting fancy."

I recoil at the thought of William being nothing more than a *fleeting fancy*, as she put it. Yet the prospect of loving him sends my heart skittering. Fluttering. A renewed sense of that giddy feeling.

It doesn't scare me this time.

It doesn't remind me of how things went with Dennis Feverforth.

Because this feeling is tethered to more than just fickle words and illusions.

It's tethered to the man who assured me my words are beautiful.

To the man who slept in a chair beside my bed the night I drank myself into stupidity.

To the man who shared his vulnerable past with me.

Who jested with me, flirted with me, and confessed his feelings in the pages of our playful book.

I rise to my feet, beautiful and terrifying words on my tongue. "I love him enough that I won't let your fears for him come to fruition. I won't let him lose himself in me. But...I won't push him away either."

Her lips curl into a smile. "You're going to forgive him?"

I search for the remnants of anger I felt for him. They're there, but they're nothing but ashes compared to the blaze in my heart. "I already have."

She rises with the aid of her cane and takes my fingers in her free hand. "You should tell him to his face."

My chest lifts. It's still full of clouds, but I'm ready to disperse them. Together. With William. I'm still scared, but it's not enough to stop me. My legs tremble with my sudden burst of eagerness to get back to him.

Cassie gives me a knowing grin. "Let's get..." She blinks. Once. Twice. Her expression slips. Her already pale complexion goes a shade lighter. Then, with a flutter of her lashes, she slips to the ground.

CHAPTER THIRTY-EIGHT

EDWINA

I'm going to miss the gala.

Night falls outside the window of the bedroom where Cassie rests. She's been sleeping for hours now, and I can't bring myself to leave her, despite her insistence that she was fine before she retired to her bed.

I understand William's protectiveness over her even more now. It was terrifying to watch as Cassie's slender body went limp. Luckily, I eased her fall and she wasn't injured. She even regained consciousness quickly and gave me the address to the house where she's staying. With my aid, we hailed a hansom cab, and I handed her into the care of her friends. They echoed Cassie's assurances that this wasn't the most unusual thing for her and that she'd be better after some rest.

I believe them, but I can't leave her. How could I? William would be furious if he knew I left her while she was still recovering. I'm already half convinced he'll rage at me for agreeing to keep her fainting spell a secret until she can tell him herself. It's a vow I'm coming very close to breaking, though I understand Cassie's reasoning. She doesn't want him to miss the gala either and refused to lie down until I agreed not to send word to him.

Though I never promised I'd leave her myself.

The room, at least, is comfortable for Cassie. It's a large guest suite in a grand manor at the edge of town, just a ten-minute coach ride from the café we dined at. Her friends have come in to check on her periodically and have laid out a tray of tea, cookies, and Cassie's next dose of medicines. She truly does seem to be in the best of care. Her friends dote on her as deeply as William does.

Just in a far less overbearing manner.

When Cassie finally wakes, I rush to her side.

"What are you still doing here?" she asks, her voice thick with sleep.

I aid her into a seated position. "I had to ensure you were well when you awoke."

She reaches around me for one of her remedies, waving me away when I offer my help. "You really didn't have to," she says as she administers several drops of a tincture into her teacup. "I told you I'd be fine after a couple of hours of rest. It was just a dizzy spell. It happens."

"Regardless, I wanted to wait until you awoke."

She takes a sip of her tea, eying me over her teacup. "Are you sure you're not procrastinating over a certain conversation you should have with a certain individual?"

"No," I say, and I mean it with all my heart. "I'm ready to talk to William, but I wouldn't feel right pouring my heart out while keeping a secret from him. I understand why you don't want to worry him, but I needed to see for myself that you're well."

She shakes her head, a mixture of amusement and annoyance on her face. "If I knew this would happen, I would have let you send word to him after all. Then at least you could miss the gala together. He's probably worried sick about both of us."

A hollow pit opens in my stomach, and I need to voice it. "There's something I want to say to you, Cassie, but it might not be my place."

She sets down her teacup and pours herself a teaspoon of her next medicine. Her eyes narrow slightly, but she gives a resigned sigh. "If you love my brother, you might as well be family. And if you're family, then it is your place to speak."

Her mention of love has my stomach flipping and fluttering all over again, but I focus on what I need to get off my chest. "Please don't hide your troubles from William. Let him see you're dealing with them. Let him know when you struggle and how you recover with the aid of your friends. Let him truly see that you're thriving. Not to convince him you don't need him but to show him he isn't missing out on anything. He isn't going to be surprised by a sudden tragedy. Let him feel like he's with you every step of the way, even when you're apart."

Cassie doesn't meet my eyes. "Is this about what my mother did?"

"I know she meant well," I say, voice gentle. "She wanted William to enjoy his university years, the same way you want him to enjoy his life without constantly worrying about you. But I can't imagine how hurt he was to find out he'd been left out of Lydia's struggles, and I'm sure there's a part of him that thinks the same is happening with you. He should have been given a choice back then, so let him have a choice with you from now on."

Her expression turns wary.

I level a knowing look. "Even if his fretting and fussing is unbearable."

She lets out a small laugh at that. "Fine. I understand what you're saying. I'll…do my best to give him a choice."

Relief uncoils inside me. "Thank you."

"But I also have a choice over whether I accept his—or anyone's—fretting in person. And I'm making that choice now. Please go to the gala. I really am all right."

"You are, aren't you?" I study her clear eyes, the color that has returned to her cheeks.

"Go," she says with a shooing motion. "Don't you want to sabotage his date?"

A shock of panic sweeps through me. I forgot about his date again! My anxieties regarding our relationship and future have lessened, and I no longer carry a fear that his auctioned date could turn romantic.

But still.

I give Cassie a wicked grin. "I most certainly do want to sabotage his date."

I'M A BALL OF FRAYING NERVES ON MY WAY BACK TO THE hotel. The coach ride takes twice as long as it did to get Cassie from the café to the manor, due to all the traffic heading toward the hotel. Even though the gala started almost an hour ago, guests are still arriving. Only once I exit the coach do I realize just how underdressed I am. Figures in evening gowns or frock coats stream toward the front doors. Meanwhile I'm still in my much plainer day dress.

"There you are!"

I recognize the voice before I locate its source. Then a woman with short black hair strides up to me, and I find Daphne's seelie form. She's outfitted in the same dress she wore when I last saw her in this body—the yellow silk gown with pink-and-white flowers she got from Zane. Her ruffled hem lands just above her knees, and her legs are covered in white stockings. Her feet are tucked into matching dancing slippers, also from Zane's closet.

She looks adorable and just a touch scandalous, thanks to her short hem. I'm almost of a mind to warn her when a female fae strolls by in a skirt even shorter than Daphne's and a top that barely covers her breasts. Even though most of the guests I've seen so far seem to favor more modest human fashions, this is still a fae event, and fae fashions are far more varied.

"You look lovely," I say to her.

She grimaces. "I'm going to try to dance. But forget about me. I've been looking for you everywhere. Where have you been? Your auction starts in fifteen minutes. Where is the personalized book you said you were going to donate?"

The blood leaves my face. "I…uh…"

Daphne shoves me toward the front doors. "We need to hurry, and you need to get dressed."

As much as I want to find William at once, I do have a commitment to fulfill; a donation item to select. I can spare ten minutes to get dressed and choose something of value that bidders might like.

We rush past the bodies funneling into the lobby and race to our suite. My heart slams against my ribs as I hurry to change. I never planned tonight's ensemble so I do the same thing Daphne did and wear the dress I got from Zane—the backless white one William untied and retied in the elevator. I don't bother doing a thing with my hair and instead put together my donation, carefully tearing written pages out of my notebook and stacking them together, but not before writing out a few final touches on the last page.

Daphne's impatience is etched over her face by the time I emerge from my room. "Hurry!"

We race back down to the first floor, and my lips curl wider with every step. My heart continues to pound, beating to the rhythm of my hurried pace, my excitement, my hope. I outpace Daphne as the ballroom doors come into view. I rush through them, but an arm comes to my elbow as soon as I'm inside.

"Finally!" Monty rakes a hand through his hair while he pulls me out of the way of the stream of guests entering along with me. "Where have you been? No, first things first. Where is your donation?"

I hand him the stack of papers. He frowns at it, but the expression soon turns into a smirk. He reads the front page. "*Fourteen Ways to Die in Faerwyvae: An Illustrated Guide.* Are these the kinds of things you're always scribbling in your notebook?"

"More or less."

He flips past a few pages, his eyes widening on one. "That's a rather unfeasible position," he says of a sketch I drew of two nude figures entangled on a pegasus.

I shrug. "Not all my ideas work out, which is why I sketch them first."

He flips to the next page. "This one though. This position I guarantee works wonders. I bet Daph would like this sketch. Speaking of..." He lowers my papers and stares at the ground with a frown. "Where is everyone's favorite feral mustelid? I told her to find you—"

"I'm right here." I startle at her voice, still not used to hearing it so close to my ear. With the crowds still pouring into the ballroom, I hadn't realized she'd come up beside me.

Monty's eyes go wider than I've ever seen. He freezes in place as he stares at her seelie form. "Daph?"

She shrinks down slightly. "Yeah."

His shocked gaze sweeps down her form, then he stiffens. "Whoa. Legs."

356

"Where's William?" I say, drawing Monty's attention both for Daphne's sake and mine.

Monty shakes his head as if to clear it, his cheeks suddenly pink. He aims a thumb toward the stage. "He's being auctioned off as we speak."

Urgency propels me away from Monty and Daphne, and I race toward the stage, skirting around the dancers circling on the floor, weaving between chatting figures and those browsing the auction tables. Finally, I catch sight of the stage. A large crowd gathers before it, so dense I could never hope to cut through to the front.

At the very center of the stage is William.

CHAPTER THIRTY-NINE

WILLIAM

I feel like an idiot. Not only because I'm sitting on a literal throne being gawked at by strangers—though that certainly has to do with it—but because I can't stop dwelling on what happened last night. I don William the Poet's smug grin as I slouch sideways in the gold-plated, velvet-cushioned chair. Inside, I can only think of Edwina. Edwina, whom I haven't seen all day. Not since she left the recreation room with so much hurt in her eyes.

I haven't seen Cassie either since she came to see me earlier. She hounded me about Edwina, inquiring about my feelings, the attraction Zane told her about via telegram. I crushed her hopes when I relayed Edwina's reaction to my confession. Cassie was so crestfallen afterward. Perhaps she decided not to come to the gala after all. I do hope she doesn't blame herself for what happened between me and Edwina.

That was entirely my fault.

Edwina was right. I should have told her sooner. In fact… maybe I never should have agreed to this arrangement with Cassie. Maybe I'm robbing my sister of the empowerment she'd feel if she kept trying to publish her book on her own. Maybe I'm betraying my fans by presenting someone else's art.

But the money.

Our debts.

Cassie's dream.

The ticking clock of her prognosis.

Blooming hell. I don't know what the right choice was. All I know is that I want to do anything to inspire Edwina's trust in me again.

"Do I have twenty sapphire rounds?" The auctioneer stands beside my ridiculous throne, calling out bids and encouraging higher ones.

"Twenty," calls a young man at the center of the crowd.

"Twenty-one," shouts a woman at the front, her hungry gaze locked on me. I try not to grimace as she licks her lips, though I do hope no one misunderstands the purpose of this date or expects it to be anything but chaste.

"Twenty-two," says another.

The bids rise higher and higher in rapid succession.

Thirty. Thirty-five. It jumps to forty. Then fifty, with a trio of bidders battling to get the better of each other.

"Fifty-two," says the woman at the front, her eyes still locked on me as she fans her ample bosom with her dancing card.

"Fifty-three," her rival shouts.

"Fifty—"

"Two hundred."

The voice calls out from the very back of the crowd, and my heart lurches as I see the auburn head peek above all the rest.

Edwina.

She's here.

Our eyes lock across the crowd and I rise from my seat.

I can't see her fully, but from how she's grown two heads taller and the way she splays her arms, she must be balancing on a chair. It reminds me of the first day we met, when she stood on a chair to spout awful poetry before getting tangled with me in a bet.

She raises her hand, empty without a bidding number. "Two hundred sapphire rounds," she shouts, almost breathless. "Did I do it right?"

Silence echoes back as the bidders turn to look at her.

"That's Edwina Danforth," someone whispers. "The romance author."

The woman at the front huffs. "Two hundred and one—"

"The bet," Edwina shouts. "I bid the dissolution of our bet."

I take a step toward the edge of the stage, my mind spinning to comprehend what she's saying, what she's doing.

More whispers break out in the crowd, and even the auctioneer looks puzzled.

"What is she talking about?" someone asks.

"Can we bid intangibles?"

Edwina raises her hand again. "My heart." Her voice cracks on the word. "I bid my heart, Will."

My breath hitches at the sound of my name. Not my full name. Not my stage name. Just...me.

I race down the stairs at the edge of the stage and make a beeline for her. The crowd parts in gasps and startled exclamations, but I only have eyes for her. Finally, the sea of bodies parts enough to give me a full view. She's outfitted in that gorgeous fucking dress that I once had my hands beneath, and the way her crooked updo spills loose frizzy tendrils all around her shoulders only enhances her beauty.

Because this is a bold and uncaring kind of beauty that eclipses all else.

I stop before her. With the height of the chair, she stands slightly taller. My fingers yearn to touch her, but I don't dare until I know she wants me to.

Her eyes glaze behind her lenses, and her bottom lip quivers. "I'm sorry I'm so stubborn, Will. You're right about me. I get so high on my ideals that I judge others for not following them too."

"You don't ever have to apologize for being stubborn," I say, my voice as rough and uneven as hers. "I love that about you."

Her eyes widen.

"I love *you*, Edwina, exactly as you are."

"You love me?"

My mouth curls. "I love you."

A tear spills over her cheek, and her lips break into the widest, sweetest grin. She reaches for me then, winding her arms around my neck while I wrap mine around her waist. I press my mouth to hers as I lift her off the chair. Our kiss continues as I set her on her feet, neither of us willing to release the other.

"By the way," she whispers when she finally breaks away for breath, "I love you too."

I press my forehead to hers. "I figured."

"I'm sorry I was late."

"It's all right, love. I'm not going anywhere."

"I hate to interrupt."

Edwina and I separate just enough to find Aubrey standing before us. My muscles tense as I notice every pair of eyes in the crowd is locked on us, some in confusion, others in amusement or awe.

"We are still in an active auction," Aubrey whispers. "If you didn't already know, I should inform you it is magically binding. And you, Miss Danforth, just bid your heart. A bid that could get gruesome if the auctioneer interprets it the wrong way. I highly suggest we return to your first bid of two hundred sapphire rounds."

Edwina and I exchange a horrified look.

"Yes, I agree," Edwina says.

"Two hundred rounds," Aubrey shouts to the auctioneer. "Let us return to that."

The auctioneer nods. "Do I hear two hundred and one?"

I wince, expecting the aggressive bidder near the stage to pipe up again, but only silence echoes back. Well, silence and music and the curious whispers of those around us. No one tries to top Edwina's bet.

"Sold," the auctioneer says, "to...the woman in white."

Edwina purses her lips to hide her amused grin. "Did I just purchase you?"

"A date. You purchased a date." I smirk. "You already have the rest of me anyway."

"You're right," she says, pulling my lips to hers again. Her breathless tone sends a shiver up my spine. "I already told you you're mine."

IT TAKES ALL MY RESTRAINT NOT TO DRAG HER OUT OF THE ballroom and prop her against a wall in the first empty corner of the hotel I can find. Or better yet, inside the elevator. Or back in our suite on the billiards table. Or any number of the places I want to devour her.

But after Edwina's tardiness and the stir we caused during my auction, it's best we stay. This may not be a signing, but it is one of our official tour stops. We have fans who've come to see us.

Edwina confesses about where she was this afternoon, which explains where Cassie has been too. My stomach bottoms out when she recounts my sister's fainting spell, but I manage not to lose my head. It certainly helps that Edwina stayed with Cassie until she was sure my sister was well.

We part ways to chat with our respective readers, and once the gala comes to an end, Edwina and I meet in the lobby to return to our suite together. We take the stairs, which are less crowded than the elevators, stopping to kiss in the stairwell when we're alone. I manage to slip a hand under her bodice, exploring her beautiful breasts while my cock strains against my trousers. The sound of footsteps on the flight below has me biting back a frustrated groan, and we proceed the rest of the way to our floor.

Once inside our suite, Monty and another woman are already there. The latter is perched on the kitchen island, swinging her stockinged legs over the edge of the counter while she sips ruby liquid from a tumbler. Monty's elbows are propped on the other side, his cigarillo perched between his lips and filling the common room with a faintly sweet aroma. I've never seen Monty with a friend or lover, and the shock at seeing a stranger in our midst cools my ardor.

Then the woman speaks in a familiar voice. "Ah, they're back."

My mouth falls open. "Daphne?"

She shrinks down, as if only now realizing why the sight of her might be surprising. "Yeah," she says, tugging on the short hem of her skirt.

"Did you dance?" Edwina asks as we approach them. She's not at all surprised by Daphne's appearance, though it makes sense considering she's already seen Daphne's seelie form.

Daphne takes a sip from her cup. "A little."

"She filled half her dance card," Monty says, and there's a strange look on his face when he stares at Daphne. Something soft and open I've never seen before. Then he dons a crooked smile. "This little weasel is a terrible dancer."

Daphne scoffs. "You're worse than I am."

Edwina casts a surprised look at Monty. "You danced too?"

"Only once," he says. "I'm not one for dancing, but one of Daffy's partners was getting a little too touchy."

"You didn't have to crush his shoulder," Daphne says under her breath. "He thought you were going to murder him."

"I haven't a clue what you mean," Monty says, a humorless grin on his face. He looks much more like his flippant self now.

"Wait, why do you have this?" Edwina lifts something off the counter. It's a collection of pages that bear her handwriting.

"I won the auction," Monty says.

"Why?"

Monty takes a drag from his cigarillo. "What do you mean, why? I placed the highest bid."

Edwina gives him a scathing look that's betrayed by the humor in her smile. "Yes, but why did you want it? I thought this would go to a dedicated fan of mine."

"You wound me in suggesting I'm not a dedicated fan. Besides, I thought Daphne would enjoy your drawings. The sexy ones, in particular." He winks, receiving a growl from Daphne, before he turns his gaze to me. "And what a waste it would be if William never got to see the final page."

I glance from Monty to the stack of papers in Edwina's hands, then to my beautiful lover's face. Her cheeks are flushed, and her smile is suddenly bashful.

"Well, now I'm intrigued." I reach for the papers and she hands them over with only the slightest hesitation.

"Don't skip the beginning," Monty says.

I flip through each page, starting with *Fourteen Ways to Die in Faerwyvae: An Illustrated Guide* at the beginning. Then a few lewd drawings. After that, I find a page entitled *Fourteen Ways to Die in Faerwyvae: Arrogant Poet Edition*. Beneath it are several crude illustrations, most of which I can't make out, though I believe one is supposed to be a glass vial. Next to it is her handwriting: *Poison?*

I snort a laugh and cast a questioning glance at Edwina. "Death threats?"

"I was drunk," she explains with a grimace.

I flip through more pages of drawings, then another How To list, this one *How to Seduce a Stranger*. Several bullet points are listed below, such as *Act coy and demure* and *Cleavage*. In the margins, her sloppy scrawl reads *I have no idea what I'm doing*. More drawings follow, and then I reach the final page. My throat tightens at once.

Fourteen Ways to Fall in Love with Faerwyvae.

Beneath the title are bullet points numbered one through fourteen.

All of which bear my name.

William Haywood.

William Haywood.

William Haywood.

William Haywood.

I set the papers down and face Edwina. "You were going to auction this away without ever showing me?"

She gives me a hesitant grin. "It was the highest value item I could bear to part with."

It's so much more than that. This collection of papers is the story of us. From her first arrival in Faerwyvae, to her horrible first impression of me. All the way to the blossoming of love. With several drawings of unattainable sexual positions interspersed between, of course, but I can't expect to be the only thing to have taken up residence in my strange little lover's mind the past couple of weeks.

I step closer to Edwina, my eyes locked on hers.

"I appreciate you winning the bid, Monty," I say without sparing him so much as a glance, "but I'll have to repay your thoughtfulness by warning you and Daphne to fuck off for a while."

Edwina looks puzzled at first, but then a sly grin curves her mouth.

"Oh, I know what this is," Daphne mutters as she hops off the counter, swiping a bottle of cordial on her way.

Monty releases a long-suffering groan. "For fuck's sake, Daph, we are never sharing a suite with them again for the rest of this tour."

"Agreed," Daphne says.

As soon as the common room door closes behind them, my lips crash into Edwina's. My fingers find the ribbon at the back of her dress, and her bodice falls away. I waste no time tugging the skirt over her hips, then sliding down her undergarments. There's no slow teasing this time. No waiting. Edwina reaches for my cravat, tugging it loose while I shrug off my jacket, then my waistcoat. In a matter of seconds we're both naked.

I prop her on the kitchen island, and she falls back, hooking her legs around my hips as I position myself before her. She's already dripping wet for me, eager and open. I pause with my tip at her entrance, coating my head with her arousal, before I slide into her with a single thrust. I take her there on the counter, over the loose papers, over all the evidence of her love for me. I slam into her until she quivers with release. Then I slide out of her and carry her to my bed, where my kisses turn tender, my pace slower as I lower myself on top of her and enter her once more.

I grasp her hands in mine, pinning them to the mattress

as I breathe in the scent of her skin, the taste of her lips. She holds my gaze as I make love to her as slowly as I can, in tandem with the languid rock of her hips, sating her every need with my movements. Only when she tightens her legs around me, her walls squeezing my cock, do I quicken my pace. Her moans rise, mingling with mine as she writhes beneath me. She throws her head back, lips parted, as the sweetest fucking whine I've ever heard escapes her throat. She unravels around me, her warm slick heat tightening in her orgasm. My next thrust has me spilling into her, my moan in harmony with her final whimpers. I shudder with the euphoria of our shared climax, a sensation that tears through me like never before. It's so potent I can barely hold myself up in the wake of my spend.

I lay back with her cradled against my chest, but almost as soon as I close my eyes, I'm aware of a floral scent and something that tickles my neck.

Edwina notices it at the same time, lifting herself halfway and plucking something out of my hair. "Is this…"

I squint at it through the darkness of my unlit room, but it isn't hard to guess what it is. "A flower petal."

She lifts a handful of more petals she finds beside my head, then lets them fall.

I look to the side, finding more petals all around us.

Edwina arches a brow. "Will, did you just ejaculate flower petals all over the bed?"

I bark a laugh. "First you ask if it's poop, now you ask if it's cum. It's neither. More like…spontaneous unintentional flower creation. I swear, that doesn't normally happen."

She takes another handful and lets them slip through her fingers. "Well, you said the same thing about the three-second handshake I gave your cock, and you were right. You've lasted much longer ever since."

I shift her onto her back again. "You are not supposed to bring that up."

Her grin turns mischievous. "I said I wanted it on a plaque over my mantle, and I mean it."

"You're a vulgar woman."

Her smile softens. "But you love me anyway."

"Yes, Edwina," I whisper, planting a kiss over her temple, then her cheek, then her mouth. "I love you anyway."

CHAPTER FORTY

EDWINA

The next day, I get to collect my auction prize—my date with William. It also means I must part with two hundred sapphire rounds, which is practically everything I have on my person in that currency. At least it's for a good cause, serving not only the Faerwyvae Literary Society but also keeping William all to myself.

However, he insists on delivering the date exactly how he'd planned if I were a stranger. I'm even required to sign an agreement when I hand over my funds, promising not to engage in a number of behaviors with my chaperone, including kissing, hugging, or any form of touch outside of that between a proper escort and his charge.

Furthermore, he refuses to ride with me to our meeting place. Instead, I hail a hansom outside the hotel and give the coachman the address. As unfamiliar as I am with Darlington Hills, I haven't a clue where our date will take place.

My cab heads in the opposite direction from where

Cassie is staying, taking me down roads I haven't traversed yet. There are more storefronts and lovely buildings with those sloped tiled roofs, more flowering trees. Then the buildings become sparser, the plant life more plentiful, and I catch sight of crystal-blue water in the distance.

The coachman lets me out before a gated sidewalk lined with swaying willows. I can't see what lies beyond the gate or the trees, but many of the pedestrians around me carry picnic baskets and blankets. I follow their lead as they head through a towering archway in the gate, composed of latticed wood sprouting tea roses. As I cross under the arch, I find a sprawling green lawn surrounded by more willows and a wide rippling lake at the center. A promenade circles the lake, and all around it are the most beautiful blossoming trees in the most stunning pink hues, casting shade over the walkway.

I lightly lift the hem of my blue walking skirt as I make my way down the stone staircase that leads to the promenade, awed by the beauty around me. The water is as clear as the sky, dancing beneath the most perfect gentle breeze. Swallows swoop from flowering branches, chirping and chittering. Lovers stroll arm in arm or lounge on picnic blankets. It's not unlike a public park in Bretton, yet it's somehow a thousand times more dazzling.

"Love at first sight yet again?"

I'm so distracted I momentarily forget why I'm here. But now the sound of William's voice has me shivering with joy.

I whirl around and find him with a sly grin on his face. He's dressed in the same ensemble I first saw him in, an emerald-and-sage suit with a cream cravat. Just like that first glimpse I had of him, at his table in Flight of Fancy, I'm struck by his beauty. Will I ever not be struck by it?

With a shake of his head, he dons a more serious expression. "Pardon me, Miss Danforth. That was a brash thing to say to a stranger."

"A stranger?" I echo with an arched brow.

He holds out a gloved hand. "Allow me to introduce myself properly. Greetings, Miss Danforth, I am William Haywood, the poet you have so kindly bid to date for an afternoon. Thank you for taking the time out of your day to enjoy the Darlington Hills Promenade with me."

I place my own gloved hand in his. "Are we acting?"

"A little," he whispers with a wink.

"Pleased to meet you," I say in a formal tone, though I'm sure my smile betrays my shoddy efforts.

He releases my hand and proffers his elbow. "Shall we?"

"We shall," I say, placing my palm at the crook of his arm.

We keep a chaste distance as we stroll along with all the other proper couples around us. The promenade seems to cater mostly to humans or seelie fae, as everyone maintains the formalities I'm used to seeing back home. It's a strange blend of familiarity and novelty, and I'm enjoying it.

William guides us to a food stall, much like the vendor we bought Lumies from in Lumenas. This time, the treat is one of those doughy bean-filled confections Cassie and I had at the café.

Cassie came to visit us at our suite this morning, proving she's fully recovered from yesterday's debacle, much to William's relief. She apologized for not sending word to him and promised to be more transparent in the future. She said this while giving me a knowing look, demonstrating that she is taking my advice.

I almost wish she was here with us now, for I'd like to get to know her better. But I can say the same for William —there's much about him I want to know. As we continue our walk, we ask questions between bites of our sweet treat. I learn more about his childhood, how he moved from city to city both before and after his father met Lydia. Before Lydia, William's father was always chasing the arts and following a revolving cast of muses. After, they lived wherever Lydia's career took them. Most recently, William and Cassie lived in the Earthen Court, as that is where Lydia chose to settle down during her final years for medical care.

I collect every story he tells me, treasuring the sweet and bitter alike. Every new fact fills in the fabric that is *him*, and I'm hungry for all of it. We may have fully fallen for each other, but there is still much to know about one another. It's the opposite of how it was with Dennis Feverforth. With Dennis, we got to know everything about each other via letter. Then we fell in love. Then we met. And it all fell apart.

With William, neither of us were looking for romance. If anything, we sought the opposite with each other. But our attraction was inevitable. As I learned more about him, saw new sides of him, I fell in love. Now I get to learn the beautifully mundane details that make this fae male who he is.

We circle the lake slowly, stopping often, and by the time we reach where we started, William faces me with a formal bow.

"We must part ways," he says. "Thank you for your company."

My heart sinks, swept up in his act, until I remind myself I'll see him back at our suite. I sink into a curtsy. "Likewise, Mr. Haywood."

"I bid you a good day. Though I suggest you visit the bridge before you leave."

"The bridge?"

He points not far down the promenade, near a heavily forested side of the lake. "Take the walking trail there and you'll see it."

I squint to where he's pointing until I spot the trail in

question, but by the time I glance back at William, he's gone. Quiet bastard. When did he sneak away?

I'm too curious about this bridge he's mentioned to ignore his advice, so I march back down the path until I reach the walking trail. I note several more on the way, but I stick to the one he pointed out. The trail leads me through more swaying willows, between flowering hedges, and finally to another paved path. A beautiful garden stretches before me, filled with miniature trees, weathered statues of forest critters and fae creatures, water fountains, and several ponds. It's empty compared to the main promenade, with only a pedestrian or two in sight. I wonder if few know about the hidden garden.

I follow a winding path through fragrant hedges until a red arched bridge comes into view. It's suspended over a trickling stream, and a figure already waits at its center. My lips pull into a grin as I quicken my pace and meet William on the bridge.

"What are we doing here?" I ask as I close the distance between us. "You bid me good day."

"William the Poet bid the auction winner good day," he says, pulling me into his arms at once. "Now it's just us."

I encircle his neck with my arms, tilting my head back to meet his eyes. "What was that all about? Were you trying to prove something with that act?"

"Yes," he says without shame. "I wanted to prove you had nothing to worry about, even if you hadn't won the auction. I created that form you signed from the start. Before I had any inkling that you might forgive me."

My heart falls. "I'm sorry I ran the other night. I'm sorry it took me a while to come to terms with my feelings."

"No, Weenie," he says, and I realize it's been quite a while since that nickname irked me. Now it only sparks warmth. "You're allowed to take your time when you're upset.

However much you need. You came back, which gives me hope that you'll come back again and again, even if conflict arises between us."

I recall what Cassie told me. About the promise I made to her, that I wouldn't let him lose himself in me. About his guilt over Lydia's death. About the pain he must have felt when he discovered her health had deteriorated after his father left her, and that she'd suffered while William was gone.

"I will come back," I say. "I will always come back. It's safe to let me go a little, and it's safe to follow your dreams as well."

I don't know if I'm making much sense to him, but I don't know how else to put it. Our love is still too new for bold promises and lifelong commitments, no matter how my heart beats for him. We still have careers to enjoy and goals to pursue. I want to pursue them together, but independently as well. We can forge strong pillars of love without collapsing into each other.

To reach that place, we'll need to learn from each other. Build trust in each other.

William must learn we can depend on each other without growing dependent. And I'll have to trust that he won't suddenly change his mind about me, even when I show the worst sides of myself.

"I love you," he says, holding me tighter. "I want to experience everything with you, no matter what happens with the contract."

Another sinking of my heart.

There's still no getting around the inevitable. One of us will win the three-book deal. One of us won't. But one thing is for sure. I will love him and support him no matter what happens, and I know he feels the same about me.

I pull back slightly. "It's time, Will. Let's dissolve our bet."

His eyes widen. "You're sure?"

"I'm sure."

"Then let it be done. I hereby revoke our bargain, dissolving every condition of the bet we agreed to, including all amendments and additions verbally agreed, and now deem it null and void."

I expect a shudder of magic to wash over me, or some tangible sign that our magically binding bet is no more. Yet there's nothing. "That's all? It's done?"

"It's done."

"Then it's a fight for sales from now on."

His lips quirk in a sly smile. "A fight to see which of us is really the most popular."

Our competition has never felt as good as it does now. His taunting grin sparks only excitement in me. Because I know we'll be all right no matter what happens. Cassie too. Should I win, I have ideas of how we can all benefit. And I know—without him saying a word—he has ideas of his own, should he come out the victor. We're in this together.

Yet rivals nonetheless.

And I wouldn't have it any other way.

I want to compete with him all the way to the end.

Lifting my chin, I mirror his teasing façade and release my hold around his neck. I press one palm to his chest while I tap the tip of his nose with my forefinger. Just like he did to me the day we met. "I hope you don't cry when I win, Willy."

His arms remain around me, and he pivots until my backside presses against the side of the bridge. Then he plants his hands on the railing, bracketing me as he leans in. "Hey, Weenie."

"What?"

"Free pass."

I scoff. "We don't have a free pass anymore."

"Maybe not officially, but I still like the game."

The heat in his gaze has my chest flipping. "All right. What do you want to do with your free pass?"

"Kiss. Touch. Fuck you right here on this bridge."

I bite back a whimper at those words. My rational side has me casting a glance around the garden. It remains as empty as it was when I entered, not a soul in sight. "What if someone comes?"

He brushes his mouth over the corner of my jaw. "What if you come?"

"I thought you didn't like doing intimate acts in public," I say, my voice already breathless.

"There are a lot of things I don't like to do with anyone else but you. What do you say, love?"

Heat pools between my thighs, an ache I can't suppress. I tug the front of his coat, pulling him against me. "Free pass accepted."

He lowers his lips to mine.

CHAPTER FORTY-ONE

TWO WEEKS LATER

WILLIAM

I don't know when I became so certain of my own defeat, but maybe I always knew, deep down, that I never stood a chance against Edwina. Not even my actor's charm combined with my sister's lovely words can hold a candle to Edwina's genuine passion. She's the full package. She puts her heart and soul into her work, and her readers respond in a way I don't think they ever will to me.

So it's no surprise when Edwina strolls into Barley and Mint Public House with an enormous grin on her face. Monty, Daphne, and I are already waiting for her at one of the booths. Monty and I rise from our seats as she approaches, and Daphne hops onto the table in her pine marten form.

Edwina trembles from head to toe. "I got it. I got the contract."

I pull her into my arms at once. "Congratulations, love. You fucking deserve it."

There isn't a part of me that doesn't mean every word.

She does deserve it. She deserves the world.

Today was our post-tour meeting with Mr. Fletcher at Fletcher-Wilson's headquarters in the Earthen Court, located just down the street from the pub. Even though the sales for *A Portrait of June, Etched in Solace* were massive during the tour, I knew he wasn't going to offer me the contract. Even if he did, I was prepared to reject it unless subsequent books were published solely under Cassie's name. I'm not certain that's the right choice. Maybe my sister is happy with our arrangement. Maybe she even claims it's what she wants. But what she deserves is recognition for her work. She deserves to be valued without my face stamped over her beautiful creativity.

Whatever the case, my career as a poet is over. I want to act. I want to return to the stage. Edwina has given me that courage. That burning ambition. A renewed competitive drive.

Maybe this time I'll aim for roles I'm better suited for.

"I'm so happy for you," Daphne says as Edwina and I break apart. "I urged Mr. Fletcher to pick you during my tour review—no offense." She says the last part to me.

"None taken."

"Oh, I think we were all rooting for Edwina," Monty says, clapping his hands. "I was on William's side for an entirely other purpose. Speaking of, how would you rate my match-making skills?"

Edwina arches a brow. "Matchmaker? You're going to try to take credit for our relationship?"

Monty shrugs. "I'm building my portfolio."

"What is with you and matchmaking?" Daphne says.

"Love is torture," Monty says, "and I like torturing people."

"There is one problem," Edwina says, looking at me side-long. My stomach falls, but I can already guess what she's about to say. "It's going to take six months for Mr. Fletcher to secure my citizenship. I'll have to return home in a couple of weeks when my visitor's pass expires."

I squeeze her hand in a gesture of comfort. "Will you be able to keep your apartment in the meantime? Or will you stay with your parents?"

"I'll stay with my parents. They'll let me live at the estate without pressuring me to marry, so long as I assure them my career is secure. Besides, I want to spend time with them before I move. I won't get to see them as often anymore."

"And you're sure you want this?" Even she must hear the unevenness in my tone. "To live here?"

She faces me with a serious expression. "With all my heart."

Her words convey so much more than surface level. She wants this. Living here. Us. She'll come back.

I may worry every minute she's gone, fearing something might befall her while we're apart, but I need to learn to let go. To stop feeling so responsible for those I love.

"We'll write," she says, and this time she's the one offering the reassuring squeeze to my palm. "I'll write until you're sick of me."

"That will never happen."

Her lips quirk with mischief. "I'll write dirty poetry and send you naughty drawings."

Daphne raises a paw. "Send some to me too! Tide me over until your next book comes out."

Monty snorts a laugh and saunters toward the bar. "I'll get everyone some drinks."

Daphne darts after him, leaving me and Edwina momentarily alone.

"I really am happy for you," I say, framing her shoulders with my hands.

"I know you are. But there's something I want to say. Or...offer. I want to help pay for Cassie's education." At my frown, she rushes to add, "At least a semester. I want to help her, and I won't take no for an answer unless it's straight from her."

My first instinct is to refuse, to tell her she doesn't need to spend her hard-earned advance on us, just because I lost the contract. But I know her desires aren't out of a sense of pity or charity. Edwina is no longer an outsider when it comes to me and Cassie. Every day, our relationship grows. Every day, we work to build something of substance. Something that makes Edwina more than a lover.

Someday, whether she opens to the idea of matrimony or we pave our own way as a committed couple, she's going to be family. Maybe she already is.

I breathe out a shaky sigh. "All right."

Her expression brightens. "You're not going to fight me on this?"

"No," I say, pressing my lips to hers. "You've won this round."

She grins, her eyes crinkling behind her lenses, and I think I just fell in love with her all over again.

"Drinks," Monty says, setting a tray upon our table. As we settle into the booth, Monty takes his usual glass of water and Daphne predictably reaches for the cordial and a tiny cup. I select a glass of wine while Edwina reaches for a tumbler filled with blue liquid—indigo on the bottom, pastel on the top.

I nearly choke on my wine. "That's Cloud Dive," I rush to say.

Edwina pauses, then narrows her eyes at Monty.

He shrugs, leaning back in his seat while taking a long drag of his cigarillo, a crooked smile on his face. "I thought you might want to reminisce. We all had such a good time that first night, didn't we?"

Edwina casts a longing glance at the libation. "I admit, it was really fun."

"Just don't drink more than one," Monty says. "Switch to regular wine after."

"Cordial is nice," Daphne says, raising her little cup.

Edwina looks at me, and the temptation is clear on her face. "I kind of want to try it again. Maybe if I drink in moderation I'll get a truly brilliant idea for my book this time."

I level a scowl at her. "Do you never learn? Don't do it."

Her grin turns devious. "Do *you* never learn, love of mine? Never dare me not to do something."

"That wasn't a dare—"

But already, she's taken the glass and brought its contents to her lips. In a matter of minutes, she's chatting incessantly to Daphne, boasting about how brilliant she was at her meeting with Mr. Fletcher.

I cut a lighthearted glare at Monty across the table. "She's going to be incredibly annoying tonight, thanks to you."

"Yes," Monty says with a wink, "but you love her, even when she's annoying."

I heave a sigh and angle my body toward my belligerent, mischievous, beautiful beloved. "I really do."

EPILOGUE

SIX MONTHS LATER

EDWINA

J'm bouncing on the balls of my feet as I wait to disembark the ship. My trip back to Faerwyvae—to my new home—was perfect. No storms, no delays. My citizenship has been approved and processed by all necessary means. I'm already cleared by customs. Everything has been so easy, I fear something will inevitably go wrong.

And if anything were to go wrong, it would be…

William.

Not that I have any reason to believe that will happen. We've exchanged letters as promised over the last six months, and even though his physical distance was a constant ache in my chest, our emotional proximity never wavered. Not once. If anything, we've grown closer. After three months of our correspondence, Will sent me a poem. It was a humorous limerick harkening back to the poems we edited in my annotated copy of *A Portrait of June*, all about the baby carrot in love with the redhead. In this one, the carrot asked his lover to share a home with him.

Which is when I realized…

That was Will's way of asking me to live with him once I returned.

I've never kicked my feet so hard or squealed so loud as I did then.

That excitement hasn't abated in the slightest, nor have William's reminders of his affection and anticipation of our life together.

But I've felt this before, haven't I? Certain of a man's affection based on his words in writing?

William isn't Dennis, I remind myself, and my anxiety eases. This isn't the first time I've faced fears regarding our relationship, and it's gotten easier to move past them. It helps that William has already seen and loved the real me.

His face is the first I see when I finally emerge from the ship onto the pier. He stands amongst all the other figures waiting to greet loved ones. Everything inside me yearns to race ahead, but that would break protocol. Not only that, but without the escort of a full fae immigration officer to usher me through the invisible perimeter of protective magic that surrounds the isle, I'd find myself slamming into an unseen wall. I do my best to maintain my composure as the officer slowly walks me down the pier.

William's eyes lock on mine, his grin as wide as my own. As soon as the officer nods for me to proceed, I run the rest of the way to my beloved. He lifts me in his arms at once, pressing his lips to mine as he spins me in a circle. Our cheeks are wet with tears, my spectacles crooked as he sets me down on my feet.

"You're really here," he says, voice choked. "I missed you so damn much."

"I missed you too," I say, swiping at my cheeks and eyes to get a better look at him. He's even more beautiful than I remembered, his dark hair in windswept disarray, his earrings sparkling in the midday sunlight, his eyes as bright as the sea behind us.

He pulls away and pushes an enormous bouquet of peonies into my arms. "These are for you."

"Are these intentional," I ask with a wry grin, "or are you just happy to see me?"

"Both."

I stand on my tiptoes and kiss him again.

"All right, all right. You've had your sweet reunion."

I recognize Cassie's voice and angle my head to see her strolling toward us, cane in hand. My heart stutters as my eyes fall on the three other figures with her.

"Can we interrupt now?" Zane asks, a bright smile on their face.

"Welcome home," says Jolene. She has her arm linked through an unfamiliar—yet incredibly handsome—man's arm.

"Jolene!" I say. "This must be your husband."

William and I aren't the only ones who kept a correspondence while I was in Bretton. I wrote to Jolene too, sharing details of my romance with William—details I admit I may have laced with boasting—while she told me about the start of a very happy marriage.

"Edwina," Jolene says, "this is George. George, this is Edwina Danforth, my dear friend and romance author."

I greet him with a handshake, then pull the others into hugs, one at a time. I've never been one for hugs, but I've also never really had friends either. Even with my college friends, I was always the odd one out due to my own choices, valuing writing over socializing. After we graduated, I never reached out to keep in touch with any of them.

Now, more and more, I'm learning to value other things aside from my career.

"It's so lovely to see you all again," I say, though my chest tightens at Monty and Daphne's absence. We've kept in touch, but I doubt either could be here today. Both have been quite busy at Fletcher-Wilson headquarters lately. I'll still see them plenty when I meet with my publisher.

With more passengers being escorted down the pier, the sidewalk is getting crowded. Zane links their arm through mine, and we make our way toward the heart of Port Dellaray, the busiest port town in the Summer Court. William and I will be staying here for a night while we wait for my luggage to be brought from the ship to our hotel. Then after that...

I glance over my shoulder at William. He walks with Cassie, his hands behind his back, probably to keep his over-protective tendencies at bay. "Where will we go after this?"

He knows what I mean by the question. We may have agreed to live together, but we haven't finalized every detail. Since we couldn't exchange letters while I was on the ship, he may have news I've yet to hear. Good news, hopefully. Last I heard, he'd auditioned for a part in a play. If he got the role, we'd temporarily relocate to Lumenas, where the play is set to premiere for three months.

Cassie elbows him in the side. "You didn't tell her?"

"I haven't had the chance," he whispers back.

Hope blossoms in my chest. "Don't keep me in suspense."

"I got the part," William says.

"Tell her *which* part," Zane says.

He gives me a crooked grin. "The villain."

My knees go weak just thinking about my handsome beloved playing the role of a villain. "You'll make the perfect arrogant asshole, Will."

"Your faith in me knows no bounds."

"Any kissing scenes?" I ask.

"None."

William's answer fills me with a flutter of relief. Not that I would stop him from taking on a role that had a kiss. We've even come up with some ideas for how he may be able to navigate kiss scenes in the future. We're willing to bet if I stand off stage and he meets my eyes, he may be able to perform such a feat. First, it's best he establishes himself in roles he can astound the audience with.

"So Lumenas will be our home for a while," I say.

He nods. "Rehearsals start next week, so we'll be catching a train north tomorrow."

I could leap for joy. Of all the places we visited, Lumenas was my favorite. I'm so happy we'll be returning sooner rather than later.

"Your stay will be extra comfortable," Zane says, "considering you'll be at my place."

"You're going to host our stay?" I ask. "Won't we be a bother?"

"I won't be there," Zane says. "I'm headlining a three-month tour around the isle. I'll have sung in every major city by the end of it. I'll be sure to catch a train back for at least one performance, of course."

"As will we," Jolene says, and her husband voices his support.

"I'll be there on opening night," Cassie says. "For obvious reasons."

Thanks to the funding I provided, Cassie was able to attend the Borealis School of the Arts, on the south end of Lumenas. It took some convincing to get her to agree to let me pay her tuition, but she relented in the end. Based on the weekly letters I got all about her college experiences, I know she's grateful. And I'm grateful we'll be so close to her, at least for a while.

"What I want to know," Jolene says, arching a brow at me, "is if you finished your manuscript."

"I did, on my way here." I heave a sigh. "What a relief. My deadline is next week."

Jolene releases an impatient groan. "I'm so eager to read it. I've already read through your backlist."

"My wife is quite fond of your work," her husband says. "I can't say I've read any of it, but she's always in a rather... exhilarated mood after she finishes certain chapters."

I purse my lips to hide my smile. I think I know what kind of mood he means, and Jolene's blush only confirms it.

"George," she whispers, "not in front of others."

"What do you mean?" His frown looks genuine, which gives him the aura of someone adorably dense.

Jolene rolls her eyes, but there's a sweetness to the expression.

"Don't worry," I say to her. "I'll let you read an early copy."

Our party reaches the hotel William and I will be staying at, which turns out to be everyone's place of lodging for the night. We settle into the public dining room, ordering drinks and food, and catch up on all that we've missed.

William squeezes my hand under the table, and I squeeze his back. I'm giddy over his touch, his proximity, the mere thought that he's mine. I no longer shy away from that excited feeling, or even the spark of terror that comes with it. Excitement and terror often go hand in hand. I'm ready to face it all now that I'm exactly where I'm supposed to be. With the man I love. The people I cherish.

This is the start of our adventure. Our relationship. Our story.

Wherever we go, whatever we do, I'm home.

BONUS EPILOGUE

ONE YEAR AFTER THE HEARTBEATS TOUR

MONTY

*B*ased on my history of destroying every good thing, I should have known when Mr. Fletcher called me into his office that this would be the day I royally fuck up.

Mr. Fletcher stands behind his desk and slams a paper down before me. "What is this?"

"Broadsheets, sir," I say, lounging in the chair on the other side of the expanse of mahogany that takes up half his office. "This particular paper is the Cedar Hills Gazette."

"I'm talking about this," he says, tapping my black-and-white portrait at the bottom of the front page. "Your interview with Hansel Bonesmith about two of our authors."

I shrug. "He asked for insight into everyone's favorite real-life love story."

Mr. Fletcher rubs his brow. He's a burly man with dark hair and a thick mustache. I've always considered him a respectful employer, though he is a bit of a stickler for rules. Something I've never been too fond of. Unless we're talking about the rules of a game, bet, or sport. In that case, I'm fully invested. Honestly, I'm surprised he agreed to publish *A Portrait of June, Etched in Solace* at all, considering it came with a dash of deception.

He lowers his hand and taps the paper again. "You claimed to have played matchmaker for Edwina Danforth and William Haywood during their tour."

"I did. Well, I think I did. Ask either of them and they'll say I had nothing to do with it."

"It's clear you had something to do with it, thanks to this interview."

"Thank you. At least someone believes me."

"That's not a good thing." Mr. Fletcher lowers himself into his seat, elbows propped on his desk. "You claimed to have overseen a bet between them."

"Fact."

"A seduction bet."

"Also a fact."

"You offered to sleep with Miss Danforth."

I hold up a finger. "Only to make William jealous. She turned me down besides."

"You assaulted a fae male in an alley."

"He tried to take advantage of Edwina. I have zero tolerance for such behavior."

"You smoked drugs."

I bite the inside of my cheek to keep from laughing. Who calls the act of imbibing herbal substances through inhalation *smoking drugs*?

I don an innocent expression. "You mean Moonpetal? Moonpetal is not a drug; it's a relaxing fae herb, no different from what's sold at the market. It just so happens to be unregulated."

"Then you took them to an orgy."

"A voyeurism club just so happened to be at the same respectable university party we—is that really what the reporter said? He better not have misconstrued my story."

He rubs his brow again. "Mr. Phillips, just one of these actions alone is serious enough to qualify for your dismissal from Fletcher-Wilson. This compilation of unprofessional behavior cannot go ignored. How do I know you haven't done worse during the other tours you've managed?"

"I assure you, every tour I've managed since has been incredibly boring."

"Boring," he echoes. "Are you saying you acted like this for the purpose of entertainment?"

"And the name of love?" I say it with a flourish of my hand, but he isn't at all amused.

He heaves a sigh. "I gave you this job because I respect your father."

All former mirth drains from me at the mention of my father. My fingers clench around the arms of my chair. "What?" I say through my teeth.

"He requested I hire you."

My blood boils hot, and everything inside me seeks to lash out. It's all I can do to keep my voice level. "That isn't possible. I didn't tell him I applied."

"He knew anyway," Mr. Fletcher says with a worn shrug. "How else did you think that you—an aristocrat's son with no work experience—earned the position of junior publicist?"

"My charming personality," I say, but I can't force more than a flat tone.

"I promised your father I'd give you a chance, but making a public spectacle of Fletcher-Wilson is the last straw."

"You're dismissing me?"

"Yes."

I'm almost relieved. If I knew my father had any part in getting me this job, I would have quit long ago. Fucking bastard still seeks to control my life, even after I did everything I could to get myself disinherited.

Yet being disinherited means I have no backup plan and no finances should I become unemployed. Not unless I want to return to my father, beg on my knees for him to take me back, and become the perfect son he wants me to be. Keeping his secrets. Pretending he isn't the person I hate most in this world.

"You no longer have a place at Fletcher-Wilson."

"Salt in the wound, but thanks," I mutter.

He glares at me. "But…I may know of a job that may better suit your…inclinations."

I narrow my eyes. "Is my father involved?"

"I admit, if you weren't your father's son, I wouldn't give a damn, but this recommendation is all mine." He opens the broadsheets toward the back and pushes it toward me. Then he writes an address on a slip of paper and passes it across the desk. Tapping the top of an advice column titled *Ask Gladys*, he says, "Go to this address. Third floor. Ask for Charlie Michaels."

I frown, first at the column, then at the address he's given me. "What is this?"

"You're the new Gladys."

I study the column with fresh eyes. Then I return my attention to Mr. Fletcher. "It's a romance advice column."

"For starry-eyed lovers," he says. "People write this so-called Gladys, seeking answers to relationship conundrums. Your answers are allowed to be somewhat sensational, but please keep things appropriate. I'm recommending you for this position in good faith."

A twinge of rage pierces me, knowing said good faith is for my father's sake. It's almost enough to make me refuse.

And yet...

Me. A romance columnist. Surely, I can stir some mischief and mend some hearts. Not mine, of course, but maybe someone else's.

"I'll take it. Thank you, Mr. Fletcher."

"Great. Now please get out."

I LEAVE MR. FLETCHER'S OFFICE WITH A SKIP IN MY STEP. Getting fired never felt so good, and I lost three jobs in quick succession before I landed the position here. What great fucking luck I have, and just when I thought I'd ruined everything. Maybe things are turning around for me after all.

I twirl a cigarillo between my fingers as I stride down the hall and through the lobby. The sunlit streets come into view beyond the glass windows—

"Monty?"

The voice has my lungs tightening, and I steel myself before turning around. At the other end of the lobby stands Daphne in seelie form. She's dressed in loose trousers, a white blouse with puffed sleeves, and a mauve waistcoat. It makes me uneasy to see her like this. I haven't witnessed her in her humanoid form since the night of the gala. After we returned from the tour, she was promoted from intern to editorial assistant. With our departments separate and me volunteering to manage as many book tours as I could, we haven't seen much of each other. I wonder when she started favoring her seelie form.

I tuck my cigarillo behind my ear and shove my hands in my pockets, my posture slouched and casual. "Hey, Daffy."

Her shoulders are hunched as she strolls toward me. It seems she still isn't fully comfortable in this body. "I haven't seen you in a while."

"Well, this is hello and goodbye. I got fired."

"Why doesn't that surprise me?"

"You did warn me," I say with an easy chuckle. I pivot on my heel. "Well, I'm off."

"Wait, that's all?"

I freeze at the frantic note in her voice, though I should have run from it.

She shifts from foot to foot as I turn back to face her. "Do you maybe want to...share a meal? Catch up?"

I saunter closer to her, then lift a hand. She flinches as I pat the top of her head. "Nice knowing you, Daffy Dear."

Her eyes narrow to a glare. "You really do think of me as a pet, don't you? Even when I look like this."

I wink. "A really cute pet."

"You're an asshole."

I give her a mock pout. "And here I thought we were friends. See you around."

I exit the front doors before I can think better of my cold farewell. Before my chest tricks me into thinking it would be better to feel anything but a void. Before I can hope.

Daphne's better off if she forgets about me.

And I'm better off if I forget about her.

Edwina and William's story may be complete, but Daphne and Monty's romance is just getting started. Fall in love with the next fantasy romcom in the *Fae Flings and Corset Strings* series with *My Feral Romance*.

NOT READY TO LEAVE
FAERWYVAE?

YOU'RE IN LUCK! The next fantasy romcom in the *Fae Flings and Corset Strings* series follows Daphne and Monty's love story in *My Feral Romance*. Get ready for more banter, spice, and feral-yet-cozy vibes.

You can catch more cozy fantasy romance with the *Entangled with Fae* series! Every book in this series is a standalone new adult fairytale retelling with a HEA guarantee. You'll see some familiar faces that you met in *A Rivalry of Hearts*! Read all about Gemma Bellefleur, Edwina's biggest fan, before she became queen in *Curse of the Wolf King: A Beauty and the Beast Retelling*. Or read all about the mischief Monty Phillips got into when he set up his best friend with his fiancee in *A Dream So Wicked: A Sleeping Beauty Retelling*.

If you're in a stabby and angsty mood, take a trip to Faerwyvae's past with *The Fair Isle Trilogy*, an enemies-to-lovers romantasy. It's set twenty-four years before *A Rivalry of Hearts* and lays the foundation for much of the isle's world building.

ACKNOWLEDGMENTS

Some books are torture to write. Beautiful torture but torture nonetheless, yet always worth it in the end. This was not one of those torturous books. This was one of the most enjoyable books I've ever written. I've never cackled out loud so often while writing than I did while working on *A Rivalry of Hearts*. Writing this book was pure magic and I'm so grateful I got to write the book of my heart.

But even easy books can become torture without a support system. So I have many to thank for encouraging me along the way.

Thank you Valia Lind and Hanna Sandvig, who were my loudest cheerleaders as soon as I shared my idea and longing for this book. You reminded me that this book would be my reward while I was writing the much more difficult books that I wrote before this one. Thank you besties!

Thank you to my critique partner, Alisha Klapheke, for being the first to read the early draft and sending me your reactions! Knowing this book was as funny as I wanted it to be kept me going.

Thank you to all my other author friends, including my Queens of the Quill besties, as well as all the authors who voiced their excitement whenever I shared about this book, whether during 1:1 convos or on my social media posts. That support and encouragement means the world to me!

Thank you to my husband who read this book and chortled at "the testicle cupping scene" and didn't bat an eye at my increase of spiciness in the love scenes. I was pretty embarrassed for you to read this one, but you're a champ. I love you!

Thank you to my daughter who is never able to read this book. Ever. I love that you encourage me anyway and tell me I'm cool!

Thank you to my agent, Kimberly Whalen, for taking a chance on me this year. I'm so happy to have you in my corner and can't wait to see where we go!

Thank you to Kristen at Your Editing Lounge and the rest of my proofreading/typo hunting team for this book: Claire, Emily, and Bea. I treasure you!

Thank you to my PA, Emily and Elyse at Luna Blooms, for helping me stay organized and navigate the most stressful parts of my book releases.

And most of all, thank you to all my readers for supporting me, encouraging me, and falling in love with my worlds and characters. So many of you were just as excited as I was for this book. I hope to create many more swoon-worthy stories for you in the future!

Happy reading!
Tessonja

ALSO BY TESSONJA ODETTE

FAE FLINGS AND CORSET STRINGS - FAE ROMCOM

A Rivalry of Hearts

My Feral Romance

— And more —

ENTANGLED WITH FAE - FAE ROMANCE

Curse of the Wolf King: A Beauty and the Beast Retelling

Heart of the Raven Prince: A Cinderella Retelling

Kiss of the Selkie: A Little Mermaid Retelling

— And more —

THE FAIR ISLE TRILOGY - FAE FANTASY

To Carve a Fae Heart

To Wear a Fae Crown

To Spark a Fae War

STANDALONE FAE ROMANCE NOVELLA SET IN FAERWYVAE

Married by Scandal

PROPHECY OF THE FORGOTTEN FAE - EPIC FANTASY

A Throne of Shadows

A Cage of Crystal

A Fate of Flame

YA DYSTOPIAN PSYCHOLOGICAL THRILLER

Twisting Minds

ABOUT THE AUTHOR

Tessonja Odette is a Seattle-based author of fantasy romance, epic romantasy, and fairytale retellings. She especially loves to write about brooding fae and the fierce women who hate-to-love them. When she isn't writing, she's watching cat videos, petting dogs, having dance parties in the kitchen with her daughter, or pursuing her many creative hobbies. In her books, you'll find enemies-to-lovers, witty banter, cozy vibes, and a delicious dash of steam. Read more about Tessonja at www.tessonjaodette.com

instagram.com/tessonja
facebook.com/tessonjaodette
tiktok.com/@tessonja
x.com/tessonjaodette

Made in the USA
Monee, IL
14 July 2024